THE

FOX

AND

THE

BRIAR

CHESNEY INFALT

BookDragon
PUBLISHING

The Fox & the Briar
A Fae Sleeping Beauty Retelling

Cover Design by Lydia Russell.
Interior Design and Formatting by Nicole Scarano.

BOOKS BY CHESNEY INFALT

Once Upon a Reimagined Time

~The Heart of the Sea

~The Fox and the Briar

A Different Kind of Magic

~A Different Kind of Magic

CONTENTS

Mom, thank you for sharing your love of reading.

PROLOGUE

THE UNSEELIE KING

*D*arkness ripples about me as I step through the portal, traveling from the black-and-grey tones of Unseelie to the brightly lit throne room of the human palace. There are many human lands in this dimension, the various kings clutching to the bits of land they call their own while trying to snatch more from enemies and so-called friends alike. But most of them either fear us Fae too much or think we are merely folklore. This is one of the few kingdoms left that willingly interact with us.

And so, that is how I can easily conjure a portal between my world and theirs, barely expending much magic with a quick flick of my fingertips.

It is good to be King.

My first steps in the human lands leave me nearly breathless, gasping. I'd been told that they are devoid of magic, but I'd not expected to feel as though someone had ripped the air from my lungs.

Even as I stop to regather myself, I keep a smile plastered across my face, relishing the surprised looks as humans and faeries alike notice my entrance. For most, their surprise turns to confusion, but for some, especially the faeries now standing near the cradle, it turns to horror. I straighten my stance—this is going to be fun.

"You were not invited here," hisses Queen Vivienne of the Seelie. Magic crackles in her words, and a breeze whirls about the room, making the torches flicker. Humans stand still, eyes flitting about as if there can be any explanation other than magic. If they are frightened by a harmless trick meant to intimidate, they will be wholly unprepared for whatever comes next.

Although Vivienne looks the part of a Faerie Queen—red-gold locks braided back in an intricate knot, a simple golden circlet matching the embroidery at the neckline and sleeves of her forest green gown—she does not carry the power of a ruler of Seelie. No, that rightfully belongs to the child trembling beside her, reaching for her hand. My half-brother, Loren.

One of the faeries beside Vivienne picks up the child, whispering sweet, comforting things into his ear while her silver eyes remain locked on me. They match her hair well, a stark contrast to her beautiful dark skin. Evanthe is her name, well-known throughout all of Faerie because of her strong magic and even stronger loyalty to the Seelie rulers. I have little doubt that if Evanthe had followed my mother instead, Faerie would still be united, and my mother still alive.

Instead, she chose them, an acting queen and a faerie prince they intend to make king when the time comes. I intend to never let that happen.

The amber-eyed boy in her arms has the same curly red-gold hair as Vivienne, our aunt, and the late King Oberon—from what I can recall of him.

"I noticed I was overlooked," I say, taking a few slow steps forward. The portal behind me closes, and the shadows that formed it bleed onto the floor and rise around me to become wolves whose heads reach my elbows. Gasps ripple through the nobles as they scurry backward, tripping over each other. The shadow wolves pay them no mind, walking beside me, waiting for my command. They are just my magic, after all, and can do nothing without my say so.

If the Queen of Seelie wants a show, I will be more than happy to oblige.

The human king and queen rise from their thrones, the queen moving toward the cradle.

"You were *not* overlooked—"

I cut off Vivienne, speaking to the human queen: "Come now, Your Majesty. You accepted gifts from everyone else; I merely want to bestow one of my own upon the princess."

She halts, hand in midair. Her wide eyes move away from me for a second to look at Vivienne. I want to laugh at her blind, innocent faith. If it came down to a one-on-one battle between Vivienne and me, I would destroy her in a matter of minutes. But the fact of the matter is that she keeps powerful faeries like Evanthe around her and Loren at all times. I am content with letting them ease into a feeling of security for the time being.

"The gifts are from Fae nobility," Vivienne states.

I know she is expecting me to feel the sting of her words—and I do, but I let them harden my anger, a cold, sharp iron that could pierce any faerie and poison them as they bleed to death. Just like my mother taught me.

"Then you should know more than anyone that I have the right to be here," I reply in challenge, maintaining a grin.

Her expression slips, but is quickly replaced with a glare. "You, *boy*, will not taint my brother's memory with—"

"With what? The truth?" I laugh, dark and bitter. "My claim to the crown is stronger than that child's. But surely you recognize my power, since you have yet to pluck the crown from my head."

A few more steps forward. I am nearly at the bottom of the stairs leading up to the throne, but I wait, relishing the way the anticipation tenses their movements and shortens their breaths.

"I have a gift to give your daughter," I tell the king and queen, "and then I will be on my way." Before Vivienne can interject, I add, "I will immediately return to Unseelie after bestowing the gift."

Vivienne reluctantly closes her mouth. We faeries speak lies in things that are unsaid, unable to speak lies outright.

"You may give her the gift and then leave," the human king agrees, suddenly finding his voice. "If you do not—"

"I know I am greatly outnumbered," I tell him, growing impatient. My wolves growl and snap at those who are still a little too close.

Vivienne brought eleven faeries with her, including Loren. Ignoring the child, I still would not do anything remotely as idiotic as going against eleven faeries at once. Perhaps if we were in Unseelie, but not here, where our magic is limited.

"Let him pass," the king orders Vivienne. "The sooner we let him, the sooner he will leave."

Her disbelief apparent, Vivienne obeys nonetheless. Half a step, no more.

I pass her, wolves snarling while I pay her no heed. The rest of the faeries stay behind Vivienne, and the queen reluctantly sits when her husband gently takes her hand.

The cradle is ornate, painted with nature scenes of foxes and deer and butterflies and birds. She will, after all, be wedded to Loren and become Queen of Seelie, according to the long-upheld agreement between Fae and Humans... if she lives that long.

The child inside is smaller than I expected, the blankets swallowing her tiny form, leaving only her face uncovered. She stares upward, not at anything in particular. If human babies are anything like faerie ones, she is barely a week old. Various spells in brilliant colors wrap around her like they are becoming part of the blanket, but they are already seeping into her skin. Spells of beauty... kindness... luck...

Vivienne tenses as I touch the baby's forehead.

"What will I gain from harming an infant?" I ask.

"Give your gift and leave," the king warns.

The wolves melt back into darkness and coil around me once

more, slithering up my body until they reach my arms. Every eye is on me as I trace the side of the infant's face. She squirms.

"Princess Briar Rose will indeed be beautiful and kind, loved by many," I begin, voice taking on a storyteller quality. Magic slips down my hand and pools on her forehead before seeping in like the rest. I feel its absence like a deep ache, like someone scraped out my insides. Mighty magic for a mighty gift... "But when she turns eighteen, she will prick her finger on the spindle of a spinning wheel... and die."

Everyone is in uproar, moving toward me. I feel the spark of Vivienne's and Evanthe's magic, but I envelop myself in darkness, holding to my promise. It swallows me whole, blocking out the shouts, and then I am tumbling backward, air and magic rushing back into my lungs. My feet land on the floor of my bedchambers; I find my balance and greedily inhale, Unseelie slowly soothing my aching insides by restoring my depleted magic, drawing from everything within range.

I did what I set out to do, but I am not yet done—if any of the faeries have gifts left to give the princess, they will attempt to soften the curse I bestowed upon her, but they will be unable to break it.

I lock my bedchamber before any of the other residents or servants notice my return. There are not many of them, but every so often more defect from Seelie or the Solitary Fae to join me. Given enough time, the Seelie might be weak enough that they will have to bow to me, making the Courts united once more.

In the meantime, I want to see what happens in my absence, so I go to the mirror. I place my hands on either side of its frame, the edges resembling the rolling waves of the sea it was crafted in by merfolk. Power trembles within it, but nothing happens until I command, "Show me the throne room of King Faustus."

The surface ripples, changing from my reflection until the throne room appears on the glass like I'm looking through a window.

"Your Majesties," Evanthe interrupts the boisterous arguments and exclamations, "I still have a gift to give Princess Briar Rose."

That quiets the room. The queen clutches her child, tears

streaming down her cheeks, her husband gripping her shoulders from behind. She meets Evanthe's steady gaze with a glimmer of hope.

"Can you... can you reverse it?" Her voice is fragile, almost inaudible.

Vivienne takes Loren so Evanthe can go to the queen.

"I cannot," she answers gently. "But I might be able to alter it."

I smirk, curious to see what she comes up with.

The queen shifts the baby in her arms so her little face is exposed. There is a furrow in her brow where I touched her, like she is deeply concerned about something. Evanthe places her hand over it.

"I cannot stop her from touching a spindle," Evanthe says slowly. Her hand glows a faint pink. "But instead of dying, she will fall into a deep sleep that will only be broken by True Love's Kiss."

I snort. Of course one of the Seelie would use such a term. Granted, since the curse is powerful, she had to come up with something specific and difficult as a loophole. Who knows if she will even ever meet her true love?

That thought doesn't seem to cross the king's and queen's minds —they hold each other and their little girl, crying and thanking Evanthe for their shred of hope.

I let the magic dissipate, leaving me in a lightless, silent room once more.

The princess has eighteen years to find her true love so he can break the curse when she falls asleep. And I have eighteen years to plan the reunification of Faerie.

This is going to be fun.

CHAPTER ONE

BRIAR ROSE

*H*is footsteps nearly match the pace of my rapidly beating heart. I keep the hem of my gown lifted and continue to run down the stone hallway, sunlight casting a myriad of bright colors through the stained-glass windows.

Against my better judgment, I dare a peek over my shoulder and squeal. He grabs me, and we tumble together. Just before we hit the stone, I imagine a field of flowers and hold tight to him. We land and roll onto soft grass… and biting cold soaks into my sleeve.

With a yelp, I yank out of his grasp and sit up. "Snow?" I ask, not bothering to hide the judgment in my tone. "Really, Henri?"

Henri laughs and rolls off the snow, onto the grassy knoll I conjured, the stone hallway long gone. "It was softer than stone."

"And freezing!"

"I could keep you warm." His brown eyes sparkle with mischief, and he grins at me boyishly.

I hope he doesn't hear the catch in my breath.

With a wave of his hand, the snow dissipates, replaced by more flowers. A slight chill remains, but it is always present in the dreamscape. He raises his brows expectantly. "Better?" The way he scoots closer to me tells me he definitely noticed the effect he has on me.

"Marginally," I reply, dragging my gaze down to my dress sleeve. A mere thought has it dry once more, but I pretend to fuss with it anyway. It shimmers in the warm sunlight, and I change the color of my dress from pink to blue… then back to pink again. If only it were so easy in the real world.

"You mess with colors when you're nervous," Henri whispers, his forehead nearly touching mine. I don't look up at him, even though everything in me wants to. It would be all too easy to look up, all too easy to give in to his charms, all too easy to let him kiss me.

"Fleur…" he calls me softly, the same way he has for the past year. Well, almost a year.

Guilt knots my stomach, enough to make me conjure a tree to lean back against, putting distance between us, if only a little. It appears the instant I picture it in my mind, just as I imagined it, with the abundance of vibrant green leaves overhead. I put on my best no-nonsense expression as I look up at him, trying to ignore the chill that always clings to me in the dreamscape, no matter how warm I make it. He watches me, a curious expression on his face.

"You caught me," I say. "Ask your question."

There is a flicker of disappointment in his eyes, but he obliges me. "Very well." He shifts so that he's sitting cross-legged in front of me. A lock of dark hair falls onto his forehead as he stares, pondering.

"Here I was under the impression you had lots of questions," I tease when the weight of his gaze becomes unbearable.

The corner of his mouth twitches upward; I force myself to look back up at his eyes. "If I'm to have only one question for today… and I'll not see you for some time…"

My pulse quickens again. I dig my fingernails into my palms to keep from fidgeting. *Ask me something easy… Something I don't have to avoid. I can't lie to you.*

Finally, he asks, "What is your real name?"

The words repeat accusingly in my mind as I draw my knees to my chest, hugging them tightly. "I…" My throat feels too tight to say anything. It should be simple, sharing your name. I want to tell him, want to trust him with it.

But in a world with faeries, sharing your name with the wrong person can sign your life away. Henri looks to be a normal human, but here, in the dreamscape we have created together, we can look any way we wish.

I certainly change my appearance, making myself taller, with less curves and more volume to my stick-straight hair. Change the color too, depending on my mood. Today I chose black ringlets, but as I twist one around a finger, it shifts to auburn, then blonde.

"That was unfair of me," Henri says gently. "I beg your forgiveness. I only thought to ask for something I can hold onto until I can see you again."

I bite my bottom lip. "Would… would you tell me your name, if I told you mine?"

Seriousness snuffs out the mischievous glint in his eyes. "I would."

Courts help me… but I believe him.

No, I tell myself sternly. *You can never tell him.* Because even if I could be assured he isn't Fae, giving him my name now would mean more than just that. It would mean opening myself up to him completely, letting him get to know me, letting myself hear my name from his lips…

I flush. Silly as it seems, there is something unspoken between us, and if I give him my name, it might make these feelings undeniably real.

And I am promised to someone else.

Henri patiently watches me. He has not moved, yet it feels like there is a great distance between us, something I'm not quite willing to bridge the gap for. It really is silly. Almost a year, and we have only offered each other fake names and inconsequential (albeit honest) answers to random questions about ourselves. We are strangers. So why do I care?

"I… cannot." I try to offer a sympathetic smile, but all I can manage is a wobbly one as I try not to let emotions take hold. "I hope you understand."

"Of course." He sounds genuine, but his shoulders sink slightly. "Another question…"

To lighten the mood, I say, "What makes you believe you get another question?"

I am rewarded with a small, half-hearted smirk. "Because I caught you, and you have yet to give me an answer."

I gave you one, just not one either of us wanted.

For a moment, I close my eyes, listening. Not to the river or Henri's breaths or my heartbeat that refuses to slow, but to the world just outside of this place, the one that is waiting for me to wake. There is a soft humming from the kitchen, which tells me Evanthe is preparing morning tea, and she will rouse Delphine, Irit, and me soon.

Henri does not speak until I open my eyes again. "Are you safe?"

He always asks that. "Yes, I am, but you should ask your question quickly, for I am running out of time."

"In that case…" Henri stands and offers his hand, helping me to my feet. Then he gingerly presses his thumb between my brows, to unfurrow them, or so he's said before. "I will save my question for when next we meet."

"You… you want to wait?"

Slowly, he brings my knuckles to his lips. The kiss lingers, and then he says quietly, "You are worth waiting for."

CHAPTER TWO

LOREN

*W*armth tingles across my skin as I step from Seelie to the human lands. Everything here feels heavier, like the ground wants to keep you pinned to it. No matter how many times I have crossed, it never seems to get any easier.

Seeming to be in agreement, Toussaint snorts in annoyance and picks at the back of his hand, as if we could pluck the sensation away. "We should take the princess and return immediately. Why waste time on a ball when you have been betrothed to be married since you were children?"

I am of the same mind, but I say anyway, "We have dances as well."

He shoots me a disdainful look, one he'd dare not make if anyone else were around, especially not Aunt Vivienne. "Ours are revelries, full of passion and freedom. These are dull, restricting affairs."

I huff a laugh. "Then it is a good thing Briar Rose will live with us in Seelie once we are wed." Her name still trips my tongue, as if I am speaking something I have not been given permission to. She nearly gave it to Henri—it was there in her eyes, the war between desire and sense. Always there when she is with Henri, never when she is with me.

Not that I can much blame her for it.

"Very good." He adjusts his jacket and smooths stray locks away from his forehead. "I do not think I could stomach living here."

"You would do it for me." I smirk at him.

He smirks back, but there is nothing in his tone other than utter devotion when he replies, "Where you go, I go, Prince Loren."

Luckily the portal brought us close to the castle, just within the walls, in the rose garden. There is a statue of Remi and Avalee, the original lovers who brought Fae and humans together... at least, before the Courts split into Seelie and Unseelie. Despite our ongoing war with the Unseelie, we have kept our alliance with the humans, kept the tradition alive of Fae royalty marrying human royalty. And, just as Remi joined Avalee in Seelie and became one of the Fae, so the same fate has been set for Briar Rose since she was born.

We walk through the rose garden, courteously nodding our greetings to the nobles strolling by us. Some of the young women giggle and stare at us from behind their fans, but we pay them little heed. That is how the women seem to react to High Fae like us. Well, all except Briar Rose.

The guards bow and let us into the castle, a herald excitedly announcing our presence. One of the servants steps forward to take my cloak, but I dissuade him with a dismissive wave of my hand. He bows and mumbles an apology before stepping away, even though we have moved far past him. Where everything in Seelie is open, wild nature growing around the pillars and even the throne itself to create a harmonious scene, humans keep the castle enclosed, nothing but stone and wood and glass. There are vases of flowers placed on tables and near windowsills, but they are small, their life waning from being cut off from the earth. I flick my fingers in the direction of a pot; the wilting daisies stretch upward, basking in the colored light coming through the stained-glass window. That will give them a few days longer at most.

Toussaint raises a dark brow, but I refuse to give him the satisfaction of meeting his gaze. He will no doubt remark on that frivolous use of Glamour later. In Seelie, the land refills our magic capacity, but in the human world, we are limited to what we have, and then it is gone until we return home once more.

There are more guards stationed at the doors to the throne room, and they bow as we pass by. Inside is a long purple carpet that leads directly to the thrones on the other side of the room, atop the steps. Many nobles stand on either side of the carpet, most faces bright and in awe as they watch us, but some bear scowls that I have learned to ignore. They are the ones who speak in hushed whispers they think we cannot hear, whispers of blame, saying we are stealing their royalty for our own dark purposes.

Yes… what a dark purpose marriage and children are. Although I am not overly excited by the idea, I do not agree with their suspicion and disdain of us. That is the fault of the Unseelie, whom we split from nearly fifty years ago, going by the way humans count time. It flows differently in Faerie, leaving it difficult to judge the time passing between the two lands accurately.

Human lives are short, but their memory is long and bitterness nearly eternal—there are still a few among them who remember the days when the Courts were one.

The room is filled with people, and yet I see no sign of my betrothed.

BRIAR ROSE

Evanthe has already rushed me through breakfast and gotten into a far-too-long spat with Delphine and Irit over what dress I should wear and how my hair should be styled to meet Prince Loren. They have put me in five different dresses and done my hair each time to match, all without magic. Even though we are in a cottage that borders Seelie, we are still far enough away that it will not refill their magic. They have resorted to using it sparingly over the years since they rarely visit their home, each trip only a few days to replenish their magic and see their friends and family. With the curse looming over me, my faerie guardians loath leaving me unprotected, taking turns when leaving does become necessary. Sometimes Queen Vivienne will send others to replace them, but these three are the ones who have been with me most, since as far back as I can remember. Flora and Fauna used to come, but something happened to their magic—none of the faeries will tell me exactly what, only that it is enough to keep them bound to Faerie, unless they want to risk losing their lives.

Secretly, I wonder if that is only part of the truth; I saw how my people treated them because of their less-than-human-like appearance. Evanthe, Delphine, and Irit are constantly watched by wary eyes, and they are High Fae, as close to human as a faerie could get. Only their pointed ears and ethereal beauty mark them as otherworldly, not to mention the magic they can use with a flick of their long, elegant fingers.

At the cottage, we are close enough that I can use dream magic, which is why we come. That is all I can use until I marry Prince Loren and become Fae, allowing me to have Glamour at my command in both wake and sleep.

At least there is one upside to marrying that pompous prince.

"Put her in the blue one! It's a good color on her," Irit says, holding the silk sleeve against my cheek. "See?"

Delphine sighs loudly. "You always want her to wear that one."

"Why wouldn't I? I made it, and it looks lovely on her!"

"But pink is her favorite color," Evanthe cuts in, reaching for one of my favorite gowns. She, at least, tries to make me feel a little more comfortable when seeing Loren. As she carries it to me, I note how well the color looks with her dark skin and silver hair. Not grey, but silver, and always shimmering like bits of starlight got caught in the silken strands. The three of them claim they have lived for multiple centuries by human reckoning, but they appear to be not much older than I am: eighteen. Well, eighteen soon, in a little over a month.

"She wore pink last time," Delphine points out, fists on her curvy hips. As dainty as her name sounds, she carries herself with strength and boldness, just like she speaks.

Irit sighs, shoulders slumping. "Then what about green?" Her voice is naturally gentle, suiting her petite frame and softhearted nature.

"Och! The color doesn't suit her."

"There is no pleasing you!" Evanthe snaps.

The faeries continue to bicker. I yawn and try to ignore them, knowing this could go on for a while. My eyelids are heavy, but I cannot bring myself to regret spending time with Henri in my dreamscape instead of actually sleeping. Because I have to use magic to enter the dreamscape, my body does not truly rest, not as much as it would if I were asleep. I should have resisted, but I wanted one more chance to be with Henri before Loren arrives, because now I will be expected to spend all of my free time with him. It is probably for the best that I do not see Henri in the meantime: I will probably be too irritable from being around Loren to be much fun anyway.

Their argument gets louder, all of them speaking over each other and waving dresses in their clenched fists. In my tired state, I lack the sense not to comment, "Why should it matter? He's seen me many times and still is unimpressed."

The three faeries instantly go silent, eyes pinned on me.

"Did that brat say something to you?" Delphine asks, voice sharp as a blade.

I stammer, "Y-yes. I mean, no. Well, we've said things to each other over the years, and he started the pranks but I continued them, and—"

Evanthe waves a dismissive hand. "He was a child."

"That was last year!"

"He was probably not sure how to express his feelings properly," Irit suggests, to which Delphine whirls on her.

"That is no excuse—"

"Enough!" Evanthe commands with enough force that even Delphine stops. "We are late as it is, so we will have to make a decision and leave now. Brat or not, Loren is our prince and her betrothed. Come now, hurry."

They rush to ready me, but still Delphine states plainly, "I will not stand for either of you to torture each other."

Before I can reply, Evanthe tugs a brush through my hair and responds, "Of course not. Princess Briar Rose will be absolutely pleasant, and if Prince Loren is anything less than charming, he'll have us to answer to."

"I'm sure everything will go smoothly. After all, a person can change a lot in a year," Irit adds with a smile as she fixes my neckline. The dress flatters my curves well, with tiny gold designs throughout the skirts that are old Fae wishes of good luck, but they look like mere golden swirls to the unknowing eye. The three of them swear there is no magic in it, but I do not quite believe them. There is a confidence I feel when I wear it that I've yet to find in any other garment.

Evanthe clucks her tongue. "We are too late to travel by carriage now."

Delphine rolls her eyes. "Yes, by an hour or so, dear. I'm certain the prince has already arrived and everyone is waiting."

Evanthe takes a breath before replying, "Well, then I suppose there is only one option left. We can hardly keep them waiting." She strides to the wall, her index finger beginning to glimmer. She bends down so that she can trace the outline of a curved door on the wall. The moment she steps back, the wood inside of her tracing turns white, then into swirls of color.

"Come now, no time to dawdle." Gently but firmly, she takes my hand, leading me through the portal with her. In the back of my mind, I wonder why she dared spend so much magic when she has no idea when she'll return to Seelie next, but I'm too in awe of the magic to say anything. It radiates warmth, beckoning me to step closer and let it envelop me. As we step through, it dances across my skin like a hundred little playful pixies excited to see me. I want to close my eyes and rest awhile, to bask in it… but all too soon, we step through to the other side, and it is like someone dumped cold water on me. The air is the same as before I stepped into the portal, but now it feels… like it's void of life and excitement.

The portal brought us just inside of the castle entrance. Nearby guards stare in confusion and surprise, hands reaching for their swords, but they relax when they notice me.

The four of us hurry down the hall while still looking dignified, and I trip on the hem of my gown. Delphine catches my arm.

"Thank you," I whisper. As I right myself, I notice one of the potted plants I'd put on the windowsill is much healthier than I remember it being. The others need to be replaced, but that one is somehow thriving. Odd, especially since I am the one who normally replaces them. Perhaps one of the servants has… but why have they not done all of them?

Delphine tugs me along, but when we reach the throne room, the faeries form a half-circle behind me. Even though all eyes are on us, I am not the least bit nervous—I have been raised as the perfect princess after all—until I see Loren.

CHAPTER THREE

LOREN

$\mathcal{T}$he way Briar Rose crosses the room with such grace and dignity is almost faerie-like. It seems not to matter to her that she is late… but that is also a typical faerie characteristic. Perhaps she will fit in after all.

No, it was never about whether or not she would fit in: it was about whether she would be safe. With the curse nearly upon us—

I refocus my mind, realizing she is looking directly at me. Her cheeks flush slightly—or were they pink before?—and her step falters for just a moment. I flinch where I stand beside her parents, almost taking a step toward her before my mind can make sense of what my body is doing. But Toussaint grabs my arm, and Briar Rose continues as if it never happened, dipping into a curtsy to honor her parents. Evanthe, Delphine, and Irit follow suit, ever the princess's loyal protectors, caregivers, and teachers. Very rarely have I seen her without them, or them without her, and I wonder how much they miss home after being stuck in the human lands for so long.

"Welcome home," greets her father, King Faustus. Although his tone remains courtly, there is a warmth to his hazel eyes, almost the exact same as Briar Rose's.

"We are glad you could join us, dearest," her mother chimes in.

King Faustus looks at me. "Prince Loren, you are free to greet your betrothed and share your news."

A flicker of confusion crosses Briar Rose's expression, quickly replaced by a calm, collected demeanor. The weight of her gaze makes my steps heavy as I descend the few stairs and stop in front of her. The grey of her hazel eyes has gone from a soft, warm color to that of steel, hard and cold and edged.

With a gentle touch, I raise her hand to my lips, brushing a kiss over her tense knuckles. Briar Rose trains her sight on me, not once blinking. Odd, how someone can keep their stance and face pleasant while their eyes bear the weight of their true feelings. Yes, she will make a good faerie when the time comes.

"You are lovely as ever, Princess Briar Rose."

Her pupils shrink, a sure sign she is searching my words forward and backward and inside out to understand their meaning and find any tricks. We faeries cannot lie, not outright, and she caught onto that quickly. I suppose I left it open to interpretation, but the words are already said, and it would be strange to change them now. Besides, she never seems to believe me.

"I hope you enjoy your stay as much as last year, Prince Loren," she says in return, lifting her chin slightly.

I cannot help a small smirk. Last year's visit was one of the most memorable, with both of us coming up with ingenious pranks to use on each other. But she had the advantage of being in her home, and that is all about to change.

"I'm afraid this visit will be brief." I raise my voice so everyone can hear. "In three days' time, I will take Princess Briar Rose back to Seelie with me, so that we may prepare for our wedding and her transformation into Fae."

BRIAR ROSE

Three days. *Three days.*

Delayed applause fills the room, but his words echo in my mind. Three days means I will be leaving shortly after the ball, the one meant to celebrate Loren's visit and my birthday. I wondered why Father and Mother planned it a month before my actual birthday, wondered if it had to do with the curse…

Of course. They want me to be in Seelie, where I might be safer with their magic to guard me from the curse the Unseelie King placed on me when I was an infant: after I turn eighteen, I will prick my finger on the spindle of a spinning wheel and die. Luckily, although she was unable to break the curse, Evanthe was able to alter it so that instead of dying, I will go into a deep sleep until True Love's Kiss breaks the spell.

Which makes me think I might be forever asleep unless I can either find a way to break the curse or find my true love before it happens. Neither seems very likely.

Henri's face invades my thoughts, and I shove it away. It is ridiculous to think I could fall in love with someone I have never actually met. I don't know his name, have never even seen his true face.

Then it hits me: I am going to Faerie, to the Seelie lands. They have not brought me there since I was a child, back when Loren and I actually got along for the most part.

Despite my feelings about being with Loren, I find myself excited to be in Faerie again, to see the brilliant colors and meet mythical creatures and feel the magic in the air—

And they will finally make me Fae. I have yet to find out what all that will entail, but the idea of having my own magic outside of the dreamscape is something I crave. If I have to marry Loren to get magic… that very well might be worth it.

The applause dies down, and Father insists that we have a celebratory dinner this evening, welcoming Prince Loren. Other than his personal guard Toussaint, Loren has brought no one else. Normally a few others of the Seelie Court visit, sometimes even the Queen of Seelie herself, Vivienne, Loren's aunt. But she rarely can leave, for fear of what the Unseelie could do to Seelie without her magic there to protect the land.

I do look forward to seeing her, with her genuinely kind and fun-loving nature. One of the last times I was in Seelie, Vivienne had taken Loren and me through a portal to visit mermaids—well, mermen, two princes who were friends with Loren. Loren, Toussaint, and I always had the best adventures until...

I shake the memories away before they can sour my mood. Although I find myself being led to the gardens by Loren, so I suppose there's a chance my mood will be soured regardless. For the sake of the kingdom believing we are the lovestruck pair whose union will strengthen both humans and Seelie, we have to pretend to at least like one another, which means being together. An unspoken understanding between us is that being outside, especially in the gardens, is the best option. A neutral ground of sorts.

It's hard to miss the way passersby openly ogle Loren. Thankfully, they leave a wide berth for us to walk. I breathe in, letting the scent of earth and flowers melt a bit of the tension in my shoulders. His grip on me loosens but doesn't let go.

"Are you upset about the news?" Loren asks quietly. Toussaint is a few paces behind us, but I'm sure he can hear the conversation regardless.

Nothing in Loren's expression clues me in on why he is asking. Could it truly be concern for my feelings? Has he changed in the past year? He keeps his gaze forward, eyes flicking about to the different flowers. They never stray to any of the women fanning themselves as they watch us walk by.

"I wish I was told in private beforehand," I admit. I should give him the benefit of the doubt—Irit especially would be appreciative.

He nods, still not looking at me. "Perhaps if we had arrived earlier, it could have been arranged."

That prickles my anger. I tighten my hold on his arm. By *we*, he means *me*. "There were some difficulties preventing our arrival from being punctual." The words come out strained, trying to maintain an even tone. It was not my fault we were late, but I would hate to blame Evanthe, Delphine, and Irit. They were merely trying to help me look presentable.

He side-eyes me, brows furrowing in a way that I cannot quite tell if it's meant to be confusion, worry, or the beginnings of a scowl. "Since you are here safe and whole, I assume the difficulties were dealt with appropriately."

I barely hold back a snort of derision. "Your concern is noted, Prince Loren."

He studies me for a few moments longer, then returns to the flowers.

If I were walking with Henri instead, this would be a lot more fun. We'd chase each other or share jokes or—

My stomach knots. Like it or not, I am betrothed to Loren. He doesn't deserve a fiancée who is pining after someone else. I need to give him a chance. If he were pursuing someone else, I...

An uncomfortable feeling pinches my chest. Why would I care? I don't like Loren. But we are betrothed to be married, and the thought of him looking—

"Shall we return indoors?" Loren asks, breaking my dizzying thoughts. "You look as though you are about to be ill." He stops, actually meeting my eyes. A couple locks of auburn hair have fallen forward, curling at his brow, and I fight back the urge to tug one. He used to let me when we were children. He'd pretend to be irritated by it, but he'd always smile.

I still don't quite understand what happened between us. The deep heartache I've long stuffed down rises to the surface once more, demanding attention, threatening to overtake me.

No. I will not let it.

"I am fine, thank you," I reply, wishing my tone sounded more at ease. I am unused to his gaze, so I look away and try to continue walking. His grip remains firm. Toussaint keeps his distance, but I can tell he's concerned, trying to decide if he needs to step in.

"Lying will do neither of us any good."

That brings my attention right back to him. "I am surprised a faerie could say such a thing."

His amber eyes darken, his expression sharpening.

Not looking at each other, we walk in silence for the rest of the afternoon.

CHAPTER FOUR

LOREN

*A*fter the disaster of a conversation earlier, dinner cannot come soon enough. I bring Briar Rose to her room so that her faerie guardians can get her ready with plenty of time to spare. All three of them eye me as Briar Rose hurries into her bedroom with barely a goodbye.

Delphine frowns, making my pulse quicken, but Irit thanks me and shuts the door before anything can happen.

Toussaint gives me space to think while I go to my own quarters and ready myself, but I can feel how jittery he is.

"Say it," I demand finally, tugging a new shirt on. This is a little less comfortable than the other I was wearing, meant for special occasions. My aunt insists that uncomfortability is the price for beauty. I hate it.

"You should tell Briar Rose how you feel."

"Do you really think that will go over well?" I tug on a jacket that seems to have one purpose: squeezing the life out of me. And being stylish, I must admit, with its stitching and gold buttons stamped with falling leaves, no doubt to symbolize autumn, my Glamour's affiliation. Two purposes then. Perhaps I can make this work.

I stare at my reflection, fixating on the clothes so I can avoid looking into my own eyes... and avoid letting Toussaint see them. Although I am certain he already knows my thoughts before they fully form in my mind.

"I believe she will take it better than the childish remarks and pranks you play on each other."

Unable to help myself, I glare at him in the mirror. He stands near the door, arms crossed, corner of his mouth twitching upward, but everything in his stance tells me he is alert to everything going on around us, just like he always is.

"Either you explain everything and work through the consequences, or let this tear you both apart and make the rest of your lives miserable," he continues, his tone softening a touch. "I know you are more than willing to pay the price, but I also know you would spare her whatever sorrows you can."

I break eye contact, focusing on undoing the jacket. It's far too tight, even with it undone. But the king and queen had the outfit made for me, including the crown, and I dare not slight them, especially given their hospitality and generosity over the years. I am supposed to become King of the Seelie in a short while—I thought I would be used to being uncomfortable by now, having prepared for this my whole life.

Just make it through tonight... and the next few days... and the next few decades...

"Loren..."

"Leave it, Toussaint." I will my hands not to shake as I pick up the crown, twisted metal meant to look like overlapping vines with leaves and berries and small flowers. Fitting for a faerie prince, even if I cannot quite muster up the spirit to play the part. Aunt Vivienne would tell me to smile and do it anyway, if only for a few hours.

Instead of listening to me, Toussaint presses, "She will come to understand in time. Tell her before we return home, before she can find out from someone else. She said so herself that she wished you had told her about the new arrangement in private beforehand. You have to give her a chance."

"I avoided telling her beforehand because I was uncertain it would actually happen."

Toussaint pauses. "What do you mean?"

"I asked my aunt to wait longer, to find another way."

Another pause, this time longer. Even without looking at him, I know he is trying to figure out my reasoning. "You do not want her to come to Seelie."

I press my thumb into the sharp point of one of the metal leaves. Golden blood wells, and when I wipe it across the crown, it shimmers.

"Loren, Briar Rose will be safe—"

"She was not safe last time." The scraps of sunlight coming through the window gleam off the crown in a myriad of colors. I used to do that to Briar Rose's crown, the iridescent effect making her smile. But she found out how I did it and made me stop, pressing kisses to my fingertips. "I could not keep her safe..."

"You were a child! You both were."

I whirl around to face him finally, the points of the crown biting into the flesh of my tight fist. "The Unseelie King is getting stronger every day. She is safer here, without magic for him to track and use against her."

As my voice raises, his expression turns sympathetic. It simultaneously makes me want to shove him, to get him to fight back, and to hide away from my childishness.

Before I can apologize, Toussaint whispers, "The curse will happen one way or another. If True Love's Kiss is the only thing that will break it, you have to give her a chance to fall in love with you."

What if I'm not the one?

I stuff that thought back down as I have every time over the past thirteen years, since the Unseelie King put that doubt in my mind. I can do this. I am the Prince of Seelie, and I have a role to play, duties to perform. Steadier than I expect myself to be, I place the crown atop my head.

"We have a dinner to attend."

Keeping the rest of his thoughts to himself, Toussaint follows me out of the room.

BRIAR ROSE

The dress chosen for tonight brightens my mood significantly: it was created with magic, sparkling like it is made up of tiny stars. The fabric itself is a soft purple, the skirts flowing perfectly. They would be fun to twirl in if we were dancing.

Alas, it is just a dinner, and I will have to sit with Loren. Hopefully I can come up with a better conversation than earlier.

"Don't frown." Evanthe lifts my chin. "No one is worth the frown lines humans get."

I almost laugh, cracking a small smile.

Delphine snorts. "She'll be Fae soon enough; she won't have to worry about that."

"What did he say that bothered you so?" Evanthe asks, ignoring Delphine.

"It wasn't anything in particular," I answer carefully, trying to keep still as Irit pins flowers into my hair. "He just… he is so cold. I thought that we were best friends when we were younger, and after…" I swallow the lump in my throat. "Now he hates me."

"He does not hate you," Evanthe insists as Delphine snorts again, rolling her eyes. "The boy needs to learn to be charming, but he does not hate you. I guarantee it."

I nod to appease her, and she lets it go even though she knows I don't yet believe it. Perhaps I can find a way to smooth things over with Loren, to at least make things between us less tense. Maybe pretend he is Henri? How would I act if I were going to dine with him?

My room suddenly feels warmer as I imagine actually meeting him in person, being able to feel his hand in mine—

"Are you feeling ill?" Irit asks, pressing the back of her hand to my forehead. "Your cheeks are flushed."

"She is well enough," Delphine interjects. "The excitement of the evening is all." She makes sure she has my attention before she puts her hands on her hips and adds, "If he gives you any trouble, wave us over, and we'll deal with him."

"Delphine!" Irit squeaks.

"What? Prince or not, I'll not let him treat her any less than she deserves."

"You know he—" Evanthe cuts herself off, takes a moment to inhale. "You know things are different now. He and Briar Rose will be married soon, and I cannot fathom that he would want to make anyone's life more difficult, especially his own."

My heart leaps at the knock on the door. Delphine and Irit stand near me as Evanthe lets in Loren and Toussaint, gracefully curtsying. They bow their heads in return, and then Loren's eyes immediately seek mine, the weight of his gaze pinning me to the spot as he takes me in.

Faerie clothes are generally thinner and looser, much less to wear than human clothes, so it really doesn't surprise me that he has his doublet open, exposing the white shirt beneath, and has completely forgone gloves. Still, he carries himself like royalty, unmistakable even if he were not wearing the crown atop his loose red curls.

"Princess Briar Rose is beautiful, is she not, Prince Loren?" Evanthe asks, her hint of amusement clueing me into the fact that we might have been studying each other for far longer than socially acceptable.

"She is," Loren answers, voice soft, taking me completely by surprise. He crosses the room and takes my arm before I can remember to thank him for the compliment, and then we are headed toward the dining hall.

Perhaps Evanthe is right: perhaps things are different now. Why, I do not know, but I intend to find out.

CHAPTER FIVE

LOREN

I try not to look like I'm walking too quickly, but I can feel Evanthe's eyes boring into the back of my head. And possibly Delphine's. Irit is too sweet and polite to follow suit.

I couldn't help staring at Briar Rose, and the way Evanthe all but dragged the compliment out of me has me irritated. I should have thought to say something. That's what Henri would have done, regardless of who was around. He is charming, confident…

…and doesn't exist. A creation from my imagination, a mask I wear when I am in Briar Rose's dreamscape. Or my own, which I have had little need of since I started visiting hers. I have thought of telling her many times over the past year, but I hate the idea of losing this connection with her. I lost it when we were children, purposefully putting a wall between us to keep her safe, and these secret meetings in her dreamscape have been a salve to that still-bleeding wound.

But now I have to take her back to Seelie, where we are to be married and she is to be turned into Fae. Despite my arguments, Aunt Vivienne has decided that Briar Rose will have the best chance of breaking the curse if we do all of that before she turns eighteen, before the curse can go into effect. I understand her logic, but the thought of the Unseelie King finding her again knots my insides— all of the Faeric Lands are wild, full of magic, and if she turns Fae, then she'll have her own magic he'll be using against her. I wasn't strong enough last time, but this time I'll be ready. I'll have to be. As much as I fear becoming king, that may be what will give me enough strength to stand against my brother.

The dining hall is already full by the time we arrive. The herald announces us, and those in attendance raise their drinks, cheer, and clap. Briar Rose's grip on my arm tightens. I sneak a glance, noting that, although she has her princess smile on, there is tension in her mouth. Briefly, I consider slipping out into the garden so she can have a moment to regather herself, but Toussaint discreetly taps the back of my arm, reminding me that we have duties to attend.

I put my hand over hers in what I hope is a comforting manner. Her fingers twitch, and she looks up at me, but I'm already leading us forward, between the two long tables stretching across most of the room. If I dare look back at her now...

Seeing her anger earlier was more than enough for one day. Toussaint is right: I have to find a way to open up my heart to her again so that hopefully she'll do the same.

Be more like Henri...

Easier said than done. Henri is not who I am, and acting like him will raise her suspicions. Best I come clean to her soon, before she finds out on her own and hates me even more.

BRIAR ROSE

The way Loren puts his hand over mine makes my heart skip a beat —but when I glance at him, he is expressionless, focused on bringing us to the small table prepared for just the two of us, nearby my family's table.

Loren isn't trying to comfort me; he's trying to keep me with him. I have no idea what gave him the impression that I was going to pull away from him or flee the room, but now both sound like wonderful plans.

Give him a chance, I remind myself. He did actually comment on my beauty—well, Evanthe did, and he agreed. Still, that is the nicest thing he has said about me in a long time. And the way he'd been staring, lips slightly parted, eyes alight...

Father and Mother greet us without getting up from their seats. Father's cheeks are already pink, the goblet in his hand nowhere near full. My younger brother Jovan sits near them, his scowl disappearing when he sees me. He waves enthusiastically, to which Mother calmly reaches over and puts his arm down.

Servants pull out our chairs for us, and I maneuver into it carefully with my dress, the skirts barely fitting. Loren waits until I am seated before he follows suit, finally releasing my arm.

Father raises a toast to our impending nuptials, his words beginning to slur. Mother has a pinched smile but refrains from saying anything. Thankfully, he keeps it short, wishing us well and thanking Loren for taking me "off his hands," a joke that lands well with the other nobles but not with me or Mother. Or Loren, who has already half-drained his goblet of wine by the time the others have stopped laughing enough to drink.

The arrangement of food would normally be tantalizing, but I only nibble at the roasted pork and peas. Loren finishes his first goblet of wine, and a servant dutifully refills it before stepping back toward the wall, where Toussaint, Evanthe, Delphine, and Irit are waiting, watching us from under the large floral arrangements hanging from the ceiling. Everything seems to be decorated in flowers, like someone tried to make the dining hall feel like a garden, and I cannot say I dislike it. The roses on our table are a range of pinks, which means they must be from Mother's special garden. I lock eyes with her and smile, and she smiles back briefly, interrupted by the need to stop Jovan from tossing peas into one of the vases in the corner of the room.

"I was not expecting so many flowers," Loren says in between bites of food. It seems he has hardly touched his dinner too.

An odd thing for him to say, but we are a far cry from the friends we were as children, and I suppose we have to start somewhere. "Do you like it?" I ask, unable to tell from his tone, and lacking any other safe conversation topics.

"Yes," he answers, sneaking a glance at me. "It reminds me of Faerie."

The ache returns with a vengeance. It has been thirteen years since my last visit, and I can only recall bits of memories: a sweet scent, bright colors, Loren smiling at me, hugging me...

I take a sip of wine, trusting that will wash the anger and sadness back down. When it doesn't, I take another. And another. "I believe that was their intent." My voice comes out even, with just a hint of an edge. I hope he doesn't notice.

But of course, he does. A muscle in his jaw twitches, his expression on the cusp of a frown. I try to remember the last time I saw a true smile out of him. He has his charming, courtly smile, but I think the last genuine one had to have been in Faerie.

That is an awfully long time for someone to be unhappy.

"If they did it justice, then I look forward to seeing how beautiful Faerie really is."

Loren side-eyes me, pondering. "You have been to Faerie before."

"I have... but it has been so long, I do not remember many details." *Just the things that keep my heart aching.*

He turns toward me, shifting in his seat. I want to look away, but there is a heaviness to his countenance that I cannot quite understand, and it draws me in. He opens his mouth, then shuts it, swallows, and tries again to speak. "I hope you like it."

Is that what he meant to say? "Why wouldn't I?"

"I only meant that if it is to be your home, it would be tragic if you did not like it."

Home. I hadn't thought of Faerie as my home, but it will be

soon. From what I remember, I can't imagine not loving it, the land thrumming with magic and teeming with creatures and adventure. Another reason marrying Loren might not be as bad as I fear. Besides, surely I will be able to visit my family every so often when I get homesick, although it will be under the guise of us royals keeping the human-faerie alliance strong by regular meetings.

Then it hits me: Loren said he hopes I like Faerie. If he were human, that could be disregarded as polite pleasantry, meaningless conversation. But he is a faerie, incapable of lying with his words.

Does a part of him care?

CHAPTER SIX

LOREN

"*L*ast night was not… terrible," Toussaint says as we stroll through the gardens, waiting for Briar Rose and her faerie entourage to join us. I'd thought we were going to have breakfast together, but servants were sent with food shortly after I woke up. Having spent a lot of time in Briar Rose's dreamscape recently, I had not realized how tired I was, sleeping well past the sun's rise. Granted, it seems she also slept in.

I wonder if she misses seeing Henri.

"It was not," I agree. Uncomfortable, certainly, but not terrible. If the worst we have to get through is stilted conversation before we can be on good terms again, I can suffer through that. Although I know that is not the worst—I have to tell Briar Rose that I am Henri. She clearly likes him and is conflicted about that, being betrothed to me. I should have spared her the guilt a long time ago.

"It was the first time neither of you pulled a trick on each other."

My laugh sounds forced. "That is a very low standard for judging how well a dinner goes." I scuff the toe of my boot in the dirt. Chances are, someone will notice but not say a word, just like they said nothing last night about my doublet being open and my crown being slightly askew. They are too fascinated by the fact that I'm Fae, or perhaps do not want to be rude. Over the years, almost nothing has been brought up about the antics between Briar Rose and me, not even when I used magic to give her pink dress brown dots before an important ceremony, or when she slipped herbs into my tea that turned my skin orange. I'd had to use what little magic I'd had left to undo it, yet another frivolous choice, in Toussaint's opinion. But he wasn't the one who had to go around looking like that. And if he didn't want me fixing it, he shouldn't have made all of those jokes about it.

"Still, it is an improvement." I don't miss his small smirk.

"Most anything is." I sigh, turning my face up toward the sun to bask in its warmth and closing my eyes.

Quickly, I lean back, feeling something move past me. When I open my eyes again, Toussaint is readying his next attack, smirk more apparent now.

"Good to see your wallowing hasn't made you lose your edge, Fox," he teases, using a childhood nickname that has stuck into adulthood. I assume it has to do with the color of my hair, but Toussaint tends to give a different answer every time someone asks him.

I dodge the next one just as easily as the first. But he's just getting warmed up, trying to goad me. It works, and we slip into that familiar dance, knowing one another's tells and strategies from years of sparring with each other. While the high bushes block us from the view of passersby, they also add the challenge of close quarters. Quick steps, precise movements.

A soft gasp has us both halt mid-strike. I crane my neck back to see Briar Rose and her entourage of faeries watching us with rapt attention. Her hazel eyes are pinned on me, her expression something uncomfortably close to awe. But then she looks at Toussaint the same way, and my gut twists.

We lower our hands and move toward the women. Evanthe, Delphine, and Irit dip into curtsies, and I vaguely acknowledge them as I stop in front of Briar Rose. Her attention snaps back to me, and I freeze.

What would Henri do?

Gently, I take her hand, noting she forewent gloves, surely so she can enjoy the feel of flower petals. Her eyes flit across my face, that all-too-familiar furrow between her brows present. The Henri in me wants to press my thumb to it, to smooth it out, but I am not him, and definitely not ready for her to figure out he does not exist.

Instead, I kiss her knuckles. The furrow softens but doesn't completely go away. I suppose I should take that as a win, all things considered.

"Good morning," I greet.

"Good morning," she parrots in a rushed manner, her cheeks flushed. "I apologize for my tardiness. I hope I haven't kept you waiting long."

"Not long," I reply, trying to figure out what has her so flustered.

Briar Rose clears her throat and pulls her hand away. "I am glad. What would you care to do today?"

"Whatever your heart desires." I inwardly cringe at how sappy that sounded. Henri does much better at sounding charming than I do. Besides, her heart's desire toward me is probably to get me back for the years of pranks.

Briar Rose ponders a moment, and I do my best not to fidget. Toussaint and the other faeries remain quiet, but I can only imagine their restraint to keep from laughing at how uncomfortable this is.

Something flies overhead, casting a small shadow over Briar Rose that is gone as quickly as it came. By the time I glance up, the dark creature is too far away to make out. A bird, most likely. No need to be jumpy.

"A walk in the woods sounds nice," she suggests finally.

Woods. Outside. Yes, that is a good choice. Even with the dining hall being as large as it is, last night's dinner left me feeling like the walls were closing in, especially after King Faustus declared his eternal gratitude for me marrying his daughter soon. He hadn't gone into detail, but I know he and his wife—the entire kingdom, really—hang their hopes for breaking Briar Rose's curse on me. True Love's Kiss. What Evanthe thought she was doing in making that the way to break the curse, I have no idea. It feels like something so far out of my control...

But I have to try.

CHAPTER SEVEN

THE UNSEELIE KING

In the midst of a gloomy grey sky, a black figure swoops over treetops, careening toward my castle. I watch through the window, the diagonal panes giving the glass diamond patterns. The figure is now clear, a small wyvern about the size of a cat making her way toward my window as if she means to crash through. She unfurls her wings, and the moment before she makes contact with the glass, I flick my fingers. The wyvern disappears in black smoke-like tendrils and reappears on my shoulder in the same fashion, magic reshaping her.

"Asra," I murmur in greeting, and cautiously place my hand near her head. She leans into it and chirrups when I scratch under her chin. Her tail coils loosely around my neck, claws digging into my shoulder for balance.

"What news do you have for me?" I ask, resting my thumb against her forehead. The wyvern's slit-pupiled eyes close, her barriers lowering as my magic travels into her mind. Even if she'd kept the barrier up, I would have been able to break through without much effort, but I prefer removing the risk of fracturing her mind, something irreparable, even with the help of magic. Good informants are hard enough to come by, and I trust her more than any of the Unseelie. They were, after all, going to hand me over to Seelie Queen Vivienne after my mother was murdered, in hopes that she would spare them and allow them to return despite the years of bloodshed. They had thought me too young to lead, too young to have much power.

I'd proven them wrong.

I close my eyes so I can focus on the images unfurling as my mind connects to Asra's. It takes a moment to adjust to the bright colors and the way things of magic have a shimmer overlay. Oh, to be able to see magic as easily as a wyvern.

I piece together that she was flying over the human castle, home to that self-important King Faustus. While he is nowhere to be seen, there are six forms Asra fixated on, daring to dive closer. Five of them shimmer, some more than others, but the sixth... her colors are muted, darkness clinging to her. My own magic.

Princess Briar Rose. In the last almost eighteen years since I cast the curse, it remains just as strong, circling her like it is waiting for the right moment to pounce.

Eighteen years... the curse will enact any day now. Everyone is aware, and they must be preparing to bring her to Seelie. I am sure of it, since my half-brother Loren is with her. They believe they stand a better chance of breaking the spell if she is Fae, and they are sorely mistaken. That will only make it easier for me to find her, but whether or not I do, the curse will... sooner or later.

The six of them walk toward the woods. I skip ahead in Asra's memories, to where she is awaiting them, nestled in the branches above. Birds and squirrels scatter at her presence, but when Loren and the others look up at the noise, they do not see Asra in the shadows.

This close, I can better see Loren and Briar Rose. Both are much older since I last saw them—granted, they were young children then. While our father's likeness is obvious in Loren's features, there is also a softness to his expression I never saw in Oberon. An agony whenever he glances at Briar Rose. But when she looks his way, it turns to stone, unreadable. They break eye contact quickly, turning their attentions to various parts of the forest.

"They can barely stand to look at each other," Irit whispers to Delphine and Evanthe, trailing behind to give the betrothed couple their space while also keeping watch over them.

Toussaint keeps pace with the three female faeries, shortening his strides. He sighs. "Perhaps they need a nudge in the right direction?"

"I'm not sure how many more 'nudges' we can give," Delphine grumbles. "If we 'nudge' them any more, they're bound to either break or fall off the edge."

"Edge of what…?" Irit asks. "And if you're breaking something, you're doing a lot more than nudging."

Asra hops from branch to branch, following them. As is typical of adult faeries, Evanthe, Delphine, and Irit have not changed a bit since they were my caretakers, neither in appearance nor in their squabbling.

But I have certainly changed.

"We have today and tomorrow to fix this," Evanthe says after she hisses for the other two women to cease their bickering. "Wedding preparations are already underway. I doubt Vivienne will be convinced to postpone it yet again, no matter what Loren says."

I hold the memory still so I can ponder for a moment. Loren wants to postpone the wedding. But why, I wonder… Does he think she is safer in the human lands? I could easily bring her here if I desired, but kidnapping is not my taste. And, again, I do not need her here, or to even be near here, for the curse to take effect.

If True Love's Kiss is supposed to break the curse, then he should be trying to get her to fall in love with him.

She said they have two days, which means they will bring Briar Rose to Faerie, directly to the Seelie Palace, no doubt. They will also have all spindles gone by then in an attempt to thwart the curse.

I smile. Really, I can sit back and do nothing, and everything will still fall into place. But I have other plans, an idea forming. I want to see Briar Rose, in person, and talk with her.

The memory continues on, giving me nothing more of consequence, although I do appreciate witnessing Loren's awkward attempts at conversation and Briar Rose's witty, barbed responses. Truly, they are both awkward, and I wonder what has caused such a divide between them. They seemed inseparable before, Loren ready to throw himself at me to defend Briar Rose the last time I saw them…

"Good girl." I slip out of Asra's mind and gently pet her wings. "Let's get you a treat."

BRIAR ROSE

I can be nice, I can be nice, I can be nice… That has been my mantra the whole day so far. It was easy to follow it this morning. Loren seemed like a different person then, someone relaxed and… happy. He was actually smiling as he sparred with Toussaint, both of them moving quickly and fluidly, like they knew each move the other would make. It looked almost like a dance, although it was a bit too aggressive to be. Plenty of times, their strikes almost landed, and when one had come too close to Loren's jaw, I gasped involuntarily.

And just like that, they stopped. Loren's gaze on me was intense, and I had to look away. But then he took my hand, kissed my knuckles, reeling my attention back in…

We went from a tentative truce as we walked through the woods —me thinking he might be more charming than I'd given him credit for—to this awkward silence. Surely we have *something* to talk about.

"They're whispering about us."

I peek over my shoulder to see that Loren is right, except I would have described it as hushed bickering. The other faeries are far enough behind us that I cannot hear them, but I wonder how much Loren has heard.

"What are they saying?" I can't help asking.

"I am not entirely sure," he says, the tips of his ears turning pink even though it is much cooler in the forest, with the trees shading us.

"But you have some idea," I press, adjusting my grip on his arm.

He holds a branch out of our way so we can pass without our clothes getting snagged. That would have put me in a sour mood, but Irit would have mended it quickly, even without magic.

"For a faerie, you are a terrible liar," I tease him.

"I would think you'd appreciate that."

I blink, processing his response. "I'd appreciate no lies at all."

Loren clenches his jaw and refuses to look at me.

I can be nice... Only "nice" is the last thing I want to be right now. I want to be away from all of them, at the cottage on the edge of Faerie, where I can sneak into my dreamscape and wait for Henri to find me again. Because somehow, he always does. Like a gentleman, he never leaves me waiting long.

Enough about Henri, I chastise myself, tucking him away in a secret corner of my heart. I can't leave all of them, not right now, but...

An idea comes to me, reminiscent of something Loren and I used to do as children. Maybe I can spark something in both of us if I recreate one of our better days, back when we were friends. I lean toward Loren, tilting my mouth up toward his ear. He tenses but leans in, slowing his pace slightly.

"We could lose them," I suggest as quietly as I can.

Loren straightens and casts a glance behind us before locking eyes with me. "Lead the way."

I wait a minute, sneakily sliding my hand into Loren's. To his credit, he doesn't flinch this time, just waiting to follow my lead. It reminds me of times long ago, back when his hand could completely envelop mine. Not the same now that we are grown up, but the warm, comforting feeling takes me by surprise. I find myself waiting for the familiar assuring squeeze, but it doesn't happen.

Being nice doesn't mean looking for things that aren't there anymore. I'll only end up hurt, and really, it isn't fair of me, when neither of us is the same as we were as children. I have to lay the old Loren to rest and get to know who he is now.

Checking behind me again is tempting, but I don't want to clue the other faeries in on our plan. So, I take a breath, and then bolt into the thicker part of the woods.

CHAPTER EIGHT

LOREN

*B*riar Rose grips my hand tightly as we create our own
path through the trees, which are so close together that
they block out a lot of the sun. I have a flicker of concern about her
being able to see well with her human eyes so reliant on light, but
she doesn't slow down, darting back and forth, ducking under
branches and weaving between trees and bushes.

Toussaint calls out for me first, then Evanthe for Briar Rose.
Certainly, they saw us running, and if they really feel the need to
find us, they will resort to magic.

I find myself grinning, intrigued to find out where we will end
up; hopefully, they will wait to use magic.

With her free hand, Briar Rose holds her skirts, using her
forearm to bat aside anything in her way. I would have thought her
dress would have slowed her down, but she seems to be managing
well. Granted, I may have used a bit of magic to move things before

they snagged her hair or cloak. It leaves a half-empty feeling in my chest, a reminder that I am still in human lands, that my magic here is finite.

Eventually, we slow to a halt near a river that cuts through the woods. She pants as she looks over my shoulder.

"I think we lost them."

"For now," I agree.

Her eyes dart to my face, then to our still-interlocked fingers. She pulls away, toying with a lock of her hair. If we were in her dreamscape, she'd be absent-mindedly turning her hair different colors.

"There is a grove on the other side of the river," she says hesitantly, eyeing the rocks protruding from the water. "We could cross over there."

I recall those being bigger the last time we'd crossed them. A side effect of growing up, I suppose. If we are careful, we should be fine…

Briar Rose is already marching toward them with determination, so I follow. If we are to get ourselves in some sort of trouble, we might as well do it together, right?

The first isn't far from shore, so she jumps onto it easily. Wind plays with her hair, loosening the pinned updo and blowing strands in her face. She ignores it and hops to the next one. I keep behind her, watching her footing. While the river isn't going too fast, the rocks are slick, and her heeled shoes are better suited for indoors. I fear if I warn her to be careful, it'll be taken wrong and irritate her.

Luckily, we make it across after having only gotten the bottom edge of her cloak wet.

"Could have been worse," she says, and pushes her hair back out of her face. For a few moments, she tries repinning it, but gives up quickly. "The grove is that way."

"I remember," I reply without thinking, and am not sure what to make of the appraising look she gives me. *If you are wondering, I remember all of it, every moment, good and bad.*

The words are stuck in my throat, and before I can find a way to say them, Briar Rose nods. "Good."

Even though I know where we're going, I let her take the lead. It feels a little too presumptuous to walk beside her like we are friends again, like nothing happened.

My aunt wants me to wed Briar Rose as soon as possible, to have the two of us take over the Seelie throne, strengthening our position against the Unseelie. While I agree with the logic of it, the thought of marrying Briar Rose against her will makes me sick. Either way, it has to happen, so I have a short amount of time to tear the wall down between us.

If I were really Henri, this would be easy. Which, I am, sort of, but I doubt that Briar Rose will be thrilled about it when I tell her, so I'm hoping to be at least on better terms when I do.

The glade is the same, surrounded by trees and wildlife, bunches of flowers in random spots... and on the far side stands a tiny, poorly-built house. Barely big enough for us when we were children, I doubt I would even be able to get my torso inside.

"Is something wrong?"

"No." I clear my throat. "I just... I wasn't expecting it to still be here."

Puzzled, she asks, "Where else would it be?"

I don't have a good answer for that. Because really, I had not thought about our playhouse in a long time.

Aware of her eyes on me, I kneel in front of the playhouse. Just a few pieces of wood and sticks placed haphazardly, the only thing keeping it upright is the spell I'd cast on it. A ragged blanket hangs over the entrance in lieu of a door, and all the flowers we decorated the house with are long gone. The paintings remain, messy hearts and misspelled words. She painted flowers and pixies and even a kelpie we narrowly avoided. The horse-like creature had wanted to drag us to the depths of the lake, but Toussaint and I managed to scare it off long enough for us to flee. After that misadventure, Briar Rose gave him the highest honor she could think of at the time: permission to paint something on our playhouse.

With a cheeky grin, he wrote "Toussaint was here" in our language. Spellbound by the beautiful flourishes of the foreign lettering, Briar Rose asked me what it said. Since I didn't have the heart to tell her, Toussaint did, making her burst into a fit of giggles.

So many of our adventures, memorialized on bits of wood tied together with string and magic. And in the middle of it all, under the fox and rose I drew, are our names in childlike writing:

LOREN + BRIAR ROSE

I fight the urge to trace the letters. I didn't know how to read any of the human languages at the time, but she'd told me what she'd written.

"I have nothing to fear," she'd said with a kiss to my cheek, "if True Love's Kiss is all it takes to break the curse."

If only it were that easy.

Briar Rose settles beside me, freshly-picked flowers in hand. Silently, she offers me a few. Our fingers brush, and we quickly look away from each other, focusing instead on decorating. It looks ridiculous, having flowers sticking out between the gaps in the wood, but for some reason it brings a small smile to my face that gets even bigger when I notice she's smiling too. Barely there, but it counts.

I wonder if there is something I can say to bring out one of her dazzling grins, the ones currently reserved for Henri alone.

Of course, my mind blanks when she catches me staring.

"How long do you think it'll be until they find us?" She picks a few more daisies, angling her face away from me, but not fast enough to make me miss seeing her blush.

"Hard to say," I admit. "That depends on whether they use magic or not."

"You mean whether they cheat or not."

I chuckle, which surprises her. Well, both of us. I clear my throat. "That's an apt way to put it. It would completely ruin the game."

Why am I so terrible at this?

But she tentatively gives me a nod of approval and goes back to adjusting her floral arrangement, so I guess I'm not too terrible, but not great either.

"Can I ask you something?" She still won't look at me for more than a few seconds at a time.

"…Yes."

The pause she takes adds to my anxiety. "Why now?"

I wait a moment to see if she will finish her question, but she picks at her dress like there's something stuck to it that I can't see. "Why now what?"

"Why are you taking me to Faerie now? It's been years, and now all of a sudden you want to take me there with barely any time to prepare." She speaks calmly, but her motions are tense. "What changed?"

I'm not sure how to answer that in a way she'd like, or at least accept. "The curse is nearly here. We cannot wait any longer."

"But why did we wait?" Hesitantly, she looks my way. "I thought… I thought it was supposed to happen sooner."

I swallow. How did we get to talking like this, so serious so soon? We were on the cusp of old times, and it feels like one wrong word could pitch us both over the edge. "It was," I confess reluctantly. "But Faerie is dangerous by itself, even more so with the Unseelie King after you."

The furrow between her brows is back. "After me? He already cursed me, and as far as I understand it, it's inevitable unless we find a way to break it. Why would he still be after me?"

"I do not know." Just like none of us know why he was there, in Seelie territory, watching Briar Rose and me as we played and explored. He could have been following us for hours, waiting until we were alone, hiding from Toussaint and the other children… He had barely lifted a finger—

"He is powerful, isn't he?" she asks, then shakes her head and sighs. "I mean, I know he's powerful, considering the curse and all of that. But any mention of him seems to have everyone terrified. I would have thought you'd want to steal me away and turn me into a faerie so I could stand a chance against him and his curse. There is only so much preparing in the dreamscape I can do as a human."

Steal her away…? I hadn't considered the fact that she might not *want* to go to Faerie. She used to love it, and no one who has ever gone has been able to fully hate it. There is a lure that cannot be denied once you have stepped foot inside our lands, like a piece of its magic latches onto you, goes with you however far you may travel.

Briar Rose could also be referencing the Unseelie and the way they used to steal humans. There have been very few reports of lost humans as of late, or so King Faustus has told us. How could she liken our betrothal to kidnapping?

She keeps her gaze steady. "What is everyone hiding from me?" she asks in a hushed tone, so light the breeze could have carried it away before it reached my ears.

Not everyone, I should tell her. *I am the only one. If others keep secrets from you, it is at my behest.*

But I don't.

CHAPTER NINE

BRIAR ROSE

*L*oren and I walk back toward the river. He lags behind, eyes looking anywhere but me. I only glance over my shoulder a few times. Maybe more than a few.

What could he possibly be hiding? I don't understand why he can't just tell me.

But maybe I pushed too hard too soon. Whatever is between us is delicate, something to prune and nurture, not rip out of the ground. Besides, he's not the only one keeping secrets…

I grimace, wondering if I should tell him. Although what good could come out of it, I don't know. What I do know is I need to talk to Henri, to break things off between us before anything truly starts. He deserves at least that much, and Loren, as closed off and aggravating as he can be, doesn't deserve to be marrying someone who longs for another. Once I reach Faerie, I'll have access to dream magic, and I can talk to Henri then. One last time…

I pull my cloak tighter around me, as if that would shield me from that line of where those thoughts will lead. I know what I have to do, but dwelling on it right now will do me no good.

Honestly, I am surprised the others haven't found us yet, and wish they would. My idea was a terrible one despite my good intentions, and I need time to myself to be ready to socialize at the ball tomorrow night.

Tomorrow is my last day in the human lands. Who knows when Loren and I will be wed, but I bet it will be soon. One day to say goodbye to my family for who knows how long, one day to get ready for my new life of becoming a wife, a faerie, a—

It sinks in that I will become Queen of the Seelie. Me, a human. Even when I transform into one of them, will they accept me wholeheartedly, or secretly despise me? If roles were reversed and Loren were becoming a human and taking my father's crown, I can only imagine the amount of bitter whispering. Possibly even open disgust and resentment, or a rebellion.

I peek behind me to make sure Loren is still there before hurrying back across the river. If I hadn't been doing this since I was a little girl, the wet stones and quickly-flowing river would make me nervous, especially with these shoes. Even so, I consider asking Loren to hold my hand just to be safe, but after not talking for so long, it feels strange to say anything at all. I should be fine.

You would have asked Henri regardless, my thoughts nettle me.

Yes, I think, *but I wouldn't have taken him to see Loren's and my playhouse.* At least, I hope I wouldn't have. That would be an ultimate betrayal, if not to this Loren, then to the boy I used to know. Although judging from the way he fixated on the playhouse today, perhaps that boy isn't fully gone. It might be a desperate wish, but I cannot bring myself to let it go.

Crack!

I throw my arms out to balance myself, but pain lances up my leg, and the world pitches askew. Loren calls my name the second before the frigid water knocks the air out of me in a burst of bubbles that quickly disperses. Instinctively, I breathe in, flailing my arms above me and kicking my legs even though the sharp sensation in my ankle keeps stabbing me—

There is a muffled splash nearby. Despite the weight of my water-logged gown, I breach the surface, hacking up water, my mind reeling with wild ideas of what could be in the river with me.

"I have you." Loren pulls me to him, and I latch on. His feet reach the bottom easily, the waterline at his chest. He walks us to shore and carefully sets me down. "Are you hurt? I saw your heel break."

Just as he said, I see that one heel of my shoe is completely missing, no doubt on the bottom of the river. With them being covered in grime and broken, I see little point in trying to fish it back out. I remove one shoe, and when I get to the second, I bite my lip to stop from squealing.

Loren grabs higher up my leg and eases off the shoe, then my stocking. If he were human, this would be considered scandalous, but so would us being caught out here alone. Faeries do not seem to care as much, and since we are already betrothed, I doubt anyone would make much of a fuss other than chastising us, which our guardians are already bound to do when they find us anyway.

My ankle is swelling.

"Stay still" is the only directive Loren gives me before, cradling my leg, he slides his hands down toward my foot. By the way the air shifts around us and the warmth that seeps into my skin, I know he is using magic. It soothes the pain, stealing it away bit by bit, and eases the tightness in my chest I didn't realize was even there.

Loren concentrates on my ankle, head bowed, movement slow and steady. The sun hits his hair just right, causing the red in his loose auburn curls to be more prominent than usual. I'm halfway to touching them before I catch myself and hold my hand against my chest.

He looks up and frowns. "Did you hurt your wrist too?"

"N-no," I assure him. "I am just a little cold." He studies me a little longer, as if trying to decide if he believes me or not, so I add, "Thank you. For using your magic, that is. Or is it Glamour?"

"Glamour is a specific type of magic more commonly used by

faeries, mostly enchantments and illusions," he explains, helping me to my feet. "How does that feel?"

I tentatively shift my weight and move my ankle around. "No pain at all." The feeling of wearing only one stocking while the other is in mud and dirt is a strange feeling, so I peel it off. "Thank you, Loren." No titles, no hostility in my tone, it's odd to hear his name said that way, but it makes me smile.

His eyes flick up from my feet to my face. "You are welcome, Briar Rose." He is not quite smiling back, but there is a lightness to his eyes that I'm sure wasn't there previously. "We sh—"

"*There* you are!" Delphine bursts through the trees and instantly pulls me this way and that so she can inspect me for injuries.

"We are very glad you are safe," Irit manages to say just as Evanthe litters me with questions about what we were possibly thinking and why we ran off. Toussaint merely looks over Loren and settles into his normal stance near his prince, whispering, "Glad you are safe, Fox."

Fox. Seeing the drawing on our playhouse reminded me that is his nickname, but I'd forgotten Toussaint is the main one who calls him that. It does suit him still, but the way his real name rolled off my tongue—

"Are you even listening to us?" Delphine snaps.

I scramble for an answer, having missed the last bit of what they'd said.

"We should return to the castle immediately," Loren interjects, gesturing to our dripping clothes. "We tumbled into the river and should get indoors before we fall ill."

Faeries can get ill? I wonder. They must, because even though Delphine continues to grumble things under her breath, our guardians hurry us back to the castle.

CHAPTER TEN

THE UNSEELIE KING

My dark magic collides with the double doors to the throne room, forcing them to swing open with what would have been a jarring clatter, had my soldiers not been boisterous already. Cackling, cheering, drinking. A lute player strums enthusiastically as he sings off-key, feet shuffling and body swaying off-beat as if he thinks he is actually dancing.

The song tells of a princess falling victim to the Unseelie King, who then obliterates the Seelie and restores Faerie to its former glory. It's a dream my mother instilled in them.

A few heads turn my way anyway, those wise few sobering up enough to jab those closest and hush them. It takes on a rippling effect as I draw closer, more and more of them falling silent and dropping to their knees. Asra tightens her tail around my neck and hisses when a faun's horns nearly graze my arm as he hurries to bow, his furry, hoofed legs bending differently than ours do.

Normally, I would murmur comfortingly to Asra, calming her so she doesn't decide to maul someone she thinks is threatening my well-being, but I have no comforting words to give at the moment. What little I have left right now is being used to keep control of myself.

Using extra magic to make it visible, my Glamour skitters across the ground like snakes. My subjects scramble backward, and the musician finally notices me and stops mid-strum. The final note is cut short, echoing dully in the now-silence. My boots tap on the stone floor. I can practically feel everyone holding their breath.

Good. Now they are ready to listen.

The musician tumbles on his way off the throne platform and gives a grunt of pain. Then he picks himself back up and rushes to hide amongst his peers, who dare not look away from me as I settle onto my ivory throne. In the entire castle, this is the only thing that is white, crafted from the bones of our enemies. Mother said she did it so that any blood she spilled was obvious, a stain she would leave for days afterward, sometimes weeks. I will admit that it does strike a fearsome image, a good trade-off for how ridiculously uncomfortable it is.

Once I am still, Asra crawls down onto the wide armrest to sit within range of my hand so I can pet her. Which I do, the slow, steady, repetitive motion grounding me.

Quick steps click from the hall and into the throne room, letting me know that my captain of the guard has arrived. Not much to be captain of, not if I cannot get these fools out of their wine cups before they inadvertently drown themselves.

Unlike most of my soldiers, Margaux walks with purpose, shoulders back, head held high. She stands a good bit higher than all of us, myself barely reaching the middle of her upper arm. From her skin to her hair to her eyes, she is as white as my throne, a stark contrast to the black and red of her uniform and cloak. Brisk movements bring her before me in a matter of moments, and she sinks into a graceful bow.

"There are still some at their stations, My King. All are accounted for."

I nod, and she moves onto the platform to position herself near me as a bodyguard. Her head nearly brushes against the silk drapery hanging from the ceiling and hooked into the nearby walls.

With as calm a voice as I can manage, I ask, "Would someone care to tell me why the majority of the castle posts are unmanned, while you party in my hall?"

A few of them glance toward the doors, no doubt wondering why Rolfe and Jean did not announce my arrival when they were supposed to be on guard.

"Your friends were passed out, drunk," I announce. "If we were attacked, they would have been of little use, just like the rest of you." The Seelie have not come this far into our territory since I took over and drove them out, but desperation is a strong catalyst to inspire the stupid and insane. If I allow myself—and my followers— to become cocky, we could miss a small string that snags and unravels our plans. My mother and I have worked too hard keeping the Unseelie fight alive to let it fall to ruin.

The majority of them have either ashamed or stony expressions. No one has drunk or eaten since I began speaking.

"What, pray tell, are you celebrating?" I know they are all too drunk or intimidated to have invited me, but I do find it curious that I, their King, did not know about it. Neither did Margaux. All very odd.

A slender woman rises from amongst the various types of Fae with their wings and tails and horns, and makes her way toward me. Chimere, a fairly recent newcomer to the Unseelie, originally living amongst the Solitary Fae, those refusing to choose a side in the war between Courts. Why she decided to join us, I have yet to figure out.

She could almost pass for High Fae if not for the sunset-colored scales on the backs of her arms, and her snake-like eyes that dare flick up to meet mine once she is at the bottom of the stairs leading up to my throne. She sinks into a graceful curtsy, making the slit up her red dress obvious that it almost reaches her hip. No scales to be found on that leg.

"Your Highnessssss," Chimere addresses me respectfully, forked tongue flicking between her sharp teeth. My mother warned me that the snake-like faeries carry venom in those fangs, enough to kill even a mighty troll with ease. "We were told to celebrate, jussst as the humansss are celebrating the princesss'sss birthday, for the cursse isss sssoon to overtake her and hand the Faerie Courtsss to you, our rightful King."

"Who told you this?" At the slight edge in my tone, Asra lowers her head and growls.

"No one," answers another voice, a male, the faun much like the one who nearly bumped me earlier. Only his coloring is darker, especially the shaggy hair covering everything on his lower half except for his hooved feet. Odilon is his name, one I have known since I was but a child toddling after my mother. One I have learned to watch, his name continuously connected with all gossip and rumors, even if only distantly. I would not be surprised to find out he played a part in my mother's downfall.

"Your Highness," he quickly tacks on, moving to stand beside Chimere. "We merely heard of the human princess's birthday cele-bration and thought to raise our own celebration in your honor."

To the Unseelie, parties and sacrifices in one's name are the highest honors one could receive. And yet, as I stare into his goat-like eyes, I sense nothing close to honor or respect.

Intentionally slow, I get to my feet. Asra leaps onto my shoulder, latching on with her claws, but I refuse to flinch. All eyes on me, I descend the stairs, knowing fully well that Margaux will be only a few steps behind me, leaving any potential attackers a split second away from their lethal demise. Odilon lifts his chin slightly, and I cannot help the smirk tugging at the corner of my mouth. He knows my power, has seen it for himself as I strangled a would-be assassin with my magic in this very room. If he wishes to undermine me without consequences, he will be utterly disappointed.

But, I must admit, I do enjoy a challenge.

Chimere shrinks back a bit as I stop in front of them; Odilon remains unmoved.

"Odd," I say after a long, tense moment has passed, "that I was not in attendance of a party thrown in my honor. It is almost as if I were not made aware of it."

Odilon's eyes narrow infinitesimally. "You are the King. You can do as you wish."

"Yes," I agree, drawing out the word a beat longer than necessary. "And yet I would loathe to insult the one who started the party in my name by not making an appearance."

Wisely, Odilon has no more replies, his stance becoming rigid.

"The princess's eighteenth birthday is not for another month," I state loudly enough for all. "Until you hear the command come from my own lips, you will do well to stick to your posts." I step past them. Asra jumps to my other shoulder just so she can glower at Odilon a few moments longer. At that, he does flinch.

"We have not gotten this far by letting down our guard," I continue. "The Seelie foolishly believe that they will be able to undo my curse and stand a chance against us. Let us not give them a foothold with which to destroy everything we have worked so hard to build."

A fire nymph starts the cheer, throwing a fist into the air and causing embers to fall off her skin and hit the stone floor, sputtering out. Quickly, the others join her in a chant: "Blood for the throne!"

Another tradition my mother started that I have kept alive, although not quite in the same vein. She allowed for small respites where they could go wild, which often ended in multiple deaths. But we cannot afford to lose even one faerie, because even the smallest pixie is useful.

Instead, I retrieve an ornate knife from my belt and swipe across my palm. Their chant grows louder and more urgent with each step I take back toward my throne, almost deafening when I smear my blood across the top.

A wordless oath that I will do whatever is necessary to protect Unseelie and restore Faerie to its former glory.

CHAPTER ELEVEN

BRIAR ROSE

*M*y faerie guardians fuss over me all the way back to my room, eventually wrangling the truth out of me.

"You *broke* your ankle?!" Delphine exclaims.

"I don't know for sure," I answer quickly, trying to pull my foot away from her, but to no avail. "Whatever happened, it's fine now."

"The prince's magic is on her," Irit states quietly. Another thing I will enjoy when I am a faerie: being able to sense magic.

After a moment, Evanthe says, "See? He's not terrible."

That doesn't stop Delphine from poking and prodding my ankle.

"I'm *fine*!" I insist.

"Delphine…" Irit rests a hand on her shoulder. "She had an eventful day. She needs rest before the ball tomorrow."

Delphine grunts in response, reluctantly releasing me. I cautiously get out of the chair and head toward my bed. They already changed me into a nightgown and had food brought to me, telling everyone that I will be fine enough for tomorrow's celebration as long as I have some time to recuperate. Father and Mother always defer to their judgment when it comes to the matter of my wellbeing.

"I promise that I am well." I try to add a smile, but I can tell she doesn't quite believe me. Physically, I am fine, but how do I explain to them that my emotions are all over the place, when I don't fully understand them myself? First there was strained silence between Loren and me, then we seemed to start to connect at our old playhouse, then he shut down, refusing to speak…

But I cannot be mad at him. Not when I am harboring a secret of my own. A secret that I have a feeling will be a lot harder to keep once I am in Faerie. Who knows how quickly Queen Vivienne will expect me to marry Loren and become a faerie myself?

"Before you leave…"

The three faeries stop at the door, turning to look at me. Keeping this secret from them for so long has been hard in and of itself; how do I lie to them this one last time? I just need enough time to put everything to rest, to end things before they can turn into a problem.

"I…" These three faeries will do—have done—so much for me. But I have to do this. Ignoring the knot in my gut, I clear my throat and start again. "Can we go to the cottage tonight, practice my dream magic? With the curse fast approaching, I'm nervous to enter Faerie and not be ready." The wavering in my voice surely helps me seem more pitiful, and will at least tug on Irit's heartstrings.

As I guessed, Irit is the first to speak. "Lovely, you do need rest… but I suppose a quick trip might not be terrible."

"It is an hour ride just to get there," Delphine points out, crossing her arms.

"But it is still early yet…"

They bicker a few moments longer before Evanthe interjects, "No one is going to the cottage."

"Finally, someone who speaks sense." Delphine nods approvingly.

I open my mouth to argue, but Evanthe holds up a hand. "I will take you briefly into the dreamscape."

"But... but your magic."

Appreciating my concern, she smiles and touches my face affectionately. "That is why I specified it will be a brief visit."

A brief visit... and she is going with me... Surely, I can figure out an excuse to be there alone so I can call upon Henri.

"This is not wise—"

Evanthe silences Delphine with a raised brow. "You have my permission to pull us out if my magic gets too low."

That seems to satisfy Delphine and Irit enough for them to back down. Evanthe gestures for me to lie back on the bed, and then takes her place beside me, holding my hand. We close our eyes, and I focus on the tingling of her magic against my palm. When I'm in the cottage, it is close enough to Faerie that I can reach out with my mind to connect with it and use its magic by myself, but since this belongs to Evanthe, I let her direct it.

There is no quicker way to anger a faerie than to take control of their magic.

The tingling warmth spreads up my arm, across my chest, and floods the rest of my body like I am being submerged under a hot spring. I inhale, feeling my soul tilt forward, like it is leaning over the edge of a cliff. Ready for the dizziness, I don't fight it: I exhale and let myself fall, my soul tumbling out of my body, still holding onto Evanthe. The soft light behind my eyelids is replaced by swirls of color, dark and bright and pale—

Evanthe squeezes my hand, one of the limited motions we have while in this state, being away from our bodies but not fully disconnected. It anchors me in the midst of the reeling, giving me enough presence of mind to picture my dreamscape.

I stumble, my knees giving way and hitting the grass, but Evanthe lands on her feet with a grace I have yet to master when traveling to any dreamscape. Hence why I always choose a grass glade as the entrance of mine.

I stand, and with a mere thought, the green stains on my dress are gone, as if they were never there to begin with.

Evanthe scans the area, takes in the trees I will into existence, their forms twisting and growing until they appear exactly how I imagine them, tall and strong, their leaves a myriad of oranges, yellows, and reds. In my dreamscape, I can have it always be autumn, my favorite season. Sometimes I mix it up, enjoying the pastel flowers of spring or glittering white snow of winter, but I always return to autumn.

"I will leave you to visit your friend."

I whirl around, desperately seeking an intelligible answer that doesn't come to me. "What?"

Evanthe leans toward me, presses a soft kiss to my forehead. "I know about Henri," she whispers even though it's just the two of us. "Do you think I wouldn't monitor your dreamscape?"

I should have known she knew. She was the one who taught me that each person carries a different feeling that taints every dream-scape they visit. Besides, did I really think I would be able to keep this secret from her for a year?

Still, it stings, makes me want to squirm. If she knows about him, then she must see that I am falling for him, someone I don't really know.

"You know who he is?" I ask finally.

"Yes."

"Who he truly is?"

Evanthe does not reply, which is an answer in and of itself.

"Then he must not be dangerous, otherwise you would have driven him away." If he even is a he, I realize. With all of this power, why wouldn't I be able to appear as a man, or a baby, or a little old lady? I could even make myself look like a faerie or a mermaid if I so desire.

I really know nothing about Henri.

Again, Evanthe declines to reply.

"I want to say goodbye to him," I manage. "He deserves that much. They both do."

Even though I don't clarify, Evanthe seems to understand. She nods. "I wish I could tell you to take your time, but… you will have to make it quick."

"Of course." I have no intention of taking any more magic from her than necessary. I'll find a way to thank her later. "Are... are you upset with me?"

Touching my cheek, Evanthe kisses my forehead again. "You have to make choices for yourself. Even if I do not agree, I will always love and support you."

That does not answer my question, but it starts to unwind the knot in my stomach.

"Be quick," she reminds me before stepping off the edge of my dreamscape. Instead of falling, she simply winks out of existence, no doubt waiting in her own dreamscape nearby.

I am sure we will be talking more about this later, but for now, I have to gather the courage to end this. To say goodbye to Henri.

Summoning what inner strength I can, I walk through my glade. As I imagine a beautiful white castle, it forms itself, everything in pristine condition, down to the stained glass windows and gold sconces lining the walls. I could reach out to him, calling his magic at any moment I wish, but it only seems right to say goodbye in the place we met.

A grand ballroom takes up most of the bottom floor of the castle, so long that you cannot stand at one side and see where it ends. Even though there are no musicians, a bittersweet tune plays, as if echoing the ache of my heart.

This is for Loren, I remind myself. Loren is real, and I know him, and we are promised to one another. We will not be as close as we once were, but we have a chance to start something new. He is still closed off, but the tender way he healed me and the nostalgic expression he got when seeing our playhouse... There is hope for us. I know it.

I *want* there to be hope for us.

After changing my appearance and exchanging my nightclothes for a ballgown, I take another deep breath.

Then I reach for Henri's magic.

LOREN

The all-too-familiar tug takes me by surprise. Cards fall from my hand and flutter to the bedroom floor as I put a hand to my chest. Toussaint already has his cards facedown on the table, one hand near the knife at his belt—one of the few unhidden weapons he has on him.

"I'm fine," I say quickly, noting the way his eyes are darting about the room, as if there is an invisible entity trying to attack me. "She is calling me."

That answer doesn't settle him any. "You've spent enough magic as it is, Fox."

Another tug, this time more insistent. "We return to Faerie the day after tomorrow. I can replenish then."

"What if that time doesn't come?" He leans forward, pinning me in place with his intense gaze. "With the curse nearly upon us, who knows what the Unseelie will do to be certain of their victory?"

I know he has a point—I can see the Unseelie King's icy eyes, the dark magic slithering around him like snakes, lashing out at Briar Rose…

I squeeze my eyes shut and pinch the bridge of my nose. One cleansing breath, then another, just as Aunt Vivienne taught me. Unfortunately, instead of cleansing anything, it just seems to give me enough of an edge to stuff things below the surface.

"She has to be using one of the faeries' magic," Toussaint says, not letting it go. "Unless they rode for the cottage, but that would take them much more time."

"They could have used a portal," I offer up.

"Not if they want to risk alerting the Unseelie King with that much magic at once."

I finally open my eyes so I can stare back at him, rising to his challenge. "I am well aware of the risk I put us in by healing her, but I couldn't leave her like that." There are rumors that the Unseelie King is tracking the magic of certain faeries, namely mine, Aunt Vivienne's, and Briar Rose's faerie guardians'. Probably Toussaint's as well, if that is, in fact, true.

Regardless, using that much magic in human lands does tend to leave its fingerprint, a ripple that can alter places, events, and even sometimes people.

"No," he concedes, "but you can leave her this time." Before I can even open my mouth to argue, Toussaint cuts me off. "You have very little magic left, and we are going to take her with us to Faerie shortly. If you want her to fall in love with you, it needs to be here, not in the dreamscape."

"Maybe Henri should be the one to reveal who he is." I know how pathetic it sounds, even before Toussaint responds. And I know that it's wrong—I should be the one to tell her, in person, not wearing a mask.

"Henri. Doesn't. Exist."

Other than the servants walking about the hallway outside of my door, there is nothing but tense silence. Neither of us moves, or blinks. We rarely disagree like this, and when we do, it tends to end in an uncomfortable staring contest until one or both relent. You would think that we could have come up with something more mature and interesting since our childhood, but no.

A few more tugs. I send a bit of my magic toward it, a flicker to let her know I will be there in a moment. Toussaint must sense it, because resignation settles over his features.

"I have to go to her," I say, as if that explains everything. "She wants me." Thankfully, Toussaint is not cruel enough to point out that she wants Henri.

Instead, he dips his head. "As you wish, Prince Loren." He settles back in his chair and begins playing with the coins, letting them fall back onto the table and clink against one another. "Be quick about it. I almost have you beat." He gives a half-hearted smirk. "There's no honor in leaving a game you're sorely losing, even if it's on behalf of a lady in distress."

I shake my head at him with a small smile, and settle onto the bed. As I start to answer Briar Rose's call to her dreamscape, it doesn't escape my notice that Toussaint has angled himself so that I'm in his peripherals.

CHAPTER TWELVE

LOREN

*T*he sweet scent, like blooming flowers in spring, reaches me before her dreamscape comes into view, even before I realize I'm feeling Evanthe's magic holding everything together. She has yet to say much to me since our last serious conversation a few months ago.

Tell her, Prince Loren. Free her of the guilt, tell her you are the one she is falling in love with.

Only it's not me, it's Henri. Regardless, I hate when she's right.

Briar Rose—Fleur, as she introduced herself—isn't waiting for me at the edge of her dreamscape like usual. So I walk through the autumn woods, wondering yet again why she chooses to make trees like this, and not daring to assume it has to do with me and my Glamour affiliation.

I can hope though.

The moment I open the castle doors, music meets me, trailing sorrowfully. I hurry, trying not to let my mind run amuck with ideas of what could be troubling her.

At the doorway to the ballroom, I panic, remembering at the last second to change myself into Henri: dark hair and eyes to match, and more human-like features, especially rounded ears and shorter stature. Not too much, or else I'll look like a ridiculous painting come to life. I'm not sure if that would make her laugh or terrify her. Probably both.

By the way the music begins to swell, I can tell Briar Rose knows I'm here. Just as I suspect, she is standing there in the middle of the ballroom, waiting for me. As usual, she has made herself taller, thinner, with pale skin and blue eyes, blonde hair twisted up and held in place by her sparkling diamond tiara. The ball gown is simple, only a few tiny gems on the bodice and scattered on the top layer of her skirts, matching her tiara and dangling earrings.

I suddenly find myself looking forward to seeing her—the real her—dressed up tomorrow. We will be expected to dance for at least a few songs, and I hope I've practiced enough that the experience won't be too terrible. If I step on her toes or spin her too hard or—

"Henri." Briar Rose takes a few faltering steps, then stops. She swallows, blinks, and fidgets with her dress, its color bleeding from pink to red to a purplish blue.

I go to her, leaving only a bit of space between us. There is something off, something more than the flickers of sadness I see in her eyes on occasion. The tension makes me think that if I reach out to her first, if I try to comfort her, it will not be taken well. "Fleur? What is it?" Hiding my anxiety is harder than I anticipate, but of course Henri would be worried about her. I can show some of it, just not all: Henri has no reason to suspect anything terrible will happen. Henri is overall calm and charming and easy-going, not an anxious mess.

Candlelight gleams in her watery eyes, eyes that will not quite meet mine. "I owe you an answer."

How do I respond to that? Opting for a more light-hearted tone to keep her from crying, I joke, "We can race again, double or nothing. Then you have the chance to ask me two questions." Two questions that I will have to answer truthfully. With all of my maneuvering and careful responses, I'm shocked she has yet to figure out that I am a faerie. Still, she has been just as guarded thus far.

She smiles with quivering lips, and shakes her head. "I don't mean that. I mean you deserve to know… well, at least the bits of truth I can give you."

My pulse is about to leap out of my body. "Fleur, you do not have—"

"Yes," she interrupts, "I do." Rolling her shoulders back, she looks up at me. For a split second, I swear I catch a glimpse of the real her, and it steals my breath away. I lock my knees before they can falter. If she is really saying goodbye to Henri, then I need to come clean, to tell her everything, and I don't want to do it now, especially not here. It needs to happen in the real world, where it comes from Loren's lips, not Henri's. If I am going to salvage any sort of trust from her, this has to be in person, where she can see the truth of it in my eyes and scream at me and storm off. Maybe hit or shove me if she is angry enough.

As much as I hate it, it *has* to happen in person.

"I can't tell you everything—"

"Fleur, please, stop—"

"Henri—"

I cup her face in my hands and rest my forehead against hers. She tenses but doesn't pull away. It hits me just how close we are, how easy it would be to tilt my head, to angle my mouth…

"Please," I implore her before I do something stupid and make it so much harder than it already is. "This needs to be done in person."

After a long moment, she barely shakes her head. "I can't."

"We can." I breathe in to steady myself, but catch the scent of her, the real her, and nearly give in to the temptation just a small movement away. But this isn't her, and when—if—I get to kiss her, I don't want it to be in the dreamscape when she thinks I'm someone else.

"I *can't*," she repeats. "I wish I could, but I can't."

Tears slip down her cheeks, and I gently wipe them away.

"I'm betrothed," she manages, speaking in a rush, like she is afraid she will never get the words out if she lets herself think too much about what she is saying. "I thought I had more time, but they are taking me away in two days and I'll be married and…" She chokes on the remainder of the sentence, trembling, gripping my forearms like I am her anchor.

Emotion overtakes Briar Rose, collapsing her in sobs. I catch her, holding her upright. She crumbles against me, burying her face in my shoulder.

They are taking me away… I wish I had more time, but they are taking me away…

I don't know how I've been so blind: even Briar Rose sees faeries as all the same, thinks that we Seelie are no better than the Unseelie, stealing whatever we want. Marriage contract or no, to her, she feels like she is just a pawn, something to be bartered with.

We sink to our knees together. She continues to sob into her hands, and I sit there, unmoving, my heart more hollow than the almost-depleted magic in my chest.

If she doesn't want to fall in love with me, why should I even try?

An invisible ripple travels throughout the dreamscape, no doubt a reminder from Evanthe that Briar Rose needs to go.

"I'm sorry," she sniffs. "I must leave. I wish it were on better terms." Briar Rose stands on unsteady legs, and shakily inhales to say, "Goodbye, Henri."

BRIAR ROSE

I don't look at him, don't dare let myself stay a moment longer. It is cowardice and terrible and I am the worst person to ever have existed, but it had to happen. If I dared meet him in person, it would only hurt both of us. Like it or not, I am betrothed to Loren. I should never have let things get this far.

I tumble back into my own body, not bothering to try to make the return gentle. It jolts me, reverberating, stinging all over, inside and out, like falling onto water the wrong way. But I deserve it: for entertaining the idea of betraying Loren, for breaking Henri's heart—

Tears pour out of their own volition; I roll over, burying my face into a pillow.

"What happened?" Delphine urgently wants to know, but Evanthe hushes her and rubs my back.

"My sweet," she murmurs, settling close to me, the bed sinking slightly under her weight.

I curl into myself. Everything in me wants to return, to try to make things the way they were, but there is nothing to be done. All I can do is hope Henri can forgive me and move on, find someone else who could love him the way I was starting to.

If only I got to meet him one time, in person... But no, it is better this way. Either he is as wonderful as I imagine, and it would hurt worse to break things off, or he isn't who he says he is at all, and those memories would be irreparably scarred forever... just like the memories I have of Loren.

Evanthe holds me, gently tucking hair behind my ears and pressing kisses to my head. The mattress shifts again, Delphine and Irit joining us.

"I'm a stupid girl," I manage between broken sobs. "I have to... I have to tell Loren."

The pats and caresses pause. The faeries exchange puzzled looks.

"Tell Prince Loren what, my sweet?"

My throat aches, and swallowing doesn't help. "I have to tell him that I was falling for someone else. I can't marry him but still have secrets."

They exchange another look, this time like they are having a silent argument. I sit up.

"What is it? I know he's hiding something from me too."

With a heavy sigh, Evanthe kisses my temple. "Faeries barter in secrets, love. That is our currency and greatest treasure. Get a faerie to tell you their secrets, and you know you have their heart." She wipes my cheeks and offers a kind smile. "Sleep now."

She knows Loren's secrets, or just that he keeps them? I wonder, my eyelids slipping ever lower, my head sinking back into the pillows. Then a horrible thought hits me: *Does he know about Henri, and that's why he hates me?*

Sleep takes me before I am ready.

CHAPTER THIRTEEN

LOREN

*T*oussaint pulls a chair near the bed the moment he knows I've returned to my body and realizes I don't plan on moving from the bed anytime soon. But he says nothing as I stare up at the canopy, not even to comment on how little magic I have left.

A distant thought in the back of my mind wonders if there is a spell to fill the hollow feeling, to numb the bone-deep ache. But even if there is, perhaps I deserve to endure it. I'm the one who pushed her away and didn't explain. I put up the wall between us. And somehow, in my pride, I thought I could fix this. Instead of protecting her, I gouged both of us.

"Don't sink too far into despair," Toussaint says quietly. "There is still hope."

I don't have the energy to retort or lash out, which is for the best, really. Less I'd have to apologize for later when I'm in a better state of mind. Instead, I tell him, "She thinks we are stealing her away."

A confused pause. "What?"

"Briar Rose told Henri that she was going to be taken away in two days and married off… and she burst into tears."

"She…" Toussaint leans forward, resting his arms on his knees, frowning. "She said that?" My silence is answer enough, so he adds, "Humans can say things they do not mean. Maybe she felt emotional about having to say goodbye to Henri, and that is how it came out?"

"She is not in the habit of saying things she doesn't mean."

An urgent, rapid knock interrupts Toussaint's response. I peer out the window, seeing how dark it is outside, and wonder who could possibly be visiting this late.

Toussaint is already on his feet, in a stance that allows for a quick transition into fighting if need be, but is still peaceful enough to not make the visitor assume they are about to be attacked.

The knock comes again, insistent. "Prince Loren, I request a moment of your time."

Evanthe. I let her in, not wanting to draw out any more of her ire. Before I even have the door closed, she whirls on me, barely giving Toussaint a quick glance.

"What happened?"

I fight the urge to take a step back to put distance between us. "She said goodbye to Henri." Something I am wholly unprepared to do. To lose that escape where I can relax and breathe…

Evanthe pins me with her scowl as she takes a few slow, steady breaths. If we were in Faerie, certainly her Glamour would crackle around her like lightning. I can taste a hint of it in the air. "You did not tell her."

"…No…"

"And why not?" she asks, but does not give me time to answer. "She is feeling *guilty* because she is keeping this secret from you and trying to make things right. If I were you, Your Highness, I would relieve her of this guilt as soon as possible."

I can feel Toussaint's eyes boring into me, willing me to speak up, but what can I possibly say? The bottom line is that I do need to come clean with Briar Rose.

"I will."

Evanthe lifts her chin, giving the illusion of looking down at me even though I am taller by a decent amount. "See to it that you do. Good night, Your Highness." She barely lowers her head in an almost mocking version of a bow before taking her leave. I half-expect her to slam the door, but it shuts quietly.

"So, you will tell her?" Toussaint presses after a few moments.

"Yes." I walk past him, stepping over his mattress, and climb into bed. I had a second bed brought in just so Toussaint would not have to sleep on the floor. He refuses to leave me alone all night outside of Seelie, and I had to explain that to King Faustus years ago so that he didn't go on believing that Toussaint thinks he is too good to sleep in the servants' quarters.

But right now, I almost wish he would, because some time alone sounds nice.

"Get some rest," Toussaint says, blowing out the candles one by one. "I'll finish beating you in the morning."

I huff a laugh for his benefit and roll onto my side so my back is to him. If I cannot be truly alone, I can at least be alone in my thoughts. Tomorrow, I will tell Briar Rose everything, put the final nail in the coffin of her hatred toward me.

And then I will try to find a way to release her from our betrothal.

I AM awake before the sun rises the next morning. Granted, I did not do much sleeping, slipping in and out of consciousness throughout the night, never quite committing. My thoughts bled into nightmares that tormented me, visions of Briar Rose in tears, of her running away, of her falling into the curse, terrified and alone, with no hope of being set free because I couldn't give her True Love's Kiss.

And I was too selfish to give her a chance with anyone else. I hadn't even considered it until yesterday. If the thought of marrying me wants to make her burst into tears… then trying to get her to fall in love with me seems fundamentally wrong.

In Faerie, I would stroll through the woods or venture into caverns, whatever I was in the mood for to pass the time and escape my mind for a bit. But here in the human lands, they do not take kindly to faeries "skulking about" in the dark, not after how much the Unseelie have terrorized them. To most humans, a faerie is a faerie, all strange, dangerous creatures. Which, I willingly admit, we are dangerous. I cannot fault them for being unable to differentiate between Seelie and Unseelie—we can tell by the tang of their magic—but I would greatly appreciate it if they would stop hovering their hands near their weapons.

"Go see her," Toussaint orders from the other side of the room. I turn from the window to see him still in his bed, arm flung over his face. "I know you are trying to decide when it is proper to check on Briar Rose."

Even though he isn't looking, I glower at him.

"I'm saying go see her. Continuously walking back and forth from the window to the desk is bound to wear down the floor at some point."

He still won't look at me. I cross my arms and debate kicking his ribs. Not hard, just enough to be a fair warning. "Humans would find that improper, considering we are not yet married." I've spent a good amount of time figuring out a way to release her from the betrothal, but no such luck yet. It is too important to our peoples, especially the Fae. If we are going to win against the Unseelie, we will need the power my union to Briar Rose will bring.

"But you will be soon." Toussaint rolls away from me and springs to his feet. "Come on, I'll join you. Then you won't be improper. Besides, you want to get the confession over with, right?"

I stifle a sigh. "Right."

Toussaint fixes his tousled dark brown hair with a few quick run-throughs with his fingers. If I did that with my curls, they would poof and become even more unruly.

"Hey." Toussaint pokes my chest. "No more magic, got it?"

I bat his hand away. "I'm fine."

He snorts and tugs on his jacket and boots. Then he straightens and starts tapping his fingers as he lists off, "You aren't radiating power like you usually do, there are dark circles under your eyes, you're sluggish and irritable... Is that the definition of 'fine'?"

This time I let the sigh escape my lips. It may take a few days because of how low I let it get, but my magic will replenish. I'm not in danger of dying. Getting sick, perhaps, if I use any more, especially since the human lands carry illnesses we faeries are not used to. Of course, Toussaint is right, but I cannot bring myself to admit it or agree to stop using magic. What if another accident happens?

If I argue, he'll point out that any accident at a ball will surely be a minor one, nothing that he or Briar Rose's faerie guardians cannot fix if need be.

"I'm watching you," he reminds me, knowing he'll get no promises.

"Always," I reply, to which he gives a lopsided smile that has made many faeries trip over themselves. Humans, too.

Dawn light seeps through the windows, casting a soft glow. Servants work as silently as possible, cleaning and putting final touches on decorations for tonight's celebration. Royals will soon wake and convene for breakfast, or else they will have food brought to them in their bedchambers.

I hope we are catching Briar Rose before she leaves her room. Better to find her here than to have to track her down and pull her away from her family to give her this news.

I barely knock thrice before Delphine throws open the door. She squints at me, her grip on the door handle tightening.

"Your Highness," she greets through gritted teeth.

Evanthe and Irit look at us from over their shoulders. They are inadvertently blocking Briar Rose from view, one fussing with her dress and the other dabbing her face with a handkerchief.

Is she crying?

They take a step back, and Briar Rose turns toward me. No tears from what I can see, but there is a heaviness to her posture.

"Good morning, Loren."

It takes me too long to return the greeting, and it sounds awkward, forced. This seems to be destined to be a terrible morning through and through.

"My ankle is well, if that is what you came to ask," says Briar Rose, as if feeling the need to fill the gap in conversation. "Thank you again. Well, I am not sure I actually thanked you in the first place, so I suppose a simple 'thank you' would suffice."

Her babbling almost makes me smile... until I remember why she is so nervous.

"I thought perhaps you would care for a brief stroll through the garden before breakfast," I find myself offering. "I have something I need to share with you."

The look Evanthe gives me from behind Briar Rose could almost be categorized as approving, but there is still enough of a warning to it that has me on edge.

Briar Rose tilts her head slightly. "Oh, well, yes, that sounds like a... good idea." She crosses the room and hesitantly takes my arm.

I hope she can't feel my heart banging against my ribcage.

CHAPTER FOURTEEN

BRIAR ROSE

*L*oren's movements are stiff, awkward, not as graceful as usual. Toussaint trails behind us, and by the time we make it outside, my nerves are ready to snap.

What if he knows about Henri? That thought has wound itself around my chest and continuously squeezed, making it hard for me to breathe. But how would he know? I doubt Evanthe would have told him—she would want me to do it myself.

Unless Henri is someone Loren knows… If Evanthe knows who he is, it's not far-fetched to assume Loren could.

I peek at Toussaint. Even his demeanor is subdued, serious. There is no spark of mischief in his eye, no bounce in his step. No, I cannot see him being Henri. His personality could easily match Henri's, but the bond between Loren and Toussaint is too deep for me to believe that Toussaint could ever consider being interested in me, his best friend's betrothed. While other faeries might find it fun to toy with a human's emotions, I do not see Toussaint going that far.

I know very few faeries, so the only other option I can think of is Loren. But he and Henri are very different, and I have a hard time picturing Loren being affectionate and flirtatious like Henri.

Or, I desperately hope, Loren wants to talk about something else entirely, although I have no idea what that could be.

Loren stops near the rose hedges, where Toussaint and he were sparring just yesterday. He releases my arm and tugs the bottom of his doublet like he's straightening it, but open as it is, it does nothing.

Toussaint waits far enough away that I do wonder if he is able to hear us, even with his heightened senses. We are still in sight, so I suppose he is content with that.

Loren actually faces me. His skin is paler than normal, with bruise-like circles under his eyes, something strange to see on a faerie, their appearance almost always beautiful and perfect. Right now, his eyes look as tired as mine; Evanthe and Irit had used a lot of cosmetics this morning to cover them.

What has kept you from sleeping? A possible answer leaps to mind, but I bat it aside even as my stomach rolls and twists. *How could he be Henri? Surely there is another reason. Perhaps it took too much magic to heal me?* That guilt would be easier to deal with, easier to recover from.

If Loren were Henri…

Stop panicking, I berate myself. *He hasn't said anything yet.*

No, but his amber eyes are filled with a thousand unsaid words, ready to brim over. In this moment, he looks so much like the boy I knew, the boy who liked me and went on adventures with me and shared his hopes and dreams and fears…

"What is it?" I ask quietly, afraid of the answer but unable to stand the anticipation any longer. I told him I wanted no secrets, no lies, and this is how it will have to begin, with a freefall and the hope that we can either catch each other or mend the broken pieces.

"Briar Rose, I…"

"…Yes…?"

His throat bobs. "This… this has been long overdue. I am sorry it took so long, and I never meant for it to last as long as it did, but…"

I study him as if that will help me piece together what he is trying to say. The cold facade is down, exposing the mess he is sorting through, but I don't know what to make of it. I stuff down the panic as best I can. *Let him finish, then you can say what you need to.*

Loren reaches for me, and everything stops. Even though the autumn morning is warmer than it has been, when his thumb gently presses between my brows, a chill snakes down my spine and solidifies in my stomach.

No. No no no no no.

The touch is undeniably the same, something I recognize without being in the dreamscape. But the faerie standing in front of me is a far cry from the person that gesture belongs to.

Loren reluctantly lets his hand fall away. "I am sorry, Briar Rose."

I shake my head, no words coming to me. At least, no sentences, and certainly not words a princess should be saying.

"I am Henri," he confesses, as if I needed to hear it. And maybe I did. Maybe I should give him credit for telling me, but what I really want to do is kick him. Scream at him. Rant until my voice goes hoarse. Run away and never see anyone again.

The worst part is that I know he's not lying, because he *cannot* lie. Not directly. He left no loopholes and gave no insinuations.

My eyes begin to sting, and I blink furiously.

"I thought you should know before…" Loren clenches his fists at his sides. "Before we leave for Faerie tomorrow."

Tomorrow. After that confession, it feels like a punch in the chest, knowing I will be leaving with them, with *him.*

"How magnanimous of you," I snap. "All this time, and now you tell me?" Loren's stunned expression only seems to fuel my ire. "How wonderful for me, that I get to be taken away to live with such manipulative creatures."

"I—"

"No." I step away from him. "Do not touch me."

Clearly wounded, Loren obeys. I turn on my heel and sprint

back to the castle, my vision blurring. Blinking doesn't stop the tears, only frees them. Luckily I know the way back to my room, and I care little about what the servants think of me. Let them talk. I'll only be here until tomorrow anyway.

I choke on a sob as I reach my doorway. A hand grabs my arm, and I whirl around to see Loren, Toussaint not far behind.

"Please," he begs, voice raw, "let me—"

"Leave me alone," I seethe. "I do not wish to speak to you or see you until tonight. Am I clear?"

I hear the door open but keep my glare locked on the faerie prince who still has his hand on my arm. He looks over my shoulder, then back at me. If he thought he was going to get help from my guardians, he was very wrong. He may be their prince, but I am their charge, like a daughter to them.

Hesitantly, he lets go, his fingers twitching so briefly I consider that I did not actually see it.

"Until this evening, then." Loren dips into a stiff bow, then leaves without turning back around.

I storm past my guardians, kicking off my shoes in lieu of punching the wall and bruising my knuckles. Bruises to a ball would be unsightly, as would a bandage, so they would resort to using magic to fix it, even if I told them not to.

I cannot handle any more magic right now.

"What did he say?" Irit asks meekly, although I am sure she already knows the answer.

"He is Henri." I shake my head at Evanthe. "How could you not tell me?"

While Irit and Delphine look confused, Evanthe bows her head. "I am sorry, my sweet. That was the prince's secret to tell, not mine."

Of course. No matter how close we are, Loren is still their prince, soon to be their king.

And I, their queen.

Still, it smarts. I bite my lip to keep from spitting venomous words at her, one of the women who has cared for me since I was an infant, who has loved me like I was her own.

"Leave me," I order them. When they linger, I say, "Return in an hour to ready me for tonight."

"As you wish," Evanthe says first, heading toward the door. Irit and Delphine follow suit, still clearly puzzled and concerned with the whole situation, but I am sure Evanthe will explain. Or maybe not. Either way, I do not want to see any faeries right now. No one at all.

I start to walk to my balcony so I can stare at the horizon, but the flower on my vanity catches my eye. Before I left with Loren, it had been wilted, and I had intended to replace it. Now it stands tall, pink petals vibrant and full of life. I cannot feel it, but I know it has to be magic.

None of my guardians would spend their finite magic on something I could replace so easily. Before I can think too much about it, I climb into bed and pull the blanket over my head.

THE UNSEELIE KING

"You called for me, Sire?" Margaux is silent, even for a faerie, when she positions herself behind me on the castle wall. For the most part, the giants have repaired the damage the Seelie had left… when they can be persuaded to work, that is. It seems as though my recent blood oath inspired more than just them: instead of laughter and lewd stories, I hear the clanging of hammers on metal and the grunts of laborers. Since that night, I have yet to find any of the guard posts unattended. The guards always straighten in my presence, their eyes shifting to Margaux. I have no doubt that if I lost Margaux's loyalty, I would lose theirs with it. Although whether it is loyalty or fear is up for debate, and I honestly do not care either way, as long as my Captain of the Guard does not abuse her power. I need my soldiers to be able to fight, after all.

"What news do you have?" I ask, staring out at the land of greys, blacks, and browns. Most of the trees are ashen, with bits of red in between peeling pieces of bark. One of the few colors in the dark and muted tones of Unseelie, almost like I bleed the vibrancy out of everything along with the magic. Even the sky is a muddled grey-blue.

Where Asra is on alert around others, she settles into a more comfortable position across my shoulders when it is just Margaux. I trust her judgment more than mine.

"The Seelie have sent scouts, but they do not cross the border," Margaux informs me, confirming what Asra has already shown me. "Our spies have sent word that Princess Briar Rose will be brought to Faerie tomorrow. The wedding details have been kept secret, but it seems that she will marry the Seelie Prince shortly after her arrival."

Just as I suspected. "Continue to monitor them, and station two guards at every post. Have scouts watch boundary lines in case the Seelie get a little too confident in themselves." Which they are certain to do.

"As you wish, Your Highness." She leaves just as silently as she came.

"A few more days," I murmur to Asra, scratching under her wing. She curls into my touch, purring. "The humans got rid of their spindles a long time ago, as if that would stop the curse. They do not realize that I can draw her here."

Asra chirrups as if agreeing, almost like laughter, and then nuzzles her face against my hair.

"A few more days."

CHAPTER FIFTEEN

LOREN

*N*ot long after I make it back to my room, Evanthe comes in with barely a warning knock, a mere graze of her knuckles against the doorframe as she steps through. This time Delphine and Irit are with her, expressions twisted in a mixture of confusion and concern.

"Thank you for telling her, Your Highness," Evanthe says after she bows. "I imagine it was difficult."

I nod, my throat too tight to speak.

Evanthe crosses the room to me but keeps a respectful distance. "I would like to offer to help ready you for tonight, if it pleases you."

"Where is Princess Briar Rose?" Toussaint voices my question for me.

"She is taking a moment to herself. It is a hard truth to process."

Evanthe means no slight, but I feel the sting of it anyway. "I would appreciate the help," I make myself say. Because, if nothing else, Evanthe's presence is a comforting one when she intends it to be. She was one of my caregivers for the few brief years before she was assigned to Briar Rose.

And before me, she took care of my brother. I wonder if that is why she watches me closely when she can, that way I do not end up like the Unseelie King.

"Toussaint, bring a chair here," she orders as she walks to the vanity. He obeys instantly, and she pats the seat. "Come, Your Highness. You are far too tall for me."

"Should he not change into his clothes now?" Delphine suggests. I'm impressed she has yet to press for details on what I had to tell Briar Rose.

"He can after I am done." Evanthe waits for me to sit, then runs her fingers through my curls. Cool, sweet-smelling magic seeps out of her hands and onto my scalp. I grab her wrists; she raises a single brow.

"Save your magic."

"You need it, Prince Loren. You have spent far too much."

"And I do not need you spending any of yours. We return tomorrow—I can wait until then."

We lock gazes in the mirror. I know how wretched I look, and I want to lean into the tension-melting magic, but spending someone else's magic frivolously does not sit well with me. I am their prince, soon to be their king, but I do not want to take from my people like my father did.

Evanthe leans toward my ear. "Then you must stop bringing flowers back to life, My Prince. That will not heal the wounds between you."

She takes a bottle from the vanity and puts some oil on my curls. All the while I ponder her words, and come to the conclusion that, while wounds may be healed, I worry it is not just wounds between Briar Rose and me, but scars.

BRIAR ROSE

My faerie guardians return and prepare me for the ball. We speak little, which is fine with me. I cried enough to leave my chest hollow, and if I am to socialize tonight, I need to reserve as much energy as I can.

I wear a new lilac purple ball gown, made just for tonight. Irit braids tiny purple flowers into a section of my hair, leaving the rest down in soft waves to the small of my back. I look every inch a princess, but I feel detached from what I see in the mirror.

He was Henri the entire time. I was falling in love with *Loren,* who was pretending to be someone else. Of all the conniving faerie tricks—

I cut off that thought before the anger can rise again. Tonight, I am Princess Briar Rose, human betrothed to the Seelie Prince. Tomorrow, who knows what will happen, but I can handle tonight. One day at a time, or else I might collapse in on myself.

Loren fetches me on time. He does not look at me, and I loosely take his arm. In silence, we make our way downstairs, where the festivities are already starting.

Like the dinner party, the ballroom looks like a forest scene, full of plants and flowers on the walls, the tables, even woven into the chandelier.

If this is at all like Faerie, I will love it. My heart twists, and I swallow down the sadness before it can creep up too far.

I can make it through tonight.

Father and Mother cross the floor to greet us. Loren's courtly smile lacks its usual charm, not quite reaching his eyes, but Father doesn't take notice. He kisses both of my cheeks and wishes me a happy birthday. Mother barely gets in a hug and concerned squeeze to my upper arm when Father announces, "Clear the floor! The soon-to-be groom and his bride will have the first dance."

The music pauses and the conversating groups disperse, leaving Loren and me alone in the center of the room. Slowly, he unwinds his arm from mine and turns toward me, raising a hand between us.

His eyes look past me, but give the illusion of looking at me, a flicker of pain in them.

While I don't want him looking at me, I also hate that he won't.

The meeting of our palms sends a thrill up my arm, making me flex my fingers. He straightens a bit.

Music starts again, slow and inviting, and we follow its soft, imploring tug. My skirts twirl as we sway and spin, our synchronized steps calling and answering one another. We circle around each other, only our palms touching, until the song picks up. Then Loren grasps my hand fully, pulling me into him, his other hand hovering so close to my waist that I can feel its presence like a tingle.

I firmly place mine on his shoulder, hoping he will take the hint. There is not supposed to be any awkwardness between us. We are supposed to be the faerie prince and human princess, betrothed and smitten and not at all angry at each other.

The tempo quickens, and we match pace, his hold on me more sure, but Loren keeps a rigid distance between us, no closer, no farther. I take a bigger step toward him than the dance allows; he retreats the same amount. I try again, and he repeats the response.

Then Loren pulls me against him in one quick, fluid movement. I inhale sharply, seeking his gaze, and find it a split second before he dips me. The song's end takes me by surprise as I stare up at him, heat rising in my cheeks.

Attendees clap for us. Loren rights me, takes my arm, and leads me off the dance floor. I go without hesitation, hoping no one notices me blush.

"Are they not a handsome couple?"

We make it to our designated table in time to see Father raise a goblet in our honor.

"To my daughter's birthday, to her happy marriage to Prince Loren, and to our kingdoms prospering together, united."

Everyone repeats the sentiment, but Loren and I say nothing, separating abruptly and reaching for our wine before we have fully seated ourselves. The next song starts, and couples flood the dance floor in a sea of brightly-colored gowns.

I only allow myself a few sips of wine, but Loren drains half the goblet, or so it seems from the corner of my eye, being unable to bring myself to look directly at him. My cheeks are still aflame, and I hate that a small, traitorous part of me wants to ask him to dance again. But I don't.

We eat in silence, watching the celebration play out in front of us. A few nobles break away to congratulate us and wish me a happy birthday, to which I respond with what I hope is a convincing smile. Thankfully, none of them linger.

My faerie guardians and Toussaint stay near each other, not too far away from our table. They will not approach us unless they deem it necessary, and if I ask for an excuse to leave, none of them will give in. It would be strange for a princess to leave her own ball not long after it starts.

But, somehow, it feels like I would not be missed by many. Mother sneaks glances my way, but she is too busy making sure Jovan is behaving. He breaks away from her and races toward me, weaving through the dancing couples.

"Rosie!" He throws his arms around my neck, not giving me a chance to stand up from my chair. "Mama says you're leaving tomorrow," he whispers. "I don't want you to leave."

"I have to," I reply, very aware of Loren next to us, able to hear our every word no matter how quietly we speak. "But I will come to visit. I promise."

"You'd better." Jovan finally relaxes his grip and retrieves something from his jacket pocket: a leather cord with a pendant of a crudely whittled rose surrounded by briars. "Happy birthday," he says, pressing a kiss to my cheek. "I hope you wear this, so you don't forget me."

"I could never forget you." The smile I give him is completely genuine. I lift my hair, and he ties it around my neck so that it rests just below my collarbone.

"You could," he whispers again, sneaking a peek at Loren as if the faerie prince can't hear him. "I hear faeries are tricky, Rosie. Be careful they don't take your memories and replace them with others." He grows very serious. "Forget everyone else if you must, but please don't forget me."

"I won't," I promise. "And we will be back to visit soon. Besides, you are coming to the wedding."

Jovan grins widely. "I get to go to Faerie!"

Mother appears behind him, putting her hands on his shoulders. "It will be a beautiful wedding."

"And fun! Mother, can we see a kelpie?"

"You do not want to see a kelpie," I interject. In my peripherals, I notice Loren tense.

"Come now, Jovan." Mother urges him back toward the party, and throws a look at me that tells me she knows something is off and will want to talk about it later. I merely nod, and she is satisfied with that for the time being.

Neither Loren nor I say a word for another three songs. I nurse my wine and pick at the pork and potatoes on my plate. It's not that I have nothing to say to him, but everything will either end in us bickering or a deep discussion that should not be had in a public setting.

I could ask him to dance again. Talking takes too much effort, but not dancing. The way we moved together, it was easy, simple. If we cannot quite communicate well yet, at least this will be a good starting point. If I am to marry him, I don't want to spend however many centuries I have left being angry with him. We won't have what we used to, but maybe I can find a way to forgive him and move forward to something new.

We could start with dancing.

"You must hate that you are destined to not only wed one of the 'creatures' you despise, but also become one yourself."

Surprised he spoke, I turn to him, trying to decide if he is serious. In his formal attire, a circlet of golden leaves atop his loose red curls, sitting back in his chair with a wine goblet in one hand, he is every bit the faerie prince everyone expects him to be. I suddenly find myself unable to look away, the conversations, laughter, and music of the party fading to the background. Like this, he looks like a painting come to life, and the urge to touch his cheek, to see if he is real, hits me out of nowhere.

But this is **Loren**, I remind myself. He is very much real, and I would still very much like to tip that wine onto his lap, for starters. The very least of what he deserves.

"I quite look forward to becoming Fae." The words escape me before I can stop them, but I realize... I spoke true. Becoming Fae has its appeal for many reasons—having magic when I am awake is the foremost of them. I'd rather not have to draw from someone else's like a leech. And then I'll have my own magic to combat the Unseelie King and his curse, and not have to feel like I'm relying on something so far out of my reach as True Love's Kiss.

Loren pauses, the rim of the goblet at his lips. A mirthless smile, a huffed sigh that could almost be mistaken as a laugh. Although what the joke is, I do not know. "Ah. So it is I alone who stirs your ire."

I have no idea how to respond, so I just watch him sip his wine, and he tilts his head back, downing the rest of it swiftly. He sets the glass on the table with strained care, and his amber eyes finally flick to mine. For the first time, I notice the flecks of bright gold in them, how they catch the light like bits of flame come to life.

There is a flash of pain in them, but he tears his gaze away before I can read further into his expression. A servant refills his goblet, and Loren drains that one as well, snatching the man's sleeve so he can get a third.

No more dancing for us tonight, I lament. "Continue that way, and you'll be too drunk to return to your bedchamber," I warn him.

This time he snorts derisively and shakes his head. "Your concern is noted."

Now I want to strangle him, to wipe that scowl from his too-pretty face. Why did I promise Evanthe, Delphine, and Irit that I would behave? They know how infuriating their prince is.

"You are making it too easy for me to retaliate."

I draw his attention back with that threat. The number of ideas for pranks I'd come up with earlier swirls in my mind, but at the moment, none of them seem good enough, not after finding out that he was Henri the entire time. Besides, there is no way for me to pull them off without drawing attention, not with the whole court in attendance in the great hall.

Loren smirks at me, leans toward me. I cannot move, cannot breathe, cannot think—

"Give me everything you have, Briar Rose," he whispers, his voice like silk over my skin, leaving goosebumps in their wake. This close, I could count his long, red lashes if I so desired. But I am frozen, lost in those molten eyes, heart thrashing in my chest as I await his next move. Because if it is my turn to move, I am uncertain I can do so.

Abruptly, he stands, goblet rim dangling from his ringed fingers. Wine sloshes over the side and drips onto the stone floor.

"Seems you might not have the upper hand as you thought." Loren pivots and leaves the hall, only a few heads turning to watch. Toussaint instantly strides toward him, but the Fae prince dismisses him with a wave of his hand, and Toussaint reluctantly returns to his post, eyes narrowing on Loren.

My feet carry me toward Loren before I can consciously decide to follow him. I ignore the confused looks the guards exchange as I hurry past them, down the hallway, and snatch his arm. Loren jolts, looking down at me like he is surprised I actually came after him.

Truth be told, I am too—I just know I cannot allow him to have the last word. But now that I have his attention, I have no idea what I want to do. And he is standing here, *waiting* for me to do something, anything.

His surprise hardens into something akin to disappointment, then annoyance, but he doesn't pull away. "What are you waiting for?" he asks in challenge.

His tone fuels my ire again, and I yank him toward me, intent on telling him exactly what I think of him.

Instead, I find my lips pressed to his. He goes rigid, and I hear his goblet hit the floor.

Loren. I am kissing Loren.

I should pull away, I should be mortified by my actions, but instead I lean into the softness of his mouth, the way it suddenly yields to mine. Then Loren pulls me against him, kissing me back with a hunger that steals my breath and leaves my knees weak. He tastes of wine, and it leaves me dizzy.

A few steps, and he has my back against the wall, his hands cupping my face. I gasp, and he pulls away just far enough to look into my eyes. His look dark, the pupils nearly swallowing the irises. His throat bobs, and, with a sigh, he buries his face in my hair. We stay there a few long moments, saying nothing, doing nothing.

"I thought you hated me," I say breathlessly. *And I started to believe the lie that I could ever truly hate you.*

He takes a long time to respond, so long that I wonder if he will at all. "Hating you would be far easier," he finally whispers into my hair. Abruptly, he leaves me there, no longer holding me up, so I sink to the floor, the skirts of my dress tangled around my legs. I watch him disappear around the corner with long, hurried, erratic strides.

He doesn't once look back.

CHAPTER SIXTEEN

LOREN

I *diot, idiot, idiot.*

    I hurry away as fast as I can, feet faltering as my head spins.

We kissed. We *kissed.* I know she's furious with me and I'm not liking myself much either… So how did we end up *kissing?*

The cool night air soothes my burning skin. Chasing after it, I stumble down the steps, put my hands out as I pitch toward the ground—

Toussaint catches me under the arms and heaves me back. "What did you think you were…" He lets me go, then instantly grabs me again when I sway. "You are burning with fever. Magic sickness is starting to set in."

"I'm fine." I try to shove him off, but it takes so much effort that I barely brush him and end up falling into his arms. He grunts.

"I have seen you better, Your Highness," he mocks, getting me upright and pulling my arm across his shoulders.

Why does everything hurt? "You have also seen me worse."

Toussaint chuckles. "Yes, Fox, I have. But let's get you inside so you can rest. Maybe I can convince Evanthe to let me take you to Faerie early, and they can bring Briar Rose tomorrow."

"Nonsense." I try to hit him, but it ends up a light tap. "Hey! Stop that."

"Stop what?" He walks us back toward the castle, taking the stone stairs one at a time, half-dragging me.

"You know what." Leaning away from him has me nearly falling on my face. His magic soaks into my skin, hot and sharp, the scent of cinnamon tickling my nose.

"As much as you seem to enjoy wallowing, I'm not leaving you like this."

"I'm—"

"With all due respect, shut up, Loren."

A bubble of shocked laughter escapes me. Toussaint shakes his head and sighs.

A few figures meet us in the doorway of the castle entrance. It takes my eyes a few moments to adjust.

"What happened?" Evanthe demands.

It's a struggle to hold my head up.

"He's used too much magic," Toussaint tells her. Delphine rushes forward to grab my other arm, and the two of them carry me inside. I try to walk, but Toussaint snaps at me to quit trying to help.

"And he might have had too much to drink," he adds, further proving his point that I have lost too much magic: human wine should not have been able to intoxicate me. Not like this.

There is a shout in the distance, followed by rapid hoofbeats. I look where the others are looking, but my head lolls to the side, and my vision won't quite focus. Everything is starting to spin, churning my stomach.

"Briar Rose!" calls out Delphine.

The horse rider continues on, a blur in the darkening distance.

"We have to go after her," someone says. I only realize it's me when Toussaint argues, "You have to rest. We will go after her."

"No," I insist. "I have to… talk to her. It should be me." Not very convincing, having to lean heavily on my best friend to stay on my feet, but I know I have a point. She is upset because of me, and I should be the one to atone.

One mistake after another… And the Seelie want me to be king? Maybe all of my mess-ups are proof that I am the wrong child, that the firstborn is supposed to take the throne. Because, as dark and twisted as he is, he seems to know how to be a ruler better than I do. Or if he is a mess too, then he's hiding it far better.

Shocking me to my very core, Delphine looks me up and down, and states, "He is right. He should be the one to talk with her."

Evanthe is frowning, and I'm sure Toussaint is too. Even subtle movements have my head spinning, so I don't dare check.

"She has to be going to the cottage," Irit points out. "It will be close enough to Faerie that Prince Loren can at least recover a little, so we can take him with us."

Good to know they do not entirely loath me.

"Well?" Delphine says, pointing in the direction Briar Rose fled, the sun casting its final bits of light into the horizon before it finally disappears. "We need to catch up with her."

Evanthe glances at me, then nods. "Delphine and Irit, you stay here. Toussaint and I will take Prince Loren to retrieve Briar Rose."

BRIAR ROSE

I have no idea where else to go. All I know is I have to get away from the castle and people. Especially *him*.

If I asked—or even ordered—anyone to take me to the cottage, they would have said no and informed my faerie guardians. So, I took the fastest horse—my father's prize stallion, Armand—and fled, the stableboy's shouts fading the farther away I got.

First I lost Henri, then… No, that's not true. Henri was not the first one I lost, and he was never real enough for me to lose him. Not truly. But I do not want to unravel those feelings, at least not yet.

I cling to Armand, my fingers and toes starting to go numb in the quickly-dropping temperature that accompanies nightfall. In my rush, I hadn't grabbed a cloak, too nervous that someone would stop me. At least we have a couple of months yet until winter arrives, so I am fortunate that I should be able to reach the cottage before the cold fully claims my extremities.

Hopefully.

In the dark, it is difficult to make out the silhouette of trees against the shadowy forest, so I have to urge Armand to slow down. He huffs as if to say, "Finally." I pat his neck, noting that I cannot feel my hands.

"I'll get you carrots from the garden," I promise him. "Please get us the rest of the way there. It should not be far now."

It will be different, I muse, *to be a faerie. I will have to be more careful about how I craft my untruths.* It would be wonderful to be one now, to have magic I could use to warm myself. And to have a light source of some kind.

Armand walks carefully through the forest, ears twitching this way and that, while I dig through the bag I swiped from the stable on my way out. I have seen hunters take them for their trips, supposedly full of all of the supplies they need other than their bows and quivers. My fumbling hands find bits of jerky, twine, a small knife, a blanket—

With a sigh of relief, I manage to balance the bag on my lap while I pull the blanket around my shivering shoulders, then return to rummaging through the supply bag.

Howls send my teeth chattering for a whole new reason. Armand's ears flatten completely, but he presses on.

Please, I silently beg, *please let there be a faerie light in here.* There is supposed to be one in every bag, a last resort. They are one of the gifts the Seelie provide us as protection against the Unseelie. Well, not against them, exactly, but against their tricks to guide us the wrong way and make us stumble into Unseelie. And after how this day has gone, it would only make sense that I would be the poor unfortunate soul to end up there.

More howls and growling, this time closer. Armand stops completely.

At the bottom of the bag, I find the smooth stone and almost cry in relief. Hands trembling so badly I almost drop the faerie light, I lift it to my mouth and exhale. My breath rips from me, leaving me gasping, and illuminates the stone in a soft, dim glow.

Are the shadows moving? The faerie light is growing brighter, but I still cannot see much past the nearest trees and shrubbery. There can be any number of creatures prowling about, and my imagination is in no short supply.

When I suck in enough air, I bring the faerie light back to my mouth and whisper, "Take me to the cottage."

It takes its payment again, this time enough to have me fall forward onto Armand's neck, pressing my face into his mane to muffle my wheezes.

The growls seem more like rumbles now, and I swear I hear rustling.

Keeping my breathing shallow, I slowly raise my head and open my eyes. Like twinkling stars, there is a pathway curving between the trees.

Thank you. I nudge Armand's sides, and he reluctantly walks forward, his hooves making soft sounds that I hope the wolves either do not hear or ignore. I also hope they are wolves, and not faerie monsters that sometimes find their way into human lands, because I know I would have much better luck surviving the wolves.

Partially to calm Armand and partially to keep myself from giving into the rising panic, I gently pet his neck. He is a mighty stallion, trained for everything including war (or so Father claims), so the gesture should seem ridiculous, but he leans into my touch.

A low growl is our only warning before a wolf lunges from the bushes. Armand instantly bolts; I barely grasp the reins in time, the supply bag gone in an instant, taking the one small weapon in my possession. The blanket flutters away after it as if not wanting to be left behind.

The wolves snarl as they gain on us. I cling to Armand, the faerie light so tight in my fist that my whole hand aches.

At least it's wolves, I tell myself. That gives us a chance, however small it may be.

Branches snag my hair and skin and dress, whatever is within their reach, and still I press my knees harder into Armand's flanks, willing him to go as fast as he can.

Jaws snap near my leg, catching the hem of my dress and tearing it instantly. Armand shrieks and wrenches to the right. My cry is cut short by the impact of the ground; I roll, my numb fingers scrambling for purchase, and hit a tree. A sharp, burning sensation erupts throughout the left side of my ribcage.

Armand's screams pierce the air as he flails, too far away from me and the illuminated path. All I can see are black shapes struggling against one another.

I move to stand, but the stabbing pain sends me back to the earth. It would be enough to keep me there if not for the horrible noises: the ripping, the gagging—

Using my right arm, I drag myself toward where the faerie light tumbled into the grass, still shining, a small beacon of hope I focus on instead of the thrashing shadows that could turn on me at any moment.

Armand's final whinny rattles, its echo cutting off abruptly.

I force myself onto my knees and hobble, keeping my left arm tight against my injured side. The growls turn toward me as I snatch the faerie light and hold it to my mouth one more time. I exhale everything I have left, and the faerie light seizes it all.

Bright like fire, I plead, like it would be able to hear me and understand.

And somehow, it does.

Brilliant light floods the area. I squint, barely able to make out the retreating shadows that snap and snarl at the edge of my vision. My lungs spasm, attempting to inhale but unable to for more than a split second at a time, and not wanting to release what precious little it has acquired. Tremors wrack my body as I hold up the stone, which is beginning to wane.

No, please no.

There are no fallen branches or sharp rocks at my disposal. I can draw shallow breaths in between coughing fits that shoot fire through my ribs, nothing that will charge the faerie light again. The pathway remains, as if taunting me, and in the back of my mind, I wonder if it will disappear when I take my final, rattling breath.

The wolves close in, skirting the outside of the faerie light's circle of illumination. Awkwardly, I push myself to my feet and bite back a cry of pain. If I am to die here, I will not give in easily.

Stumbling on the glittering path, the wolves maintaining pace with me, I go as fast as I can, letting branches rip at my arm and cheeks because it is too painful to try to dodge them. My face is wet, and I cannot tell if it is tears or blood or a mixture of both.

If I die here, the curse was all for naught, I muse bitterly, dark laughter bubbling up my throat, taking me by surprise. *What a terrible ending to a terrible tale… I never got to fix things with Loren.*

The faerie light flickers twice more, then drops to a dim glow that barely shows what is in front of my face. Everything falls to shades of black except the shimmering path and the faerie light, which seems almost as drained as I am. Regardless, I press on, frantic.

The first teeth rip through my skirts and sink into my calf, only a mere heartbeat before the second find my arm that is still pressed against my wounded side. I slam onto the ground, losing grip on the stone. There is no air to scream, to cry, to beg.

Then something in the air shifts, and they are gone. I hear the impacts, the struggles of newly joining creatures that appear almost invisible against the darkness. Whatever they are, the wolves stand little chance, torn to shreds and left in lifeless heaps along the path.

The world rocks back and forth, sometimes doubling, hitting me with waves of nausea and making it difficult for me to focus on reaching for the faerie light. But I can do it. I have to. I…

Someone steps into view.

"It has been a long time, Princess Briar Rose."

CHAPTER SEVENTEEN

THE UNSEELIE KING

The princess manages to look up at me, pupils shrinking and expanding like they cannot make up their mind. Her breathing is mere gasps, sucking in air like a fish; by one look at her, the faerie light, and the path, I know exactly what happened. She is lucky to be alive, not even considering the wolves.

Her elegant dress is in tatters, her hair knotted with bits of twigs and leaves. The scent of blood is strong, although I know most of it is not coming from her.

My Glamour tearing apart what remains of the wolves, I kneel down next to her. The faint light is just enough for her human eyes, and recognition sets into her expression as pure dread, the embers of hope dying out.

Consciousness flees her swiftly, her head falling back to the earth.

"This is not your time, Princess." I place my hands on her back, recalling my magic so that it can wrap around her. It does so gently before seeping into her wounds, knitting them back together until no evidence of their existence remains. The loss of magic is like scraping my insides raw, a painful reminder that I am in human lands. For the time being, it is necessary.

Asra swoops down and lands on my shoulder, chittering urgently. She opens her mind to me, showing Loren, Evanthe, and Toussaint heading into the woods on horseback.

"Good girl," I praise, pressing a quick kiss to her head. Then I turn my attention back to the passed-out princess. "Well, Your Highness, I suppose we must make haste."

I lift her into my arms easily enough. "Asra, darling, fetch the faerie light for me, please."

The wyvern obeys instantly and settles back across my shoulders, faerie light clutched between her claws. Gently, she turns Briar Rose's hand over so she can drop the stone into it. The faerie light brightens a little in response, as does the glittering path. Asra folds the princess's hand back over it.

"Let us see where you intended to go," I say aloud. If we were in Unseelie, I would use magic to whisk us toward the destination. It is probably not far, but the risk of draining my magic is too great, especially with my half-brother on my heels. Of the three of them, Evanthe would be the worst to combat. They might be drained of magic from being in the human lands, but I decide against using mine regardless. I've bided my time wisely this far; wasting it would be a great tragedy.

I decide on walking quickly, Briar Rose limp in my arms. At least she is breathing more evenly now, but her skin is too pale, lacking the rosiness human faces tend to bear. That should return once she is warm and gets some rest.

Every so often, Asra flies off to scout the area and check on the others' progress. After her third trip, we find the end of the path, which leads to a small cottage nestled between two towering trees whose trunks' widths are greater than that of the cottage itself. It is a simple building, with ivy climbing up the sides, delicately wrapping around the windows.

I inhale deeply. A border between human and faerie lands is nearby, magic trickling in where the divide is blurred. Invisible to humans, we faeries see the warping of colors that signify there is a passage, much easier than using a portal. But from where we are, I am sure it would take me to Seelie, and I have more than enough magic left to make a portal home.

The cottage door opens easily. Evanthe and the others must not have expected anyone to come here, or else they figured there is nothing inside worth protecting. It has two floors, the bottom hosting what can barely be considered a kitchen and dining room combined, as well as an open area with a fireplace and a few chairs. I carry Briar Rose up the stairs to find two rooms with only beds and a few decorations.

Does she not spend much time here? For a princess, I assumed she would have had many more possessions. This is much closer to what I imagine a peasant girl would have, necessities with some simple comforts, nothing more.

Gently, I lay her on one of the beds. She looks like she is sleeping peacefully, save for the slight furrow in her brow. Taking that as a sign that she may soon wake, I settle down beside her, almost falling off the edge, my forehead touching hers. Asra hops off me and curls up above our heads, already alert, watching and listening without me having to ask her to.

"Come with me, Briar Rose," I whisper. Then I slip into my dreamscape.

LOREN

Despite my protests, Toussaint has given me some of his magic, just enough to get me out of my sickened state. Although the jostling of the galloping horse Toussaint and I ride on is keeping my stomach in a state of being perpetually unsettled. He tells me to hold onto him, but warns he is going to tease me relentlessly if I throw up on him.

Sunlight gone, my eyes adjust to the darkness. Certain Unseelie creatures thrive in the absence of light, seeing as well in darkness as we can in daylight. The rest of us Fae are not as blinded by it as humans, but it is like being in a dimly lit room, and entering the forest doesn't help matters.

The first howls set my veins to ice. I listen carefully, and by the way Toussaint tenses, I can tell he is too. Evanthe's horse falters, but she whispers a few Fae words to him, and he perks back up, no longer disturbed by the heightening sounds. From what I can tell, they are not faerie creatures that found a way into human lands— however, there are many that can mimic whatever they hear, and many more that can shapeshift as well.

Let them just be wolves. Between the three of us, I do not know how much magic we have left to combat any faerie creatures, especially if they are of the monstrous sort.

Nothing like danger to sober me up.

A scream pierces the air; images of Briar Rose jump to mind...

We press the horses to go faster, but they are already sweat-soaked. At this point, I would consider making a deal with a phooka just to get to her in time, my own safety be damned. I'd give years off my life, my sweetest dreams, my blood, my teeth—even my bloody crown if the vile creature demanded it—just to save her.

Blinding light flashes. Our horses falter to a halt, nearly throwing us.

"What was that?" Toussaint asks.

"Faerie light," Evanthe breathes, urgent hope lacing her words.

And then I feel the hint of magic in the air; we must be on the outer edge of its effect. We press forward, watching through squinted eyes as the glow dims significantly. The horses refuse to go faster than a tentative walk, so I let go of Toussaint and slide off.

"Hey!" Toussaint grasps my arm.

Yelps and snarls in the distance. More violent, heart-wrenching imaginings plague my mind.

"We don't have time!" I tug away from him and sprint, stumbling as my legs try to remember how to work properly.

"And you do not have magic!" Toussaint hops down after me, catching up within a few seconds. Without me having to ask, he rushes ahead, already drawing his throwing knives, and disappears around a bend.

Evanthe hurries to my side, trying to help me, but I wave her off. "Save Briar Rose."

After only a moment's hesitation, she nods and follows Toussaint.

Once they are out of sight, I fall, catching myself against a tree trunk, and stop fighting the nausea. When my stomach is finally done, I groan. Of course, instead of being the charming prince to her rescue, I am the idiot who got himself magic-deficient and drunk. Wonderful.

Feeling a little steadier albeit shaky, I take off after Evanthe and Toussaint. I expect them to be far ahead of me, possibly having reached the scene already. The sudden silence is panic-inducing.

I turn one corner, hop over a fallen tree, make it to the next turn—

Toussaint and Evanthe are standing there, staring at the aftermath. My knees want to give way, but I force myself to take a few more steps, to stand with them. I have to see this for myself, have to know what exactly my stupidity has cost me.

All I can make out in the shredded remains are a horse head, some hooves, and bits of wolf carcasses. By the looks of it, it is King Faustus's horse, the one he uses in parades and on hunts. There are gouges in the ground, which are painted in smears of red...

It takes me far too long to process that I do not see her. Relief knocks me forward, and I catch myself before I faceplant. "She's alive..." I whisper, fingers digging into the dirt.

"Possibly," Evanthe replies, voice devoid of emotion. "No faerie light stone, no pathway left. She must be just ahead of us."

The area is thick with remnants of recently-used magic, the faerie light effects faint, almost gone. The rest is strong, overpowering, sharp.

I jump to my feet, fresh panic pumping adrenaline through my veins. The three of us exchange concerned looks, but none of us dares speak the obvious: that is the magic of the Unseelie King.

Evanthe conjures a tracking spell, and neither of us argue with her.

CHAPTER EIGHTEEN

BRIAR ROSE

Spinning. Darkness. Never-ending falling. Trying to scream but only able to whimper, I grasp for something, anything, to stabilize myself—

"Shhhh…" Strong arms catch me, cradle me. "I would have thought your guardians would have taught you to land in the dreamscape better than that. I can teach you, if you wish."

The black recedes to reveal a fair-skinned man holding me, one arm behind my back and the other under my knees. A faerie, as indicated by the pointed ears sticking out from his ink-colored hair, as if his unfairly perfect beauty were not explanation enough. His ice-blue eyes stare into mine studiously, a hint of amusement tugging at the corner of his mouth.

"It has been a long time, Princess Briar Rose," he said before I lost consciousness. And then I woke up here, in… a dreamscape? A shadowy place, all I can make out in the light of the few lone torches hanging on the walls is that he is carrying me through a stone hallway. It forms more as we make our way closer to a set of double doors. The soft, pliable feeling of magic surrounds us, urging us to create, endless possibilities at our fingertips...

"Put me down," I order, struggling against his grip. This is the Unseelie King, the faerie who cursed me—does he intend to kidnap me? If he does, why did he bring me to a dreamscape? To make me prick my finger on the spindle of the spinning wheel and force the start of the curse? ...Would that work in a dreamscape, or does it have to be in the real world?

The fact that I am not yet eighteen is my only brief solace, but he could keep me captive until then.

To my surprise, he obeys, but before I can run away, he takes my arm and presses it tightly against his side, as if he were escorting me.

"Let me go." I yank, but he holds fast.

"Not just yet, Princess." He is irritatingly calm, continuing toward the doors.

First wolves, then the Unseelie King... I never should have left the castle on my own.

Before we reach the doors, it hits me: I can feel the tug of magic, meaning he has allowed me to conjure in his dreamscape. His mistake.

With a single thought, a dagger forms in my fist, and I press it against his pale throat. He pauses, the only indication that he is surprised. Although when he looks at me out of the corner of his eye, there is no surprise, only more amusement.

"You will release me."

The dagger disappears, just as I suspected he would do, and I conjure a hundred more, all surrounding him, hovering in the air at various angles. He takes his time scanning them, even daring to move a bit to get a better view.

"So, they have taught you almost adequately," he says without a hint of nervousness. "I will admit that this much control is impressive for a human."

For a few seconds, I consider skewering him. But would that kill him in the real world? How could I handle killing someone? The thought leaves a bad taste in my mouth. Maybe I can wound him enough to drop the barriers so I can escape?

His gaze flicks to mine. "Have they taught you what happens when you kill the host of a dreamscape?"

Fighting the urge to blush, I shake my head. Why would they? They only thought to keep my mind and soul alive in the dreamscape until True Love's Kiss wakes me from the sleeping curse.

"It makes sense that they would want to keep you from such drastic measures, but I thought Evanthe would eventually find the lesson necessary, all things considered." His mouth quirks, the smile lacking the mirth of earlier. "If you were to kill me here and now, it would kill me in the real world. Since the dreamscape is anchored to me, it would disappear until you are swallowed by nothingness, your soul forever lost."

For a moment, the Unseelie King seems like he is looking past me, pain etched into his expression. He looks young, far too young to be the bloodthirsty monster everyone paints him as. But faeries do not age like humans, and so even though he appears to be not much older than I am, I know he has to be, considering he had just taken over the Unseelie when I was born, and he was there to curse me at the celebration of my birth.

Like shutting curtains, his expression snaps back to an unaffected calm air. "What will it be, Princess?"

This is his dreamscape: he could make all of my daggers disappear just like the first one. He could take away my ability to conjure anything in this place, leaving me powerless. Instead, he has chosen to give me a level of control, leaving me with the question of *why?*

"If you want answers," he says as if having been privy to my thoughts, "we will talk civilly, no threats. Agreed?"

The last time I saw the Unseelie King, I was a young child, about five years old. I remember him being taller, older, scarier. Well, scarier in an obvious way, like a monster. Now I wonder if my mind has fashioned that over the years.

But he can also take on whatever appearance he wishes in the dreamscape.

Still pointed at him, the daggers roll slowly as I ponder. "You will not force me to prick my finger and start the curse?"

He grins. "You are starting to think like a faerie," he states approvingly. "No, I will not force you to prick your finger and start the curse. Unless you find a way to break it before it happens, the curse will find a way on its own."

Why not ensure your victory? I wonder, but decide against giving him reasons to do it. Reluctantly, I dispel the daggers.

"A wise choice, especially since we are running out of time." He releases my arm and briskly walks to the double doors. They throw themselves open, and he passes through into the darkness.

I want to ask what he is talking about, but that would waste what time we have, so I follow after him, braving the dark. The moment my foot passes the threshold, the room fills with a soft, dusky light. Fog covers the floor in a thick layer, coiling around me as I make my way to the center, where he stands with his back to me. I position myself beside him, leaving enough space between us so that he cannot reach out to touch me.

"This is what Faerie is like now," he says quietly, staring into the never-ending distance. "After the split of the Courts, many parts of Faerie have become wastelands, voids where nothing can thrive, only shrivel into nothingness. The In-Between is taking over, slowly but surely, because of the division."

The fog creeps toward us, bringing with it despair.

"Then why not find a solution with Loren?" I question, hating how tense my voice sounds.

Without looking at me, he answers, "We know the solution: one of us must bow to the other for Faerie to be whole again." After a pause, he continues, "I assume you do not know everything, that you feel like a pawn in a game to which you do not know the rules and consequences."

I turn to him, only to find him already studying me. *Am I that easy to read?*

"I have a proposition for you, a way that will restore Faerie and break the curse."

I roll his words over and over, trying to find the loophole, the hidden meaning that will surely stab me in the back.

Slowly, the Unseelie King steps toward me. When I do not recoil, he takes my hand and brings it to his lips, leaving the cool tingle of magic and bringing heat to my cheeks. "Call for me if you wish to hear more."

LOREN

I can taste the bitterness of my brother's magic as I nearly trip rushing up the stairs of the cottage. There is nothing out of place, and yet the chill in the air has my every nerve on alert.

Evanthe and Toussaint make it to the room first, and when I peer over their shoulders, I see the last bits of dark Glamour dissipate on the bed beside Briar Rose's sleeping form.

Evanthe rushes to her, reaching out as Briar Rose gasps and sits up, hand pressed to her chest. There is dried blood on her temple and hands, and her dress is torn and dirtied beyond recognition, but I can see no obvious wounds. I wish that gave me more relief.

Jovan's necklace is still there, slightly dirty but otherwise fine. When Briar Rose sees that, she will be happy.

Evanthe smooths back Briar Rose's hair, checking for injuries on her head and neck under the guise of comforting her. She barely glances at her guardian before she meets my eyes; under the weight of her gaze, I find myself having to lean against the doorframe.

I want to go to her, but the room barely allows for three people, and I am the last person she wants tending to her. *She is alive,* I tell myself. *Let that be enough for now.*

Yet she continues to stare, pondering something.

"Did he hurt you?" Evanthe asks, now more obvious about checking as she inspects the princess's arms and hands.

Abruptly breaking our eye contact to stare at her lap, she only shakes her head in response, her brow furrowed and mouth pinched. Even if I still could be Henri for her, I doubt I could make her feel any better. The Unseelie King's presence lingers in the room like he left an imprint on her.

If only we were a few minutes earlier... But then what? What would we have been able to do? We have no idea what he did to her, what he wanted. I was terrified that he was going to steal her away to Unseelie, yet he left her here.

My gut twists as my mind tries to come up with answers.

"We have to leave for Seelie now," Evanthe announces.

That snaps Briar Rose out of her sullen, distant mood. "What?" She leans away from her faerie guardian, scooting toward the other side of the bed so she can stand. "I have to say goodbye to my family."

"It is too dangerous to stay," Evanthe points out. "The Unseelie King may have left you here, but he just proved that you are not outside of his reach. We have to do what we can to protect you."

As much as I hate the desperation in Briar Rose's expression, I know Evanthe is right. Seelie is not safe, but it is safer than here. And if I want to talk with my aunt alone to see if there is some way to release Briar Rose from the betrothal, I'll have to do it in person.

Taking me away... Her confession to Henri rings in my ears, further solidifying my decision, as much as it tears my heart apart. *We're doing this to protect you,* I want to tell her, but I am certain she doesn't want to hear from me. The fact that she is avoiding looking at me again further proves it.

Squaring her shoulders and lifting her chin, Briar Rose says, "Very well."

Evanthe turns to Toussaint. "Take them to Seelie, and tell Queen Vivienne that I am retrieving Delphine and Irit and will join you shortly."

CHAPTER NINETEEN

BRIAR ROSE

I snatch Evanthe's sleeve as she exits the cottage in a rush.

"I will catch up to you soon, my sweet," she promises, pressing a quick kiss to my forehead. "Flora and Fauna will be in Seelie to take care of you until then. You can trust Toussaint to get you there safely."

"Wait…"

She watches me expectantly.

I swallow, gathering my thoughts amidst the rolling emotions. There is no way to sort them in just a moment, so I ask, "Please, tell my parents that I am sorry. And tell Jovan that I will not forget him." The pendant under my fingertips grounds me, reminds me that not all is lost. This is just the next step in this journey, and I am not alone.

"Of course." Evanthe hugs me, then mounts one of the horses. The other is tied to hers, forced to gallop alongside her. At least those two will make it back home... Father will not be pleased to have lost Armand.

"Thank you," I whisper into the light breeze, hoping it will bring the words to Armand. He certainly earned his status for being courageous.

"Princess Briar Rose," Toussaint calls gently, his tone as serious as I've ever heard it. "We must make haste."

I know he is right. But my body refuses to move, and I keep staring at the forest, at the bend that disappears into the trees. In my mind echoes the howls, the screams, the ripping of flesh—

"Princess?"

I inhale, but I cannot turn around, not with the tears that are threatening to spill over. I fear that, if I move, I will crumble and not find the strength to stand again. So much danger in such a short amount of time, and that was in human lands. How am I supposed to survive Faerie?

...you feel like a pawn in a game to which you do not know the rules and consequences...

I shiver and brush at my shoulders, as if that will rid me of the lingering unease the Unseelie King left. I am, after all, his enemy, someone he cursed. Why would I trust anything he says? He only wants to destroy the Seelie and conquer everything for himself.

Just as I am resolving to turn around, a jacket settles onto my shoulders. Loren stays at the edge of my vision, and when I face him, he stops moving entirely. No wall, no stony expression, just a tired faerie looking at me with a mixture of concern and... is that fear?

Loren abruptly walks away, back toward Toussaint, who is watching us intently. After a moment, I put my arms into the sleeves of the jacket and follow.

"It will be easy enough to cross here," Toussaint informs me. "But if you are feeling weak, I can carry you."

Part of me wishes he would make a joke to lighten the mood, but the other part is grateful he doesn't. He is, after all, our protector—his main duty is not to cater to our feelings.

"I can walk," I reply, my voice a little raw, giving a glimpse into how exhausted I feel in both body and mind. Utterly unconvincing, really.

Surprisingly, Toussaint nods it off. "Very well. All the same, we should hold hands, to make sure we stay together. The borders of Faerie like to play games, and it is easy to get lost."

After the way they keep referring to their homeland, I have to wonder how I was ever allowed there as a little girl, and why they allowed the three of us to play unsupervised as often as we did. Although now that I think back on it, surely there must have been someone watching us, even if we were unaware of their presence. Faeries are many things, but they are not stupid.

Toussaint offers his hand first, and I take it. Loren steps to the other side of me, but we do not look at each other. When Toussaint impatiently clears his throat, Loren finally extends his hand, brushing his knuckles against mine. An unexpected tingle runs up my arm, but I ignore it, writing it off as merely a vague remembrance of the way things used to be. He is no longer that boy, and after today, I do not know if I could summon that girl even if I wanted to.

Loren's grip is looser than Toussaint's, and I cannot help but think that if Henri—

No, I chastise myself. *No more thoughts of Henri. He does not exist, and never did.*

"Stay close," Toussaint reminds us even though we are holding hands. "It should only take a few minutes at most, unless Faerie is in the mood for tricks."

I actually look at him this time. "The land can *move*? It is alive?"

He blinks at me, puzzled. "Yes, Princess. The land itself is made of magic, and magic is very much alive and has a mind of its own."

I was five or six the last time I stepped into Faerie, and the memory of the crossing is blurry at best, so as we march directly into the trees, I brace myself. Just as I think we are about to smack straight into a tree, everything around us shimmers and warps, bleeding into a mosaic of colors that remind me of traveling to the dreamscape. I cannot tell the ground from the sky, but we keep moving forward, even as the air grows lighter and tries to lift us off our feet. Both faeries hold tightly to me now.

"Tricks it is," Toussaint mutters.

Everything feels thick, like we are wading through water, and I struggle to breathe. Unrelenting cold seeps into my bones, and I make a mental note to thank Loren for the jacket later.

"Do not stop," Toussaint orders, dragging me along. Loren keeps pace, hooking my arm under his. My legs are already shaking from the effort of walking with the heaviness of my water-logged dress, and if the two of them weren't holding me, it feels like I would either fall or get my feet stuck.

My lungs are beginning to burn.

"Almost there."

The colors bleed into each other again. With one final push, we step onto dry, even, solid ground. I topple forward, but they catch me, staggering in an attempt to keep us all upright.

Forest surrounds us, just as it did in the human lands, but the colors are richer, more vibrant. I survey the area as I suck in greedy breaths, wondering why faerie magic has a penchant for air. The only answer I can come up with is that everything seems to be *alive*. Even though the trees are unmoving, I can almost see them inhale and exhale, can almost make out faces in the trunks. A breeze moves past us, and I swear the blades of grass whisper to each other as it nudges through them. I do not know what they say, but they radiate contagious excitement that ripples down the hill to the stream.

"If she is listening to the wind, Queen Vivienne will know of our arrival shortly," says Toussaint.

"She does not expect us until later," Loren points out. Already the coloring of his skin is less pale, and the brightness is returning to his amber eyes. He stands a little straighter, a hint of a smile at his lips that disappears when he notices me staring. Clearing his throat, he gestures toward our surroundings. "Welcome back to Faerie."

Welcome back. Hints of this place stir long-slumbering memories at the back of my mind, as if the land is begging me to remember.

"The welcome might have been better," Toussaint comments

with a faint smirk, "if the border hadn't decided to play games with us." I must have a strange look on my face, because he quickly adds, "We were never in any real danger. If Faerie did not want our presence, it would have made sure we didn't make it through."

I nod, still taking in the song-like bird calls and various vibrant colors of the flowers blooming at various points along the path. A far cry from the forest we just left.

The branches above our heads shake, sending a small shower of leaves and flower petals into our hair. Two luminous green eyes peer back at me, and a grin appears just beneath them. As if slowly forming its existence, a nose, whiskers, and fur make up the rest of the creature, a long, striped tail dangling almost low enough for me to reach up and tug. I resist the urge to.

The cat shifts its weight but doesn't jump down, just stares at me with a maniacal grin that makes me want to step backward.

"Prince Loren," the cat speaks, "what a relief to see you return. And you have brought a friend...?" He sniffs. "A human. Could this be your betrothed?"

The voice sounds familiar, but not enough for me to place it. This time I do take a step back, and Loren grasps my elbow, protectively pulling me toward him.

"Hello, Cheshire," he responds. "I would recommend you keep this knowledge to yourself. My aunt will be rather cross with you if you are caught gossiping again."

The cat presses a paw to his chest, mouth open in mock horror. "I do not gossip, Your Highness. I merely leave clues for those thirsty for information." The end of his tail coils in on itself.

"Keep it to yourself, Cat," Toussaint warns. "We'll not have another mishap because of your need to complicate matters."

Cheshire sighs dramatically, and begins to disappear, starting with his coiled tail. "Very well... Until next we meet..." Then he is gone, as if he were never there in the first place.

"We have lost enough time," Toussaint says, urging us to continue our trek through the forest. Loren releases me, and I almost reach for his arm, his hand, something to ground me.

"Was that a faerie? It looked like a cat."

Loren shoots a troubled glance at me from over his shoulder. "We are… not quite certain what the Cheshire Cat is."

"Trouble is what he is," Toussaint mutters with a shake of his head. "Even before the splitting of the Courts, he liked to be a part of politics, spreading rumors and making loved ones distrust each other. He brings nothing but chaos, and it has only gotten worse since Faerie was divided."

"But… Is he not Seelie? I thought faeries had to stay in their chosen Court." I lift the hem of my dress and try to step over shifting protruding roots as ladylike as I can. I don't appreciate the trees trying to trip me.

"Like Fox said," clarifies Toussaint, "we are not entirely sure what he is. Some believe he is a creature that existed before the time of the Fae. He can go between Seelie and Unseelie without consequence."

I envy the way the two of them maneuver through the roots with ease, like they know exactly how they will move, while I trip and stumble.

"Would you like help?" Toussaint offers.

My first instinct is to reject him… but it seems more and more likely that one of these times I will end up on my face.

"Yes, please." I reach for him, but he steps backward.

"Fox?" He shoots his prince a cocky smirk, to which Loren returns a glare that is gone by the time he is facing me.

With only a moment's hesitation, Loren scoops me into his arms like I weigh nothing. Reflexively, I almost put my arms around his neck, but I settle for holding them to my chest. If Henri had done something like this, I would have swooned—or at least felt like swooning.

But he is Henri.

Loren stares straight ahead, moving quickly to catch up with Toussaint. His jaw is set determinedly, his eyes like flickers of flame whenever the light finds them through the trees, and a few curled locks of hair at his temple bounce and sway slightly with each step.

I am caught off-guard when he suddenly stops and meets my gaze. The hardness of his expression melts; his throat bobs.

"As much as I love seeing you two on better terms," Toussaint interrupts, "we should get to the castle before something with hostile intentions finds us." From his voice, I can tell he is smiling, but I can't seem to bring myself to look away from Loren. It feels like there is something fragile forming between us, and although I do not know what it is, I am afraid that any wrong move might shatter it.

But it must be in my imagination: he puts me down and continues walking, not bothering to check to see if I am following.

CHAPTER TWENTY

THE UNSEELIE KING

"My King."

I look up from my wine goblet but do not bother standing; I am far too comfortable with my feet propped up in front of the fireplace, the one source of light in my bedchamber. Besides, Asra is curled up in my lap, and I would be loath to disturb her rest.

"Yes, Margaux?" I lean my head back, letting my half-empty goblet dangle from my fingertips. Strange, how I can still feel Briar Rose's blade against my throat. Perhaps she will be more interesting than I originally assumed.

The pale faerie draws closer, stopping a few paces away. "It is as you predicted: the princess is in Seelie. The wedding and her transformation are planned to happen soon. Their queen refuses to speak of details with anyone."

As I expected. "No matter," I tell her. "Continue to watch the border."

Margaux pauses, her silence a pressing query she dares not utter, lest she appear to be questioning my order.

But Margaux has earned at least a small amount of assurance after the years of unwavering loyalty. "Like the Queen of Seelie," I explain, "I also keep details to myself."

Without a word, my Captain of the Guard bows. "Anything else I can do for you, My King?"

"None." I wave her off dismissively, grateful there is not enough left in my goblet for the wine to slosh over onto the rug under my chair. It would not take much magic to clean it, but it would be annoying to use it on something so trivial.

"Very well." But instead of leaving, she informs me, "Chimere wishes to have an audience with you."

It takes a moment for me to recall who she is, making me think maybe I drank my wine more quickly than I thought.

"Tell her I am open to meeting at a later date." I cannot bring myself to even entertain the idea of being around anyone right now. There is too much to consider, too much to plan without adding more politics into the equation.

But I will have to stop pushing this off sometime soon.

"Tomorrow," I add before Margaux can shut the door behind her. "Tell her I will meet with her tomorrow."

LOREN

Where the human castles are enclosed, tall buildings of stone, the Seelie castle is more of an arrangement of trees surrounding a glade of flowers, with a stream running through it. Enough elements that all sorts of faeries can gather comfortably, all under an open sky. Walk a small way in any direction, and you will find yourself coming upon a house, always small, always unassuming, letting the land dictate the size and shape of the structure. Open politics, closed homes, as my father is often quoted.

Unfortunately, he could not hold to his own standard, and that killed him in the end.

I sneak a peek behind me. My chest warms at the sight of Briar Rose's unfiltered awe, soaking in everything from the scenery to the harp serenading us to draw closer to the plethora of various types of Fae present for her arrival: tall, tree-like dryads that cast long shadows over everyone, easily seeing over others' heads to watch our arrival; smaller, rounder, more unassuming hobgoblins that are straining on tiptoes and peering between openings with their beady eyes; elemental sprites that are closest to the front, most avoiding fire and water that naturally emanates from them. High Faeries like myself are scattered throughout, most human-like in appearance, but we are far outnumbered by the other kinds of Fae.

Aunt Vivienne makes her way through the crowd easily, everyone parting for her without her asking. She is every bit a queen, from her beauty to her grace to her unmatched inner strength I have gotten to know well over the years. She does not command loyalty: the Seelie trip over themselves giving her whatever they can.

She should rule, I think for the thousandth time. Giving me the crown seems like a horrible idea for multiple reasons, all of which she disregards.

"Loren." Aunt Vivienne embraces me heartily, as a mother would a beloved child. I hug her back and do not resist when I feel bits of her magic seeping into me, replacing a little of what I have lost. Being in Faerie for a short period of time, I am no longer in danger of becoming sick again, but I am by no means close to capacity. All of us Fae bear the same minor marks of fatigue, the tired eyes and slumped shoulders that accompany magic deprivation. Although not true deprivation, the In-Between is slowly eating away at Faerie, tainting our magic and leaving us not quite rejuvenated as we should be. As our land suffers, so do we.

"Welcome home," she whispers, with an edge of relief. She will no doubt ask the details of what happened later, when we are in private, but for now, she lets herself be happy.

And I let myself smile.

She touches my cheek before turning her attention to Toussaint, greeting him warmly and thanking him for bringing us here safely. Then she finally addresses Briar Rose with a brilliant grin.

"Princess Briar Rose." She looks her over. "My heart rejoices to have you in Seelie once again, darling girl."

Briar Rose barely gets out a "thank you" before she finds herself in the arms of the Queen of Seelie. Her look of surprise draws a chuckle out of me, and I try to smother it, but Briar Rose notices.

I freeze, unsure what to do. Does she think I am laughing at her? I hope not.

She smiles at me tentatively, giving me a split second of relief that melts the tension from my body instantly. Beautiful in its fragility, the smile is a small, unexpected gift. Something akin to what Henri—or young me—would see often.

"Come," Aunt Vivienne says, "stand where the others can see you better."

While most are semi-patiently standing nearby, peering over shoulders and in between antlers and horns, there are others in the trees, slipping to lower branches to get closer to us. From what I can tell, the Cheshire Cat is gone, but I do not believe that for a second. This is too monumental for him to miss; I am certain he followed us all the way here. The worst I can think of is that he will tell the Unseelie King, but the cat does not seem to pick sides, and my brother certainly already knows that Briar Rose is here. Or at least suspects it.

Aunt Vivienne gestures for us to follow her, and the faeries eagerly lean in. Briar Rose latches onto my arm, her smile wavering but not yet gone. It slips into her princess expression, demure and soft and lovely, only the barest hint of a worry line between her brows.

If I were to think about it logically, I assume she is holding tightly to me because I am one of the few familiars in a sea of new, strange creatures and places... but I could easily let myself imagine she does it because she trusts me, because she wants to be with me like she used to, long before Henri.

I wonder how much she remembers. It seems greedy to hope for much, considering how many years have passed and how young we were at the time. That leaves a bad taste in my mouth, thinking she mostly remembers the cold, distant me. The me who has been trying to protect her.

Aunt Vivienne brings us to a wood platform in the center of the glade. It is flush with the ground until Briar Rose and I stand on it. Vines break through the ground and circle around the platform, rumbling and twisting as it raises us. With a startled squeak, Briar Rose lets go of my arm and instantly grips me around the middle, pressing her cheek into my chest as she stares down at the vines.

I manage to work my arm out of the awkward hold so I can put it around her comfortingly. I am tempted to lean down and kiss the top of her head, to murmur that everything is okay. In her eyes, this must be a lot to take in. All platforms in the human lands are stable, unmoving, and most have railings to prevent falls.

The vines shudder to a stop when the two of us are on display for all. Briar Rose keeps her hold on me but looks around, then down at her tattered dress. To be honest, neither of us looks our best, and I should have thought of that earlier.

Unable to help myself, I release what little magic I've replenished, letting it first coat her. Stains disappear (along with my jacket), tears repair, and for good measure, I change the color of the dress from lilac purple to rose pink, her favorite. She looks up at me, and I quickly run my hand over her hair, my Glamour undoing the knots and reforming the loose curls. As I spend my magic, Seelie trickles it back into me. If I was not already so low, it would be able to keep up, but as it is, I stop using it after she looks presentable.

"Faeries of Seelie," my aunt announces with pride, "may I present your soon-to-be King and Queen!"

That draws Briar Rose's attention away from me, steals the warmth from her expression. She appears calm, but I can feel her heart pounding against my side, and her grip on me remains strong.

"Look how in love they are!" someone squeals above the cheers and applause. "She is loath to let go of him!"

"Who wouldn't be?" another calls. "Have you *seen* Prince Loren?"

A few daring pixies fly toward us, hovering around, toying with her curls and inspecting her dress. They are as tall as my hand, so when one lands on Briar Rose's shoulder, her head reaches her ear. "Definitely human," she comments, voice high-pitched but clear, like a tiny bell. "But won't she look so lovely with faerie ears?"

Briar Rose turns to look at her, and the pixie jumps back into the air before she can get knocked off.

"Very!" the others chime in, and hurriedly zip away as the platform descends, the vines slowly worming their way back into the earth.

Briar Rose adjusts to linking our arms, more proper among humans. Her eyes meet mine briefly, and I find no malice, but she is not quite smiling either. Still, the air seems somehow lighter, like perhaps I found a small hole in the wall separating us.

My heart twists with a horrible truth: as much as I should, I do not want to try to find a way to release her from our betrothal.

CHAPTER TWENTY-ONE

BRIAR ROSE

*A*fter Loren and I leave the platform, I half-expect to take a step and find myself floating. Most of the faeries seem to float as they walk, and I wonder if I will be that graceful when I become one of them… which will be soon.

As that reality begins to sink into my mind, I furtively survey the nearby Fae under the guise of taking in the surroundings. Most of my interactions with their kind have been with what I have heard my guardians refer to as High Fae, the ones whose appearance is closest to humans. I assume that is what I will be transformed into, but I have never asked about it. I wonder if I should, seeing how many have animal-like features… but I have no idea how to bring that up. Waiting until my guardians arrive sounds like the best idea.

It feels like we have been in Faerie for a few hours, but there is no sign of any of my guardians as of yet. I wonder if time moves differently here than in the human lands. Surely Evanthe made sure to speak with my family to assure them before whisking away Irit and Delphine, but I cannot imagine that taking long. I hope they didn't run into any trouble… especially with the Unseelie King.

Don't think about him, I chastise myself. *He is trying to manipulate you into helping him win the war against the Seelie.*

I adjust my grip on Loren's arm, and he peers down at me. There is more color in his cheeks, and he moves with more ease than before, his shoulders back and head held high. We hold each other's gaze for a moment, and then I break it and clear my throat.

Queen Vivienne stops to check on me, drawing the attention of all nearby faeries, who pause their conversations and work. "Are you unwell, Briar Rose?"

"No," I assure her quickly. "But thank you for your concern."

She frowns disbelievingly.

"She is tired from the journey here," Loren supplies for me. "After a decent night's rest, she will be fine."

At this, she nods understandingly. "I meant to start wedding preparations at once, but we can start tomorrow morning instead."

Wedding preparations. Tomorrow. Then how soon is she planning on us being married? Can I forgive Loren by then?

"Have you already planned the day? When is it?" Loren seems just as concerned as I am, and I can only imagine his inner monologue. I thought he *hated* me, but his confession has left me as confused as ever.

Hating you would be far easier.

"Such things need not be discussed in open places," his aunt replies quietly.

Outside of the glade that makes up the "palace," there are buildings and houses that work with the lay of the land, not against it. I wonder how some people deal with slanted houses. The woods make it feel less open than the palace, but I suppose she would know better than I would. Besides, I keep checking the branches above us, expecting to see glimpses of the Cheshire Cat, who sounds like he would find ways to spread information. The last thing we need is the Unseelie King stopping our wedding.

He could have, by taking me to Unseelie when he had the chance... Why didn't he?

"Take Princess Briar Rose to her temporary home so she can rest." Queen Vivienne gestures to two handmaidens following us, and I take the scrap of relief when I recognize them: Flora and Fauna, sisters who bear great resemblances to their names. They are two of my other guardians, although I have not seen them in a while—they look the same as I remember, save for the ink stain black that covers their fingers up to the third knuckle. Maybe the faeries were telling me the truth about why they have not returned to human lands.

Temporary home? I find myself hesitating to release Loren, despite my simmering anger.

Flora and Fauna wait patiently, looking between me and the Seelie Queen. But it is Loren who speaks softly, leaning close to my ear: "I will see you in the morning. Sleep well, Briar Rose."

I get the urge to look at him, but his face is too close to mine. He lingers, breath warm on my cheek, and I wonder what he is thinking. Maybe I can ask him to walk with us. I'm sure he wouldn't deny my request.

No, I can be strong. Evanthe, Delphine, and Irit will be here soon, and I can rest and sort out my feelings in the meantime. Hopefully.

I bid them goodnight and follow Flora and Fauna, vaguely aware of the eyes following me. But I have two amber eyes etched in my mind, that sometimes gleam like fire and sometimes are liquid like honey. I refuse to turn around, but a small part of me wonders if they are watching me leave. And if I want them to.

The sisters bring me to a grassy knoll, where a small door is the only indicator that there is a residence inside. The three of us duck under the doorway to enter, where the scent of earth hits me instantly. Somehow, it's comforting, and I take a deeper breath.

Thankfully, I do not need to hunch over inside, although it would take very little effort to touch the dirt ceiling. There is a table with chairs, a fire pit, and an area with a few beds. It naturally has an earthy scent that I welcome, although I wonder how I will keep the hems of my dresses from getting dirty. There are far too few rugs for me to only stick to them.

"You will join Prince Loren once you are wed," Fauna explains. "For now, Queen Vivienne wishes to keep you hidden in case anyone seeks you out."

Anyone, meaning the Unseelie King. I stifle a shiver that creeps along my spine. If he had wanted to take me, he would have. But I still have no idea why he decided to leave me, knowing I would go to Seelie with Loren.

"There is no need to worry," she adds with a smile that might have been reassuring had I not had a run-in with the Unseelie King.

"Everyone already considers you one of the Seelie," Flora chimes in, her voice melodious. When she moves, the flowery vines that make up her hair shift, and she faces me, her pink irises looking like blooming roses. "You will soon be a queen; you already have many who would be honored to die protecting you."

I stare at her, shifting uncomfortably at the weight of her words, said so matter-of-factly. "Die? I... Why?"

The two of them exchange confused glances with each other.

"Because you are to be the queen," says Fauna, as if that explains everything. Her facial structure and body type seem exactly the same as her sister, but her hair is a thick mane, her eyes cat-like, and she has claws where her fingernails should be. Her legs are like that of a feline, down to the paws, and a tail lazily moves back and forth behind her as she studies me just as intently as I study her, years having passed since I last saw both of them. "Your transformation to Fae and marriage to the rightful ruler will restore much power to Faerie, breathing life back into the land."

"Power that will give us enough of an advantage to end the war of the Courts." Flora lifts her chin, a hint of a determined smile at her petal-shaped lips. She curls her black-tipped fingers into fists. "And stop the In-Between."

Noting that I am staring at her sister's fingers, Fauna lifts her own. "The In-Between did this to us. We got too close, and it stole most of our magic. Faerie seeks to bring balance to itself, but it cannot until the In-Between is stopped."

For my entire life, I have known I will marry Loren. But I thought it was for an alliance and tradition, nothing more. Suddenly, that thought seems silly: why would faeries, who are powerful, magical creatures, possibly need an alliance with humans? To have enough power to end the war and restore their broken land.

Will they forget the alliance if Faerie is reunited? Guilt eats at me for even thinking it, but, as I recently learned for myself, faeries are tricky creatures with their own motives. *You will be Queen of Seelie, possibly Queen of all of Faerie. You will not let the alliance break.*

"We should have started with saying how good it is to see you again," Fauna says, breaking my spiraling thoughts with a tight hug. "It has been far too long, Princess."

Of course it has, since humans are far more comfortable with the High Fae. I had thought Flora and Fauna stopped coming to replace my other faerie guardians after having too many hostile responses from humans who do not like creatures that look so different... But now I know that something more happened to them, preventing them from returning. It was not a half-truth Evanthe and the others concocted to keep me from asking too many questions. While other faeries radiate power, the two of them almost feel as powerless as I am.

I embrace Fauna, whispering, "It has been. I am glad to see you two again."

Flora joins in on the hug, unable to help herself. "We are glad to have you back, Briar Rose. Faerie needs you."

Those words sink into my soul, dragging it to the pit of my stomach.

Before I can say anything, they let go of me, and Fauna offers, "Let us know whatever you need, and we will do what is in our ability to make it happen."

"Thank you." Between these two and my other three faerie guardians, I will always have a small crowd following me. Especially if I am with Loren, who has Toussaint with him wherever he goes.

"Feel free to rest, Your Highness," says Flora. "We will be here when you wake."

The two of them sit at the table, talking quietly, and I curl up on the bed closest to the fire, pulling the fur blankets around me.

I can feel the magic in the air. If I wanted to, I'm pretty sure I could step into my dreamscape without help.

Henri's face flashes in my mind, and I shove it away, but the pinch of pain in my chest refuses to leave. I feel like an idiot. How could I ever believe that Evanthe didn't know I was seeing someone, and how could I believe that he was real? Why did I hold on for so long when I knew the only way it could possibly end was in tragedy?

Silly girl.

I know the answer: I wanted love, for someone to want me, to make me feel wanted. I wanted the possibility of a choice, the unknown, not something arranged for me to a person who, until just a few days ago, acted like he could not stand me.

And now... Now Loren seems different. I don't know if it's out of duty or guilt or some tiny bit of affection, but he has been toying with the line between cold and distant, and warm and open. He has almost been *nice* to me. Hasn't quite crossed the line fully yet though.

But he might be *trying*, and that has to count for something... right? Or am I drawing conclusions out of a desperate hope that I am not going to be shackled to someone who doesn't want to be with me?

Hating you would be far easier...

After wading through these muddled feelings and thoughts, I resolve to find time alone with Loren tomorrow so I can ask him why he made up Henri. I am going to get answers, even if I don't like them, and hopefully from there, we can start to rebuild something between us. Probably not love, but I might be able to settle for friendship.

LOREN

Aunt Vivienne takes me to our home, a castle made up of multiple trees that grew together over hundreds of years. My room is toward the top of one, where I can sleep under a canopy of stars. Butterflies and pixies often come to visit, as if checking on me to see how I am faring. Once I am king, I will transfer to Aunt Vivienne's chambers, which are in the roots of the trees. And Briar Rose will stay with me.

I look about my aunt's room, the reality sinking in that it will soon be mine. I wonder how long it will take until it no longer feels like hers. And if Briar Rose will even share it with me.

"You seem heavy-hearted, nephew," Aunt Vivienne says quietly. She removes her transparent spider silk cloak, and the butterflies that were resting on it fly about the room until they settle on various objects. One lands on my outstretched finger and seems content to stay there.

"There is a lot on my mind." *And heart.* I stare as the butterfly opens and closes its brilliantly colored wings that remind me of a rainbow on a misty morning.

"About the curse?" She pries, undoing her hair so that it cascades down her back in soft waves. Strands catch the candlelight and gleam red-gold. Many make comments about our hair being the same, but mine seems more orange to me most of the time, which I'm sure is why the nickname Fox stuck.

"Yes…"

She moves around her vanity to stand in front of me, gently turning my face. When did I grow taller than she is? She seems to command such respect that I often forget I tower over her.

"What worries you, my darling?" A gentle whisper that nudges my heart to respond.

"Everything," I say hoarsely, emotions raking my throat raw.

My aunt draws me close and rubs my back, and I rest my forehead on her shoulder, closing my eyes. The tension in my jaw and shoulders relaxes. We stand there, the position a little awkward from how far I have to bend, but no less comforting than when I was a child, still able to be scooped up into her warm embrace.

"I've failed her," I rasp. "I thought I was protecting her, but I made her hate me."

Aunt Vivienne takes her time replying, "I do not believe she hates you."

"No?" My laugh comes out as a sigh.

"No." She squeezes me a little tighter. "I saw how she clung to you, how she was hesitant to say goodbye."

"That was because she is frightened, and I am one of the few people she knows here."

After a few quiet moments, she asks, "Did you tell her about Henri?"

I forgot she knew, with how rarely the subject came up. I confided in her about it recently, and she took it well, not urging me to fix things as much as Evanthe. She said she trusted me to do the right thing and left it at that. "...I did."

"And she did not take it well."

I try to take a step back, but she doesn't release me. "She did not. Would you have taken it well?"

My aunt looks up at me, pondering. "No... but you did tell her the truth. Give her time to get past it."

"How much time? I assume there is very little time between now and the wedding." We do not have months to spare, given how hungry the In-Between is to devour Faerie. How can so much damage over the years be fixed in such a short period of time? How can I possibly be prepared to become the King of Seelie and Briar Rose's husband?

At this, she lets go and moves away with slow, small steps backward. "It will not be long," she admits reluctantly. "But she will forgive you and come to love you over time, I am sure of it. Just let her get to know the real you again."

I stare at her. For all I know, Briar Rose and I could be getting married tomorrow. Will letting her see who I truly am help her forgive me? I can't imagine being married to someone you despise makes getting past it any easier.

"What if..."

She tilts her head slightly. "What if...?" she urges me to continue.

I don't want to. I want to stay quiet, to dream that maybe there is hope for us. But if I were in Briar Rose's place, would I forgive so easily?

This isn't about what I want.

"What if we call off the betrothal?" I force myself to say before I can lose my nerve.

Her eyes widen drastically. "We cannot."

I know better than to ask why—I know the answer to that. This is about more than goodwill between us and the humans, more than whether or not Briar Rose and I hate each other. Much more hangs in the balance, and if we do not wed and transform Briar Rose into a faerie, we are all but certain to lose to the Unseelie.

Aunt Vivienne draws near again, cups my face in her hands. "You will marry Briar Rose and assume the throne," she states. "All will be well, I promise. You will figure out something, my clever little fox."

If it is not too late.

CHAPTER TWENTY-TWO

THE UNSEELIE KING

*I*t has only been a day and a half, I remind myself when I fixate on the fact that the princess has yet to reach out to me. She must be in Seelie now, surrounded by faeries preparing her for her wedding and Ascension into becoming Fae. Undoubtedly, my half-brother knows I was there, even if she did not tell him about me taking her into my dreamscape.

Intriguing would be the best way to describe Princess Briar Rose. On one hand, she possesses more control of dream magic than I anticipated, and yet on the other hand, it is far less than I would have hoped Evanthe would have taught her. After all, am I not the reason they have been teaching her to use dream magic?

I knew she would not kill me, but it was unexpected to see her emotions dancing in her eyes, fully on display even when her face remained unreadable. The princess was *conflicted* about killing me, even wounding me. And she was curious, hanging onto my every word and turning them inside and out. That alone tells me that she will reach out to me, desperate to find a way to stop the war... and possibly a way out of a marriage she has no say in.

I just need a little more patience. Everything is coming together in its time.

In the afternoon on the second day, I pull myself out of my chair in front of the fire, which has been mere embers for hours. A goblet sits on the small table beside my chair, with empty bottles of wine littering the floor around it. Enough pondering and wallowing. Time to act.

Asra curls up on my bed, watching me intently as I clean myself. Normally she would be scouting, but I dare not risk sending her to Seelie, and she dares not risk leaving me when I'm drinking.

"I'm fine," I mutter to her for the third time since this morning, and she snorts in response. I can imagine her pointing out how I reprimanded my people for doing this very same thing, neglecting responsibilities.

"I needed a break," I add, as though she had voiced her concerns. Her eyes narrow; her tail flicks. Part of me wonders if wyverns are distantly related to cats.

I wash up and dress in finery, adding a silver crown atop my head, the only part of my ensemble that is not black. The reflection in the mirror shows me nothing new, but I look all the same, searching for the little details that I've seen in Loren, what we got from our father. Perhaps the shape of our eyes, or the slant of our brows. To anyone who did not know us, they would never guess we were related. Where Loren took after our father, my mother always said she was too prideful to let Oberon claim me as his alone, so she was glad I ended up with her dark, cold, sharp features. There was no mistaking who I belonged to—I was the one thing he could never take away from her. Not that he even tried to get me back.

Turning around with my arms out in a dramatic fashion, I ask Asra, "Do I reach your standards?"

The small wyvern with scales like bits of onyx blends in with the darkness of the room, save for her glowing violet eyes, which roam over me appraisingly. She takes her time, and I raise my brows.

"Well?"

Asra pops to her feet, then leaps from the bed to my shoulder.

"I'll take that as acceptance." I scratch under her chin, and sigh. "We'd best not leave Chimere waiting any longer."

At the name, Asra digs her claws into my shoulder the slightest bit, her tail coiling around my neck as if claiming me as hers.

"A brief meeting, that is all," I say, unsure if I'm assuring her or myself.

Margaux awaits us in the hall, just outside of my bedchamber. Even though her eyes are completely white, I get the sense they are roaming over me, assessing that I am, in fact, well.

"I am alive," I tell her. "Can't very well succumb to death before I've restored the Courts. Someone would be bound to mess everything up trying to fix it, or they'd do something as ridiculous as trying to bring me back from the dead."

"Chimere is waiting for you in the throne room," Margaux states, making sure to keep one step behind me, just on the edge of my vision, as we make our way through the dimly lit hallway. Not the way I ordered it, but how my mother did, and Margaux holds to those traditions, serving me just as well as she did my mother, if not better. My pale guardian, my wingless angel of vengeance. A strange, human concept angels are, but I find I like the idea all the same. Margaux does not feel Fae, but something else entirely. And when she snaps… I have witnessed it once, when I lost my mother. Some of the Unseelie thought to assassinate me—Margaux answered in blood.

And when the others thought to overwhelm us while she was engaged in battle, I answered with my Glamour, forcing them to their knees. They finally bowed to me then, but I am far beyond believing that they are loyal. The Unseelie serve self above all, and if I do not continue to prove to them that serving me is to their benefit, they will find someone else, someone who would assuredly lose focus of what is truly important: restoring the Courts so that Faerie can be united once more.

Your father let us rot, let Faerie break apart, Mother told me repeatedly. *Do not let his foolishness be the end of the Fae. We will do whatever it takes to bring Faerie to its former glory.*

So I do whatever it takes… which means meeting with Chimere today. Odilon has made it clear that he is not to be trusted, but if I can convince Chimere that I am worth giving her loyalty to, then she could convince other Solitary Fae to join us. Even if she doesn't, getting her loyalty is one less person I have to worry about.

This time the guards are where they are supposed to be, and they stiffen, backs stick-straight when they notice us coming toward them. They give quick, respectful greetings, and I am grateful not to smell alcohol. Sweat, certainly, but nothing sweet like faerie wine.

"As you were," I tell them as my magic blooms forth, pushing open the doors for me and rolling out like a black fog at my feet. The guards suck in a breath. Little displays like this remind those watching of the power I have at my disposal. I barely have time to feel the ache of the magic being gone from me before Unseelie restores it, the land filling me back up, as if assuring me that I am the one it wants ruling it.

Chimere is standing in the middle of the room with a selkie in human form and a fire nymph. A few other groups of faeries are scattered about, no doubt here seeking an audience with me—to be expected after my absence. Besides, I am not the only one getting restless that the time of my curse is at hand.

No matter how far they are, all bow when they see me enter the throne room. There are a couple of goblets here and there, but nothing of the debauchery I witnessed previously. The musician begins to play his lyre, an ominous tune that somehow makes me feel even more powerful.

Thank the Courts he decided against singing.

I head straight toward Chimere. A tree-like faerie steps forward, and Asra hisses at him, wings snapping open in warning. He retreats, and she closes them slowly, tail coiling even tighter around my neck, the spines pricking my flesh. I refrain from reacting, feigning indifference as I approach the snake-like faerie. Her slitted pupils slowly rise to meet mine from under thick, long lashes.

"Your Highnesss," she greets with a soft smile, fangs barely visible behind her full, red-painted lips.

"Would you care to join me, Chimere?" I ask, offering an arm.

"I would be honored," she answers, locking arms with me.

The others watch us leave. They will wait to see if I will return soon, so that they can speak with me over various matters. I will get to them eventually—I must not spend much time with Chimere, but also not make her feel like I am rushing through this meeting.

I lead her toward the meeting room, and she tugs gently on me.

"I thought perhapsss we could do thisss outdoorsss."

"Why is that?" I raise a brow, looking down at her.

"I thought to get to know you better, Your Highnesss." She smiles shyly. "That isss why I requesssted the meeting. We could take a ssstroll through the beauty that isss Unsssseelie."

I glance out the window and try not to frown. "There is not much beauty to take a stroll through." Unseelie faeries are every-where, manning the walls and gates, repairing the castle, making weapons, and preparing the storehouses. Since the Faerie was split, Unseelie land has become more and more of a wasteland each year, devoid of color, and what little lives manages to off of sheer stub-bornness. Nothing fragile or beautiful, no blossoming flowers or lush trees.

Chimere chuckles as though I have made a joke, and I can't help but frown in confusion.

"Thossse meeting roomsss are a tad ssstuffy," she whispers. "I meant I wanted to get to know *you*, persssonally, Your Highnesss." With a wink, she adds, "I believe I can undersssstand sssomeone'sss politicsss far better if I know the persssson, rather than let them try to sssell me their ideasss and goalsss."

The end of Asra's tail flicks, scratching the back of my neck. Interestingly enough, she has yet to growl or even bare her teeth, so the wyvern has not decided what she thinks of Chimere. Odd, seeing how easily she tends to read everyone else.

But when Asra and Margaux are with me, I have little to fear.

"Very well," I concede. Refusing would be ungentlemanly, after all, and I find myself intrigued by her thought process. Much like another woman… but I am trying to keep my mind off of her for the moment.

This should do as a short distraction.

CHAPTER TWENTY-THREE

BRIAR ROSE

I did not expect to sleep much, but after all of the excitement of the last day or two, I sleep soundly until Evanthe kisses my forehead.

"You're here," I mumble, groggily sitting up and hugging her neck before I fully make the conscious decision to do so.

She chuckles and returns the hug, running a hand down my hair. "Of course. I told you I would be."

"Did… did my family say anything?"

She pats my back. "Your parents look forward to seeing you soon. Jovan said to remember your promise to him."

My laugh falls apart into a soft sigh, my heart growing heavy at the thought of my family. They must have been so worried about me, must still be. No proper goodbyes…

I will see them soon. Does that mean that the wedding will occur in the next few weeks? I assumed it was a possibility—that leaves me little time to fix things with Loren first. Or at least get everything out in the open so that we don't feel like enemies.

When I finally let Evanthe go, I greet Delphine and Irit with kisses on their cheeks, and they smile delicately in response.

"What is wrong?"

Their exhaustion is evident. "The curse will begin soon," Evanthe explains. "There is much to be done, and we are hoping that we have enough time to do it."

I wait for more answers, but none are forthcoming. "Do you mean my transformation and wedding? How will they help against the curse?" Before they can answer, I say, "I mean, I can see how magic would help me, since there might be a way I could break the curse myself…" I trail off at their sympathetic faces.

"Unless the Unseelie King himself breaks the curse, only True Love's Kiss will save you from it." Evanthe tucks a strand of hair behind my ear and smooths a few other strays.

I have asked them over the years why True Love's Kiss is the answer, the key to my salvation. Evanthe always explains that it was the only thing she could think of that would be powerful and rare enough to change what the Unseelie King cast.

Again, I have to wonder *why* he chose not to do anything to me. He had me at his mercy, could have kidnapped me and forced the curse to happen. Is there something preventing him, or a darker plan in play? He told me he has an offer for me…

No. I cannot reach out to him, no matter how curious I am. It's not safe, and I doubt anyone has enough luck to survive that many dances with death—that is surely what is awaiting me if I seek him out. If not true death, then at least death of the life that I know, because being forever asleep doesn't sound like life at all to me.

"Then how will becoming a faerie or marrying… help?" I cannot bring myself to say his name, not right now. Hopefully, after we talk, I will be less angry. I thought I was, but a fresh wave of hurt —and grief over a lost love that never was—washes over me.

Flora joins us, leaning in to set a plate of berries and fruits on my lap. I didn't realize she or Fauna were with us, although I should have. Her magic is too weak for me to feel, especially with how strong the others are.

She insists that I eat, and then she answers: "You see, Princess, Fae mates can sense one another, even from great distances. They share magic, and are stronger for it."

My other faerie guardians know better than to suggest it, but Fauna chimes in, "And Prince Loren could be your True Love. Who knows? Maybe when you kiss on your wedding day, it will break the curse." She sighs happily, resting her head on her sister's shoulder. "Wouldn't it be so romantic?"

I take a large, unladylike bite into a golden fruit that resembles an apple, filling my mouth so I don't have to respond. I have already kissed Loren, and I feel no different. But no one else knows that...

What if we have to be in love for it to work? I reason. *Could I make myself fall in love with Loren?* It seems far out of my reach at the moment, but I did fall for Henri, who was Loren, as much as that realization pains me.

Henri was *Loren.* All those moments I was falling for Henri over the sweet compliments and brief touches and playful teasing, that was Loren.

In a strange sense, I was falling for *Loren.* But that is not the true him... is it? It seems like that would be far too easy.

But the only way I will ever find out is to try.

"There are lots of preparations to do today!" Flora announces in a sing-song voice, clapping excitedly. "Queen Vivienne has requested your presence immediately."

"Immediately?" I repeat, Delphine pulling me out of bed while Irit fixes the blankets.

"There is much to do!" Fauna says as though it were obvious. But how would it be? I know human marriages are a grand affair for royals, but I have no idea what happens in a faerie marriage. My faerie guardians have kept quiet about it, refusing to give details... as if I am not nervous enough already.

They change me into a pale green dress made of a soft, light fabric that shines blue and purple in certain lighting. No corset, no shift—I am not quite sure how I feel about being so unsupported. It's almost like being naked, but also freeing.

The shoes that go with the dress are flat with thin soles, as if the faeries cannot bring themselves to be too separated from the earth. When I wiggle my toes, I can feel the ground. They finish off the outfit by weaving tiny flowers into my hair, leaving it long and loose.

"Perfect," Irit says with a grin, and then the faeries whisk me away to meet with the queen.

As we pass by the Seelie who are already awake and going about their day, I realize that these are the creatures I will soon be queen over. How will they feel about a human becoming one of them? Will I be an imposter? This has happened many times before, but not in nearly a century. Faeries live long, and time flows differently here than in the human lands... King Oberon originally married a human princess, but then cast her out when she wanted to take the throne from him. She took their son—who is now the Unseelie King —with her, and instead of trying to get him back, he married another faerie and sired Loren. At least, that is how much of the story I have gathered from the snippets I've wheedled out of my faerie guardians and Toussaint. I avoided asking Loren, since I could see talking about his parents hurts him.

After the disaster of last time, are the Seelie wary of me? I do not blame them if they are. But Flora and Fauna believe that the Seelie are happy about my arrival, so I shouldn't be nervous.

There are so many different types of faeries, with wings, horns, fangs, scales, some more humanoid while others resemble animals or plants. They are all beautiful in their own way, eye-catching. I wonder what I will look like when I transform.

Instead of bringing me back to the glade like I assumed they would, they take me to a group of mighty trees that have grown together into a massive one. It makes sense that the Queen and Prince would live here. Not as big as a castle, but impressive none-theless, and I have to keep myself from picking up the pace in my excitement to see the inside.

Calm. Regal. Fit to be their Queen.

With barely a touch from Evanthe, part of the trunk opens, a wide and tall enough gap to let us through one at a time. Inside are floating lights—tiny faeries, but I cannot remember what they are called. So small and their light so bright, they look like little glowing orbs. A few of them hover near my face, and I whisper, "Hello."

They flicker brighter, making me squint.

"Let her pass before you blind her," Delphine says, batting at them. She misses on purpose, but they scatter nonetheless.

The hall is carved into the tree, a narrow way that splits into multiple paths. I think my mother would feel claustrophobic here, but I almost find it comforting, like the tree is protecting me, keeping me close, like a mother cradling her child.

Evanthe takes the front, guiding us down the center path. The tiny faeries follow, bobbing above my head, casting their soft lights around us.

The path opens up into a large room, which has far more of the tiny faeries. It is like floating snow without the cold; I find myself beaming at the sight, shoving down the urge to touch one. If I put out my hand, perhaps—

Queen Vivienne and Loren are in the center of the room. Their coloring and the way they move makes it undeniable they are related; I would have believed that she was his mother had I not known better.

She touches his cheek fondly and then turns toward us with a brilliant smile. "Briar Rose! Good morning." She pulls me into a hug, which I reciprocate with a little less awkwardness than yesterday.

I try to meet Loren's gaze from over her shoulder, but he refuses to acquiesce. When his aunt releases me, he steps forward to press a chaste peck on the back of my hand.

"Loren, darling," Vivienne says with a shake of her head, "that is not how we greet loved ones."

Her word choice escapes neither of us. Hesitantly, Loren drops my hand and opens his arms, leaving a little room between us, as if I would reject him. Aware of everyone watching, I close the distance, and have to turn my cheek so my nose doesn't collide with his chest. He tenses slightly, then relaxes, and I relax with him, leaning into his warmth.

When was the last time we hugged? We must have been children, because he used to kiss the top of my head...

"Good morning," he says quietly, head bent, and I half-expect him to fall into our old pattern.

But he doesn't, and I whisper "Good morning" back to him despite the ache in my chest. How can something from so long ago still hurt?

We separate but remain near one another, as is expected of us.

"Better," Vivienne says, with one brow raised at her nephew. Then she addresses everyone in the room, including the faeries behind her inspecting colorful fabrics: "No more delays! We can finally get the wedding and transformation clothes together."

I start to ask if that means one set of clothes or two, but Vivienne orders Irit to find colors suitable for me, so Irit gently takes my hand and brings me to where the other faeries already have a plethora of fabrics laid out on one of the tables. The room is filled with long tables just like it, with faeries working with fabrics, flowers, and magic. From what I can tell, this wedding is going to be just as elaborate—if not more than—the one I would have had in the human lands.

Irit helps me up onto a stool, and Delphine and Flora hold up fabrics by my cheeks. After they choose one, they bring their pointer fingers together and then spread them apart, a silver thread of magic appearing between them that they take to lay against the cloth.

Evanthe and Fauna don't make Loren stand on anything, seeing as he is taller than both of them. He fidgets every so often, and when he catches me staring at him, he immediately looks away, turning a bit and garnering a chastisement from Evanthe about moving while she's trying to fix his outfit. Toussaint snickers from the corner of the room, where he is leaning against the wall, contributing absolutely nothing. Either Queen Vivienne is ignoring him or assumes that he won't be helpful with preparations, because she continues to flit about the room, inspecting progress and giving suggestions.

It seems like an eternity passes. I finally take a deep breath by the time Vivienne sends Loren and me off to take a break to eat. Fauna supplies us with a basket, and Toussaint follows us outside, keeping his distance.

No one else is taking a break.

I can feel every pebble, every root, every dip in the land through the thin shoes, and I consider taking them off. Most Fae stroll about without them. Loren and the other nobles are the few who do wear them, more of a fashion statement than a necessity.

"Is there a reason you are staring at my feet?"

Loren's question jolts me back to the present. Odd, that that is the first thing he has said to me today of his own volition. Does it really take me acting strange for him to talk to me? *I* am the one who should be mad at *him*, not the other way around. And I am… sort of. Not the kind of mad that I don't want to talk to him. In fact, it's infuriating that he's trying to avoid me.

I almost let it out right then and there, but decide we should probably eat first. I'll be a little less likely to strangle him if I'm not hungry.

"Very few faeries wear shoes."

His brows tick upward in surprise that quickly recedes. "There is little need for them. Besides, they tend to block our connection to the earth."

So, I was correct in my conclusion. "What do you mean by connection?"

We walk without touching, and we haven't stepped closer to each other, but somehow the gap feels a little smaller.

"Faerie itself supplies magic," he clarifies. "It fills us, the pulse of magic obvious under our feet and in the air." He moves lighter, his complexion healthier than before, no more sickly paleness to his hue. Even his hair shines a more brilliant red.

"It'll make more sense when you…" Loren trails off, shooting me what I can only assume is an abashed look.

"Do you know when?" I ask, so softly that it's almost inaudible.

But, of course, he hears it. "I have my suspicions."

I stare at him. We've stopped in the middle of the woods; Toussaint stays back, but I know he's watching intently.

Realizing his error, Loren looks me in the eye and assures me in no uncertain terms, "I do not know when. My aunt has kept it a secret from everyone."

Then he breaks eye contact and walks away, assuming I'll follow.

Loren gave me a direct answer. A small truth that cost him little to nothing, but… something eases in my chest, and I find I can breathe a little easier.

CHAPTER TWENTY-FOUR

LOREN

*B*riar Rose and I sit beside a stream and silently share lunch, which consists of fruits and nuts. Toussaint pointedly watches us from a distance, and I can practically hear him begging me to say something to her, anything at all.

What can I possibly say? I have been waiting for her to explode, whether that means bursting into tears or screaming at me or flat-out attacking me.

I should let you go... but even if that were an option, I know I wouldn't.

She pops a berry into her mouth, chewing thoughtfully, eyes glazed over. Her profile is soft lines I am itching to draw, and the sun reverently shines on her, giving her olive skin an ethereal glow. Faerie suits her. Everything seems drawn to Briar Rose, from the light bathing her to the grass and flowers reaching for her to the pixies following us not so discreetly as they might think. Even the earth seems eager to share magic with her, pressing it against her skin even though she has no capability to absorb it. She is completely unaware of it all, that achingly familiar furrow forming between her brows. I grab another piece of fruit to distract me from the temptation of reaching for her.

Henri knew her that way; I do not. Young Loren was closer and might have been able to get away with smoothing her brow, but I messed up that closeness a long time ago.

Still staring into the distance, Briar Rose asks, "Can we be transparent with one another? If we are to be married, I would at least like to be on civil terms, and to do that, there are things between us that need to be discussed." Her eyes slowly drag to meet mine. She seems calm and collected, but the way her jaw is set and her fingers keep twitching tell me otherwise.

A number of responses cross my mind, but I know better than to speak any of them: she wants clear and concise answers, leaving no loopholes or shadowy areas. To lay myself bare as just me, no masks, no alternate personas. What she asks would be considered a high price to any faerie, especially to me. And yet... I find part of me longs to indulge her, on the small chance that perhaps she might see something in me worth taking a second look at.

"What do you wish to know?"

Her eyes narrow. "I want your assurance that you will be honest with me, Loren."

It takes a lot of willpower to hold her gaze and reply, "I will be honest with you for every question you ask that pertains to us."

She is silent for a beat longer than I like. "Why not all of my questions?"

"That would make me beholden to answer you always, from now through eternity," I explain. "If I am given information that I am expected to keep secret, that would nullify it if you were to ask me directly." A faerie's worst fear: to be held to an obligation that leaves them feeling controlled and vulnerable. She must know this, because she decides to drop it.

"Very well. You will answer my questions about us directly and immediately."

She will fit in well here. "I will answer your questions about us directly and immediately... and you will give me the same courtesy."

Lifting her chin, Briar Rose sticks out her hand. "Agreed."

I could be a jerk and insist that she repeat the words as I did, but that wouldn't hold her to it regardless, being a human. Knowing her, she will keep her word.

Awkwardly, we both shift to face one another, I cross-legged and Briar Rose daintily tucking her legs beside her, adjusting her dress so that it covers them down to her ankles. In the corner of my eye, I see Toussaint disappear into the shadows of the trees, giving us the illusion of privacy.

"What is your first question?"

Her eyes dance across my face, like that will help her make up her mind on which of her many questions will be the first. I fight the urge to look away. How does her gaze leave me feeling absolutely naked, down to my very soul?

"What happened between us that made you... not like me?"

Starting out strong... "I... have never not liked you."

She gives an exasperated sigh. "You know what I mean. Why did we stop being friends? Why was I suddenly not allowed to come to Faerie?" Before I can answer, she starts, "I suppose those are two separate questions—"

"With one answer," I finish for her. "Do you remember your last day in Faerie? The Unseelie King found us."

Frowning, she says, "I remember... we were playing, hiding while Toussaint was trying to find us. It got cold, and I saw the Unseelie King, and then... and then I woke in your arms, and you were crying." She searches my face again, this time with renewed intensity. "Why do I not remember what happened?"

I don't want to tell her. I don't want her to live in fear, to feel that nowhere is safe, even though that is the truth. But I promised I would be honest. "He put you to sleep so he could talk to me without frightening you. It was one of the few times I was alone, without someone of great power nearby to combat him. I thought he was going to take you to Unseelie with him, to enact the curse early, but instead he tried to convince me to hand over the crown, in exchange for him undoing the curse."

I wait, steeling myself for the onslaught of "why didn't you?" and "how could you be so selfish?" But she ponders, absently toying with a strand of hair. This is where Henri would tease her to lighten the mood, and she'd shyly smile and dip her head to hide her blush.

Enough. You are not Henri. If you were, everything would be so much easier. No tension between Briar Rose and me, no kingship for me to step into that I am clearly not cut out for. I wouldn't have an older brother who hates that I was born to the woman who seduced our father into betraying his mother. Because somehow that was the only requirement for me to take everything that was originally his.

"You couldn't hand over the crown," she says slowly, processing aloud. "Handing over all of Faerie to him would have been dangerous for everyone, even us humans."

The knot in my chest unwinds a bit at her understanding. That is the only solace I have for keeping the crown away from my brother.

"But why was I suddenly banned from Faerie?"

"For your protection. He rarely visits the human lands, as it makes his magic finite."

"But he still could have used it against me there."

I nod reluctantly, trying not to imagine him attacking her. She said I had to answer her honestly, not that I had to show all of my emotions. "Yes, but the chances were less."

"But aren't there many powerful faeries here in Seelie to protect me?" She tilts her head to the side.

"You bear the mark of his curse, his magic. Every time you cross into Faerie, it alerts him."

"So he knows I am here." Both hands are playing with her hair, braiding and unbraiding one small section.

"I assume so." To ease her, I add, "There are many here devoted to protecting you. Myself included."

Briar Rose pauses. Again, the impulse to look away is strong, but I refuse. If I am extremely lucky, this might be my final shot to win her trust back—not all of it, but at least a scrap.

She bites the inside of her cheek. "At the… party… you said hating me would be far easier. I thought you did hate me."

I want to deflect by pointing out that that is a statement, not a question. "I have never hated you." In fact, if I knew she would not object, I would kiss her now, which would surely be a much more pleasant experience now that I am sober and not magic-deficient. I have relived that moment time after time, and I still cannot figure out why she kissed me.

Or did I lean in when she pulled me to her?

"Then why did you push me away?" Her voice grows quiet, wavers toward the end. Despite knowing we haven't moved at all, it suddenly feels as though we are far too close.

"I…" The words catch in my throat, then come out in a rush. "I thought I was endangering you. And it broke my heart when you'd cry every time I left, begging me to take you to Faerie with me." Blistering heat floods my cheeks at my candor. *This is why faeries are reluctant to agree to promises they didn't come up with themselves.*

Briar Rose is as still as a stone; I wonder if she is breathing. She has to be, since her heartbeat has increased in pace.

"Then why Henri? Why did you pretend to be someone else?"

Wincing like I have been stabbed, I take solace in the fact that this should be the worst of the questions, that this means this conversation has to be close to over.

I just have to make it through exposing the very essence of who I am first—and hope it does not scare her away.

Her hazel gaze remains steadfast, softening into a version of the girl I used to know. A girl I want to know again.

"I do not think you will like the answer any better than I do." She gives me time to collect my thoughts, but the magic my promise carries tugs at my tongue, bidding me to answer. "I created Henri shortly after I put distance between us. Visiting you was the one pure bright spot in my life, and when that was tainted, I felt there was no escape from who I am and what is expected of me."

Briar Rose frowns. "You do not like yourself?"

I sigh, but it does little to ease the tightness in my chest. "Not entirely. I do not hate myself, but there is not much about me that does not feel like a fabrication to fill expectations."

Her shoulders slump. "I... can understand that."

That confession cuts deep. "I wish you didn't," I whisper.

To her credit, she does not look away, not even as her emotions begin to rise to the surface, brimming in her eyes. I want to give her time to process—and respond, if she so desires—but I have not finished upholding my end of the bargain. The magic coaxes the words from me: "To find reprieve from expectations, I created my own dreamscape, as well as a person to become. Henri was a simple human, unburdened, loving life simply because he could *be*." I take a deep breath. "One day, I was thinking about you, and suddenly you were there. I thought I'd somehow conjured an illusion of you, so I flirted and teased and enjoyed the moment... until you quickly changed your appearance and told me your name was Fleur."

Remembrance lights her expression, but she keeps quiet. What I wouldn't trade to hear her recall aloud her first time meeting Henri...

"It was then I realized you were real, and that you had the scent of Evanthe's magic around you, helping you into the dreamscape. We had already touched, already melded magic, so Evanthe recognized it instantly and sought a private audience with me. I thought she was going to berate me, but instead she said, 'For now, I think you need it. And so does she.'" *But do not take too long to gather the courage to tell her the truth,* she had added.

"I knew it was wrong," I admit. "But she was right: I needed that escape."

Briar Rose nods.

"And you," I add, "I needed you, too."

Simple words, yet so weighty. When she finally speaks, it is barely a whisper. "Why did you not make amends yourself?"

"I was afraid. I thought you hated me." This has to be what humans mean when they use the phrase "wanting to crawl out of my own skin." If I could be anyone else right now, I would. Faeries aren't vulnerable by nature: we play games, we speak riddles, we dance around the truth.

"I never hated you," she whispers. "I wanted to love you, Loren... but you never let me."

The confession hangs between us, and I stare at her, now unable to look away. I have no idea how to respond.

I wanted to love you...

Then is it really too late?

"I am sorry," I tell her, fervently hoping she believes me. "For Henri, for pushing you away, for everything. I know I don't deserve it, but I want to start over."

My heart sinks as she shakes her head. "There is too much history for us to start over," she explains. "But I think we can start from where we are right now, choose a different direction." Tentatively at first, she extends a hand. "Let me have the chance to get to know the real you, and I'll let you get to know the real me. Deal?"

I try not to seem too eager when I take her hand. "Deal."

CHAPTER TWENTY-FIVE

THE UNSEELIE KING

*C*himere visits the next day, after having spent quite a few hours talking about seemingly inconsequential topics, mostly likes and dislikes. She acts as though everything I say is interesting, to a strange degree. Margaux remains in the shadows, her uncanny ability to disappear extremely comforting to me.

When people think we are alone, they tend to reveal things they wouldn't otherwise.

Asra is helping scout Seelie, determined that she can find Briar Rose and update me on happenings. From what I have gathered from her mind, she doubts the effectiveness of our spies. While I have more faith in them, I have no desire to argue with Asra; I let her go where she pleases when she pleases.

Strolling about Unseelie, just outside of the castle grounds, Chimere holds my arm so tightly that her cheek is grazing my shoulder with every step. I cannot imagine that it is comfortable.

"You were telling me about your mother yesssterday," Chimere urges. Bits of ash, like snow, fall from the sky and catch in her lashes and carefully done-up hair. There is no fire nearby—the ash is proof that Faerie has been thrown into chaos since the split of the Courts.

The trees are wider apart than they should be, keeping their distance from each other, and the shrubbery is sparse at best. What little wildlife there is makes brief appearances before returning to their reclusive state.

No, I was not telling you about my mother. You were incessantly asking questions about her, and I was trying to avoid answering them. Trying to cut our time short yesterday only served to have her invite me to visit again today. If she is hoping for an intimate relationship of some sort, I will have to find a way to reject her without angering her.

Why is it easier to manage politics than social interactions?

"We have spoken a lot about me," I say, hoping my tone remains unaffected. "Tell me about yourself."

Chimere adjusts her hold on my arm, tilting her face to look up at me. "There isss not much to tell. My parentsss became part of the Sssolitary Fae, and that wasss what I wasss born into. There are few rulesss, and far too many clansss." When I do not meet her gaze, she stares ahead again, picking a few bits of ash from her lashes.

I have heard about how split the Solitary Fae are. They have no allegiance to either Court, so why would they hold allegiance to each other?

But if we can reunite Faerie…

"What is your clan like?"

For a moment, I fear I have crossed a line, but she seems nonchalant as she says, "My clan isss sssmall, mossstly made up of nymphsss and dryadsss. We have two bansssheesss, ssso we are normally left alone. Besssidesss, we have an alliance with the dwarvesss."

Chimere stops; I turn toward her. There is a crease between her brows, and she takes her time continuing. "There are… othersss who are waiting for word from me. They are not interesssted in joining the Unssseelie, but are open to an alliance."

So, this is why she insisted on "getting to know" me. I thought it was going to take more time before she revealed her intentions, but I much rather this turn of events.

"What kind of alliance?" I keep my voice low even though there is no one nearby other than Margaux. The castle is barely in sight, almost blending into the various shades of black and grey the landscape provides.

"They want to keep their freedom," she says simply. "But they want to sssee Faerie whole again, and they think you might be their bessst chance." She tilts her head, watching me ponder her words. "All of Faerie knowsss of your curssse. It isss coming sssoon, yesss?"

"Yes."

Chimere nods decisively. "We mussst do what isss for the good of Faerie, no matter the cossst." After a beat, she adds, "Will you meet with them?"

"With who?"

"My clan," she clarifies. "They will meet you in your cassstle, provided that you give your word that none of them will be harmed or taken prisssoner."

"None of them will be harmed or taken prisoner as long as they are not a threat to the Unseelie or my crown."

A small smile crosses her lips. "Agreed. I will reach out to them and inform you of their arrival ssshortly."

We stand there, and it takes me a moment to realize she means to contact them now, that I should return to the castle alone.

"One thing, Chimere: you gave your fealty to me. Do you not want your freedom?"

The smile grows, a little flash of fang. "I do not think you will chain me, Your Highnesss." Then she continues on without me, the hem of her cloak leaving a trail through the dusting of ash on the ground.

BRIAR ROSE

I spend most of the night dancing the line between being asleep and awake, pondering Loren's responses and letting them recolor the sour memories between us from harsh, agonizing reds and blacks to softer, bruised blues and purples. Where I was mad at him, he was caught between his feelings for me and wanting to keep me safe. When I tried to pull him close, he pushed me away, holding me at arm's length until we slowly sank into our bitterness masked by indifference, sometimes even loathing.

Can I forgive him and move on? I want to. And just as importantly, I also have something to apologize for.

With my eighteenth birthday in a few weeks, I imagine that I am not only running out of time before our impending wedding, but also before the curse finds me.

We go to Queen Vivienne's home once more, and this time I am more than prepared for her warm, enthusiastic greeting. But when she steps aside and Loren approaches, it feels like the whole room is holding its breath.

He looks me in the eye and slowly opens his arms. A silent question, he's letting me set the terms of how we move forward.

I step into his embrace. "Good morning, Loren."

"Good morning, Briar Rose," he responds in kind, with a hint of warmth that fills my chest.

The moment we part, the other faeries have us back to standing still while they work on our outfits.

"I thought my wedding dress was going to be gold," I say to Irit. "Didn't you already have the bust done?"

"It is," she confirms with a smile. "But royal weddings are a grand affair: your dress will change based on what part of the celebration you are in." She takes the bodice from the table and brings it to me. The intricate stitchwork of loops and swirls is stunning, and it takes me a moment to notice the foxes near the bottom, with briars behind them. "Watch." With a tap of her finger, one of the foxes changes from gold to pink, which bleeds into the rest of the bodice. The neckline transforms from a straight line across to curved, the fabric silk and without the many flourishes the gold one has. Still, the foxes and briars remain, this time in white stitching.

"Beautiful," I breathe, running a finger along the fox's tail.

"It will also have a dress for your Ascension," she informs me. "That is why this is taking so long—complicated spellwork takes time to do it right, especially with so many people involved."

"Would it be easier to have only one person work on it?"

The corner of her mouth dips slightly, the closest I have ever seen to her frowning. "Easier? Perhaps. But it would take far longer."

And we do not have the time. I hear the unspoken words, hanging heavily like a chain around my neck.

After a few more hours, Loren and I are allowed to have a break like yesterday. We go to the same spot and eat together under the soft sunlight peeking through the tree branches. Toussaint lounges across one of them, back resting against the trunk, fingers interlocked behind his head. If I didn't know better, I'd think he was napping. But I've seen him leap into action in barely a second's notice—he'd take an assassin's blade to the heart before he let it touch Loren.

He relaxes comfortably, seemingly just out of reach of the unease between Loren and me.

"There is a lot more preparation for weddings in Faerie than I thought there would be," I confess to break the silence.

He pauses in his chewing, swallows. "There is definitely a lot."

Well, that conversation starter was a dead end. What did I think, that because we laid everything out in the open, now we are going to be best friends again, like we used to be?

Only I haven't laid everything out in the open quite yet…

I clear my throat, his attention darting to me so quickly that it takes me a moment to drum up the courage again. "Loren, I… I appreciate your candor yesterday. And your apology. I… I feel I have an apology of my own to make." My face burns, especially my cheeks. At his puzzled expression, I explain, "I should not have allowed myself to even entertain the idea of abandoning our betrothal and falling for someone else. It was unfair to you, and—"

"You have no reason to apologize," he interrupts softly, looking down at the ground. "I am the one who pushed you away, and I am the one who charmed you as someone else."

I draw my knees up to my chest to squelch the feeling of being utterly naked, body and mind and soul. "Still, I am sorry."

The tension between us rises, and I consider saying something, but I have nothing else to say. He finally meets my gaze again. "If you feel you need to apologize, then I accept, but know that in my mind, you have done nothing wrong."

That should make me feel better, but the naked feeling hasn't gone away. Taking one more plunge, I tell him, "So you know, I accept your apologies from yesterday too."

"Thank you." Not quite a smile, but the harsher lines in his face ease and his amber eyes brighten like a candle was lit inside his soul. I wonder what I would see in them if I scooted closer, and if he'd be able to see in mine. What he'd see in mine.

Part of me wants to find out.

His throat bobs, and I think he is going to turn away, but he doesn't. He is just as uncomfortable and intrigued by this moment as I am, and I want to lean into the exhilaration of not knowing what is going to happen.

But Delphine appears, surprising us. "Her Highness awaits your return." Then she cleans up our mess with a flick of her wrist, magic enveloping what remains of the food like hands picking them up and tossing them back into the basket, which, when full, floats to her arm.

Delphine narrows her eyes at Toussaint as he hops down and makes his way over nonchalantly. "Normally we can rely on you to keep to our planned schedule."

"Who am I to rush the prince and princess before they are ready?" he asks, shaking a few leaves from his hair.

His question goes unanswered. But it repeats in my mind as I keep sneaking glances at Loren for the rest of the day.

And I catch him doing the same.

LOREN

By Briar Rose's third day in Seelie, I am fully convinced that every Fae creature is enamored with her. No word or movement goes unnoticed, seemingly all of Faerie watching her. If they thought they could without angering my aunt, I am sure many would try to join our lunch breaks.

I wonder how many of them notice how small her smiles are, that her wonder at being here is weighed down by a sadness that has slowly become more and more a part of her with each passing year that brings her closer to the curse.

To her, we have taken her away from her home, her comfort and safety.

Knees drawn up to her chest, she stares into the brook. She has barely eaten anything.

A far cry from the plethora of warm, stolen glances of yesterday. Are we at a place where I can ask her what is wrong and get a truthful answer without it feeling forced? I know our agreement of honesty only truly binds me, but she will hold to it undoubtedly.

Instead, I ask, "Is there anything you wish to see in Faerie?" When her attention shifts to me, I add, "I know we have done little but wedding preparation. I'm sure you'd like to see more than the royal home."

The heaviness cloaking her lifts a bit, temporarily replaced by a ponderous expression. I silently count down to the exact moment she bites the inside of her cheek, knowing she would once she was deep in thought.

"I would like to go to the ocean."

I frown. "That might have to wait. It is a long way to go."

She looks confused. "Are the... shimmering mirrors not working?"

Shimmering mirrors...?

As I puzzle together what she means, she sighs and gestures toward her legs. "Where the... creatures have tails instead of legs? You were friends with some of them." She huffs. "I swear I know the word for them..."

It suddenly clicks. "You mean the merfolk?"

She brightens, shifting so that she's facing me. "Yes! They were quite fun, the brothers. And they were friends with the human prince and princess, right?"

I'm surprised she remembers that much, but also glad for it. Lowering my voice, I say, "Perhaps we can find time to sneak away and visit Caspian and Devere."

She snaps her fingers. "*Those* were their names! What about the others?"

"Sabine and Oliver?"

"Thank you!" She sighs in relief, like I have just unwound a knot that had been agitating her greatly. "Do you really think we can slip away?" she whispers.

"If I allow it," Toussaint says from his perch in the trees. "I'm sure something can be arranged."

"Arranged?" I raise a brow even though his eyes are closed, head tilted back to bask in the sunlight. "You have to go where I go. Besides, I do not know you as someone who would pass up an adventure, short as it may be."

"Please, Toussaint," Briar Rose implores him. "I would love to go through the shimmering mirrors to visit the merfolk."

"Portals," he corrects gently. "I'll see what I can do. Although your aunt will be livid, Fox."

"I'll talk with her."

"Now?"

"After."

He smirks. "This will be fun."

As much as I'm sure my aunt will be upset, it is hard to care much about the consequences when I see Briar Rose's face light up like this.

I do have a chance, I tell myself. It is a small one, but I will take it.

CHAPTER TWENTY-SIX

BRIAR ROSE

That night I lie awake in my bed, visions of merfolk swimming around my mind. I close my eyes and try to recall the feeling of sand under my feet, the coolness of the water, the weightlessness as I swim. There are rivers and a lake in my father's kingdom, but nothing that quite matched the life that the ocean brought. Merfolk are magic creatures just like Fae, and yet they live in the human world.

I wonder why then my father has not been in contact with Oliver and Sabine's father. Surely their kingdom must be flourishing if they have an alliance with the merfolk as we do faeries.

Instead of pondering all of this, I should be sleeping, but sleep feels far out of reach. So I decide to make use of the time, which I should have been doing since I arrived in Faerie.

Based on the silence of the house, it seems like all of my faerie guardians are asleep, or at least trying to be. I listen carefully for a few more breaths before I squeeze my eyes shut and search for the dream magic. Evanthe always calls it "opening your consciousness", so I open my hands, palms facing upward, ready to receive. The subtle action does nothing to initiate the dream magic, but somehow it prepares me for it.

Instantly, I am met with that familiar fuzzy warmth, only this time it is much more intense, like a heavy blanket covering me. It smothers my gasp as it eagerly sinks into my skin and yanks me from my body. I tumble forward, swirls of color nothing but blurs as I try to right myself, but there is nothing to stop me, nothing to hold on to.

Except magic.

I imagine a field of soft grass beneath my feet. The abrupt stop has me wobble, but I manage to stay upright. Of course I land decently well when no one else is around.

The last time I was in a dreamscape, it was the Unseelie King's, all muted tones and darkness. I suppress a shiver and make the green grass a brighter hue, and add yellow and pink daisies sporadically. Still, his offer niggles at me. Why would he want me to reach out to him? It has to be some sort of trick. He *cursed* me, and I will not trust him. Ever.

Ignoring the chill that refuses to go away, I picture a castle. It begins to materialize, spires piercing the blue, cloudless sky...

Henri flashes across my mind, all the times we spent in the halls of the castle. My heart twists, and I flinch. The bits of the half-formed castle pause, then crumble into nothing. Taking a calming breath, I refocus the magic, bringing into existence a much smaller building, if it can be called that. It is nothing more than pieces of wood haphazardly kept together by twine and magic, but I move toward it reverently like I would a holy place.

Sinking to my knees in front of the playhouse, I stare at it, watching as the paintings appear one by one. *Which one was Loren fixated on?* Not the kelpie, or the roses. Was it our names?

The chill gets more intense, snaking between my shoulder blades. I conjure a cloak and pull it tightly around me. The Unseelie

King is not going to make me call for him. He can haunt me all he wants, but this is *my* dreamscape, not his.

I trace Loren's name slowly. "Maybe there is hope," I whisper. Maybe we can find a way to fall in love with one another, and maybe I can strengthen my dream magic enough to at least survive the curse until Loren can get to me—

"Hello, Princess Briar Rose."

I stand and whirl around in one fluid motion, conjuring daggers in my hands. The Unseelie King stands only a few steps away from me, just out of range.

"What are you doing here?"

He raises his brows. "Generally, greetings are in order before the interrogation begins." I assume he is joking, but he doesn't smile.

I try to shove him out of the dreamscape with magic, but he doesn't budge. It's like pushing against a stone wall. "I did not call you. You shouldn't be able to be here."

"My magic is tied to you via the curse, basically a part of you because of how long it has been since I cast it. And anytime you use magic, it tugs on me."

I hate the idea of having any sort of connection to him. Despite myself, I ask another question: "Then why didn't you visit before?"

He shrugs. "There was little need to. I've let you live your life until now, enjoying what you can before the curse fully awakens."

"*Let me?*" I hiss between my teeth. "My life was never yours to control. You stole it from me."

He studies me silently, pale eyes hard as ice. "It was a tactical decision, not a personal one. I told you that I have a way to undo the curse and restore Faerie."

"You could undo the curse without my help."

"Yes," he concedes, "but I doubt I would be able to restore Faerie with the least amount of bloodshed without your help."

Least amount of bloodshed? That response does not fit the image of a monster I'd made him to be in my head. "You curse a baby, but you don't want bloodshed?"

He remains in place, but his Glamour winds about his feet, its darkness leaking into the bright colors of my dreamscape. "Like I said, it was a tactical decision. With Loren marrying you, he will have the power to conquer and enslave the Unseelie, even the Solitary Fae if he so desires."

Such dark, aggressive colors to paint Loren with. Yet... the more I hear about the war and my marriage to Loren, the more I feel like a pawn, though I hate to use the Unseelie King's words.

Faeries cannot lie, but he is definitely trying to poison me against Loren. "Loren would not enslave anyone. He wants peace."

"Does he?" He tilts his head, gaze locked on me. "Has he sought to make peace with you?"

How does he know? Hoping the Unseelie King cannot feel it, I reach out for Loren's magic, what I used to think was Henri's. "What would he have to make peace for?"

The Unseelie King huffs a laugh. "You are already responding like a faerie even though you are still human." He glances down at my hands, which are white-knuckling the daggers. "Calling my half-brother, are you? Does that make this a party?"

LOREN

I am tugged out of sleep. Even with my mind not quite awake, I answer Briar Rose's call immediately, barely hearing Toussaint say my name before I eagerly stumble into her dreamscape. The clashing sensations of heat and cold send a shock that wakes me fully, and somehow I manage to land on my feet, albeit ungracefully.

There is something wrong with her dreamscape, like frost covering summer grass. It doesn't quite feel like her magic, too sharp and unsettling. When I look up, I find the source: my brother.

"What are you doing here, Tristan?"

Briar Rose peeks at me, then back at him, clearly surprised. But by what, I'm not sure.

"Loren," Tristan greets me coolly. He must have guessed that Briar Rose was calling me here... Is he intending to take us to Unseelie? There is no aggression in his stance, just a haughty lift of his chin and the folding of his arms as if he is getting irritated by waiting for something.

How did he enter here? Briar Rose would not have invited him. Although he seems to have a knack for getting into places uninvited.

"Call for me when you wish to hear my proposition, Princess," Tristan says, and without waiting for her reply, he vanishes, taking most of the darkness and chill with him. Some lingers, and we stand in stunned silence.

This is the second time they have been in a dreamscape together that I know of, and yet he's done nothing to her.

This time, she called for *me*.

Breathing slightly uneven, Briar Rose finally turns toward me. From what I can tell, she is unharmed but trembling, putting a hand on our playhouse for support.

Our playhouse. An exact replica, paintings and all. And she is completely herself, no change to her appearance other than her ankle-length dress shifting colors from one moment to the next, each one darker than the last.

"I'm sorry," she rasps.

Taken aback, I ask, "Why?"

She opens and closes her mouth a few times, not quite looking me in the eye. "I don't know," she answers finally. "For some reason, I feel as if I should apologize." Her breath shudders; the dream-scape shifts into a starless night, unintentionally, the magic following her mood. Only faded pale moonlight remains, barely enough for me to make out her features. I wonder if she can see me, or just my silhouette.

"I suppose I worry it's awkward to have brought you back here, but I... I didn't know what he was going to do, and..."

She could have called for Evanthe. Or Delphine. Or Irit. But she called for me. I don't dare point these out to her.

A few tears slip down her cheeks. She still can't quite look at me.

"Do you..." I try not to wince at my awkwardness but fail. "Do you want a hug?"

My heart races, certain she'll reject me, but when she nods, it doubles its speed, painfully slamming into my ribcage. I close the distance between us, then carefully envelop her in my arms. She hesitates reciprocating, and I almost let go, but she wraps her arms tightly around my torso, gripping the back of my shirt in her fists. Her ear is pressed against my chest; if she feels my heartbeat, she doesn't comment.

Besides, I can hear hers is almost as fast as mine.

Tones of black fade to greys. Taking that as a good sign, I contemplate kissing the top of her head like I used to. The urge tugs at a secret part of my heart, so packed down that I almost believed the lie that I don't remember, or even remember to care.

Don't, I dissuade myself. *This is a big step. Enjoy it for what it is.*

The urge is persistent, so I rest my cheek atop her head. Pastel colors replace the greys, making me smile.

I break the silence with a whisper: "Are we still being honest?"

"…Yes."

I pause to regather my courage before admitting, "I'm glad you called me."

She inhales shakily, then relaxes her shoulders, keeping her hold on me. "I'm glad too."

I shouldn't let that fuel my hope. But I do, as we embrace each other and vibrant hues return, new flowers sprouting around our feet as if the moon's glow nourishes them just as much as sunlight.

Briar Rose steps away first, fingers trailing down my arms. For a moment, I think she is going to hold my hands. Instead, she shakes her head and wipes at her cheeks, then crosses her arms. "Thank you."

"You're welcome." I offer her a small smile, and thankfully, she returns it. "I should go."

Her smile dips into a frown. "Or… you could stay. Just for a bit. If you want." She clears her throat and tucks a lock of hair behind her ear, subconsciously changing the strands from brown to bright red.

"I'll stay. If you want."

We end up sitting by our playhouse, facing each other, knees not quite touching. Briar Rose has her legs tucked to one side, her dress smoothed out so that it settles nicely, no wrinkles. She picks flowers and spins the stems between her fingers.

"Is there something you wished to talk about?"

She takes her time responding, having gone back to not meeting my gaze. I shift my focus to the flowers as well, choosing a few and weaving their stems together.

"His name is Tristan."

It sounds more like a statement than a question, but I confirm, "Yes."

"It sounds silly, but I never thought of him having a name."

"I don't think that's silly." I twist a little too hard and end up breaking a stem. Grabbing another, I add, "He does not make it easy to think of him as a person."

A few beats pass. "But you do," Briar Rose says quietly.

"I do." My fingers work faster now, remembering this childhood pastime. "It is hard for me not to when there are constant reminders that everything I have and everything I am supposed to be once belonged to him… It feels like I stole his life."

Her eyes are on me, but I dare not look up. There are too many emotions shoving their way to the surface already, and looking her in the eyes might break the last of my defenses.

"You didn't though," she says, speaking carefully. "If I understand the story correctly, your father made some decisions that put both of you into the positions you are now."

I dip my head in agreement. "He did. He abandoned his first wife—the one Faerie chose for him—and his firstborn son." It hurts to swallow, but I do it anyway, hoping to regain some sort of control by shoving the jumble of sorrow and grief and anger back down. "By abandoning them, he gave me this life. It doesn't feel deserved or earned; it feels tainted and wrong, like I cheated Tristan, and I think he views it the same way." Now that I cracked open that door, everything is trying to flood its way out of me. I blink back tears. "My mother was not the one Faerie chose—so how could it want me to be king?"

My hands go still as Briar Rose places hers on top. "Just because things do not go the way we expect, does not mean that they are bad." She is so close, her forehead is almost resting against mine. "Maybe things will turn out even better this way."

I want to meet her gaze, but if I do, I'm afraid I might kiss her, pushing this fragile bond between us too far. Before I can come up with a response, she pulls away, returning her attention to the flowers.

"I don't know what he wants with me," she says, breaking the silence.

"I… do not know either." I wish I did. It seems like he is trying to torment her, but… what was that about his proposition?

"He told me he has a way to reunite Faerie…" Her sentence sounds like it is going to continue, but it doesn't.

I keep my mouth shut instead of telling her not to trust him. Why would she trust him? He cursed her.

"I'm not going to call for him," she says, as if to reassure me.

"I didn't think you would."

We sit in silence for a little while, and it isn't uncomfortable. Eventually, we say goodnight, sharing a quick hug. I set the crown of flowers on the playhouse, not nearly brave enough to place it on her head, and take my leave.

Toussaint is still awake when I return to my body, a lit candle nearly just a pool of wax. "Is everything okay?"

I nod and keep the details to myself, processing as I drift off to sleep for a few hours.

CHAPTER TWENTY-SEVEN

THE UNSEELIE KING

*P*rincess Briar Rose's confused response sticks with me hours later, when I am preparing for another day of politics. As does the fact that Loren used my name. Only my mother ever used it, and Loren... the last time he did, it was to beg for *her*, the human princess.

Tristan, please... Don't hurt her.

Fear made his eyes well as he grasped her sleeping form; even then, as a child, he knew not to make a bargain with me. Not to offer up anything he could not give.

But I saw it in him then and I see it in him now: he is almost at the tipping point, where he would find a way to save her, no matter what it takes. A dangerous place to find oneself, indeed.

Shaking off my thoughts, I fasten my cloak about my neck and place the crown upon my head, careful not to let the sharp edges prick my scalp or fingertips. It settles nicely, completing the kingly look; however, my sullen expression ruins it. I adjust my frown into a thin line by pressing my lips together. Better, but not by much.

Asra growls something from my bed, although it sounds more like a grumble.

"She will call for me," I insist, staring at her via the mirror. She flicks her tail, knocking a pillow onto the floor. I roll my eyes.

"She will call for me," I repeat, quieter, more solemn, and place my hands on the smooth curved sides of the mirror. "Show me Princess Briar Rose."

For a few moments longer, I stare intently into my own eyes. Then the mirror ripples and blurs, replacing my reflection with the royal home of Seelie. The great hall is filled with tables of faeries working on clothing and decorations quietly in the background while Traitor Queen Vivienne herself strides forward to hug someone: Princess Briar Rose.

Asra hops onto my shoulder, curiously craning her head forward.

"May I?"

She chirrups her agreement, and I let my magic connect with her mind, closing my eyes so I can see what she sees.

Even with the little yellow and orange enchantments on her skin her guardians no doubt cast this morning to brighten her mood and put color in her cheeks, there is an edge to her expression, a haunting just below the surface. It matches my Glamour so well, the curse almost as tall as she is, scraping the tops of her round ears.

Perfect.

I release the spell, and the magic is invisible once more. Watching with my own eyes, I see Vivienne step back, and Loren takes her place. There is little hesitation before the prince and princess embrace and greet one another, with small, tentative smiles of shy could-be-lovers.

"Enough."

The mirror returns to its normal state, and I quickly turn away. There is no such thing as True Love's Kiss. Even if they do fall in love with one another, they will not find a way to break the curse.

I leave my bedchamber, Asra and Margaux accompanying me through the halls of the Unseelie Castle. There is no time to brood over what-ifs—I have Solitary Fae awaiting me just outside the castle walls. I must focus, must do what my mother never got the chance to do.

The gates are already open, Chimere standing inside while her visitors remain outside.

"I can give you an essscort," Chimere insists, her back to me, unaware of my presence.

"We'll not step foot inside without the Unseelie King's permission," declares a dwarf, one of three in the group that is closely huddled together. A dryad towers behind them, her appearance tree-like as all of that kind of faerie are, her skin made of bark. Only instead of the normal hair made of leaves or pine needles, hers is a thousand tiny pink flowers I am not sure I have ever seen before.

The last of the group are one earth and two water nymphs, and a banshee, who lingers at the back ominously. Long, stringy hair obscures her face and reaches to her waist. Thankfully, she is silent, although her presence is weighty.

"As long as you harm neither me nor my people nor my kingdom, you have my permission to enter the castle."

The Solitary Fae study me as Chimere whirls around and dips into a low curtsy.

"Your Highnesss," she greets. "Thessse are membersss of my clan, asss well asss a few of the dwarvesss. They decided they wissshed to meet you."

She avoided giving names, I notice. While not uncommon for faeries to keep their full names secret, a first name or even a disguise name is normally given out of respect. But I am not their king, and I will not demand it of them. After all, I can understand being wary, and wishing to keep names secret.

They scrutinize me, then Asra and Margaux.

"You could decide anything is harmful," the first dwarf says, locking eyes with me from under bushy brows that have a little more white in them than his hair and beard. He exudes self-importance, although his clothes are more patched and ragged than the others, and the soles of his boots look ready to give way.

"Keep your hands away from your weapons, and we should not have a problem." At my tone, Asra tightens her tail around my neck ever so slightly. As still as stone, Margaux remains a half a step behind me, just within my peripherals.

No one says anything. We do not break eye contact. Chimere shifts nervously, trying to catch my attention but too afraid of my response if she dares interrupt outright.

"You will not demand our allegiance?" the dwarf presses, narrowing his eyes.

"I will not." For good measure, I add, "Allegiance is preferable, but I will not scoff at an alliance."

Thoughtfully, the dwarf nods. "A warmer welcome than your mother ever gave."

I grit my teeth, willing myself not to react outwardly. I have to be smart, to play this carefully. "Follow me. We can discuss our matters privately inside."

I leave without waiting for their response. Chimere's heeled shoes click on the stone as she hurries to catch up to me.

"Sssire, I—"

I turn around to see Margaux has caught Chimere's wrist, preventing her from touching my shoulder. Chimere's slitted pupils shrink, and she looks to me helplessly. To my pleasure, her "friends" are behind her, following us to the steps of the castle entrance.

"Is there a problem, Chimere?"

She swallows. "I only meant to walk with you, Sssire. Asss we have many timesss." A glance at Margaux, then back to me.

"Perhaps we will take another walk later," I say to appease her. "Margaux, release her."

Face as unreadable as ever, Margaux obeys and falls back into place behind me. I continue to lead everyone inside like nothing is out of the ordinary, but Asra maneuvers around to watch the newcomers, and possibly Chimere. For a highly judgmental crea-ture, she has yet to make up her mind about the snake-like faerie. As long as I can keep Chimere from spending too much time with

Odilon and prevent her from falling in love with me, she should be no more than a minor irritation.

The meeting room is already prepared with faerie fruits and wine in the center of the long table. I take my seat at the head, Margaux at my right. Asra hops up onto the top of my chair, glaring at everyone, tail flicking near my head every so often.

Once everyone is settled, I invite them to partake in the refreshments. No one takes any until Chimere does. If they think I would resort to poison to kill them, they lack imagination.

And must think I take after my mother, The Mad Queen.

"What would you want from an alliance?" I ask, preferring not to dance around the subject.

The dryad leans forward, petals from her hair floating down onto the table. "We want protection. Resources."

Understandable, predictable. I wait a moment before replying, "How am I to offer protection? I assume you do not wish to reside here in Unseelie."

The Solitary Fae exchange looks of nervousness.

"What if..." the dryad proposes, "...we were willing to move our habitation close to the borders of Unseelie territory? We would take nothing from your lands that is not offered to us, and when another clan attacks, you would come to our aid."

"I am in the middle of a war," I remind them. "There is very little I can spare. How often do you find yourselves in those circumstances?"

It is the elderly dwarf from earlier who speaks in her stead: "We made an alliance with this clan three years ago. In that time, they have required our aid five times with minimal casualties."

"Define 'minimal' for me." I idly stroke Asra's tail when the end of it comes to rest over my shoulder, careful to avoid the line of small spikes along the length.

The dwarf lifts one gloved hand. The outer two fingers sag, unlike the rest. "For me, lost these and got this here scar that nearly left me dead." He gestures to his neck, where a scar winds from just below his jaw to over his collarbone and disappears beneath his shirt collar. "Three dead. The rest only got scrapes, cuts, and broken bones. All mendable." He speaks with the nonchalance of listing ingredients for a recipe. I decide that he must be fascinating to watch in battle—and relish the fact that I might be able to witness it.

"The battles would be naught to you but minor skirmishes," the dwarf concludes.

"And we would follow you into battle as well, sending whom we can spare," the dryad clarifies. "We are few, but we have much power."

We spend time figuring out the smaller details before we reach an agreement. To my surprise, Chimere remains silent, allowing us to discuss as we need.

Once everything is settled and we stand, the dwarf says to me, "We also would like to make the same alliance with you."

Asra crawls from the top of the chair to me, leaning forward to get a better look at his face. Also probably to make him ill-at-ease, knowing Asra.

The dwarf briefly glances at her before refocusing on me. "What say you, King of the Unseelie? There are not many of us dwarves, but we are strong in body and spirit. You have a war you want to win, and having us at your side will only increase your chances of success."

We both know he speaks truly. "You have an alliance." And I should have more than enough to reunite Faerie.

CHAPTER TWENTY-EIGHT

BRIAR ROSE

*T*he way Loren hugs me this morning doesn't have the same intensity as last night, yet it sends a wave of contentment through me, so much that I don't want to let go. But there are still more things to do for the wedding, and so we break apart and let the faeries do what they need to.

Instead of more clothing fittings, Evanthe and Toussaint take us to another room, a library with walls that span greater heights than I can see. Ivy grows throughout it, and more of the tiny faeries float about, providing soft light.

Evanthe has Loren and me stand near the door while she and Toussaint stand at the other side of the room.

"Must we practice *walking*?" Loren gripes.

"Presentation is key," Evanthe responds. "If you are so graceful, it should not take long to master." She gives us a few more instructions: "Match your pace, keep your palms together at about shoulder height, and your other hand over your heart. Chins high! And don't forget to smile." She eyes Loren.

"I haven't forgotten," he mutters, pressing his palm to mine. His hands are larger, and I feel the urge to interlock my fingers with his. As if he can hear my thoughts, he looks at me, scowl softening to what could almost be a surprised smile.

"Better," Toussaint comments with a smirk. "But you're supposed to be facing forward."

Evanthe shoots him a warning look. "Let me handle the directions."

"Then what am I here for?"

"I do not have an answer for you."

With a sigh, he leans back against the wall. "I suppose I'll stand here and look pretty, as usual."

"Whatever keeps you quiet."

Loren and I chuckle, and thankfully Toussaint doesn't seem put out by Evanthe's cross mood, content to watch as Evanthe has us walk across the room time and again, always with some sort of tiny feedback that to her is crucial to us starting all over.

"What was wrong with that last one?" Toussaint questions, breaking his silence after what feels like our fiftieth try.

"They are not walking *together*," she snippily replies.

He blinks at her. "Who were they walking with?"

Huffing, Evanthe has us go a few more times, then temporarily gives up so we can eat. "We will try again after."

Not needing to be told twice, the three of us hurry outside, going toward our usual spot until Loren tugs on my arm, leading me down a different path. Toussaint slips ahead of us, tossing back a few pieces of faerie fruit.

"Where are we going?" I quietly ask Loren, thinking I know the answer but afraid I will be wrong.

"You wanted to visit the merfolk," he answers simply, a sparkle in his eyes. "You'd better eat before we get there. Using portals requires a lot of energy." He takes his own advice, wiping at the juice that dribbles down his chin.

Merfolk. Unable to hold back a grin, I gobble down the succulent fruit in a way that would horrify my mother—most unladylike. But I am far too excited to care.

The landscape looks mostly the same to me, but Toussaint and Loren know the way. The trees grow thicker through here, the path disappearing entirely. I pause, noting a bit of fog peeking out from between two trees that begin to crumble at its touch, disintegrating to ash.

"We'll keep clear of it," Loren assures me with a hand at my back. But I note that his lighthearted mood has dampened as well.

When we make it to a hill, Loren offers his arm as we half slide down. Somehow, he remains steady despite the uneven ground; I swear, the rocks and roots and bushes are trying to trip us for fun.

Toussaint makes it to the bottom well before we do, witnessing our awkward descent with an amused expression. I expect him to make a joke, but he picks up speed again, bounding over a fallen tree with the same ease as hopping across stones in the river.

I stare up at it, trying to decide whether it would be best to try to climb over it or find a way around.

Instead of following Toussaint's example, Loren leaps on top and extends a hand, pulling me up with him.

"Couldn't you have used magic?" I ask.

"Not if we don't want them tracking us so easily." He lands on the other side and offers both of his hands this time. "I can use some to make this easier for you, if you want."

I shake my head. This is starting to feel like an adventure from our childhood, and I find myself wanting to savor every moment.

I take his hands, but when I'm halfway down, he catches me by the waist, softening my landing and snatching the breath from my lungs.

"Are you all right?" His touch lingers, and his gaze dances down my face, then back up to my eyes.

All I can do in response is nod.

He nods back, as if reassuring himself, and lets go of me. Clearing his throat, he says, "Toussaint is this way."

Loren walks away quickly, then slows his pace when he realizes I haven't caught up to him yet. I draw closer to him as the forest gets darker, and he takes my hand.

"Through here." He pulls me into a cave so small I wouldn't have noticed it, tucked away and almost buried under the vegetation surrounding it. We pass through the ivy, Loren ducking slightly so his head doesn't brush the ceiling. From his pocket he retrieves a faerie light, blowing gently to get a soft glow. It doesn't seem to wind him in the slightest—is it because he is Fae? Or did I not use mine correctly?

The cave is narrow, and we walk carefully down, down, down into deeper darkness. I grip Loren's hand, grateful he hasn't let go yet.

"Do I have to come back for you?" Toussaint calls from farther in, voice echoing. I stand on tiptoes to peek over Loren's shoulder, noticing a dim light coming from around the corner.

"We're here," Loren answers. We round a bend to find Toussaint standing in front of a glowing oval in the wall, shimmering with a wide range of bright colors that are warring with one another to be at the forefront. On the walls surrounding the portal are hanging necklaces, all with luminescent blue crystals of varying sizes and shapes.

"Good. I got it working again. Ready?" Toussaint asks, putting on one of the necklaces and tossing two more to us. He leaps into the portal before we even slip them over our heads.

The stone rests with the rose my brother whittled for me. I try to remember exactly what it is for... something to do with swimming...?

"The water will be cold," Loren warns me. "It might feel like you're drowning at first, but try to take a few seconds before inhaling." Still holding the faerie light, he taps his stone with two fingers. "This will give you more than enough air."

Vague memories rise to the surface, of deep-sea adventures, far deeper than we should have been able to go on limited air supply...

I stop fiddling with the stone, and look up to find Loren extending his free hand to me.

"Shall we have an adventure?" he asks, pink tingeing his cheeks and the tips of his ears.

We are children again, exploring and having fun together. Except it's also not like that at all, not when so much has happened and we are such different people... and the thought of taking his hand again has my stomach tumbling over itself.

I do it anyway. Our fingers interlock, and he squeezes lightly.

"It's easy to get lost in the portal. Don't let go," he orders gently.

"I won't." *I don't want to.* The thought catches me by surprise, and, as if he hears it, he gives a small smile and blushes a little more.

Together, we step through the portal. A few moments of floating weightlessness, and then we're submerged into an icy cold that shocks every part of my body into painful awareness. Instinctively, I gasp, then choke and sputter salty water as we spin and roll. Loren grips me tightly, pulls me close as we level out.

The blue crystals begin to emit a glow; water recedes, giving both of us just enough of an air bubble to breathe, keeping our heads out of the water. After I finish coughing and wiping my mouth, I take a look around. Sea in every direction, the only other source of light is the shimmer that must be the surface, but it is too dull and far away to tell.

"You didn't warn her?" Toussaint accuses Loren with a *tsk*. "Come now, Fox, pranks should not be cruel."

That's when it hits me: Loren and I have yet to play any pranks on one another. Every other visit, we have all but bullied each other, from me rubbing pork fat on his shoes so that the dogs would chase him, to him purposefully giving me a bouquet that would make me sneeze all throughout chapel, until my mother hurried me out of service before the priest stopped the chants to say something to me.

"I told her," Loren defends himself at the same time I say, "He did tell me."

Toussaint kicks his legs back and forth idly, keeping himself in place as he looks back and forth between the two of us. When I do the same, my dress ripples about, slowly mimicking my movements a few seconds later. I'll have to keep moving so that the skirts don't twist around my legs.

"The castle is this way." Toussaint takes off, leaving Loren and me to catch up again. I swim as best I can, but I feel like I'm floundering, not getting anywhere. Swimming is not a pastime I partake in often, since the closest bodies of water we have to our castle are lakes and rivers, and princesses have too much to do with their time other than something so childish and messy.

I am grateful that Loren keeps holding my hand. It is my tether as we move forward slowly into the great expanse that could easily overwhelm me if I let it. The deep is soundless, and all I can see outside of our lights are shadows. Every so often, fish swim past us, giving us plenty of room as if they are too nervous to get close.

"Hurry!" Toussaint is outside of my field of vision, but his voice barely reaches me. In the distance, there are glittering lights, what must be the castle of the merfolk, but it is too far to make out properly.

Two forms race toward us; I'm not sure if I'm squeezing Loren or he's squeezing me, but I've gone still while he reaches for a knife in his boot, dropping the faerie light in its place.

CHAPTER TWENTY-NINE

BRIAR ROSE

"There is no need for that, my friend!" a male voice calls, melodious and friendly. He swims into our light, a woman with him. About their ethereal faces floats their long hair, his dark, hers light. Small patches of iridescent scales cover random parts of their arms and torsos, becoming bigger until they become long tails. Their beauty is so breathtaking that I don't realize I'm staring until Loren lets go of my hand and speaks.

"Caspian," Loren breathes in relief, returning his knife and accepting Caspian's embrace.

Then Caspian turns to me with a questioning grin. "Who is this? Are you…?"

"Briar Rose," Loren fills in for him. "You met a few times when we were children."

"I recall." He dips his head. "It is a pleasure to see you again."

"It is," I reply, finally finding my voice. "To see you, I mean." My attention drifts to the woman, who somehow seems more unearthly than Caspian—even her skin glows faintly, like magic courses through her veins instead of blood. Who is she? Is she with Caspian? What happened to his love, the human Princess Sabine? I had hoped to speak with her, to see if she could somehow understand my trials as human royalty entangled in a world with magical beings.

"She wanted to visit before we get too tied up in courtly affairs," Loren explains. "And it didn't take much convincing for me to visit an old friend."

"Old friends," Caspian corrects. "Surely you remember Sabine?"

I feel a bit better that Loren is just as surprised as I am. Sabine grins, clearly enjoying the reaction.

"A lot has happened," Sabine states, her voice a serenading song that would easily drag men to the depths without her having to lay a finger on them. "Perhaps we should find somewhere more comfortable to catch up?"

"Not without me!" Toussaint hurriedly rejoins us, panting. "Any chance you could give me a tail like yours? You're too fast to keep pace with."

Sabine casts him an apologetic look over her shoulder. "Unfortunately, no. My magic does not work that way."

"Sorry to leave you behind. We got too excited when you mentioned Loren was here." Caspian clasps Toussaint's shoulder. "Come, we will bring you to our grotto." He links arms with Loren and Toussaint, and swims off so fast they are blurs. Sabine does the same with me, her grip gentle but strong. The water pulls, trying to slow us down, but Sabine doesn't listen to it, intent on reaching our destination. We move upward, leaving the dark valley behind us, the tip of her tail brushing against my dress and leg. Now I can make out landscapes, dips and hills, coral reefs and schools of fish. We are still too far below for me to see much color, but there are hints of it.

Sabine slows us as we descend into a small cavern the others have just disappeared into. She urges me to go first, following behind closely.

"It is a little tight in here," I comment, trying my best to avoid snagging on the jagged walls that bite into the palms of my hands as I slowly make my way down the corridor.

"A bit," Sabine agrees. "Although that makes it more difficult for bigger nuisances to enter. If you see any eels, just ignore them. They scare easily and will hide."

As if to prove her point, I notice the mouth of one poke out of a hole, then slip back in. I try to move faster, getting frustrated with the way my skirts wrap about my legs.

"Dresses could also be categorized as a nuisance," jokes Sabine, noticing my struggle. "I've generally hated wearing them. I'm very glad they are no longer necessary."

"Normally I like them," I tell her, "but they are not helpful underwater."

She snorts a laugh. We finally make it to the other side: a cave full of the same glittering blue crystals encrusted into the walls and ceiling. Water avoids the stones, and I fall onto my hands and knees, not ready to support my own weight.

I start to scramble to my feet, but the men are already sitting cross-legged on the dry floor, including Caspian, who somehow exchanged his tail for scaly legs that are vaguely human in shape, with webbing between his toes. Sabine settles beside me, her tail morphing into legs similar to Caspian's, taking up a lot less space than her mermaid tail.

"One of the benefits of being the Heart of the Sea," Sabine informs us. "I quite unintentionally came into my own power a few years ago."

"And helped restore what magic we merfolk had lost," Caspian adds. He looks at her with nothing but pride and adoration, so much that it squeezes my chest with longing.

Will I ever have someone look at me like that? Unable to help myself, I sneak a peek at Loren, who is pushing drenched hair out of his face. His curls flattened, the elegant points of his ears are more obvious, marking him inhuman. He meets my gaze, offers a tiny smile. I respond in kind.

"This is a cozy little space," Toussaint remarks, glancing about. "You even keep food down here?"

"This is where we bring my family and friends when they wish to visit," Sabine clarifies. "It is too far to bring them to the palace, but this is a nice, secluded place. Captain Bill likes it especially."

"The pirate? I remember him!" Toussaint leans back against the wall, the bits of floating water nearest him wetting his shirt once more. He either doesn't notice or doesn't care. "The way he speaks takes some getting used to, but he always has a good tale to tell!"

"That he does." Sabine chuckles. "I'm not convinced all of them are true though."

"Does it need to be true to be a good story?"

She considers for a moment before responding, "I suppose not."

"And some stories seem too good to be true." Caspian squeezes Sabine's hand, then turns his attention to me. "Briar Rose, I am honored you wanted to visit us."

"I am glad we got the chance to visit. I have missed this place, missed visiting here." I glance up at the low ceiling. "Although I do remember the cave being bigger."

"We used to take you to the one on the shore." Caspian shifts so that he's sitting closer to Sabine, their knees touching. "We can bring you there too, if you would like."

"No," Loren declines. Realizing how intensely it came out, he rubs the back of his neck. "A kind offer, but we do not want word to spread about our visit. Tensions between the Courts are aggressive at best, and we came here without permission."

Did I ask too much of them? Did I endanger us? Neither Toussaint nor Loren will look me in the eye. Surely, they would have denied my request if it had been too much...

"The curse remains then?" Sabine watches me curiously, like if she focused hard enough, she could see it trying to take hold of me. Apparently, it is not one of the newfound talents she gained, because she just frowns.

"It has not happened yet," I answer quietly, drawing my knees up to my chest. "It is supposed to on my eighteenth birthday... in a few days." The words taste like ash.

"I know I have already asked this of you…" Loren begins slowly, seriously, "but is there anything you can do to help her? Either of you?"

In that question alone, I have my answer: they did not care about the risk, as long as there was hope for a reward, some way to get me out of the curse. When I saw a chance for a brief respite from my impending fate, Loren and Toussaint saw a chance to save me, however minuscule.

Caspian and Sabine exchange ponderous expressions.

"Magic of the merfolk does not deal with curses," Caspian says somberly. "Our magic is quite different than that of faeries', as you recall."

A glint of a memory nags at the back of my mind, of a merfolk claw resting against my chest, of something invisible coating my skin, applying pressure until it made me cry. Their magic could not touch me, much less help me.

"No," Sabine concurs, "but mine might." Like Caspian's, her light green eyes are slightly too big to be human, and when they focus on me, they pin me in place. "Would you like me to try?"

Loren twitches, itching to answer for me. Toussaint shoots him a warning look.

"What if… what if it hurts you?" I ask.

Considering my point, Sabine frowns. "That is a risk I am willing to take. I want to try to help you if I can."

I stare back at her, weighing my options. It would be safer not to try, to let the curse take me alone as it has planned to since that fateful naming day. No one else would have to get hurt, get dragged down with me.

But… what if there is another way? Sabine was human, and now is something else entirely, possessing magic that is uncommon at the very least. And if she wants to help me… don't I owe it to myself to at least try?

"Yes."

With an acknowledging nod, Sabine kneels in front of me, her now dry blonde hair falling over her shoulders, reaching all the way to her waist in soft, messy waves. She places her forehead against mine, takes one hand, and with the other hand, touches my chest, right above my rapidly beating heart.

"Relax," she urges me gently. "Close your eyes. Let down your defenses."

I obey, even though everything in me wants to tense up. *What if this doesn't work?*

What if it does?

A tingling sensation runs along my body, neither warm nor cold, neither comforting nor alarming. I keep absolutely still, my breaths shallow and slow. *Shouldn't something be happening?*

The sensation slithers along my skin, leaving goosebumps in its wake. Then it pauses under her hand, above my heart.

"There are two shackles," Sabine whispers aloud, half to herself. "One in your mind, and another on your heart." She moves her hand to my forehead. "No... it used to be there, but it shifted... moved... to your heart. There is a different feeling to the magic there, as if someone else changed it."

"Evanthe," Loren offers up quietly. "The curse was originally supposed to kill her, but Evanthe changed it to a sleeping curse and gave her a way to break it."

"True Love's Kiss..." Sabine sighs wearily. "That is the crack I sense in the curse. It was not fully bonded to you, and so she could manipulate it." Her hand returns to my heart; her magic pushes against my chest, trying to burrow its way in, to grasp at the curse like it wants to yank it out of me. The pressure is bruising; I bite my lip.

Sabine releases me, gasps for breath, head bowed, barely catching herself on the stone floor. Caspian is at her side in an instant, steadying her, looking for signs of injury. I know Loren and Toussaint are staring at me, but I cannot bring myself to look away from her.

What have I done?

After what feels like a short eternity, Sabine raises her gaze, eyes red-rimmed, iridescent blood dripping from her nose and splattering on the floor. "I am sorry," she tells me, with such weighty sincerity that my own shoulders slump. "It would not let me. I tried. I gave it all I could."

"I know," I barely manage to say through my tightening throat. If all it took to break the curse were people to *try*, it would have been broken years ago.

"Are you all right?" I ask her, fearing the response.

Sabine nods and wipes at her face. "I could not hurt it, but it also couldn't hurt me."

The answer gives me a little solace. No help, but also no harm done.

"We should return soon," says Toussaint, breaking the heavy silence. "They are sure to be looking for us now."

Caspian shifts back into his merman form and, giving them new charged stones for their necklaces, takes them out of the grotto.

I stand, crouching under the low ceiling, but Sabine stays still, studying me. "I wish there was more I could do."

"I appreciate that you tried," I assure her. "Being a human princess amidst magic beings is… exhausting and complicated, to say the least."

She smiles sympathetically. "I understand that." She stands and puts her hands on my shoulders. "But do not lose hope. In the darkest moment when I thought that all was lost, that was when everything worked out for the best."

I try not to fidget. "Thank you. But I have a hard time putting complete faith in True Love's Kiss to break the curse."

"Yes… but perhaps that is not the only way out."

LOREN

We make it back to Faerie with no trouble, and promise Caspian and Sabine that we will visit when we can—when it is safer to keep a portal open between our worlds.

When, not if.

I start to cut my hand to use the magic in my blood to seal it shut
once more, but Toussaint stops me, does it himself. Without saying
anything, I know he means to keep me out of trouble as much as he can,
using his own magic instead, making it seem like his idea. No one will
believe him, but no one will argue about it either, seeing as they want me
to keep as much of my magic on hand as possible to keep me safe.

His blood glimmers over the surface of the stones surrounding
the portal, and it grows dim until it is nothing but a smooth stone
surface. We leave our necklaces hanging on the wall and exit the
cave, Toussaint leading the way again.

I slow my pace to match Briar Rose's. She is silent and withdrawn, a reserved defeat snuffing out the usual spark in her eyes.

"I am sorry," I tell her. "I had hoped that visit would have gone
better." Half-dry hair falls into my eyes, and I brush it back. Hopefully by the time we reach my aunt, we will have no more evidence
of where we'd disappeared to for the afternoon.

Briar Rose replies softly, "I am glad we went. Thank you."

More silence. Toussaint stays ahead of us, just within sight for
me. I make a note to thank him later for having given us a little
privacy. We cannot linger, so a few moments will have to do.

I aid her over the fallen tree again, and when I move to release
her, she grabs my wrists.

"Will you help me with something?" For the first time since we
visited the merfolk, she looks me in the eye.

"What is it?"

She takes a breath. "Will you help me with the dreamscape?" I
open my mouth to ask what she means, but she begins to ramble: "I
know how to enter the dreamscape, and I can manipulate the magic
there as you have seen—not to make things awkward—but with the
curse so close, I fear that will be the only weapon at my disposal. I
would like to be as ready as I can be, in case…"

I try not to wince at her implication.

"I don't mean any slight," she says hurriedly, squeezing my
wrists like she is trying to reassure me, but it comes across as a
nervous tic. "It could be that we find a way to break the curse, but in
the meantime, I would like to be prepared." Briar Rose's eyes are so

vulnerably intense, locked on mine, that for a moment, I consider pulling her into my arms.

"It will also give us a chance to get to know each other better," she adds, mistaking my lack of response for hesitation. "A chance that... perhaps we could..."

Perhaps we could what? Fall in love? Dare I hope? Instead, I say, "I will help you."

The small smile she gives me starts to uncoil the knot in my chest. We walk the rest of the way back much closer than before, our arms nearly brushing.

CHAPTER THIRTY

THE UNSEELIE KING

"Thank you for meeting with them." Chimere holds onto my arm as we return to the castle from yet another stroll through the Unseelie woods. "You handled that with tact and wisssdom."

"We came to a mutually beneficial agreement." Helpful, but nothing too great as to draw attention from the Seelie or the Troll Queen, the latter of which will be arriving soon. I'd hoped she would have already come to claim the twice-yearly taxes, to be done with her for the time being so I can focus solely on my own matters. But if I send word to check on her arrival, it will be seen as a slight, and my mother took great pains to make this alliance possible, so letting it fall apart is out of the question.

We already have supplies set aside to give the Troll Queen the moment she arrives. I hope she is in an indifferent mood, because then she will not stay and make my life utter torture. I have enough to deal with as it is, and adding a narcissistic magic-grubbing troll to the mix is more than I can stand.

"Isss sssomething the matter, Sssire?" She tries to lean toward me, but Asra hisses and flicks the end of her tail close enough to Chimere's face to make her jolt.

Before I can come up with a reply, Odilon strolls out of the gate, letter in hand. "There you are, Sire." Despite the chill in the air, he wears very little, the shaggy fur on his lower half no doubt keeping him warm. "A letter has arrived for you."

Silent as ripples over water, Margaux appears in front of me without blocking my view, hand extended. Reluctantly, Odilon gives it to her, and I have to wonder if he knows about her ability to nullify magic with a single touch.

With a flick of her thumb, the letter seal breaks. We wait, surveying with bated breath. When nothing happens, Margaux hands it to me.

To the Leader of the Unseelie,

Storms and troubles have delayed my journey to Unseelie, many of which I suspect have to do with your upcoming curse on the human. If you wish to keep my alliance to secure your victory, I suggest you send soldiers to ease my journey and be prepared to welcome me in your castle. Expect my arrival within a few days of receiving this letter, taxes and offerings at the ready.

                                        —The Troll Queen

It takes what scraps of control I have left not to rip the letter in frustration. No one can see me react in such a way, especially not Odilon. For her to demand an escort, when she knows well that I—

A plan takes form, uncurling, dissipating my agitation.

"Odilon, I have an urgent task for you."

The corner of his mouth twitches. "What can I do, Sire?"

"Margaux will choose ten soldiers that you will lead to meet with the Troll Queen and give her a safe escort here. You leave today."

After a brief pause, he dips his head. "As you wish, Sire."

He and Margaux bow and leave, hurrying to obey my command.

"Your Highnesss," Chimere whispers. "Can you trussst him?"

Asra rumbles a warning growl; I slowly meet Chimere's slitted gaze. "Can I trust anyone?"

Wisely, she does not answer.

BRIAR ROSE

After a few dodged questions about where we'd disappeared to, Queen Vivienne and my guardians left it alone, I suspect because things seem less tense between Loren and me. At least, it feels that way, the morning greetings coming more easily. Evanthe finally lets us move on from practicing our walk and starts training us on dancing.

But the real training comes at night, when all the others are asleep, and I call for Loren to join me in the dreamscape.

He is not Henri, I remind myself when I consider for the third time changing my appearance. We promised to let ourselves get to know who we are, no walls between us.

It takes only a few moments for Loren to arrive, landing grace-fully on the grassy field I conjured. No castle, no playhouse, just endless fields that take little to bring to life.

"What shall we practice tonight?" he asks politely, keeping a small distance between us. His amber eyes roam over me, noticing the way I have forgone a dress, replacing it with a shirt, trousers, and boots. We have gone over control of conjuring, and started working on control of returning to my body and back again within moments. But tonight, I have something else in mind.

"Teach me to fight."

He does nothing to hide his surprise. "To fight?"

"I know a little, but not enough," I confess. "Even if I am able to stay within my dreamscape when the curse takes hold, the Unseelie King—" I cannot bring myself to use his name "—has made it clear that we are connected, and he can come and go as he pleases. I want to be prepared."

There is no preparing for the curse, my gut tells me, but I ignore it. If I do nothing, I will go mad.

Loren's throat bobs.

"I've seen the way you and Toussaint spar. I want you to teach me how."

"Very well," he concedes.

We spend time going over the basics of stance, Loren lightly nudging me when necessary. It feels unnatural, going against my princess training of standing tall and holding my head high. I have learned a little fighting from watching the knights over the years, but having a teacher makes it very different, pointing out little mistakes when I am *certain* I copied him exactly.

Loren has me run through the same movements over and over. "Good. Again."

I scowl at him. "You're starting to sound like Evanthe."

He smirks. "Perhaps, but this *you* asked for."

I flounder trying to come up with an adequate retort, thrown off by seeing something that close to a smile on his face. My stomach does a strange flip.

"Again," he insists, thankfully unaware of the effect he just had on me. Whatever it was.

I go through the series of punches, and he easily evades each one—including the extra one I threw in for good measure. He raises a brow; I lift my chin.

"We're not sparring. Again," he orders.

"Why not? I need to learn to react—I won't have time to think about what I'm doing."

"You won't have to think if you already know the motions."

Glaring at him, I go through the motions again, this time adding a few more. Like a dance, he anticipates my movements, and when I keep going, he flows with me, as if I'm not attacking him at all.

"Loren!" Swing. "Fight!" Jab. "Back!" Lunge.

He chuckles at my irritation, making it worse, especially since a small part of me wants to laugh with him. This is wholly absurd, and I don't understand why he won't just—

It feels like my knuckles graze his side, but Loren whirls and falls flat on his face, unmoving. Stunned, I stand there far too long staring, frozen, trying to comprehend what just happened.

"Loren?"

No response.

I drop to my knees beside him, jostle him. "Loren! Loren." He shakes, and I hurriedly roll him over, promising myself he's fine, we're in the dreamscape, it isn't that bad. *He's fine, he's fine, he's fine*—

There is not a mark on him. And he is shaking with *laughter*.

"Loren!" I swat his shoulder. "I thought I actually hit you!"

"I thought you were trying to hit me?" He props himself onto one elbow, grinning widely.

"Yes! But I wasn't trying to *hurt* you!" I huff. "That was the meanest prank!"

"I beg to differ," he disagrees. "The meanest prank was when you swapped the oil for my hair with honey. I went to sleep with it in and woke up sticky!"

"What about when you magicked one of the chair legs away at the banquet so that when I sat down, I fell over?"

"You cannot prove that was me." The grin is still there, and I cannot help but share in it, no matter how hard I try to fight it.

"It had four legs before I sat down!"

"You turned my skin orange!"

"You…" I giggle. "I was rather proud of that one."

Loren sits up. "It was rather ingenious. I didn't see it coming."

"That almost sounds like a compliment."

"Don't get too excited. I have plans to exact vengeance."

"Oh?" I quirk a brow. "Care to share?"

"And give you an advantage? Not a chance." His smile slips a bit, his gaze dropping to my mouth.

When did I lean toward him? Suddenly I am very aware of our knees touching, of the erratic beat of my heart, of the way his eyes flit back and forth, meeting mine for the briefest of moments. In the soft sunlight I conjured, his lashes are dark red, framing molten eyes, and I consider making it brighter so I can see the gold of his irises gleam.

Does he want to kiss me? A flush rushes up my neck, recalling the night of the ball, the unintentional kiss that was never supposed to happen and was over just as quickly as it started.

"Hating you would be far easier." Uncertainty creeps into my chest and takes hold. *He doesn't hate me, but…*

Loren stands, shattering the moment. "It is getting late," he says quietly, and offers a hand to help me up. Reluctantly, I take it, and he pulls me into a hug.

"I am not foolish enough to tell you not to worry," Loren whispers, "but please know I will do whatever is in my power to free you from the curse."

All of my tension melts as he presses a kiss to the top of my head. Whatever happens will happen, but right now, in this moment, I am safe with Loren. My Loren. The Loren I knew as a child, the real Loren who is full of compassion and love of life, with a streak of mischievousness that inspires all sorts of misadventures worth remembering.

I look up at him, but he has not yet moved back, so our noses brush. With just a small movement, I could kiss him.

But it wouldn't be real, not in the dreamscape.

"Thank you," I tell him softly. As if coming to the same conclusion as I have, he releases me.

"Good night, Briar Rose."

"Good night, Loren."

After leaving the dreamscape and settling back into my body, curled up in my bed, I go to sleep that night with a grin on my face, dreaming of amber eyes staring into mine and auburn curls that are soft between my fingers.

CHAPTER THIRTY-ONE

LOREN

"*W*hat has you in such a good mood?" Toussaint leans in the doorway to my bedroom, fetching me for more wedding preparations.

"A good mood?" I ask, pretending to smooth out my shirt so I don't have to look him in the eye. "What makes you think I'm in a good mood?"

"Well, you greeted me before I could say anything. And you look like you're trying not to smile."

I force myself to meet his eyes for a split second, trying to come up with something to divert the subject. "Since when do I have good moods?"

"Since things have been going well with Briar Rose." He smirks and pushes off the doorframe. "We should go before your aunt sends Delphine to drag us downstairs."

Hurrying, we get there just as my aunt is hugging Briar Rose.

The princess's hazel eyes find mine, and her lips curl up the slightest bit. Aunt Vivienne steps out of the way so we can embrace, and there is no hesitation, no tension.

Then she looks up at me, bids me good morning, and I have to stop myself from being mesmerized by her mouth like I was last night. I'll not have our first proper kiss be in front of an audience, not if I can help it.

Evanthe shuffles us off to another room before we can get a good look at how Briar Rose's dresses are coming together, making me wonder what surprises they have up their sleeves. But there is no time to ask, because she has us walking again, and dancing.

Every time Briar Rose meets my gaze, pink tinges her cheeks, and she offers shy smiles I find myself returning.

"They are moving much more in unison," Toussaint comments in a mock whisper. I shoot him a glare from over Briar Rose's head.

Evanthe gives a noncommittal noise, the closest she has come to agreeing with Toussaint.

Without warning, the library doors burst open.

"Delphine!" Evanthe exclaims. "What is the meaning of this?"

"The In-Between," Delphine answers, eyes wide. "It is taking another part of Seelie, close to the castle. Come, hurry."

We scurry from the room, following Delphine all the way outside, where we can see what she means: a rolling fog is coming, swallowing everything in its path, making all it touches crumble to ash that fills the air before settling on the ground like a layer of frost.

Briar Rose grabs my hand and stands close to my side as she takes in the slow, menacing threat. "How do we stop it?"

Aunt Vivienne is already calling for everyone who can spare magic to hinder the In-Between. Air ripples as spells are hurled at it. Evanthe takes the lead, shouting orders and throwing her own magic where she can spare it. I can see the strain in both of them, the color that slips from my aunt's skin as she touches each of the faeries' shoulders in turn, giving what magic the land has given her. What will soon be Briar Rose's and my burden to bear—sustaining Seelie and its people, which only survive with magic.

"We have to restore the Courts," I answer simply, as if it were that simple. "Faerie began falling apart when the Courts split. But once we are married and you are Fae, we should have enough power to find the solution." *Which will likely be going to war with Tristan.* But I do not tell her that.

Briar Rose is silent, the furrow in her brow present. Whatever she is thinking hard about, she does not share, and I am not confident enough to ask her about it.

BRIAR ROSE

"Do try to get *some* sleep," Evanthe teases me half-heartedly as she wishes me good night. She does not carry herself with the same lightness and assurance she normally does—today has taken a toll on her, and so many others.

Others I will soon rule and be responsible for.

You feel like a pawn in a game to which you do not know the rules and consequences...

I may be cursed, but I am not the only one doomed.

Bits of a plan forming in my head, I slip into the dreamscape. I do not bother with conjuring much more than a glade, making the sky as dark and cloudy as my mood. This will do for what I have in mind.

Closing my eyes, I reach within, readying to call. After a moment's hesitation, I brush past Loren's warm, comforting magic and reach for the icy tendril that is ever-present, despite how much I try to ignore it.

As I open my eyes, a funnel of black forms in front of me, rising high, then falling in a spiral, dissipating once it unveils the Unseelie King.

"Princess Briar Rose. I must admit, you kept me waiting longer than I anticipated you would." He is far too calm, assessing me quickly, his face betraying none of his thoughts.

"You said Faerie is falling apart slowly," I tell him, not wanting to mince words. "I witnessed it today, how the In-Between ate away everything in its path. We have to fix it."

"On that, we agree." The Unseelie King—Tristan—takes half a step toward me, no farther. "Are you prepared to hear my offer?"

"What would it take for you to relinquish the throne to Loren?"

He snorts derisively. "If anything, he should relinquish it to *me*. I am the firstborn, the kingship belongs to me."

"What would it take?" I repeat.

He crosses his arms, raises a brow. "Are you ready to hear my offer?"

"Does it involve you giving the crown to Loren?"

Tristan rolls his eyes. "Come now, Princess—you really think that, after all this time, I would give in just because a pretty girl asked it of me?"

"He is your brother—"

"Half-brother."

"—and there has to be a way that we can end this peacefully."

"There is." He cocks his head to the side slightly. "Marry me instead."

I blink, trying to process what he said. "You... what?"

"Loren is turning you into Fae so that Faerie can repurpose your human body for magic, and marrying you so that your power will be tied to his, increasing what he already has." Tristan waits a second before he adds, "So my offer is for you to marry me instead. I will not harm any who decide to bow to me, and you will be my Queen, free to do as you please."

"But... you do not love me."

"I never said I did." He smirks, half in amusement and half in annoyance. "But you would not be marrying him for love either. At least with me, you would have a choice, and I would never expect anything of you that you would not be willing to give."

Alarm bells ring in my head, yet the words stick to me like thorns caught in my skin. A choice, a chance to fix Faerie.

But to do it would betray Loren.

"I cannot do that to Loren."

"Do what?" Tristan's eyes narrow. "Surely you do not love

him…?"

"I…" The phrase catches in my throat. "I don't know." I'm not sure I would be able to say that either if I were a faerie. Something is there between us, something raw and fragile, but to call it that?

"Affection might be blossoming between you, but it is not love, at least not in time for True Love's Kiss to break the curse."

I lift my chin. "You would not know that."

"I do," he argues coolly. "You and I are connected, Princess. I might not know you as one of your friends does, but my magic has been tied to you for most of your life, and so it knows you well."

"You mean your curse," I spit at him.

"A curse I already offered to undo given certain circumstances."

"And there is no other way?"

His expression hardens, the angles of his face sharper. "Neither of us will bow, so one must break." Darkness oozes from beneath his boots, quickly spreading across my dreamscape. He extends his hand to me. "The choice is yours."

I quickly undo the dreamscape, seeing him disappear seconds before it is gone. I land back in my body with a gasp, hitting harder than I intended, pins and needles covering my skin.

"Is everything all right?" Evanthe is at my side instantly, worry pinching her features. My other faerie guardians along with Fauna and Flora are crowding around, curious to find out what is happening.

"I need to see Loren." I leave no question in my tone, no room for disagreement.

"I can take you to him," Fauna offers, taking a step forward.

"No," Evanthe replies, and pulls me to my feet. "I will take her."

"It really is no trouble—"

Evanthe silences her with a look. "Stay here and rest."

Reluctantly, Fauna moves back toward her sister, gaze downcast. I know their magic is weaker than most, but she was only trying to help; Evanthe did not have to respond so sharply. Thankfully, Fauna seems to know it is out of worry from everything happening.

I change out of my nightgown and into a more suitable dress, and then Evanthe takes my hand and leads me into the night.

CHAPTER THIRTY-TWO

LOREN

I lie awake in my room, staring at the night sky. Briar Rose should have called me to her dreamscape by now. Did she fall asleep? It might be easier to believe that if she hadn't been so quiet and withdrawn today after witnessing the In-Between eat away at Seelie firsthand.

"You're still awake."

"Yes," I answer Toussaint.

After a lengthy pause, he states, "She probably fell asleep. You two have been staying up late a lot of nights in a row."

I don't know what to say in response, but my silence is just as telling.

"There is more to it than that, isn't there? What else is bothering you?"

We lie beside each other in complete darkness save for the soft moonlight and subtle glow of butterflies and pixies that pass by or briefly visit, leaving sparkling trails behind them that eventually fade to nothing.

"Fox?" he presses gently. "What is it? I can shoulder the burden if you let me."

He would shoulder anything I gave him, no questions asked or complaints given. Teasing would be certain, but nothing serious, all light-hearted.

" I..." *How is it so difficult to say this?* It is a truth I have slowly realized, and we faeries are free to speak truths. So why is it caught in my chest? "I'm in love with her." The admission eases me slightly, but there is an ache in my heart that has only gotten worse since she's been in Faerie.

"...This isn't news, Fox. You've always loved her." Toussaint speaks softly, like he is being careful not to trample my emotions as I process them.

"No, not like this. We've always been meant to end up together, so I've loved her, but now... The more I get to know the real her, the more I've fallen madly in love with her."

"That's great news!" He pauses, then when I don't respond, he adds, "Isn't it?"

"But the curse is coming... I can't lose her, Toussaint. I can't." My voice rasps; I swallow, hoping to ease the tightness of my throat, but to no avail.

"You won't. True Love's Kiss breaks the spell, remember?"

The answer to the curse that looms just out of reach. "What if I'm not her true love?"

"...Loren..."

I continue in a rush, afraid I will be unable to speak again if I stop: "As much as it kills me to even think it, I'd rather the spell be broken and she be with someone else than to keep her with me and have her stuck in that curse, sleeping forever. She doesn't deserve any of this."

My declaration hangs heavy in the air.

"This is why you pushed her away the first time," Toussaint points out. "You have to let yourself love her, and let her love you.

Don't waste what little time you have worrying about losing her, or you will lose her far sooner than you were meant to."

I turn to him, only to find him already sitting up, looking at me.

"Don't be your own enemy."

I have no idea what to say in response, but I am saved by a knocking at the door. Toussaint is up and wielding a dagger before the last rap of knuckles sounds.

"Toussaint?" Evanthe calls. "Princess Briar Rose would like to see Prince Loren."

I jump to my feet, half-tumbling off the bed. "Come in."

Briar Rose instantly seeks my gaze the moment Toussaint lets them in. From what I can tell, she is unharmed, but something distresses her greatly.

"We will give you some privacy." Toussaint takes Evanthe's wrist, tugging her with him out of the room. The moment the door clicks, Briar Rose sighs.

"Can we take a walk?"

"Too dangerous," I say apologetically.

"Right, the... In-Between." She winds and unwinds her fingers, clears her throat. "I did something... completely stupid, but I had to try."

I manage to keep the anxiety from my voice as I ask, "What happened?"

"I called the Unseelie King to the dreamscape. I know I told you I wouldn't, and I'm sorry, but I thought maybe I could reason with him, since he said he had an offer to undo the curse, but..."

As much as I hate that she reached out to him, I'm glad she's unharmed, that she is still here... and that she has come to me. "The offer wasn't what you wanted."

She shakes her head, ashamed. "I just wanted a way to fix things peacefully. There is more at stake than the curse—all of Faerie is falling apart, and I thought maybe I could appeal to him, get him to agree to a compromise." Tears line her eyes. I reach forward and press my thumb to the furrow in her brow; her expression softens.

"You did what you could."

The tears slip down her cheeks. "I just feel so useless, so helpless..."

Before I can think myself out of doing it, I embrace her, and she clings to me. "You are neither of those things," I whisper into her hair, and press a kiss to the top of her head. *If only you saw yourself the way I see you.*

"I feel like I am," she sniffs.

"But you are not. Otherwise, I wouldn't be able to say so." Only being able to speak the truth has its perks every once in a while.

Briar Rose hugs me tighter, anchoring herself to me.

"We will find a way," I promise, speaking to myself as much as I am to her. "Don't lose hope."

Slowly, she tilts her head back to look up at me. Butterflies flutter around us, settling on pieces of furniture in my room. The light from their sparkling trails glitters in Briar Rose's hazel eyes, amplifying the tones of browns, greens, and greys. I gently cup her face, wiping her cheeks with my thumbs, fully aware of the depth of her stare.

"I won't," she whispers.

I can hear nothing over our pounding hearts, nearly the same escalating beat. Her skin is soft, and I linger, unwilling to let her go. I meant what I said before, that if that is the way to break the curse, I will step aside and let her be with someone else, but in this moment, it feels like it would take every fiber in me to do that.

Unable to hold back any longer, I kiss her. At her small gasp, I pull back, but she follows me, initiating another, her hands moving up to my hair.

This is what our first kiss was supposed to be: affection, a sharing of hearts, of vulnerability, not an unintentional bumbling of confused, hurting souls.

As soon as we stop, I rest my forehead against hers. I know it might not have been True Love's Kiss and broken the curse, but it did break whatever was left of the walls I'd built between us. Her fingers wind through my curls and brush over the tips of my ears, making me smile. It has been far too long since she has done that.

"Loren?" she whispers, as if afraid speaking too loud will break the moment. "Will you promise me something?"

"What is it?" There is very little I will say no to right now. I wonder if she knows the power she holds over me…

"If the curse does come to pass, promise you'll kiss me, try to wake me?"

My heartbeat skips in response. "I promise," I murmur against her lips, "that I will do everything in my power to break the curse and bring you back to me."

She smiles a bit, then closes the small space between us. Everything is slow and tender, and I breathe her in, holding her against me. She smells of fresh flowers and spring rain—already a faerie in everything but body.

Toussaint clears his throat dramatically, blocking the doorway. Evanthe peers over his shoulder.

Briar Rose's hands fall to my chest as she turns to look at them, and I loosen my grip on her waist a little.

"Is everything… settled?" Evanthe asks, shoving Toussaint aside.

"Yes," Briar Rose answers, and bites the inside of her cheek.

"Then perhaps we should return to bed," Evanthe suggests. "We all could use some sleep."

As much as I detest the idea of parting with her, Evanthe speaks sense. We have spent too much time in the dreamscape, the exhaustion starting to show under her eyes and the way her "perfect princess posture" is a tad slumped.

"Or perhaps I could stay here tonight with Loren and Toussaint."

The request surprises me just as much as Toussaint and Evanthe, whose eyes have gone wide.

"We can sleep on the floor like we did as children," she continues. "Gazing up at the stars until we can't keep our eyes open any longer…"

Evanthe's frown softens to a grimace. She and Briar Rose stare at one another for a few moments, and then she sighs. "What do you think of this plan, Prince Loren?"

"I am for it." *Did I sound too eager?*

"Very well." To Toussaint, she orders, "You had better protect them, or—"

"No threat necessary," he assures her, stepping out of her way. "How about I imagine the worst thing you could do to me and then double it?"

"Triple it." She bids us goodnight and takes her leave.

Toussaint and I take the blanket from my bed and spread it out on the floor.

"I'm surprised you got Evanthe to cave," Toussaint remarks to Briar Rose. "She must already see the queen in you."

Briar Rose ducks her head. "Or she feels sorry for me."

We go quiet, settling down with Toussaint on one side of me and Briar Rose on the other, shoulder-to-shoulder.

"The sky is always beautiful here," Briar Rose says, furtively slipping her hand into mine.

"Do you remember the names of the stars?" Toussaint begins to share the star names and the stories behind them, some wild tales I have never heard of before. We listen, sometimes telling him how absurd they sound, but he claims they are all true, and we laugh together, the three of us.

Eventually, we fall into a comfortable silence. Just when I think Briar Rose is asleep, she turns toward me, laying her head on my chest. I wrap my arm around her, barely stopping myself from kissing her again. She needs rest.

I am listening to her soft, slow breathing when sleep finally claims me.

CHAPTER THIRTY-THREE

THE UNSEELIE KING

"*M*issive for you, Sire." Margaux drops a letter on my desk. A dwarf stands in the doorway, not one of those who visited before. Her pale hair is braided back, windswept strands loose about her ruddy cheeks. She holds her head high, scrutinizing gaze fastened onto me. Her lips are pressed tightly together, no doubt to keep from speaking until spoken to.

Peering down at the letter, I realize it is in Dwarvish—not something I read, but easily translatable with magic. Instead of doing so, I call to the dwarf, "You there, come here."

Margaux moves to the side as the dwarf obeys, each step slow and careful. She stops a few paces away from my desk, and I remain seated, resting my chin on my folded hands. Asra wakes from her nap, curled up near my elbow, but only lifts her head slightly to better watch the newcomer, who briefly spares her a glance.

"What is your name?"

Her eyes narrow. "You may call me Narda... Your Highness." She adds the honorific in like an afterthought.

"Why were you sent here, Narda?"

She peeks at the letter, then returns her attention to me. Calculating. "Shifter forces gather against us."

"Shifters?" Not the answer I expected. Normally human despite their ability to shift into animals at will, I have a hard time understanding what they are doing near Faerie at all.

"We suspect they were hired by one of the Solitary Fae clans. Ever since we allied ourselves with Chimere's clan, the others have seen us as a threat."

Chimere's clan? Interesting that they consider it her clan even though she is no longer affiliated with them... She has given her fealty to Unseelie, but perhaps Narda phrased it that way since I know Chimere's name but none of the others. Still, I pocket the information for later.

Impatience sharpening her tongue and emboldening her spirit, Narda presses aggressively with a slam of her fist on the desk, "The contract you signed states that you will send aid immediately." Her cheeks are no longer flushed from the cold, but from anger boiling within.

Asra rumbles a warning growl; I lean back, sitting up in my chair with intentional leisure. "I am well aware of the contract I signed, Narda. I will forgive the outburst this once—I am certain you fear for your comrades and loved ones—but I will also warn you that Asra is less forgiving than I am."

At the mention of her name, Asra bares her teeth in what comes across as a wicked smile. The tip of her tail flicks, and the closest Narda comes to flinching is the muscle that tics in her jaw.

"Margaux, assemble a group of soldiers to return with Narda immediately. Make sure supplies are sent with them as well."

"Yes, My King."

"You will not join us?" Narda stares me down.

"I cannot leave my land vulnerable. Soldiers and supplies will return with you, and if more are needed, then I will send more." I nod to Margaux, who escorts Narda out of the room. The dwarf resists at first, but eventually goes with a grumble.

As soon as the door shuts, I hold open the letter. Asra creeps toward me to watch as magic bleeds out of my fingertips and seeps into the paper like spilled ink. The letters flash and tremble, morphing until they are in flowing faerie script instead of sharp-edged Dwarvish lettering. As I suspected, Narda did not lie: she had no reason to. But I wanted to check all the same.

When I am almost finished reading it the second time to be certain I did not miss anything, a knock sounds at the door. "Who is it?"

"Chimere."

"Come in."

Asra throws me an annoyed glare, which I ignore. If I slight Chimere too much, she might decide to break her oath to the Unseelie and inspire her clan to do the same with their alliance.

Bits of ash cling to her loose hair and dust the shoulders of her dark blue cloak, and her cheeks are pink. "Thank you for ssseeing me, Your Highnesss." She draws as close to the desk as she dares with Asra staring at her, and curtsies, the silver silk of her dress catching the candlelight in shimmers.

"What can I do for you?"

The worry lines around her mouth soften a little. "I just ssspoke with Narda, and ssshe sssaid that you are sssending sssuppliesss and sssoldiersss to help the dwarvesss."

"I am. Margaux is putting it all together as we speak."

She nods approvingly. "Thank you."

When she makes no move to leave or speak more, I say, "There is something else troubling you."

It takes her a few moments to reply, "You are not going with them."

"I have a kingdom to run," I answer simply. "The Troll Queen will arrive any day, as will the curse. Surely you understand."

Her gaze dips to the floor. "I undersssstand."

"...But you do not think it will be enough."

She takes a shuddering breath. "Forgive me, Your Highnesss. You did as you promisssed. I jussst fear for their wellbeing." Her slitted eyes flick back up to mine. "Ssshiftersss can be brutal."

Her own clan is sure to help fight against them, so I wonder if she feels guilt for remaining safe among the Unseelie. Well, safer. Nowhere is truly safe. "Do you wish to join them? You have my blessing if you wish to."

Chimere hugs herself as if she is cold. "There isss little I can do," she whispers. "I am no warrior."

I think of the children, of the others who may not know how to fight, but I bite my tongue. I will not fault her for deciding to stay.

Margaux returns, walking past Chimere to stand by my side. "Everything is being prepared as you asked, Sire."

"Excellent." I fold the letter and stash it in one of the desk drawers. The locking spell seals over once more when I am done. "One more thing: inform Narda and the soldiers that if things get dire, they are to bring everyone here to the Unseelie castle for sanctuary."

I can tell Margaux is surprised by the way she hesitates in answering. "As you wish, My King."

Chimere gives me a thankful smile, and I dismiss both of them.

"That is enough social interaction for one day, don't you think, Asra?" I stand, and the wyvern leaps onto my shoulder. "Shall we retire to my bedchamber for isolation and wine?"

She chirrups her agreement, and we flee upstairs before anyone else can request an audience with me.

CHAPTER THIRTY-FOUR

LOREN

I wake the next morning feeling much more peaceful than I have in a long time. Briar Rose's chest rises and falls slowly, evenly, and the soft beat of her heart against my side nearly lulls me back to sleep. My arm is still around her, holding her to me. I smile.

She wanted to stay here. With me. She *asked* to.

Her breathing shifts and heart rate quickens. "Good morning," I whisper, pressing my lips to the top of her head.

"How did you know I was awake?" she asks, stifling a small yawn.

"Your breathing changed."

She turns to look up at me, and I consider kissing her. It would be an easy decision if Toussaint were not lying beside me.

"Now that both of you are awake," Toussaint interrupts, rolling onto his feet, "we'd best join the others."

I groan. "Can't the wedding preparation wait at least a little? We could go on another adventure."

"Oh!" Briar Rose squeals in excitement, and sits up. "We could see the Sanctuary of the Pixies!"

I'm surprised she remembers going to that tree, but they did adore her and treat her like a goddess come to bring them blessing and salvation. In a way, she will, if we can use the power she will receive from Faerie to restore the Courts.

"As much fun as that sounds," Toussaint says, "there is no wedding preparation today."

I prop myself up on my elbows. "What do you mean? What are we doing then?"

Toussaint crosses his arms and leans back against the wall. "Queen Vivienne decided that today is the day for Briar Rose's Ascension."

The look on Briar Rose's face is a mixture of concern and fear. Not what I hoped for, though if I were in her place, I suppose it would be a lot to take in, knowing that I would be changing from human to faerie, leaving behind my own life to embrace the new. Here I've been worrying about taking the crown, but she is doing that and more.

"No need to look so worried," Toussaint tries to assure her with a subdued smile. "Today is a day of celebrating. The Ascension will not begin until the sun starts to set."

"Celebrating?"

I sit up so I can smooth back her hair, noting how pale she's gone since the conversation started. "We have a lot to celebrate: your Ascension, our wedding... your birthday tomorrow." Oddly enough, the statement does not leave me nearly as anxious as before. All of those things I used to avoid thinking about, now I feel... almost excited for them, knowing she will be right there with me.

She leans into my touch. "That is a lot of celebrating for one day."

"This is just the first day," Toussaint corrects her. "It will most likely turn into a week or two of feasts and dancing before things go back to normal."

That seems to do little to lighten her mood, so I take her hand and squeeze it. "It will be good fun, I promise." *I'll look after you, make sure no faerie games go wrong.*

"And if it's not," Toussaint adds, "I'll be happy to make things more entertaining for you."

To my relief, she chuckles. "Of that, I am sure, although I'm afraid of what shenanigans you'll come up with."

He grins in response.

"Briar Rose?" Evanthe calls from the other side of the door as she knocks. "Time to wake, dearest, you have company awaiting you."

Evanthe brought a dress for Briar Rose to change into, and makes Toussaint and me wait outside of the door, at the top of the rounded stairway.

"She's nervous," Toussaint whispers. "Understandably so."

I nod, unsure what else to say.

He nudges me with his shoulder. "Come now, surely we can have a bit of fun, get her to relax and enjoy the day?"

"I hope so."

Toussaint is a split second off from putting me in a headlock—I manage to maneuver my way out of it before he can get a proper hold on me. But he anticipates this, fluidly transitioning into his next attack. I am already prepared.

"Courts claim you!" Evanthe snaps irritably, interrupting our scuffle. "Can I leave you alone for a few minutes without you being in danger of falling down the stairs?"

"Are you admitting you are worried about us, Evanthe?" Toussaint asks with a toothy grin, at which she snorts, replying, "I am worried for the prince."

Briar Rose steps beside Evanthe, and I cannot help but stare. She smiles back at me in shy amusement. The flowing silk gown Briar Rose wears does not catch the eye nearly as easily as her bright spirit; I am but a moth drawn to flame, grateful for the few moments I might burn with her.

"I see you did not directly deny being worried about *me*," Toussaint presses his luck.

"Because I would worry about finding a suitable replacement for protecting Prince Loren." Before Toussaint can prod her any further, Evanthe insists we hurry outside to join the celebration. "It is rude for the guest of honor to leave the attendees waiting."

Briar Rose holds my hand as we make our way outside, Evanthe leading us. My aunt is already there, as are most of the important figures at Court. They turn to watch us join them, and I catch sight of some other familiar faces. Briar Rose sees them a couple of seconds later, sucking in a surprised breath, her expression brightening.

King Faustus opens his arms, and Briar Rose runs into his embrace. Queen Ava kisses her daughter's forehead as Prince Jovan cries gleefully, "You didn't forget us!"

Briar Rose looks down at him in amusement. "Of course I didn't."

"My necklace worked!" Jovan shouts, victoriously thrusting his arms into the air, garnering a chorus of chuckles and confused looks from humans and faeries alike. There are always dangers amongst the Fae, but considering how many of us are protecting Briar Rose, there is little chance of something like someone stealing her memories happening to her. If he wants to think he had something to do with it, I won't say anything to discourage that belief.

There is something so sweet about the way Jovan hugs Briar Rose. If only I had a sibling... I mean, I do, but even if I wanted a relationship with Tristan, he has made it clear that I am his enemy, the one who stole his birthright.

I have Toussaint. We might not be related by blood, but something stronger connects us, a kinship solidified in silver and adorned in gold.

"Come," my aunt declares, beaming, "we have celebrating to do!"

More faeries have gathered, curious to see the humans who have come to visit our land. They keep a respectful distance—all except the pixies, who hover above. As we make our way deeper into the forest, where the festivities are already underway, I hear Jovan giggling and talking to the pixies, telling them to come closer so he can see them better. His mother hushes him.

Briar Rose slips her hand back into mine. Her eyes light up at the sight of the tables overflowing with bottles of faerie wine and piles of nuts and fruits nearly spilling onto the ground. There are also cakes and pastries Irit and Delphine made with magic, swearing they are some of Briar Rose's favorites and that they taste just like what we would find in the human lands. When I try a raspberry tart, I find they did not exaggerate in the least. I will always prefer food from Faerie, but I have to admit, those raspberry tarts are a weakness of mine.

I swipe another and pause before taking a bite. Briar Rose is still absorbing everything, and despite being obviously pleased by the celebration, there is a sadness that weighs down her shoulders and keeps her smile from reaching her eyes.

She must be thinking about the curse, since her birthday is tomorrow. I resolve to do what I can to give her at least some happy memories tonight, to distract her even for a little bit.

CHAPTER THIRTY-FIVE

BRIAR ROSE

*a*bundance of food, abundance of dancing, abundance of magic and wine and conversation and laughter. Where human parties are organized and have a theme and rules, this seems to be a release to do as you please, beholden to no one. Faeries that notice me cheer and smile and call out wishes of luck, some asking for blessings once I have Ascended.

Even though I knew it was coming, the news that my Ascension is in mere hours is a tight band around my chest that constricts more and more as time passes. I should be happy, excited, elated, to become one of the Fae. And I am: my own magic, long life, freedom to be in Seelie for as long as I like; they all sound splendid… But… tomorrow is my eighteenth birthday, which means the curse will begin. Will being a faerie help me… or not?

It could be that the curse is already broken… I shake off that tiny shred of hope, knowing it will only disappoint me. I feel no different since kissing Loren, other than feeling close to him. And if the curse has not yet been enacted, then how could it be broken? That seems too easy.

I chastise myself for falling into a spiral of dark thoughts instead of celebrating with those who will soon be my people. And... my husband.

Loren is watching me, amber eyes full of concern. I offer him a smile, one I know does not quite convince him. He returns the gesture.

Are you as worried as I am? I want to ask, but I already know the answer. At least, I think I do. He promised to do whatever he can to bring me back, and I believe him, not just because faeries cannot tell direct lies. His words rang true in my soul, and I locked them away for when the curse does come to claim me.

Loren extends the tart he is holding. "Here, have some."

I bite my lip and shake my head. "Thank you, but I am not a fan of raspberry."

He frowns. "Delphine and Irit said these pastries were some of your favorites." Something clicks in his head, because his eyes widen slightly as he ponders the phrasing.

I admit, "I told them to make those. I know they're your favorite."

Loren goes still, studying me. The frown disappears but doesn't quite turn into a smile. "I don't know if I should trust your judgment if you don't like raspberry." He pops it into his mouth and licks his fingers clean.

Fighting the urge to smile at him is a losing battle. "Yet you do regardless."

He doesn't argue.

Hand-in-hand, we skirt around the dancers, some in couples or groups, some alone, all somehow following the beat of the music even though the steps differ greatly. A mosaic of movements that draws the eye.

Everyone is wearing finery, silks and rich colors and lots of jewelry. Yet not a shoe in sight, other than some of the nobles, my family, and myself. I glance down at my feet, at the flats that are obvious with my ankle-length dress. Mother obviously noticed, her smile a little pinched, but said nothing about the wardrobe change. We are in Faerie, and adapting to their customs is to be expected. I am sure if I said something about being uncomfortable, other arrangements would have been made, but I am not. If I am going to become a faerie, I am going to embrace it wholeheartedly.

I kick off my shoes. The grass is softer beneath my feet than I anticipated, and I wiggle my toes. From the corner of my eye, I notice Jovan yanking off his boots; Mother starts to scold him, then gives up as he sprints toward us.

"Look! I took off my boots! This is much more fun than parties at home!" He dances, trying to mimic one of the faeries, then another. "Dance with me, Rosie!"

A giggle bubbles out of me. I toss any self-consciousness to the wind. Jovan knows how to enjoy the moment, and I follow his lead, soon trying to catch my breath from dancing and laughing as we make absolute fools of ourselves.

Loren joins us, as does Toussaint, both bare-footed and full of merriment and energy. We twirl and jump and dip and reach for the sky, however the music directs us. When Toussaint first said the celebration would last a week or two, I worried about growing tired of celebrating, but now I fear I never want it to end, especially when I see Loren beaming and laughing at Toussaint trying to be more ridiculous than Jovan—a challenge my little brother is more than happy to accept.

Loren and I step back, watching them for a bit. But my gaze is drawn to him, and something in me lights up at his grin, true happiness I'd not seen in him for far too long. And when he turns it to me, my knees go weak.

"Let's go somewhere quieter," I suggest. "Take a short break." I would stay to look after my brother, but between Mother watching him from the sidelines, where she sits with Father, Queen Vivienne, and Evanthe, and Toussaint directly interacting with him, I have no worries about Jovan's wellbeing. Besides, I want a little more time with just Loren if I can manage it.

Loren spares a glance at our families, then tugs me along the outer edge of the dancers, seeming as eager to be alone with me as I am with him.

Faerie magic flows with the music, clashing, swirling, and melding together in colorful, shimmering patterns in the sky despite it being still sunny. The sun is higher than I thought it would be—I am not sure how time here equates to human time, but it seems like it is later than I thought.

"Keep close, Briar Rose," Loren warns me as we make our way through more crowds spread out amongst the forest floor, conversing and eating and drinking and kissing. "Faerie parties may look to be harmless fun, but we have many tricks."

"Then why should I believe that I'm safe with you?" I try not to grin as he looks back at me in surprise, but fail miserably. He smirks and shakes his head.

"I never said I was safe. Just… safer." He winks.

I want to comment on the flicker of concern in his amber eyes, but I remind myself that we are here to enjoy our time, not dwell on worries.

Someone grabs my wrist with bony fingers, stopping me abruptly. "For you, beautiful human," whispers a female voice in my ear as a cup is placed into my hand. I flinch, and Loren pulls me toward him, snatching the cup.

"I meant no harm, Prince Loren," the willowy, wide-eyed faerie says with a sharp smile, contrasting the soft, round planes of her face.

Loren dismisses her, and she disappears into the shadows as if she were never there to begin with.

"Who was that?"

"One of the servants, wanting to get a closer look at their future queen."

The way he says it settles oddly in my stomach. "She said she meant no harm." But I know better: faeries lie with things unsaid, intentions woven together from the truths they can speak.

"She means no harm," Loren confirms, "but she wants fun, and faerie wine is a quick way to get a human into many troubles."

"But it doesn't bring trouble to faeries?"

His expression lightens a bit, as does his grip on my hand. "Trouble of a different sort. You can try it when you're a faerie."

"I cannot have even a taste now?" *I will be a faerie by tomorrow…*

"No," he answers without hesitation, and downs the wine as if to get the temptation away from me as quickly as possible.

I sigh dramatically, knowing I still have his attention. "I suppose kisses are off the table then."

Loren chokes. I swallow a chuckle as he coughs, trying to regain his composure. A few drops of wine spot his tunic, which disappear with a flick of his fingers. We have drawn some attention, but I fixate on Loren, watching as he wipes at his mouth with the back of his hand, and then swipes his thumb across his bottom lip. My cheeks flush; I draw my gaze up to his.

He grins as he leans toward me. "Are you certain of that?"

My heart thuds. "Are we still speaking the truth?"

His brow raises. "Yes."

I draw as close to him as I dare, ignoring the onlookers. His pupils expand. "Then I am certain they are still very much on the table." Not waiting for a response, I pivot and hurry off, knowing he will chase me. Counting on it.

Loren does not disappoint. I have to slow down to avoid stepping on anyone, and he is quick and sure-footed, easily catching my hand. But instead of stopping, he urges me along, farther into the trees, where there are fewer faeries. Pixies follow us eagerly until he bats at the air and tells them to leave. They giggle and fly away.

"Well…" Loren says, finally bringing us to a halt, "you said you wanted somewhere a little quieter, but this is the best I can do for right now. Aunt Vivienne and Evanthe made me promise that we would stay nearby, so they don't have to delay the Ascension ceremony to find us."

Music and chatter are still there, and I can see faeries from where we are standing amongst the trees and shrubbery, but it is quieter and a little more secluded. "Thank you." Hesitantly, I stand on tiptoes, moving to kiss his cheek. He turns; our breaths mingle, our mouths nearly touching. I close the distance with a slow, gentle, brief kiss that leaves a sweet taste on my lips. Faerie wine. I feel no different—the dizzying effect has to be Loren.

He rests his forehead against mine, wrapping his arms loosely around me. "Are you all right?"

I want to dismiss his question with a nod, but we agreed to be truthful. "I am worried, with the curse being so close. Are you?"

"Yes."

It seems like answering my questions honestly is becoming easier for him, or at least I hope that is the case. I have a theory I want to test, but it is far too soon, and it would mostly be to ease my anxious heart.

"We take what moments we have, and do what we can with what is available to us." Loren tucks a strand of hair back, tracing the rounded top of my ear before cupping my cheek. "I will not break my promise. I will do whatever it takes to bring you back to me."

Tears prick my eyes. I grip his wrist as if he can anchor me here and we can make this last. "Do you love me?" The question escapes me before I can stop it.

How unfair of me. I should tell him how I feel, not demand he answer me first.

He goes still, lips parting in surprise. "I do love you." His thumb wipes an escaped tear from my cheekbone. "I thought I did before, but now... I am really falling for you, Briar Rose."

I want to tell him I love him, but my throat is too tight. I should be happy, but instead all I can think is *is this enough?*

Understandingly, he smiles at me, kisses me, embraces me. My tears wet his shirt, but he doesn't seem to care. "Don't lose hope," he whispers, and I wonder if he's talking to himself as much as he is to me.

ALL TOO SOON, my faerie guardians find us, and take me to prepare for the Ascension ceremony. Loren reluctantly lets go of my hands after Queen Vivienne assures him that we will return shortly.

The queen accompanies us to the castle, leading us into her room. Plenty of space, there is very little furniture but lots of blankets and pillows, and butterflies that flit about as they please. One lands on my nose, and I keep perfectly still until it decides to cross the room again, this time settling on the mirror hanging on the wall.

If this is supposed to be the ruler's bedchamber, I wonder if she will move to another, expecting Loren and me to take it.

I try not to blush at the thought of sharing a room with him— sharing a bed.

"This time, at least we are not arguing over what you are going to wear," Evanthe points out with a smile. She, Irit, Delphine, Fauna, and Flora all wrap me in a lingering group hug I am more than happy to reciprocate.

"You can do this," Delphine declares with enough confidence that it lifts my spirits.

"Faerie already loves you." Irit stands on her tiptoes to kiss my cheek.

"And so do we," Fauna adds, as Flora kisses my other cheek. Her lips leave a lingering sensation—a hint of magic? It carries a sweet flowery scent.

"For luck," she whispers.

Evanthe holds my face in her hands. Her eyes shimmer with unshed tears. "We are proud of you, Briar Rose, and excited to see who you are becoming."

They squeeze me once more, and when they release me, I realize my dress has shifted to a forest green. The top is form-fitting, but the skirts ripple with my every movement, whisper-soft and lightweight. I graze my thumb over one of the embroidered foxes on the bodice. Whatever awaits me in the Ascension, at least I can bring a bit of Loren with me.

"It is gorgeous," I tell them. "Thank you so much."

"Not quite done yet." Facing me toward the mirror, Evanthe steps behind me to fix my hair. Delphine and Irit tuck flowers and leaves in where they can, but some of the petals slip through and fall to the floor. I look like I belong to the forest, and it makes me grin.

This person I see in the mirror is the one I am excited to be. Maybe I will feel more like her after the ceremony.

"May I have a moment alone with her?" Queen Vivienne asks.

"Of course," my faerie guardians reply with a bow, then make their way out of the room, easing the door shut behind them.

The queen reaches out, running her fingers over a small section of my hair. "You are beautiful, Briar Rose."

"Thank you, Your Majesty."

She shakes her head. "Please, call me Vivienne. I would like us to be friends, especially since we will soon be family. I feel as though we already are." She cradles my hands in hers. "I am glad that Loren stopped trying to find a way out of your betrothal."

My next breath painfully catches in my throat. Loren was trying to find a way out? Why? When?

Vivienne, clearly sensing my distress, hastily says, "I apologize, I should not have mentioned it." She sighs, then clarifies, "Loren is very happy with you; he only meant to release you from a burden he thought you did not want. But from what I have been seeing recently, I think this is something you both want." She punctuates the statement with a hopeful smile.

Unable to speak, I nod. Loren has been telling me the truth—I can talk to him more about it later. But right now, Faerie is waiting on me. I inhale deeply, and slowly exhale. "Is there anything you can tell me about what to expect?"

Her smile dims. "I have witnessed one Ascension... for my late brother's first wife. She did tell me a little about it."

She is talking about Tristan's mother. Once, she had been a human princess just like me, going through her Ascension so she could become Fae and take her place as Queen. But back then, Faerie had been whole, not split into Courts. She had been a distant ancestor of mine—I wonder why the Fae still keep the agreement between us, since she did so much damage to Faerie Lands. Perhaps because the land itself demands the agreement be honored?

"She said she got to feel how alive Faerie is," Vivienne says quietly, gazing into my eyes like she is searching for something. Similarities, maybe? If Tristan's mother told Vivienne about the Ascension, were they good friends at some point? That would make the terrible story so much more complicated. I hadn't considered Vivienne's feelings, losing her sister-in-law and nephew, and then her brother and his new wife shortly after that… Not to mention taking the crown and raising her other nephew until he can take his rightful place as king.

The weight of it all is there, in the depths of her eyes and in the rigid set of her shoulders, easily overlooked by the smiles and comfort she exudes.

"She got to see its true beauty, feel its heartbeat. It did not speak to her in words, but somehow she knew what it wanted her to do." The faerie queen looks back down at our clasped hands.

"You miss her." I don't mean for the words to slip out, but Vivienne doesn't seem to mind. She replies in a hushed voice, "I miss the person she was before everything fell apart. I miss the person my brother was too. He was not the same…" Her grip tightens; she blinks back tears. "What hurts the most is that I miss the person my nephew could have become."

As she makes eye contact again, I understand that she is talking about Tristan, not Loren. From what I know, she only had a little time with him. There are a thousand questions I am dying to ask her, but I have to save them for later, when we know one another better—and Faerie is not waiting on me to fix it.

"It sounds silly, pining for things that could have been," she begins, taking a moment to collect herself. "We cannot change the past—we can, however, do the best with what is right in front of us."

As if she can hear my rapid heartbeat, she places a hand just below my collarbone. "You are strong, and have a beautiful heart and a kind soul. Faerie has had far too much greed and bloodshed: You have exactly what it needs to start the process of healing."

I fight the urge to take a step back. "But… what if…"

Vivienne smiles sympathetically, then pulls me into a hug. "Take things one step at a time. If you begin to lose faith in yourself, remember that we all have faith in you."

CHAPTER THIRTY-SIX

LOREN

*W*hile the faerie guardians prepare Briar Rose for the ceremony, the rest of us wait. Aunt Vivienne went with them, assuring me that she will give Briar Rose counsel on what to expect from the ceremony, as well as any advice the others before her had written down about their experiences.

Like Tristan's mother. I wonder how frightened she was the day she went through the Ascension, and if she would do it all again, knowing how tragic her end would be.

Toussaint and Jovan find me idly picking flowers and weaving them together while I wait, trying not to let my mind run away.

"Here. Toussaint said you like these and it would cheer you up." Jovan offers a few tarts; Toussaint winces but says nothing.

"Thank you." I pop one into my mouth and continue making the flower chain crown.

Jovan eats one too, staring as I work. "Is that for Rosie?" His curious eyes are almost the exact same as his sister's, with all of the colors working together to make them entrancing. He will no doubt have women tripping over themselves with a similar effect that Briar Rose has on me.

"It is," I confirm. "How did you come to that conclusion?"

"Pink is her favorite color," he answers, smacking his lips. "And you're sweet on her."

"That's one way of putting it," Toussaint chimes in with a smirk.

"What's another way?" Jovan turns to him, eating the final tart.

Toussaint is spared from having to answer: my aunt and Briar Rose's faerie guardians escort her back to the party. The corseted gown fits her form perfectly, little foxes and roses stitched into the bottom of the bodice. The skirt flows, the forest green fabric not quite sheer, and her hair is half done up with flowers and leaves— making her look the part of a faerie queen already, especially with her bare feet.

The music stops; faeries go still, bowing as Briar Rose makes her way toward me. Pale light from the sinking sun gives her a rosy glow that only brightens when she smiles at me. Worry furrows her brow, so when she is within reach, I smooth it out with my thumb.

Thankfully, everyone gives us a little space, waiting patiently for us to exchange a few words before the ceremony truly begins.

"It is time," she states quietly, voice carrying a small tremor.

"Rosie, you look beautiful!"

Their mother snatches Jovan's hand and pulls him away, hushing him.

"You are pretty much a faerie already. This is more of a formali-ty," I joke, garnering a huff of a chuckle from her. Then I set the crown of flowers atop her head. "You will do well."

She peeks at those watching us, and then takes my hands in hers. "I wish I had one to give you, just like we used to at the playhouse. King and Queen of naught but sticks and paintings, with Toussaint as our knight." The smile wavers. She takes a shuddering breath, eyes welling.

"Soon to be much more," I tell her, retrieving a cord from my pocket and wrapping it around her wrist. "Jovan inspired me, I will admit, and I do not want to step on his toes…" A fox charm dangles from the bracelet. "I wish I could go with you through the Ascension, but this is the best I could do."

Now she is crying and pulling me into a hug. "Thank you."

I do not care how many people are watching. I hold her tight and kiss her brow. If this will give her enough courage and strength to make it through, then I will let her take all she needs.

"Your aunt said you were going to try to find a way out of the betrothal."

I freeze. *Where did that come from?* My aunt was supposed to warn her of what the Ascension could entail, not talk about the betrothal.

Briar Rose steps back slightly, enough to look me in the face. "I am very glad you didn't."

I don't have to ask her if we are still telling the truth. "I am too."

She bites her bottom lip. "Loren, I… Even if this doesn't work, or if… What I mean to say is…"

As tenderly as I can, I kiss her. "Tell me when you return."

Whether it is the tears or the glow from the pixies nearby, her hazel eyes are even more vibrant than usual. Taking a steadier breath than before, she nods and kisses me once more.

"I will return," she promises.

I do my best to keep a small smile on my face until she turns around and walks back to Aunt Vivienne.

"Are you ready?"

Briar Rose dips her head. "I am."

Satisfied, Aunt Vivienne leads her to the center of the glade, where everyone is gathered, giving plenty of space for what is about to happen.

"Faerie will accept her," Toussaint whispers assuringly to me. "How could it not?"

It will accept her, I repeat over and over, watching as she kneels in front of my aunt. Normally we would wait until the human is closer to twenty years in age, that way the body and mind can handle the transformation better, but with the curse looming, we are out of time and options. I delayed it as long as I could. Now I have to have faith in her strength. She can succeed. She will succeed.

The way my aunt stands in front of Briar Rose reminds me of one of the stained glass windows in her family's castle, of a queen knighting a man. One of her favorites, something she would pretend to do when we were playing at our playhouse.

"Princess Briar Rose of the Human Lands," Aunt Vivienne states, projecting for all to hear, "you are here to Ascend as one of the Fae, that you may take your rightful place as Queen of the Seelie."

Silence reigns. No one dares move, attention fixated on Briar Rose. A breeze passes over us, curling down to tousle the ends of her hair. The magic in the air shifts, gravitating toward her.

"Open your heart and mind," my aunt continues, softening her tone. "To truly become Fae, you must be willing to let everything change."

Briar Rose rests her hands on her knees, palms facing upward.

She is ready. She can do this.

One moment, she is there, and the next, her form fades until she is transparent, almost invisible.

BRIAR ROSE

Something—no, *everything*—is pressing against me, trying to find a way to reach inside. It is not painful, but it is uncomfortable, and just when it nearly drives me to push back, it stops. Then something slithers into my mind.

I snap my eyes open, hoping to look to Queen Vivienne for a hint, but in her place is a dimly glowing figure about her size, with no face or specific form, no details, just the rough shape of her.

I whirl around, getting to my feet, seeking out Loren. But everyone looks the same as Queen Vivienne, their glows varying in brightness, all stronger than hers, but none more than that of a candle. The landscape's colors are fading to hues of grey, like they are bleeding out slowly.

Whatever is in my mind leans on me, its presence heavy and

sorrowful. My instinct is to flee to the dreamscape, but that is neither possible nor helpful, not if I want to complete this.

But there is something *wrong*. Vivienne said I would see Faerie for what it truly is, its life and magic. That there would be great beauty, and I would feel the strength of the heartbeat of the land. If anything, the pulse beneath my feet is weak, pitiful. I lean down, pressing my hand to the ground, but it is no better.

"You are hurt," I say aloud, hoping Faerie will respond. "Are you dying? What can I do?"

The presence in my mind coils in on itself, as if in pain.

"Please," I plead, "tell me something. What can I do?"

One of the forms tugs on my arm, saying something. I turn toward them, trying to figure out who it could be. Where had they come from? That might have given me a clue if I knew what part of the circle they had been standing in. They are shorter, but that means little: it could be any number of faeries, or children.

They speak to me, but the sounds are like a babbling brook.

"I can't understand you," I say apologetically. *Is Faerie trying to talk to me through them?*

They speak again, and another form joins the first, then another, all making incoherent noise.

"I can't understand you," I repeat. "I don't even know who you are."

They fall silent.

"Please," I beg again, pressing the sides of my head, "please tell me how to fix this."

The presence reaches down, touching my heart, encapsulating it with a scrap of warmth. Sky darkening, I look around, seeking any sort of hint. It tugs on me, bidding me to turn in the direction it indicates.

In the distance, there is pure black. The presence squeezes my chest as if in confirmation.

"The splitting of the Courts..." I step toward it, but it is as if I used a portal, the way I am suddenly standing but a few inches from the darkness. Its hunger and agony nearly bring me to my knees; the presence trembles, gripping my heart tighter. I gasp.

"Well, well, well…" To my right, the Cheshire Cat appears just as he was when I first came to Seelie. He does not glow like the land or people; instead, his coat shimmers, and his pupils do too. "Princess Briar Rose. I thought they would have done your Ascension ages ago."

The grip eases a bit, enough for me to take a decent breath. "Why can I see and understand you?"

He grins widely. "Why, indeed?" His gaze flicks toward the wall of darkness. "I think the better question is: Why is Faerie bringing you here?"

"I offered to help."

Cheshire cackles, tail flicking. "That was awfully brave of you. What is your grand plan to save all of Faerie?"

I lick my chapped lips. *How long has it been since the Ascension started?* "I… I don't know."

More laughter. "I like you, human. You are just as mad as the rest of us."

"I…" There are no words to defend myself, and it would be useless to anyway. Toussaint called him trouble, and he doesn't seem to want to help me. I refocus on the wall of darkness. There has to be an end to it, right? This is the source of the pain, but it has not taken over all of Faerie yet.

The cat leaps, and I jump back, but it floats in the air, staring at me. "Lean into the madness." Quicker than my eye can follow, his claw scratches the side of my neck, and then he disappears.

I hear the muffled thud, but there is nothing nearby. My neck is not bleeding; I cannot even feel a scratch. Puzzled, I decide to ignore him and his ramblings. Mad, indeed.

Steeling myself, I slowly reach forward, pressing my palm against the wall of darkness. The presence digs into my mind and heart, yet tugs me toward it at the same time. I surge forward, hoping to make it through quickly. But it is too far, and the darkness wraps around me, making it like trying to wade through high waters. It soaks through my dress, dragging me down, down, down…

A chill runs over me, almost snuffing out the bit of warmth the presence provides. I stumble, hitting the ground hard enough that I should have skinned my hands and knees. Again, there is no blood, not even a scrape to validate my pain.

I have to keep going.

A sweet scent tickles my nose. I look up to see a single rose, hovering a few feet above the ground. In this pure black, it shines like the summer sun, colors vibrant, its scent alluring. Without thinking, I stand and move toward it. Thorns cover the stem, but the beauty is so compelling, I want to touch it anyway.

The darkness closes in, slowly smothering the light; the petals begin to wilt.

Is this the heart of Faerie?

I rush to it, carefully reaching, desperate to keep it from dying. I have handled enough roses to know how to pick one without hurting myself. Yet, just before I touch it, my fingers move of their own accord, as if someone jerks them—

The first thorn pricks my index finger, pain sharper than it should be, ricocheting up my arm and into my chest. I yank my hand back. Blood wells, deep red, turning black as it slides down my finger, thickening to an oozing ichor. Something I would suspect from Unseelie, haunting and unsettling.

Flickering catches my attention: the rose disappears, in its place a wooden spinning wheel. Its spindle tip is covered in red, quickly turning black.

I can't breathe more than soft wheezes; my entire body trembles. This was not how it was supposed to happen. Faerie could not have betrayed me—it *needs* me.

A layer of ice covers my skin, then seeps in. The presence leaves my mind, curling around my heart like a protective shell.

I can't help you like this! I silently scream.

Fatigue hits me, drags me to the ground, makes me stare up at the darkness as the cold claims me. I take one final gasp of a breath.

CHAPTER THIRTY-SEVEN

THE UNSEELIE KING

*C*himere insists on spending more time together, so when I tell her I am busy, she goes with me on the daily rounds, checking on the troops, castle repairs, and supplies.

"I have yet to hear word about the dwarvesss," she comments quietly as I survey the stored rations.

Barrels, boxes, and sacks are stacked atop of and against one another, the entire back wall of the storage room covered. Yet I second-guess myself: *Is this enough?*

It is hard to measure when you are not sure about the expanse of the storm coming. Once the curse is enacted, how will that affect everything? Will the Seelie attack us? Will we be able to successfully conquer them? Or would it be better to deal with the humans first, whether by fighting or bartering their precious daughter?

I expected her to turn down my offer, in all honesty. But I had to offer it to soothe my guilt—she has never once had a true choice in her life, at least not any major ones. Twisted mine may have been, but it was a choice nonetheless.

"Neither have I," I say when I realize she has been waiting for my response for far too long.

"Ssshould we sssend sssomeone?"

I pause at her use of the word "we". There is an open sincerity to her gaze, like she is waiting for me to say something that will soothe her heart, something that may or may not have to do with this conversation. Probably the latter, if I would hazard a guess based on how often she wishes to spend time with me.

There is no *we*, and I may have to make that extremely clear soon. Hints do not seem to be working.

"I cannot spare anyone at the moment," I tell her plainly. "There is too much happening. If the odds are not in their favor, my warriors have their orders to bring the dwarves—and all of the dwarves's allies, if necessary—back here for shelter."

I step around her and out the door. She follows behind me, heels clicking on the stone floor that leads through the kitchens. The warmth of the ovens is a welcome change from the biting cold, but only briefly. Too long in the kitchens, and it gets stuffy and over-whelming, with the heat and the people and the cacophony of scents.

To her credit, Chimere waits until we are back outside before pressing further. "Sssurely we can ssspare one or two."

"No." The response is clipped and quick, like the steps I take going up to the wall. The warriors seem to be in order, at their posts. Margaux is checking all of them, including the ones farther out in the woods, but I cannot bring myself to sit still while Chimere is sticking with me.

She huffs and quickens her pace, trying to keep up, and slips on a wet stone. I catch her forearm, then walk away the moment she is righted.

"Sssire! At leassst consssider sssending a ssscout."

"Feel free to take whatever is necessary if you wish to check on them." I stride across the top of the wall, taking note of the bowing guards and the finally repaired gate. At least we have defenses ready in case of a Seelie attack.

"How could you be ssso heartlesss and cruel?"

I whirl around; she nearly slams into me, shock written all over her face, her fogged breaths suddenly ceasing. She swallows, scrambling to regain her composure. Shoving open a guard tower door, I urge her inside with a hand to her lower back and do my best not to slam the door shut.

Small sanctuaries that connects the walls, the guard towers have little in them other than a fire pit, a table, some chairs, and bits of food and weapons. Two men playing cards abandon their game and rush back outside before I can say anything.

Chimere's heart beats loudly, her slitted pupils narrowing. She remains where I nudged her, stone still.

You are quite lucky Asra is not here. What I say instead: "I have done what I can. You might have taken part in the decisions of your clan, but running a kingdom is an entirely different matter. Believe what you will about me, I do not care. But do not insult me or question me in front of my people. Are we understood?"

I would be proud of how I maintain my temper, but I am too angry to be proud. I have not gone to the horrific lengths my mother did to maintain the Unseelie, but I am a force to be reckoned with. Losing what she gave everything for is not an option.

Chimere locks gazes with me, not moving for a long time. "I apologize," she says finally. "You mussst have a lot of ressssponsssibility weighing on your ssshoulderss." Hesitantly, she reaches for my hand. I go to pull away, but a large amount of magic leaves me at once.

"Perhapsss..." she begins, running her fingers over the back of my hand, "it would be easssier if you had sssomeone to ssshare it with..."

My heart stutters. I sway, trying to regain my balance. The land senses my loss and quickly starts restoring the magic, my strength along with it.

"Your Highnesss?" Chimere grabs both of my hands, worry pinching her features. "What isss wrong? Ssshall I fetch a healer?"

I shake my head, a grin spreading across my face. I can *sense* her, just like I sense the toll I paid for the powerful magic I cast long, long ago.

"That is not necessary," I state, pulling out of her grip. "But I have business to attend."

Sleep peacefully, Princess Briar Rose. I am coming for you.

LOREN

So translucent she is nearly invisible, Briar Rose stands, searching for something frantically. That furrow in her brow is present as she scans the crowd, looking right through me. My heartbeat trips over itself.

She leans down, pressing her hand to the ground. "You are hurt," she says. "Are you dying? What can I do?"

There can be no other explanation than she is trying to communicate with Faerie itself. What is it saying to her?

"Please, tell me something. What can I do?"

Hearing her desperation, I have to will myself to stay put, to not aid her. Not that there is anything within my power to help her anyway. This, she has to do alone.

Jovan breaks free of his mother's grasp, running to Briar Rose and snatching her arm. "Rosie! You can do it. Don't give up."

Surprised, Briar Rose looks at him, her confusion apparent. "I can't understand you."

"Don't give up," he repeats, and their mother rushes to pull him back, chastising, "Darling, you must let her do this alone."

"But why?"

"Yes, why is that?" King Faustus adds. "She is clearly distressed. Why can't he encourage her?"

"While she is taking part in the Ascension, she will be unable to understand any of us," Evanthe informs them, gesturing that they should return to their places. "Her focus is to be solely on Faerie."

"But it's upsetting her!" Jovan tries to tug away from his mother. Somehow, she keeps an iron grip on his wrist.

"She must do this alone, Prince Jovan," Vivienne states firmly but not unkindly. "Have faith in her."

"I can't understand you," Briar Rose interrupts, taking half a step away from them. "I don't even know who you are."

Everyone falls silent. Jovan stills, and for a moment, I consider hugging him, but his mother is already wrapping her arms around his shoulders.

"Please," she begs, pressing the heels of her hands into her temples, "please tell me how to fix this."

As if in response, the sky darkens. There is a noiseless rumble under our feet. By the startled expressions, no one seems to know what to make of it, but Briar Rose turns toward the north, staring at something.

What do you see? We all strain to look at the forest, hoping to catch an inkling of what has drawn her attention.

"The splitting of the Courts…" She takes one step, then disappears completely.

No one moves. No one speaks. We watch, waiting to see where she will reappear.

Only she doesn't.

"She doesn't remember me," Jovan repeats over and over, lip quivering. His mother holds him, doing her best to keep a mask of calm that is starting to crack.

My aunt throws out orders like shooting arrows, quick and precise. Everyone is to look for Briar Rose, and share whatever clues they find. Groups, pairings, it doesn't matter how many are together as long as no one goes alone.

Toussaint joins me without a word. We head to where Briar Rose was last seen—everyone is starting there—and choose a path a little away from where others are looking.

"Wait!" Jovan sprints after us, his parents not too far behind him. "Let us come with you!"

We would move faster on our own, but we don't have a clear direction yet. "This could be dangerous," I tell his parents. Not what they want to hear, but they deserve the truth, especially if their young son wants to join the search.

"Then we have to help her!" Jovan argues. "We have to find her fast!"

His parents exchange looks. King Faustus states, "We cannot just sit by while Briar Rose is missing. At least let us help look in the nearby areas."

I give in. There is no way someone would be able to convince me to sit by.

Briar Rose didn't leave footprints, nothing for us to follow. Faerie did not reject her, but… then what went *wrong?*

We scour everything, even try tracking spells—it all comes to nothing. It is like Faerie stole her away for itself.

"I have not seen faeries work together like this in a long time."

Toussaint and I tense, turning toward where, using his tail, the Cheshire Cat hangs upside down from a branch just above our heads.

"Briar Rose would be pleased to see how much effort you're putting into finding her."

"Where is she?" Toussaint snaps, taking a few menacing steps toward the cat. "No games. If you want Faerie to have a chance at survival, we have to find her."

Even without brows, Cheshire somehow raises them. "Appealing to my sense of self-preservation? My, Toussaint, you do have a scrap of wisdom to you after all." He drops from the tree, landing on his paws. "I am not easily surprised, so I will give you this: if you walk far enough that way—" he points with his tail, "—you are sure to find something familiar."

"What is it?" I ask, but he is already gone.

Toussaint and I sprint in that direction, Briar Rose's family huffing behind us. Some curious faeries follow as well, dodging branches and hopping over bushes and protruding roots.

Please let us find her please let us find her please let us find her—

We stop short at the sight of a small lump on the ground. I fall to my knees, ignoring my burning lungs. Reverently, I pick up Briar

Rose's necklace, its cord cut cleanly. There is no blood nearby, no evidence of a struggle… no other sign of her.

"Loren…" Toussaint's quiet urging makes me look up. The other faeries have gone still—too still—eyes wide, all staring ahead.

We are on the border of Unseelie Lands. I can feel the press of it, like it is warring with Seelie in an attempt to seize more territory, trying to force its way in to devour our magic.

"What did you find?" King Faustus demands, pushing his way through the faeries. Jovan's small frame slips through faster, making it to my side before he does.

"No…" He touches the rose he made for his sister. "Where is she?"

I swallow the lump in my throat. "We'll find her." Gently, I put the necklace in his hands. "Will you hold onto this until we return with her?" I do not have the heart to outright tell him he cannot come. Being in Seelie is dangerous enough, but crossing into Unseelie territory is akin to embracing death.

Jovan might not fully understand it, but he senses that this is not the time to argue. He reaches up, tying the necklace around my neck. It doesn't quite sit as it should with the extra knot in the cord, but it brings comfort nevertheless. "I think you should keep it. It will help you find her."

I manage a "thank you" and squeeze his shoulder before standing. Aunt Vivienne moves toward me, everyone making way for her and Briar Rose's faerie guardians. Fauna walks with them, but Flora is nowhere to be seen. It's odd to see them separated—she must be searching elsewhere.

"I have to go after her," I tell my aunt.

She snatches my arm. "We have to discuss the consequences first."

CHAPTER THIRTY-EIGHT

THE UNSEELIE KING

*A*sra finds me just as I am leaving through the gates; I am grateful I do not have to search for her. The second she lands on my shoulder, I create a portal and step through before it is fully formed, sealing it behind me as soon as I can. I hear Chimere call something, but it goes unheeded. Margaux will deal with her if need be—I have more pressing matters to attend.

I let my magic lead us, the curse thrumming as it urges me along like pulling on a rope. From the way the landscape is softer colors than the ones by the castle, I piece together that we are near the edge of Unseelie territory.

A small cottage comes into view, worn down, with rotting wood bending the frame. It is certainly close to collapse, yet the curse excitedly brings me to it.

A faerie woman walks out of the cottage, the door in pieces on the ground. Her rose-petal eyes find mine, widening slightly. She quickly curtsies. "I am grateful for your speed, Your Highness. I was about to send word."

"You have done well, Flora. Where is she?"

Flora points, but the cottage has barely three rooms in its open layout. Where there might have once been a dining table or a bed or chairs, instead lies Princess Briar Rose beside a spinning wheel. Dried blood coats the tip of the spindle.

"How did you manage it?" I study Princess Briar Rose. She is splayed out how she fell, Flora obviously having not touched her. I see no tears or dirt on her pale green dress, which is slowly losing its color. The intricate details on it (clearly of faerie make) suggest to me that she was part of an important event when the curse befell her.

"It was not difficult, Sire." Flora steps around the princess's fallen form. "I sensed her moving through the trees, and I used a scent to attract her. She did not fight it, tried to pluck the rose I put on the spindle. It made her form corporeal once more."

I tear my eyes away from the princess. "She was... in the middle of her Ascension?" That adds up. Would it have been better to catch her before it started, or after? Not that the details are within my control. How far did it get?

Kneeling, I roll her toward me and brush the hair away from her face. Asra leans down, inspecting her. Later, I will find out what she sees, because while this is my magic I sense, there is something else to it, other than Evanthe's changes. Her features still seem human, although her lashes are longer, darker, and her hair is a richer shade of honey brown, with golden strands in it. My fingers hover over her lips, which are slightly parted, as if she were about to say something.

"Yes, Sire." Flora keeps her distance, but I can tell without looking up that she is awaiting orders.

"Return to the Seelie before they notice you are missing. Send word when they decide to come here searching for their princess." The scouts will probably already have warned me by then, but it is better to be overprepared.

"Are we..." She swallows, clasping her hands in front of her.

"Are Fauna and I not to return to Unseelie? We have done as you asked."

"You have," I agree, forcing my gaze away from the princess to look at Flora. Her frame is thinner than normal, but with each passing moment in Unseelie, her breaths grow deeper and the tension in her body melts away.

"We belong here, My King," she whispers. "With you. In our homeland your mother promised us."

With anyone else, I would have stood and made a show of power to ensure they did not forget to whom they were speaking. But with her, I do not even get up. She needs assurance, not fear. After some thought, I say, "You do belong here. I will give you a choice: return now, and be among your people, or help me ensure the victory of the Unseelie, and I will give both you and your sister prestige and land, more than what my mother ever offered you. You will want for nothing."

Flora is quiet for a few moments. "Will you help us try to find a way to restore the magic the In-Between took from us?"

"If there is a way, I will do what I can to make it happen."

With a ghost of a smile, she dips into a curtsy. "As you wish, Your Majesty." Flora takes her leave.

If I were to trust anyone other than Asra and Margaux, Flora and Fauna would be contenders. But the larger the circle of trust grows, the more likely one will stab you in the back. Mother found that out the hard way.

Carefully, I scoop Princess Briar Rose into my arms and make another portal. The magic shimmers and swirls, this time showing my bedchamber. No one else needs to see her or know where she is being kept.

Asra hops onto the bed as I settle the princess atop the blankets. Her arm dangles off the side, something catching the candlelight. I lift her arm: a carving of a fox is tied around her wrist. Snorting, I move her over slightly so that she lies comfortably on the bed. If my half-brother wants to be possessive, so be it. Possession does not equate to love.

There is a furrow between her brows, as if the princess is deep in thought. Asra slinks closer, sniffing, examining.

"What do you see?" I ask, closing the portal and leaving us in soft darkness, the only illumination the candles set on random places about the room. Most are just pools of wax, so I magic replacements, wicks sparking to flame.

Asra looks at me, bids me to come to her with a curl of her tail. Through melded minds, I witness the curse swaddling Princess Briar Rose in a shroud of black, threaded through with bits of sparkling silver—Evanthe's magic, how she altered the curse.

In the center of the princess's chest is a subtle glow, like the first rays of dawn peeking over the horizon. The darkness does not touch it; because it cannot or will not, I am unsure.

"Sire," Margaux calls from the door.

"Enter." I disconnect from Asra's mind and turn to face my Captain of the Guard.

She strides in and quickly bows. "Seelie have been spotted at the border. What are your orders?"

Careful, "Fox"—move too quickly, and you will seem desperate. "Send two groups of warriors, but tell them to wait out of sight. They are not to strike unless the Seelie enter our territory." After a moment, I add, "And they are not to kill Loren. When they find him, bring him directly to me." He is sure to play the role of valiant knight, come to rescue his love.

I briefly consider sending Margaux with them, but there is too much at stake to risk not having her nearby if I need protection. The Troll Queen will arrive soon, bringing that nuisance Odilon back with her, and if the Seelie are stupid enough to try to attack us directly, I will need every advantage here.

"It will be done as you command, My King." Margaux puts a hand to her heart and bows before taking her leave.

I cast a spell to lock the door. There is something I wish to do, and having someone barge in would agitate me, to say the least. "Asra, come here."

The wyvern stops toying with the princess's hair and immediately obeys, the edge of her wing brushing against my ear as she lands.

"The Seelie are contemplating entering our territory," I tell her, even though she already heard. "I believe we should pay them a quick visit."

Asra growls, tail coiling around my neck.

Creating two portals in a short amount of time has already drained me—one more will certainly have me sleeping for the next day or two while Unseelie replenishes my magic. I straighten my posture despite the fatigue weighing on me, and gather my remaining bits of magic to make one last portal for today. At least I will not have to step through; if I lose grip on the spell and it fails, it will not leave me stranded on the other side. I can handle passing out on the floor of my own bedchamber, even if Asra will give me grief for it.

While the portal is still forming, I hear bits of heated arguing. Perfect. A divided enemy is a weak enemy.

The closest Seelie Fae are standing about ten paces from the border. At first, no one notices us as I survey the scene before me: Vivienne and Loren bickering; the human king and queen waiting close by, a small boy with them that looks too much like the princess to not be related; curious busybodies by nature, the other faeries are gathering around, intently paying attention to the argument.

"She may not have *time!*" Loren exclaims.

"As much as I hate to agree with him," I interject, "time is definitely not on your side."

Attention darts to me. Toussaint moves toward Loren with quick, silent steps that could almost rival Margaux.

"What are you doing here?" Vivienne snaps. It takes a lot of willpower to not revel in her lost temper. Asra, however, hisses, wings flaring open, then snapping shut.

"I can do as I please within my lands," I counter, gesturing. "The portal is in Unseelie."

"What do you want?" Loren asks through gritted teeth, hands balled into fists at his sides. A rose pendant hangs about his neck by a thin cord, which I recall the princess wearing previously. Interesting. Perhaps they are truly bonding.

"A simple reminder is all," I tell them. "Step foot into Unseelie, and risk the consequences." My eyelids are heavy, but I force myself to remain alert. The portal flickers for a moment. *Keep control,* I can hear my mother snapping at me. My fingers twitch, feeling the memory of the bone switch rapping across my knuckles.

Vivienne raises her chin. "If you hold one of our own hostage, that is more than enough reason for us to storm your lands."

I smirk. "Princess Briar Rose entered Unseelie of her own accord. The curse is holding her hostage; I am simply keeping her safe."

Loren takes a step closer, then stops himself. "Where is she? If you harm her—"

I move to the side, gesturing with a dramatic flair. "You can see that she is unharmed. Awaiting for her True Love's Kiss to break the curse."

My half-brother flinches but remains in place. I can see in his eyes he is calculating how quick he would have to be to leap through the portal before I close it. If it closes when he is not all the way through, the consequences would range from losing an appendage or limb to instant death.

"You will release her from the curse if you do not want a war on your hands," Vivienne threatens openly, positioning herself beside Loren. She takes hold of his wrist, a silent command for him to not do anything rash.

"I have had war on my hands my entire life," I counter, "whether in threat or actuality. Faerie is coming to ruin, so let us finish this before it is too late and there is nothing left to save."

"I could not agree more," Vivienne replies, tone edged. "Bend the knee, and return what is rightfully Prince Loren's."

I bark a laugh. Asra digs her claws in to maintain balance, which gives me an extra jolt to stay awake. "What is rightfully his? My *younger* half-brother? Everything that you claim is his is rightfully *mine*, the first-born of King Oberon whether he admitted it or not." Loren flinches as if I struck him. I pause, only long enough to stop myself from analyzing the response. There is little time left for me to complete my plan before my magic is too drained to keep the portal open.

Stepping backward slowly, I situate myself beside Princess Briar Rose.

"You do not hold the right. Oberon cut his tie to your mother when she betrayed him by trying to take over Faerie for herself. Her actions nullified your birthright blessing."

"Even if my mother sinned," I argue, "does that mean I am responsible for the wages of it?"

They are tight-lipped, stricken silent.

I run a finger down the side of the princess's face.

"Get your hands off her!" bellows King Faustus, face reddening.

I raise my brows at him, surprised it took him this long to say something about his daughter. His wife and child stand behind him, holding one another but unable to look away from us. "If things had gone according to tradition," I say, lowering my voice, "you would have been handing her over to wed me instead of Loren." My thumb rests on her chin; I glance down at her lips.

"But she is not for you!" King Faustus storms forward, stopping abruptly at Vivienne's raised hand.

"Do not let him bait you," she warns.

I think it is far too late for that. "I will make you a deal." I drag my gaze away from her face. "If I can break the curse, she will be free to do whatever she pleases."

"Of course you can break the curse!" King Faustus shouts. "You're the one who cast it!"

Vivienne and Loren remain silent, pondering my choice of words.

With what I hope looks like a wicked grin, I lean down toward the sleeping princess.

"Tristan, don't!" Loren cries, daring to take another step toward the border. But I am already pressing a chaste kiss to her soft, warm lips. For a moment, I think she is going to respond; my heart skips a beat.

She does not stir.

"What a tale that would have made," I sigh, straightening, disregarding the twinge in my chest. "Breaking the very curse I cast."

They stare at me in a mixture of shock and relief. I half expect Loren to pass out.

Instead, he locks eyes with me.

"We shall see if you have better luck, Loren." With trembling hands, I close the portal and collapse on the bed. I barely have enough energy to crawl to the other side before unconsciousness claims me.

CHAPTER THIRTY-NINE

BRIAR ROSE

*T*he chill clings to me even when I wake. Dark, cold, desolate, there is no confusion as to where I am: the Unseelie King's dreamscape. The same castle hallway, the same silent prison he brought me to prior.

The curse...

The Unseelie King has still left me control to conjure as I wish. But I do not plan on staying. If I am stuck in this curse, asleep, I would much rather be in a dreamscape of my own making.

I reach out with my consciousness. There is something soft under my body—a bed?—and someone is talking.

"Tristan, don't!" *Loren.*

I try to leap back into my body, not caring how it jars me, but I slam into the side of the dreamscape, losing the connection as I stumble back onto the stone floor. Panic shoots through me, drives me to reach out to my senses once more.

Something is pressed to my lips. Someone is kissing me... and that does not feel like Loren. There is no tenderness, just a brief press of cool lips.

"What a tale that would have made," I hear the Unseelie King say. "Breaking the very curse I cast."

I want to cringe, to run away from him and find Loren. Why did I hear him, but he is not fighting to get to me? Or is he a prisoner? How did I end up with the Unseelie King?

Where did you lead me? I ask Faerie, in case it can still hear me. *I was trying to help you.*

"We shall see if you have better luck, Loren," the Unseelie King taunts. Seconds later, the bed shifts, and I imagine him trying to curl up beside me.

I throw myself back toward my body, hoping enough force will shatter whatever is keeping me here. The impact knocks me onto my back, stealing the breath from my lungs, stars bursting in my vision. My finger aches, the prick from the spindle pulsing just enough pain to be annoying.

I will not be stuck here.

Pushing myself back onto my feet, I walk as far out into the dreamscape as I can, removing castle walls and making open fields. The edge of the dreamscape does not leave me a lot of room, unless this one is shaped longer than it is wider, but the ones I have been in tend to be circular in nature, a bubble for your imagination to run wild. And the edge should not feel like a solid thing; it should feel like a hazy line, warning you that you are leaving the space.

This is an invisible wall, refusing to budge no matter how much magic I throw at it. I hit, cut, stab, push... no results.

Exasperated, I scream. It echoes, bouncing back at me and ricocheting, growing quieter and quieter each time it passes by, until it is a mere hoarse whisper.

Calmed down enough, I check my surroundings in the real world. I cannot open my eyes, but I hear soft breathing. The Unseelie King must be asleep next to me, guilt of what he's done somehow a stranger to him.

Panic seizes my chest and claws its way up my throat. When he wakes, I will be completely at his mercy. I do not think he is attracted to me—surely, he kissed me to get a rise out of Loren— but if he decides to do something to me, I cannot fight back.

I retreat, disconnecting from my senses and taking a step away from the barrier. Let fear bring me to my knees, then onto my side, my face pressed against the ground. Heaviness settles over me, pinning me there.

I promise, I will do everything in my power to find a way to break the curse and bring you back to me.

Please, Loren, I beg, *hurry.*

LOREN

My aunt refused to let anyone step foot in Unseelie. "We need a plan," she insisted. "If we attack without weighing the consequences, we could lose everything."

I knew better than to offer up an alternative: she would only reject it and forbid me from doing it. So I let her guards escort me and Toussaint back to my room for safekeeping. She probably guessed at my plan and thought to stop it.

She should really know better than to think we will wait patiently while so much is at stake.

As quietly as we can, Toussaint and I gather what we need from my room: cloaks, packs, and extra weapons for me (he has more than enough hidden on his person). Now it is just a matter of sneaking out without drawing suspicion. We have climbed up and over the side of our home before, slipping away before someone could catch onto what we were doing, but I am certain they will be waiting for us to do just that.

"Portal," Toussaint says in a hushed tone, barely audible so that the guards outside the door cannot hear it. I nod. It is the only option if we want to make it there in time. Since I have not been to Unseelie before, I will have to bring us just outside of the border. A large toll of magic, but necessary. We will have to ration our magic once we step foot in Unseelie—I doubt the land will replenish those it cannot claim as its own. I have heard tales of it feeding off of its people to keep Tristan powerful, and I would not be surprised.

Toussaint smacks my hand when I start to create the portal. He taps his chest. I shake my head. If he thinks he is going to sacrifice that much—

A knock interrupts our silent argument. "Prince Loren, may I come in?"

Hiding the bags and cloaks on the other side of my bed, I call, "You may."

Evanthe opens the door just enough to step inside, then closes it before the guards can sneak a peek. She is solemn, mouth pinched into a thin line. "Your aunt sent me to see if you would like to join us in planning battle tactics." Not giving me a chance to respond, her hands slide against one another, and a piece of paper appears between her fingers when she pulls them apart. "She would appreciate your input."

Maintain your anger, the note says. *Refuse the offer.*

I search her expression, but she remains neutral. Mustering up anger does not take much, given the circumstances. "You can tell her I decline," I reply hotly. "We need to take action now if we want to save Briar Rose."

"She will be most disappointed to hear that. You know she is doing what she believes is best for everyone." The words bleed and reform into new ones: *Be ready.*

This time when I meet her gaze, she gives me a single, decisive nod. I parrot her, my mind wheeling at the possibilities of what she could mean. Evanthe loves Briar Rose, would die for her—but is she actually choosing Briar Rose over the commands of her own Queen, whom she is sworn to obey?

"That is all we can really do, when it comes down to it," I state.

"Is this your final answer?" She keeps the paper hovered in midair, and extends her left hand, circling it. Light forms at her fingertips and follows the motion, growing bigger until it is as tall as I am. The portal opens, displaying the dark landscape of Unseelie.

It has been a long time since I have been there. This is as safe a place as I could think of. Be careful.

"Yes," I say, then mouth, "thank you."

Thank me by bringing her home. Evanthe makes the note disappear. "Very well. I will return later to see if your mind has changed." She impatiently nods toward the portal, and we nab our supplies and step through. The temperature drops drastically, feeling much more like the heart of winter than the beginning of autumn. Snowflakes fall slowly from the moody grey sky, leaving a light dusting over everything. I hold my hand out, letting one land on it, but instead of dissolving to nothing, it falls apart. Ash, not snow.

Evanthe shuts the portal, leaving us in strange territory.

"Welcome to Unseelie," Toussaint whispers.

CHAPTER FORTY

THE UNSEELIE KING

*A*sra chatters in my ear and nudges me until I wake, swatting near her. She growls.

"I am *awake*, you little monster."

She makes a noise that I assume means she is laughing at me, very proud of herself. I glower, which she ignores, hopping onto my chest.

"What do you want?" Being a self-sufficient wild creature, it is not often she bothers me for anything, and when she does, it is for attention or treats. The latter means getting out of bed, so I try petting her first. The wyvern ducks away from my hand, chattering more.

"Asra…" I groan, throwing an arm over my face. "I don't have treats, but I can get some later if you just let me sleep a little longer." My magic is almost replenished, but my insides ache from using so much in a short amount of time. A horrible feeling, and movement only agitates it. I'd much rather be hungover from faerie wine than be magic deficient.

Asra growls and tugs on my sleeve, demanding my full attention.

The King of the Unseelie, bartering with a tiny wyvern and *losing.* Hopefully, no one finds out.

"What do you—" I yank away, only to have my arm hit something solid, something other than the bed: Princess Briar Rose. Luckily, I hit her stomach and not her face, but regardless, she does not react. The curse will not allow her to.

Asra stares at me expectantly.

"You want me to check on her?"

She chirrups her confirmation.

"I highly doubt she will want to see me." *Not that I blame her.*

More staring.

I sigh, running my fingers through my hair. "Fine."

Asra curls up between our heads, eyes on the door. My locking spell is still intact from what I can tell, but it doesn't hurt to have a fiercely loyal wyvern watching over us. Depending on how much time has passed since I fell unconscious, Margaux will come to see me soon, walking right through the doors because of her ability to negate magic. That should not be an issue since she and Asra seem to be on decent terms, respecting each other from a distance, their common goal protecting me.

Closing my eyes, I slip into the dreamscape with barely any effort, leaving my aches and exhaustion behind. Instead of landing in the castle, there is a wide field with slowly wilting flowers that are turning brown. In the middle is the princess, lying on her side, back toward me. Unmoving.

I draw closer, trying to decide what to say. Or do. *Is she asleep?* That would not make sense, not in the dreamscape. No one can sleep here.

She stiffens; I halt. After a lengthy pause, she pushes herself to her feet and faces me, eyes red-rimmed. "You," she says accusingly through gritted teeth.

I say nothing, not even as she strides toward me. She has every right to be angry: if roles were reversed, I would be livid, planning not only my escape but also my revenge. *It is not personal,* I told her, and although that is true, that does not make it any better. It would not make me hate the person who did it to me any less.

But sometimes we are unfortunate victims of situations and plots and others' need to have what they want. My life is a perfect example.

She does not stop where I expect, instead charging right up to me until we are toe-to-toe. Then she slaps me, hard.

"You do not touch me without permission," she seethes. "You have taken enough from me. Do not kiss me, do not touch me, do not even look at me. Are we understood?"

It did not occur to me that she would have felt the kiss, which was purely to taunt Loren. I can safely bet she would not take that explanation well.

"I will not kiss you again, if that is what you are worried about."

Her scowl does not budge. "Why did you do it? To make Loren angry? What good would that do for you?"

Even in the dreamscape, she has the fox charm dangling from her wrist. Things between them definitely progressed quickly. "It is all a matter of tactics," I say, to which she rolls her eyes.

"You and your damn tactics."

For a split second, I am shocked by her word choice, but it quickly passes. "Sitting idly by and hoping everything will fall into place does nothing to change the fate of Faerie. Action is necessary —and oftentimes unpleasant."

She puts a little distance between us and crosses her arms. "You cannot tell me you are referring to the curse."

The fire in her eyes makes me choose my words more carefully. "Do you truly believe I took pleasure in cursing an infant?" I was young then, broken by my mother's demise and desperate to keep what she left behind. I didn't know what to do, just knew that I had to inspire the same fear she had. To keep the Unseelie from seeing the tears, I put on a mask of bitterness and hatred, cutting down any who stood in my way. To hide the way my knees shook when all eyes were on me, I spent extra magic to make my Glamour appear as darkness, most times in the form of wolves or large beasts. It was easier to cut down the disloyal that way, to set the beasts upon them until they were nothing but shreds my magic left behind.

It only took the once to snuff out the heart of the growing rebellion. I further proved I was as ruthless as my mother the day I cast the curse on Briar Rose, solidifying my place as King.

The princess studies me, scowl easing into something akin to puzzlement. Then resolve. "Release me of the curse."

"I just told you that I do things *tactically*. Why do you believe I would suddenly release you?"

"Because you do not actually want to cause me harm." She lifts her chin. "I think I am little more to you than a means to an end. You want Faerie restored, and keeping me here, under the curse, is only splitting the Courts farther apart."

I almost smile—the way she debates brings a flicker of excitement. But then I realize why, that her intensity reminds me of my mother, and that douses the feeling. "For the time being," I relent. "But Loren will do anything to get you back, forcing a final battle to end this feud."

"If you wanted a fight, then why not attack?"

I raise a brow. "Why would I leave them with the advantage of knowing the battlefield, of being where their supplies and defenses are?"

She breaks eye contact for a few seconds, and chews the inside of her cheek. For how much humans seem to love war, it is interesting to me that her father, a king who certainly has had to fight to maintain his crown, has taught her little to nothing about it. My mother started my lessons from the moment I could respond in full sentences.

"There has to be another way other than bloodshed." She genuinely believes it—she would not last long in the Unseelie Court if she were to live here. If for some reason she does agree to become my Queen, I will have to be extra careful to protect her, or else my subjects will take advantage of her soft heart, tear it out of her chest and leave her to bleed out.

"I told you the conditions under which I would undo the curse.

It would be no simple task to undertake, and I would make it worth my while instead of signing over the fate of Faerie."

Frost covers the dreamscape as her mood sours further. "You think you are the only solution to saving Faerie. Can you not open your mind and consider that there may be another way?"

"The split of the Courts happened when our father cast out my mother and replaced her. To return things as they should be, I have to take the crown and rule as my birthright dictates. Faerie is about balance and tradition." I can almost hear my mother's voice, telling me the story over and over, demanding I repeat it twice daily, once upon waking and once before falling asleep. What is it about Briar Rose that constantly drags up my mother's ghost from the grave?

"You assume you know everything—"

"As I have said before, you are but a pawn in a game you do not fully understand."

The scowl returns, this time more fearsome. "During the Ascension, Faerie was trying to get me to help restore it. There is something wrong, and it wanted me to fix it."

Flora was correct about her beginning the Ascension. Interesting, that the curse was strong enough to rip her away from its pull before she could complete it. With a little help from Flora's magic, of course. I might have had to change strategy if she had become fully Fae before the curse began. Mother mentioned her Ascension a few times, briefly, when she was deep in her cups and feeling nostalgic. She spoke of Faerie talking to her, not in direct words, but rather in emotions and urges. "What did it tell you to do?"

Her expression falls. She shifts from foot to foot. "I... I don't know. I couldn't understand it. Faerie just gave me feelings, like it was trying to lead me somewhere." With a sigh, she shakes her head. "And it somehow brought me *here*."

Not the worst place to be, but I would not take well to being locked in a dreamscape either. "You know how to end this," I remind her.

Her knuckles turn white as she clenches her fists. "Get. Out."

I start to walk away from her, saying over my shoulder, "Call for me if you change your mind about my proposal." *I doubt she will be thinking about much else.*

"I will find another way!" she shouts as I return to my body. The words rattle in my brain, and I look over at her sleeping form, Asra curled up beside her head.

"If you do," I state quietly, "I will be impressed."

CHAPTER FORTY-ONE

LOREN

*W*e shiver as we make our way through the grey landscape. I flex my stiff fingers and rub them together, breathing white wispy air into cupped hands. At least we had the foresight to put our boots back on after the faerie dances, or else my toes might have broken off by now, especially after I stubbed my big toe on a rock I am certain was not present before I took that step.

Keeping low and weaving through the sparse trees has us constantly scanning our surroundings. There is very little noise in Unseelie, and no life that we have seen yet. We thought we might find someone in a ramshackle cottage close to the border, hoping to question them for information on the whereabouts of the castle, but there was no one there, only a spinning wheel with a bit of dried blood on the spindle.

It was one thing to know the curse started, but another to see evidence of it. I wanted to walk away, to press on, but instead I stared, unable to move, unable to look away. *But where is she?* I wanted to yell. *Why is this here while she is nowhere to be found?*

Slowly, I reached out, but Toussaint caught my wrist and led me back outside, away from it all.

Yet it still sticks with me, regardless of how far our feet take us away from it.

I try to keep my mind on the present, on what is in front of us, but that is almost as miserable. Where Seelie constantly supplies us with magic, I can sense Unseelie slowly siphoning from us. So, no matter how my fingers and ears turn numb, it is not worth it to risk a heating spell.

Toussaint and I ration our words as well, too afraid of hidden things that could be listening. Luckily there is not much to say; we keep moving forward, away from Seelie, and hope we can catch sight of the castle, where Tristan is sure to be keeping Briar Rose.

We will find her, and True Love's Kiss will break the curse. I will not let myself consider another alternative. Although I see Tristan kissing Briar Rose over and over, her unable to stop him—

Hold on, Briar Rose. We are coming for you. Like one of the stories she loved to hear about knights coming to the princess's rescue. The tales do not mention anxiety and freezing temperatures and fatigue… They really should.

Dropping his pack, Toussaint gestures for me to wait near one of the sturdier, taller trees. He scales it with some difficulty. Most of the branches are broken or close to, exposing bright red bark underneath, the only source of color so far.

I survey the area, noticing only trees and ash-covered ground. My almost-numb fingers run over the surface of the whittled rose about my neck as I wait for Toussaint. *How did things go from perfect to terrible in a matter of moments?* Briar Rose asked me if I loved her, and I did not want to pressure her into saying it back, but there is a small part of me that worries about it for the sake of True Love's Kiss. It should work without her saying the words… It should be about the heart, since a human could speak the words and not mean them. Not that I believe Briar Rose would do that.

I am drawn out of my thoughts when I hear the whistle of a sword arcing toward me.

THE UNSEELIE KING

Leaving Asra behind to watch over Princess Briar Rose, I exit my bedchamber just as Margaux is walking toward them. She looks me over—the only way I can tell is that the light shifts in her completely white eyes.

"How long?" I ask.

She knows what I mean. "Two days, Sire. The Troll Queen has yet to arrive, but the dwarves and Chimere's clan had to retreat and seek shelter here yesterday."

Good. That, I can handle. If she had arrived while I was unconscious, she would have assumed I was insulting her by making her wait, and she would have started giving orders and making changes.

"Have they been situated?"

"I had servants prepare a few rooms in the west wing of the castle for them to stay in. Some are in the healer's quarters being tended to." She then adds, quieter, "The leader wishes to speak with you, as does Chimere."

Why am I not surprised? "Take me to the dwarven leader."

Margaux leads me through back hallways to avoid most everyone, and I could sing her praises for it. My insides still ache—I would spend the next few days in bed if I could get away with it, but there is too much to do. I have missed enough.

"Rumor spread that the curse has begun," Margaux informs me. "Almost all are volunteering to cross the Seelie border and attack, starving for bloodshed."

"The Seelie will come to us," I reply. "They have no other option if they want to save the human princess."

The back hallway leads into one of the main ones, and we stop in front of a guest room. I knock.

The leader answers the door shirtless, shoulder bandaged and arm in a sling. Behind him, a woman and three children hurry to stand and bow. One of the smaller rooms, it has more than enough to suit their needs with beds and a table and even a bath. Margaux was wise to put them here, considering the Troll Queen will demand a room almost as big and luxurious as my mother's. I allow no one to use hers, especially not the Troll Queen.

"Glad you could stop by to speak with me," the leader says, stepping back. "Let me get a shirt——"

"We can speak here." I turn to Margaux, telling her, "Thank Chimere for her patience and tell her I will visit her shortly."

"This is not talk for children's ears," the leader insists.

The statement strikes me as odd. "What we are discussing will affect their future."

"They have enough trauma to sort through." The dwarf grunts and tosses the shirt aside. "Mava, why don't you and the girls go to Barma's room, give us some privacy."

Without a word, Mava urges her girls past us, all three of them keeping their heads down.

"Hurry inside, lad."

No one has called me that before, but it doesn't seem to be said in a patronizing way, so I step inside so he can close the door.

"I'd offer for you to sit, but..." He gestures to the room. "Not meant for sitting."

"I do not intend to be here long."

Another grunt. "Well, I suppose we should get down to it. You've more than upheld your end of the bargain, and I... want to thank you for it."

He looks away, and I resist the urge to fidget. "Thanks are not necessary."

"I give them regardless. We'd've been slaughtered without your help." Clearing his throat, he looks me in the eye again. "It seems you're preparing for something, perhaps a battle of your own. If there is some way we can help, we are at your service." Sheepishly, he shrugs his uninjured shoulder. "Well, best as we can, that is."

Perfect. Indebted loyalty is the best kind. "I will have Margaux let you know."

"Very good." After another awkward pause, he says, "I suppose you should know my name is Thaddeus. You've earned that much."

Why would you put this on me? The expectation of giving someone a name in return is a burden I hate to carry. So instead of giving it, I say, "I am glad for our strong alliance, Thaddeus. I hope you recover quickly."

Fortunately, he lets me end the conversation there and leave. Odd, I would have thought he wanted to go into detail about what happened, considering he sent his family out of the room. Maybe it had more to do with pride than protecting them.

I barely make it a few steps down the hall before Chimere finds me.

"Sssire," she greets with a low curtsy. The bodice of her dress is tight and low-cut. I keep my gaze on her face, noting a flicker of disappointment. She recovers swiftly, maintaining a smile. "It is good to sssee you on your feet again. I worried after our lassst parting."

"I had business to attend," I say dismissively. Then, mentally chastising myself for pushing her away too hard, I add, "How is your clan? Has everyone settled in?"

Chimere brightens at this. "They are, thank you. You sssaved them, and I will be forever grateful for it."

"I did what was agreed upon in our contract."

She tilts her head, her smile turning teasing. "Come now, you know you did more than what wasss expected of you."

Flirtatious was probably what she was going for, putting me at ease, but it makes my skin crawl. "I have matters to attend to in the throne room. Will you accompany me?" The balance of keeping her happy but also at a distance is tiresome, to say the least. A game I must play if I want to win.

She takes my offered arm. "I would be delighted, Your Highnesss."

CHAPTER FORTY-TWO

LOREN

I duck, rolling out of the way and onto my feet to face the attacker. He is dressed in all black and hooded, jagged sword ready to swipe at me again. I sidestep his thrust and slam the heel of my palm up into his elbow, forcing it to hyperextend in the wrong direction. A cracking sound—he loses grip on his weapon, which hits the ground heavily. I snatch it and block the next attacker just in time: the axe blade is much closer to my face than I would like. The impact jars through my stiff hands and up my arms.

I manage to shove him backward and knock the first one unconscious with the pommel of the sword. Out of the corner of my eye, I see Toussaint scramble down the tree and leap onto another intruder, slitting his throat before he knows what is happening to him. Dark blood spurts onto the ash, smothering it, but Toussaint is already after the others, a dealer of death with each precise, calculated movement, fluidly transitioning as if it is as easy to him as breathing.

The double-bladed axe is swung again, and I dodge it, dancing my way behind the attacker. A quick slice at the backs of his knees, and he crumbles, knocking one of his allies to the ground.

Seven down, three more to go, unless there are others in hiding.

Two more.

We each take one, pressing the offensive to finish the fight before it attracts attention. A flurry of attacks to disorient and increase anxiety—

I let out a strangled cry and fall to my hands and knees, pain like fire shooting through my calf, jarring the bone. The enemy stands over me, raising his sword—

—and falls flat on his back, a throwing knife sticking out of his eye.

Toussaint makes quick work of the one who stabbed my leg. It is a mercy, really, to have your throat slit instead of waiting to bleed out from the backs of your legs being cut.

He stabs all of them, making sure they are dead. No witnesses. Then he returns to me as I grit my teeth and tug on the knife. White-hot pain makes me release it, my hands slick with blood.

"Let me." Toussaint hands me his belt to bite. "One, two—" He yanks it out before I am ready. I stifle a scream as best I can, teeth clamping down onto the belt.

"Just one moment," he says soothingly, hands quickly covering the wound. The scent of cinnamon cuts through the air, and my leg grows warm.

Spitting out the belt, I snap in a hoarse voice, "No magic."

Toussaint does not remove his hands, does not let me tug away from him. "We do not know how far the castle is, and walking will be painful."

"We don't have much of a choice." I stagger onto my feet, leaning heavily against a tree. My leg trembles, ready to give out.

"No, we don't," he retorts, covering my injury again. This time I don't fight him as his magic seeps into my skin, knitting the flesh back together. I send some of my own too, so he doesn't use as much. Toussaint throws me a look but says nothing.

When my leg is healed, we take the Unseelie clothes and flee the scene.

BRIAR ROSE

I keep expecting the Unseelie King to send creatures after me, to haunt me with nightmarish visions. There is nothing to do, nothing to fight. I just pace and sit and *wait.*

When I wait, my thoughts plague me. How could Faerie betray me like this, trick me to prick my finger on the spindle and start the curse? Or was it not Faerie, but the curse leading me astray? Is that why I could not understand what Faerie wants me to do? Too many questions, too few answers.

Every so often I check my body, listening for clues my surroundings might give. My sense of smell does me no good, since the room I am in smells of candles. But I can hear something breathing quietly beside me, can feel that whatever is on the bed is small, not making the mattress sink. Whatever it is, it keeps to itself. From what I can tell, I have no injuries other than the persistent throbbing of my index finger, which should not hurt nearly as much as it does. It should not be considered an injury at all, really, except I am not sure what else to call it since it is the reason I am stuck in the Unseelie King's dreamscape.

Arguing with him yesterday—or whenever that was—did not go well at all. I let my emotions get the better of me, so of course the Unseelie King would not be willing to hear me out.

Tristan.

Perhaps I should be more civil, and that would mean referring to him by his name instead of his title. Less easy to demonize him that way, and more likely to have him see that I can be someone to talk compromises with. In my lessons, Evanthe said multiple times that rulers often have to put their grievances aside, and I have seen my parents do that plenty of times when hoping to reach an agreement or alliance. I imagine the first alliance between the humans and faeries did not go smoothly either.

From what I can remember, I reform the castle the Un—*Tristan* —had before, with its dim candlelight and looming halls. Then I brighten the room a bit because who truly wants to be in such darkness?

I add vases of flowers as I walk down the hall, and beautiful stained glass windows for sunlight to peek through and cast colorful mosaics on the floor. The wilting flowers outside straighten, their petals brightening and reaching up toward the sky.

The throne room is next. I leave out the In-Between that was taking over, replacing it with comfortable chairs and a table with tea and raspberry tarts. They will have no taste unless I conjure one—I could make it however I like. So I make it taste like it should, curling up in one of the chairs while I wait for… Tristan… to appear.

And I eat one of the raspberry tarts.

I DON'T KNOW how to judge the passing of time in the dreamscape, but it feels like an eternity before the Unseelie King finally arrives.

Tristan, his name is Tristan.

He moves silently through the hallways, my only indicator of his presence the chill he brings with him. All in black, as usual, but there is something off about the way he walks. Or maybe it's the way his shoulders are slightly hunched. If I knew him better, I'd be able to figure it out.

Pausing, he takes a second to survey what I have conjured. I gesture toward the empty seat. Curiosity lights his pale blue eyes; he settles into the chair opposite of mine and takes a raspberry tart, holding it up to inspect it. "I must admit, I did not come here expecting a tea party."

"You expected more yelling, I imagine." There is a small part of me that wonders if I should apologize, but I decide that I will most certainly not apologize for my feelings.

"You are within your right to be angry," he answers carefully, still eyeing the tart.

"It isn't poisoned if that is what you are worried about."

He smirks. "The only way you could kill someone in the dream-scape is by killing them in the real world while their soul is here."

I know this, but I keep it to myself. Better to let him underesti-mate me. Doubtful that he will let anything of use slip, but my chances might be better if he thinks I know little to nothing.

He eats the tart slowly. "Raspberry. Loren's favorite."

I tilt my head to the side, open my mouth to form the question—

"I do know my little brother better than most think I do. Knowing your enemy is imperative to victory." His gaze bores into me like he is calculating something, and my answer will help him solve it.

"Does Loren have to be your enemy? I think he would much prefer if you could be real brothers and allies, Tristan."

At the sound of his name, Tristan flinches, smirk faltering. I note the odd reaction and decide to continue on as if I didn't.

"I think it would be ideal to come to a mutually beneficial agree-ment that saves Faerie," I state, pouring myself some tea to keep my hands busy, so he will not notice them tremble.

"I gave you an offer."

"And I rejected it."

His expression is too sharp to be neutral, but not quite a glare. "You have nothing else to bargain with, Princess. Faerie is very different than your human lands."

"As a future Queen of Faerie, I think I have more bargaining power than you give me credit for."

Tristan stares at me. "You will not become Queen if you are not released from the curse."

I shrug, hoping it comes across as nonchalant. "Either Loren will find his way to me and break the curse, or you will release me. Both of you are offering to make me Queen instead of finding another human princess."

A muscle in his jaw tics. The agreement between the Fae and

our kingdom was sealed with Faerie's blessing—finding a princess from another kingdom will not suffice, will not bring power to the land. Since he is so set on Faerie following tradition, he would be loath to break it.

"You already have your two choices," he says, tone carefully even, balancing his temper. "Unless you are trying to get me to offer you more for your cooperation." He props his elbow on the arm of the chair, resting his temple against his knuckles. "If so, I admire your tact. What could I offer to sway you? I doubt riches or material goods would interest you. I already gave my word that your loved ones would not be harmed unless they try to harm me or my people."

"I am not—"

"Or is it that you are falling for my half-brother?" There is a glint to his eyes as he persists despite my interruption. "Unfortunately, I will have to draw the line there: I cannot have your affections so blatantly elsewhere if you are to be married to me. A matter of appearances, I assure you. For you, I have no f—"

I startle as he chokes on his words, surprise lighting his face. *He was about to lie,* I realize. *What was he about to say?*

Tristan rapidly recovers. "It would not be a marriage of love, but of convenience. However, it would weaken our authority if we are not seen united."

"You are acting as though I have no other choice—"

"Because it seems you do have no other choice," he hurls my words back at me, leaning forward. I am grateful for the table between us. "You have a soft heart, and I do not believe you would be so stubborn as to watch as Faerie and all those you love are destroyed by the In-Between."

The temperature plummets; frost forms over the food, the table, the chairs, and my tea solidifies into ice. Each breath is like inhaling icicles that scratch their way down my throat and into my lungs.

"Stop doing that," I demand, although my shivering undermines my tone. I resist the urge to cough.

"Stop doing what?"

"Making it cold," I snap, gesturing to the obvious drastic change.

He raises a brow. "I am not doing that. You are."

"…What?" It does not make sense, yet he cannot outright lie.

"You are creating the cold because of your emotions." He glances around, then amends, "Although some of it might be playing off of my magic."

"But the dreamscape is yours."

"It is both of ours. My magic has been connected to you since I first cast the curse."

"So…. none of the dreamscapes have been solely mine?" I recall hints of a chill whenever I have been in the dreamscape, nothing too obvious, just bits in the background, ever-present.

He waits silently as I test the theory, taking the teacup into my hands. The tea melts back into a liquid with a mere thought. Frost disappears. I meet his gaze, now pensive, with a hint of… a softer, rawer emotion I can't quite place.

"I cannot shut you out any more than you can me," he admits, voice solemn, barely above a whisper. "As long as the curse endures, so will our bond."

CHAPTER FORTY-THREE

THE UNSEELIE KING

I avoid seeing Briar Rose the next day. And the day after, only checking to see that nothing has changed and that Asra still adamantly wants to stay by her side to watch over her sleeping form.

I was caught in a lie that I didn't even know was one until it stuck in my throat. It plagues the back of my mind as I go about my kingly duties:

How did I become fond of her?

Truly, if we did marry, it would not be for love—would never be for love. But perhaps a certain level of friendship... or at least toler-ability.

She knows my name. Loren must have told her. A shock to be sure, but it was not completely horrible hearing her say it.

Over those few days, I make sure to spend some time with Chimere and Thaddeus. Margaux has given the clans weapons, armor, and, if they are well enough, fighting lessons in the training yard. The dwarves are especially eager to take the opportunity to wallop some of our soldiers in sparring matches.

His wife has forbidden him from joining until his shoulder heals, so Thaddeus is often found in the great hall, drinking and telling stories to anyone who will listen. Whenever he catches sight of me, he insists I join him. Which is fine by me, since it limits alone time with Chimere, who is constantly found by my side.

I take a seat next to him at one of the long tables, and Chimere settles beside me. "What is the legend about tonight? Shifters? Pixies? Merfolk?" If I were pressed to admit it, he does spin quite the story, spellbinding his audience. Last time, he tried explaining about werewolves, which, according to him, are different than wolf shifters, but I find that about as likely as the vampire creatures he spoke of living anywhere near Faerie. We would not allow it.

What little I can see of his cheeks above his bushy beard is flushed pinkish red. With a bright smile, he claps me on the back; I grimace. He seems not to notice as he says, "Well now, I thought perhaps the mighty Unseelie King could tell us one of his tales."

I am acutely aware of the plethora of eyes on me, both from our table and from others who have realized I am present, craning their necks to see me and hear my response. "I have no tales to tell."

"Nonsense! A man who has accomplished so much in such a short lifespan certainly has tales worth hearing."

Accomplished so much? My mother founded the Unseelie and paid her life to keep it safe. I have only maintained it—my greatest "accomplishment" is cursing a human princess when she was an infant. All to keep what my mother created from crumbling into ash.

Chimere places a gentle hand on my shoulder. "Come now, Thaddeusss, he sssought you out for one of your ssstoriesss, insss-sissssted we ssskip our walk to hear one. Indulge usss."

While there is no edge to her tone, I inwardly flinch.

The dwarf raises a bushy brow, then takes a long pull of his tankard. "Very well, I've got just the one. About a unicorn."

Chimere leans into me, her cheek nearly brushing against mine.

She smells of winterberry, not inherently unpleasant, but too strong with her proximity. "Thisss isss one of my favorite ssstoriesss he tellsss."

Idle chatter quiets as Thaddeus clears his throat and takes on his deeper storyteller voice. "A few hundred years ago, unicorns roamed the earth in greater numbers, not such a rare thing to behold, but a sign of good fortune, nonetheless. They were considered beasts of the gods, revered by all.

"One of the human kings fell deathly ill, so his son took it upon himself to find a cure. The prince had heard tales of unicorns blessing those they deem worthy, in some cases even healing them. So he set out in hopes of finding one." Thaddeus pauses to wet his lips and accept a plate of meats and bread from a fire nymph going around to refill drinks. He takes his time with a slice of meat, and I consider hurrying him up, but he continues, "Now, the issue was not finding one, but finding one willing to speak with him, so he sought the help of the Fae."

Wisely, Thaddeus does not mention that this was before the splitting of the Courts, but the tension in the room says it does not go unnoticed. If it was a few hundred years ago, it was before my parents' time and the chaos they left in their wake.

"The faeries told him that unicorns are as varied as any creature or person, that different things will attract or repulse them based on which unicorn he encounters. In exchange for a few of his sweeter dreams and a small vial of his blood, the faeries told him that he would have the most luck finding the unicorn as white as snow that was often found near a waterfall just outside of Faerie lands. For she was one of the more curious of her kind, and her soft heart would most likely respond to his plight."

A few faeries jeer at this part, claiming they would have asked for far more than a few dreams and a vial of blood.

Thaddeus ignores them. "What they did not give him was directions, and they disappeared before he could ask for them. Granted, the prince did not know what else he would have to pay for the information, so he set out on his own, following the border of Faerie for a month until he found the waterfall, and waiting two days before he finally caught sight of the unicorn.

"She was as white as the snow they described, her coat even having hints of sparkle in the sunlight, her eyes pale like ice. When she saw him, she kept her distance, but did not run away.

"'Please,' the prince begged, kneeling before her, 'my father is ill, and I wish to find a way to cure him. Will you help me?'

"The unicorn stared at him for a long time, studying him intently. Then she stepped forward, touching the tip of her horn to his forehead. He got the sense that he should stay put, even as she fled into the woods—he was certain she would return."

I have never heard this room so quiet. If only I could so easily command the attention of the Unseelie with mere words.

"He waited all day and night for the unicorn, but there was no sign of her. Finally, at mid-morning, a pale woman with white hair flowing to her ankles approached him.

"'I will give you the blessing you seek,' said the woman. 'Take me to your kingdom.'

"The woman explained that she had the help of a witch to turn her into a human, for her unicorn form would not allow her to leave the wildlands to be in civilization. She told him the transformation would last for a few months, long enough to heal his father and return to her homeland.

"As they traveled together, they spoke of all manner of things, from families to dreams to deepest desires. And, as does often happen, they fell in love before they reached his kingdom.

"The people praised the unicorn for what she was, and the prince for bringing her to their kingdom, giving them good fortune. Many voiced their desire for her to become their prince's bride, and eventually their queen. The unicorn knew she could not stay, for her human form would not last, but her heart yearned for the prince all the same.

"'I must heal your father and leave quickly,' she told him. 'Perhaps I can find a way to be with you again, but if I do not return home before I transform back, my heart will slow its beat until it stops completely. My kind is not meant to be here.'

"The prince brought her to his bedridden father. The unicorn pressed her lips to his forehead, whispering, 'For the sake of my beloved, you will live in good health, long enough to see your grandchildren's children come into the world.'

"The king's ashen complexion instantly gained a healthy color, his eyes brighter than anyone had seen in years. He wept, getting out of bed to kneel before the unicorn. 'Please,' he insisted, 'consider marrying my son, if he is truly your beloved. Or if there is something else your heart longs for, you have only to name it.'

"'Your son will always be my beloved,' she told him, 'but I must leave. If there is a way for me to live here without risking my life, I will find it and return.'

"The prince convinced her to stay one more night, but when the sun rose the next morning, she was gone, leaving a note behind asking him to wait for her. So he waited, but neither saw nor heard from her for a year.

"Then, one day, a human infant was brought by a witch, who refused to hand the child over to anyone except the prince. 'Take care of your child. Your beloved is seeking a way to be with you, and will sorely miss both of you until that time comes.'

"The prince raised his daughter with all of the love and care. It was discovered when she was young that she possessed her mother's healing talent, using it as often as she could. She became known as the People's Princess, loved by all, suitors flocking from far lands for a chance to win her hand. She eventually wed, passing her gift down to her children, who in turn passed them down to their children.

"And, just as the unicorn said, the king lived to see his grandchildren's children before he passed on. The prince became the new king, but he only lived a few more years, his heart too full of longing for his beloved, no longer able to sustain him. His daughter tried time and again to heal him, but how does one use magic to heal a broken heart?"

Thaddeus pauses here to take another drink, leaving me to ponder if that was the source of my mother's ongoing agony: a broken, rejected heart. But my father did not wait for her—he was nothing like the prince in this story.

That is all this is, I remind myself, *just a story.*

Yet when Thaddeus continues, he has my full attention once more. "The new king eventually passed on his crown, saying his goodbyes and telling his daughter that his final wish was to see his beloved one last time. Despite their pleas, he left, walking into the forest alone.

"Now, there are a few different versions of the ending…"

"Tell it right," Chimere warns him. "The ssstory dessservesss it, whether it isss true or not."

Thaddeus nods solemnly. "The prince returned to the forest, traveling alone, just as he wanted to. It took him months to find the witch so he could get one of the potions, and then to reach the waterfall, where he sat and waited for his unicorn. As if she knew he was coming, the unicorn appeared, gladly taking the potion from him so she could take on her human form.

"'She told me you were waiting for me,' the unicorn cried as she held him. 'I am so sorry, my love, that I have not found a way for us to be together.'

"'Be with me now' was all he said. And so, they spent his final days wrapped in each other's arms."

"Could she not heal him?" I find myself asking.

"What magic can fix a broken heart?" Thaddeus repeats. "But their legend lives on, or so it is said: there are royals that carry that healing magic, although it does not appear often."

Just a story… That is what I think, but it doesn't quite sit right with me. How many humans have come to believe that we Fae are just a story, reduced to mere myths to inspire terrified obedience in reckless children and wonder in those who want more out of their mundane lives?

Could this story have a kernel of truth?

A screech catches my attention; Chimere pulls away from me just as Asra lands on that shoulder, flapping her wings near Chimere's face before tucking them neatly against her sides.

She was intent on watching Briar Rose… what could have possibly—

Margaux's sudden entrance explains it all: projecting clearly for all to hear, she declares, "The Troll Queen has arrived."

CHAPTER FORTY-FOUR

LOREN

*A*s day passes into night—the only indicator being the charcoal grey darkening to a nearly sightless black—we press on through the first, and the second, but by the third, it feels as though Unseelie is not only trying to drain our magic, but is also trying to suck us down into the earth. I would not be entirely surprised if the ground beneath our feet opened up to swallow us into a crude grave.

"We should stop and rest," Toussaint suggests in a hushed voice. "We cannot keep going this way."

From his high perch the day before, when we were attacked, he had been up there long enough to see the castle in the distance—so far a distance, he claimed humans probably would not have noticed it. And in our current state, that could take days to reach.

Hunger gnaws at my stomach; my insides ache almost as much as my legs and feet. Little grows in Unseelie, and what does, we are wary of eating. But the rations in our packs are running low, so we may have no other choice.

Under the bent frame of a gnarled tree, we sit, hoping the sparse shrubs and rocks will be enough to shield us from predatory sight. The dark clothing we pilfered has helped, especially since I can cover my red hair with the hood of my cloak. Too bright a color for Unseelie.

After a meager meal of stale bread and a little water, Toussaint says, "I'll take first watch."

I look at him, but his focus is elsewhere, constantly scanning the area from under heavy-lidded eyes. No matter how much I drained of my magic to heal my leg, I know he used just as much, if not more. "You sleep first, otherwise you'll be tempted to take both watches," I counter.

He snorts lightly, his dry, cracked lips twitching not enough to be considered a smirk.

"Sleep," I persist, nudging his shoulder with mine.

It takes a little bit of pondering before he finally caves. "Just for a few hours." He leans back against the tree, eyes instantly slipping closed, hands resting near the hilts of the weapons on his belt: a sword and some throwing knives.

I sit up, propping my elbows on my knees as I force myself to remain alert. For a few hours, I can do this for Toussaint. We will regain a little strength, and we will make it to the castle so we can save Briar Rose. Or, I can. With True Love's Kiss.

What if I am not her True Love? I bat the thought away, tracing the outer edge of the rose Jovan made. There is no room for doubt. I promised her I would do everything in my power to break the curse and bring her back to me, and I will. I would even if all of Faerie didn't depend on it.

THE UNSEELIE KING

Everyone scrambles to their positions as I make my way to the castle entrance, Margaux half a step behind me, Chimere trying to keep up. Asra digs her claws into my shoulder, head dipped low, tail lashing around my neck.

Silently, I am praying that the visit is as quick and painless as possible.

Crisp, sharp winds meet us the moment we step outside the doors. I stop at the top of the stairs, noting that the caravan has made it to the gate. Originally, she demanded that I meet her there instead, but I am a king in my own right, not a dog to come running when she whistles. If my mother had not made a deal with her... well, the Unseelie would no longer exist, at least not in the same capacity as it does now.

The enclosed black carriage is pulled through the gate by reanimated horse skeletons. I wonder whose magic she stole to pull that off, and how long it will last. Trolls, their frames bulky and tall, stride behind the carriage on their own legs, carrying their weapons as if they suspect we will have any ideas about refusing to pay our end of the bargain. Four large wagons full of treasures bring up the rear of the party; my Unseelie watch those with greedy intensity, but none of them will dare try anything. The Troll Queen would take whatever is left of the thieves after I was done punishing them.

I wait as one of the smaller trolls scrambles to open the door of the carriage. Chimere tries to step beside me, but Asra hisses at her, making her move back. Then the little wyvern resumes her glowering in the direction of our guests.

The carriage tilts to one side as the Troll Queen makes her grand exit, the hem of her scarlet silk gown slipping down onto the ash-covered ground. Like Chimere, her dress is low-cut, and the glowing ruby stone hanging from the gold chain about her neck is almost nestled between her breasts. Tall, lithe, fair, she could pass as one of the Fae... that is, until the magic in the ruby is drained. Either she slew someone for such magic, or an expensive bargain was struck.

The ground beneath her feet trembles with each step, hinting at her true form. But I would know her no matter the form, for she always bears the same scowl, strides with the same pretentious gait, and her eyes… they are always the same never-ending black so deep it feels like they will swallow you whole. I wonder if that is what first drew my mother to her.

Her entourage follows behind, guards at her sides and back, Odilon and the other Unseelie I sent to escort her bringing up the rear. The trolls stand one and a half times my height, and three times my width, their physiques rock-like in appearance. The guards wield clubs and axes and wear very little armor, since it slows them down in combat and metal tends to only dent their skin—it is much more likely that the impact would crack the blade instead.

"Unseelie Leader," the Troll Queen greets when she reaches the top step, looking down at me through long, dark lashes.

"Welcome to the Unseelie Castle," I say in return, not reacting to her unsubtle dig at my title. A low growl rumbles through Asra's throat.

The Troll Queen glares at her. "I thought I told you to get rid of that hateful creature."

You need her alliance, I remind myself when sharp words are on the tip of my tongue. "If I got rid of hateful creatures in my kingdom, there would be no one left to rule."

She stares ponderously, lips slightly parted as if a question is forming between them. Then her attention darts to my left. "Have you finally found yourself someone to help you rule?"

Chimere takes half a step forward, but stops short when I say, "I rule alone."

The Troll Queen rolls her eyes and says to Chimere, "Sometimes we have to let men think that. I told his mother to try again for a daughter, but he was always her weakness."

My teeth ache from gritting them so hard that it feels like they are going to break. "Dinner is being served," I announce, pleasantly surprised at how even my tone comes out. "Your normal quarters have been prepared; servants will bring your belongings up while we eat."

I take my leave before she can press any harder and find a crack in my collected facade.

At dinner, she insists on having a table just for the royals brought to the front of the room, near the thrones, so that we can look out on everyone.

"And you, my dear," she insists to Chimere, "come sit with us."

Chimere catches my eye and, when I nod, settles into the seat beside mine. Trays upon trays of meats, fruits, and loaves of bread are brought to the tables, along with barrels of wine, but no one touches anything. I know what they are waiting for; I just have to bolster the will to do it.

To my surprise, the Troll Queen raises her goblet. "To the curse," she says loudly. "May it give you the restoration of Faerie, that all may kneel at your feet."

And in so doing, be subject to paying higher taxes to you. Remaining seated, I lift my own goblet, garnering the attention of the entire room. "Blood for the throne."

My Fae enthusiastically chant it and drain their cups. I barely let the wine touch my lips before I set it back down on the table.

"I did so enjoy your mother's flair for the dramatic," the Troll Queen says as the cheers die down and the feasting begins. "At least you guard her memory and legacy—your one redeeming quality, I suppose. Everyone has at least one."

I pick at my food, taking small bites so she is unaware of the way her presence twists my stomach. "The Unseelie do not pride themselves on redeeming qualities."

She snorts derisively, downing her goblet and holding it out for a nearby servant to refill.

"Perhaps you would be interested in something richer, Your Majesty?" Odilon asks, offering a bottle. "Queens should not drink the swill of the commonfolk."

She snatches it from his hand. "See, Unseelie Leader, everyone has their redeeming qualities. He has been most useful."

I accidentally squish a berry between my fingers, juice splattering across the plate and staining my fingertips a dark red. At least wearing black means the juice won't be noticeable on my clothes.

"Everyone has their uses." *What did you do, Odilon, to make her single you out to me like this?* In sending him away, have I made a bigger mess for myself? *There are no right decisions, only more beneficial ones.*

"Your Unseelie have been quite accommodating, especially this one," she continues, ignoring my comment. "News is beginning to travel fast through Faerie about the curse finally awakening. Glad to see your mother's plan is finally coming to fruition."

I do not bother pointing out that the plan was mine, a desperate attempt to keep the scraps of my mother's so-called legacy from falling apart, to buy myself more time to strategize.

"It wasss hisss plan, Your Highnesss," Chimere interjects.

The Troll Queen shoots Chimere an amused look. "I do believe he should make you his partner before you get some sense and become disenchanted with him. The Unseelie would do well with a woman ruling once more. That was why Faerie split in the first place —the man got too greedy."

I pretend to take a sip of my wine so I am not tempted to laugh at her apparent lack of self-awareness.

"He isss—"

"Regardless," I cut in, "the curse is here, and Seelie forces will be at our doorstep within days, a week at most." I look her in the eye this time. "I understand if you would rather cut your time short to avoid bloodshed. We can spare the same Unseelie who brought you here, to make sure your return trip is safe." Whatever Odilon has told her or led her to believe, I doubt he could do much more damage. If she wants him, she can keep him for all I care.

She tilts her head slightly, her gaze having just enough of an edge to scrape down my spine. I refuse to flinch.

"I will take them with me," she agrees, "but I will not leave until I have been given my due payment."

"The treasure is being put into your caravans as we speak."

"No." Her quick response throws me off, but not as much as the smile that slithers across her face. Somehow, it is eerier to see her this close as a faerie than it is as a troll. "Odilon tells me you are keeping the cursed princess here. I want her as payment."

A thousand colorful words come to mind, darts I'd love to pin

Odilon to the wall with. *But how does he know that?* Even if I could lie, there would be no sense in it—she will not be persuaded that the rumor is false.

"Absolutely not," I find myself replying harshly. I may be keeping her for my own selfish reasons, but I do not care to imagine what the Troll Queen would have in mind for Princess Briar Rose.

Her flicker of surprise is quickly replaced by predatorial intrigue, akin to a wolf scenting the blood of an injured animal. "Surely, she does not mean something to you? You have already cursed her—give her to me, and keep your war. You have no more need of her."

"I do have need of her."

"Oh? Do tell." She leans toward me, and I feel the bump of her knee against mine even though her faerie form suggests that her legs are too far away to do that. "Have you fallen in love with a human? Have you disgraced yourself, your mother, and your kind by the ultimate act of dishonor?"

Chimere tenses beside me, anticipation radiating from her.

"I am not in love with the princess. She is a ransom piece." I want to add "nothing more," but the words stick in my throat, then sink to my gut. *Apparently, she has me in the habit of trying to lie... about things I do not think are lies.*

The Troll Queen clucks her tongue disapprovingly. "That is a mistake: do not give your enemy options."

I hold her stare and state, "The princess is not an option."

Tone dropping to a warning rumble, she replies, "I will not leave without my due payment."

CHAPTER FORTY-FIVE

BRIAR ROSE

*T*he next time Tristan visits me, there is no warning of his arrival. He appears beside me as I paint Loren's and my playhouse in a forest landscape. I make it disappear and jump to my feet, trying to assess how to greet him. His stance is all angles and tension, but the aggression does not seem to be directed at me.

"Are we back to open hostility?" I ask, crossing my arms.

Instead of answering, he has a question of his own: "Have you considered the offer further?"

A startled snort escapes me. "Do you really believe that I could truly consider marrying the person who cursed me?"

"For everything and everyone you love, I do believe so."

The ache in my heart reaches for my throat, squeezing it until I am nearly in tears. I swallow painfully. "That would mean betraying them. Giving up on Loren." I shake my head. "I cannot."

Tristan frowns. "Do you really believe we will allow him to kiss you, to have a chance at breaking the curse?"

I study his expression, wondering what has him so rattled. "You believe he has a chance."

He waves away the suggestion like it is an annoying fly. "I do not make a habit of giving my enemies chances, even if they are nearly impossible."

Despite his intensity, there is nothing in me that wants to rise to it, to join him. In a gentle, quiet voice, I tell him, "Loren does not have to be your enemy, Tristan."

"No?" His eyes glitter with hatred, pain. "It seems fate has ordained it to be so."

For that, I have no good reply. How much of my life has been dragged along by fate and decisions others have made for me?

"Sometimes we are forced into things beyond our control, and we have to make the best of it."

His words are dagger-sharp, but they barely nick me. "There is always a choice," I whisper, more to myself than to him, running my fingers over the fox pendant on my bracelet. "Always a chance to start again, right from where you are."

Tristan's stare turns from intense to curious, a furrow forming between his brows.

"I will not accept your offer," I state with such peace and determination I did not realize was possible in such situations. "But I am willing to negotiate other terms for the good of all of Faerie."

The forest darkens, chilling breezes snaking their way through and nipping at my skin. For a moment, I consider adjusting the dreamscape to offset what he is doing, but that would probably only make him react worse. If he is trying to intimidate me, I will not allow it.

"Consider it," I say. "You are clever, and I suspect there is more good in you than you give yourself credit for. For while you say that you are certain I would do whatever it takes to save the ones I love, you do the same by making decisions to protect your people and land you clearly care for, Tristan."

Darkness smothers everything so thick I can no longer see him.

Breathing slowly and steadily, I remain still. He needs me, so he will not actually cause me harm. At least, not intentionally. And he cannot hurt me here in the dreamscape.

"Do not humanize me." His voice sounds like it is coming from all directions, circling me like a pack of ravenous wolves. Wind picks up, yanking at my hair and dress, and stinging my eyes.

Breathe... just focus on breathing.

"They have made me their monster, and it is a mantel I carry well."

Pulse racing, I manage to say, "I think you play at being a monster to survive. But you are not one, not in truth."

The winds die down, but true black remains. I am itching to make it warmer, to bring the sun out so I am no longer blind...

Then he murmurs in my ear, "You will not be able to speak lies so easily once you are truly Fae."

The darkness flees; there is no sign of Tristan, but a slight chill remains, frost and ice clinging to the trees and bits of the ground.

I grip the fox pendant in a clenched fist. "Please, come quickly, Loren."

LOREN

"Loren..." Briar Rose giggles. I open my eyes, slowly sitting up as I take in the misty morning, the grass in the glade covered in dew. Other than a few birds chirping, it is quiet. Our playhouse is behind her, the twine new and the paint still wet, but she is a woman now, not a little girl.

"How could you fall asleep at a time like this?" she teases, tugging on my hand until I stand. "I want to show you something." Petals fall from her flower crown, drifting lazily down to rest upon the grass under our bare feet as she leads me to our playhouse, pointing at where she has carved our names with a heart around them.

I squeeze her hand, not quite as strong as the emotions

squeezing my throat. Did she somehow find a way to communicate with me despite the curse? But surely, she would be more worried, asking me questions or telling me what is happening to her. Unless she is being watched...

"It says our names," she tells me, beaming. Not a hint of distress.

Gently, I kiss her forehead and pull her into a tight embrace.

She hesitates reciprocating. "Loren? What is wrong?"

I pull back just enough to look her in the eye and touch her cheek. "I am coming for you, Briar Rose. I promise."

She tilts her head, brow furrowing. "What do you mean? You are here with me now."

The words thud in my chest. Could it be this simple? Could I break the curse by finding her in my sleep?

Tenderly, I kiss her, and she melts into me, soft and sweet and gentle. Lingering, like she wants to make this last forever. But I have to know if it worked, so I pull away, searching her face for any sign of change. The only thing I see is that her smile is gone, replaced by a concerned frown.

"What truly haunts you?" she asks quietly, one hand sliding down from the back of my neck to my chest, stopping over my heart. I wonder if she can feel its stuttered beat, the twinges making the cracks deeper, splitting it apart even more.

That would have been too easy, I lament. Even if I had broken the curse, where would she be, all alone, having to fend for herself in Tristan's castle?

"What if my love for you is not enough?" I whisper, barely audible.

Luckily, she hears it. The smile returns, and she cradles my face in her hands. "I have nothing to fear," she murmurs against my lips, "if True Love's Kiss is all it takes to break the curse."

This time I lean into her—

"Loren," a male voice speaks hushedly. He shakes my shoulder, dislodging me from the dream. I open my eyes in time to catch the flicker of worry disappear from Toussaint's expression.

"Sorry," I mumble, running a hand over my face. After all of the sacrifices Toussaint has made for me over the years, I couldn't keep watch for a few hours?

"Don't worry about it." He stands, offering me a hand up. "It's hard to stay awake when we're so magic-deficient."

I start to say that that is no excuse, but he is already walking again, gesturing for me to join him.

We continue our journey in silence, our steps heavy and our insides aching. To distract myself, I wonder what my aunt has decided to do. She must know where we are by now. Has she sent Briar Rose's family home for safety? Has she gathered the Seelie army to march on Unseelie? There is no sign of Tristan sending troops, but seeing as he has Briar Rose, he has little need to. He wants us to bring the fight to him, I am sure.

What would I have done if I were king?

The only options I can see myself choosing are ones that actively seek to rescue Briar Rose, but having the full weight of Seelie counting on me, not to mention the human kingdom as well... I might have left Evanthe in charge and still gone into Unseelie with Toussaint, if I were wise. Maybe a few others as well, a small party that can go relatively undetected.

But if I am truthful with myself, I admit I would have spent whatever was necessary to get her back, my breath, my soul, my very kingdom—which is why I won't make a good king, one the Seelie deserve.

Maybe I am just as selfish as my father.

Toussaint walks less gracefully than usual, almost stumbling a few times. He is feeling the draining effects of the land as much as I am—perhaps it is best that only the two of us risk this.

CHAPTER FORTY-SIX

THE UNSEELIE KING

*A*sra curled up in my lap, I sleep in my chair in front of the enchanted mirror that night, keeping Briar Rose out of sight behind me, and ignoring the bottles of wine on the shelf nearby. Tempting, but I want a clear head and control of my emotions, especially with the Troll Queen here. She needs no help rattling me.

And, apparently, neither does Briar Rose.

I think you play at being a monster to survive. But you are not one, not in truth.

I flex my fingers when the urge to grab a bottle hits me. How did she come to that conclusion? I cursed her when she was an infant, tore her away from those she loves, and have given her an offer that does not benefit her much at all. Is she so optimistic that she is blind, or is the hopelessness of the situation driving her to insanity?

Asra purrs as I idly stroke her head. With Briar Rose in the dreamscape and only Asra to keep me company, I should feel like I am mostly alone. Yet my thoughts crowd me, filling the room, demanding my attention.

Leaning forward, I disrupt Asra's sleep, earning a chattered scolding. She calms when she sees me touch the edges of the mirror.

"Show me Loren."

The mirror's glass responds instantly, forming shapeless shadows that focus into two faeries sneaking their way through Unseelie woods. Their skin is paling with tones of grey, like the ash fluttering through the air around them. Instead of a determined march, their feet scrape across the ground more than step, their shoulders hunched and heads low.

Perfect.

As soon as I let go of the mirror, it returns to its normal reflective state. Staring sightlessly at myself, I ponder the pieces of my situation like a puzzle. With Loren and Toussaint in Unseelie, we can easily deal with them. No word yet on when the Seelie army is coming, but that should be soon. Getting the Troll Queen to leave is priority, and giving her Briar Rose is not an option.

What can I possibly offer in exchange for a princess? I will not let the Troll Queen have any of my magic. She has taken many things from me over the years, especially keen on magic-infused items, which have become very rare to come by...

Asra leaps onto my shoulder, anticipating me vacating the chair. She trills in my ear, and I hesitate, running my fingertips over the outer filigree of the mirror frame.

"I know, but it may be our best option, unless you have any better ideas," I point out. "She wants the princess."

Asra cranes her neck around to look at Briar Rose's sleeping form. Then she sighs and makes a noise I take as resigned agreement.

With a quick spell, the mirror detaches from the wall and floats behind me as we leave the room. I seal the door with magic. *I will return soon, Princess Briar Rose. Hopefully after having convinced this nuisance to leave.*

Margaux is already on the other side, waiting for me even

though the halls are cloaked in darkness so thick the torches along the wall cannot quite spill their light onto the floor below them. She does not comment on the floating mirror behind me.

"My half-brother and his bodyguard are in Unseelie, west of here," I inform her. "Bring them to me."

She stares at me with her pupilless eyes. "I will send—"

"No. You have to go with them. They are not far from here."

By her expression, I know she wants to warn me about how much of a gamble it is to have her leave while the Troll Queen is present. But I cannot have Loren and Toussaint being killed or taken by her, not when they can be of use to me.

Slowly, Margaux bows her head. "As you wish, Your Majesty."

We take leave of each other, Margaux heading toward the barracks while I go to the Troll Queen's rooms. Being so early in the day, there are few people about, most still sleeping soundly in their beds, leaving me free to hurry through the halls. The few servants I do see quickly bow and step aside.

I put the Troll Queen on the other side of the castle from my bedchamber, the nicest of the rooms other than my mother's. The servants often refer to it as her wing of the castle, considering how sparingly it is used other than when she visits. She revels in hearing it called that, and I let it slide because it keeps her from asking yet again to use my mother's bedchamber.

Two trolls stand outside the doorway, one snoring as he leans against the wall. The other jabs him in the ribs with his elbow when he notices me coming, and they stand at attention. Curiosity lights their features when they notice the mirror.

"Inform your queen that I would like a word with her."

His meaty hand nearly crushes the doorknob as he twists it. "Your Highness—"

"Go away and let me sleep!" she snaps from bed, plopping a pillow over her face. Dresses, shoes, and jewelry cover the room as though a storm tossed them about. Already her musty scent is taking over.

I carefully step around as much as I can as I make my way inside. "I think you will want to hear my offer."

She bolts upright, the pillow flying off of the bed and scattering a pile of rings on the floor. The lump under the blankets does not quite match the slenderness of her body, but then again, she looks like she gained fifty pounds since the night before, the Fae qualities stretched to strange proportions. The ruby around her neck pulses faintly; her illusion snaps back into place. "I told you what I want."

"I think you will find this an acceptable replacement." Magic ebbs and flows from my body as I have the mirror float beside me. With a flick of my fingers, the candles light, giving her a better view of the gilded edges and flawless surface.

She demands, "Why would I want a mirror?"

I turn it so she can look over my shoulder as I grab the sides and command, "Show me Odilon."

The faun appears on the glass, a half-empty bottle in each hand, heading toward… Chimere's room. Not surprising, but worth noting and being wary of.

I remove my hands, and it returns to a normal mirror.

"Extraordinary…" she breathes, scooting forward on the bed. The sleeve of her nightgown falls from her shoulder, but she does not notice as she scrambles toward the mirror eagerly, shoving me aside. "Show me the human princess."

Nothing happens.

"You have to know the person or place's name," I inform her when she shoots me an irritated look.

"Which is…?"

"Briar Rose," I supply after a moment's hesitation, knowing she will refuse to drop the matter. Seconds later, the image is of the princess, sleeping in a dark room, her white dress bright against the black of the sheets.

She raises a judgmental brow at me. "Do not love her, hmmm?"

I grit my teeth. "Do you accept the offer or not?"

The Troll Queen goes through a long list of options, black eyes glittering with excitement each time the mirror responds. "I will take this and triple my normal supplies in exchange for you keeping the princess."

I stifle a groan, but Asra doesn't bother holding back a growl. "You will take it and double your normal supplies."

"Triple," she persists. "You know how much I love princesses, and you are expecting me to give this one up?"

"In exchange for an *enchanted mirror*." As an afterthought, I add, "One my mother treasured." A bold move, one that leaves an acidic feeling in the pit of my stomach.

As I suspected she would, the Troll Queen takes a beat to consider this. "Add a crate of those wine bottles Odilon offered last night, and you have a deal."

I nod. "I will have it all prepared for you." As I start to leave, she snatches the mirror, clutching it to her chest.

"Leave this with me."

LOREN

The next time we check our bearings, the castle is much closer.

"We should make it there in less than a day," Toussaint says when he makes it back down the tree. "We'll have to wait in the shadows, see if we can find a good time to sneak in unnoticed."

"He could be keeping her anywhere," I sigh, discouragement slipping into my tone.

"The portal made it look like she was in a room, possibly his." He winces. "Sorry. Not that I am implying anything, I just…"

I wave it off even as the thought sinks its teeth further into me. "Then it would probably be on one of the upper levels, since I doubt he would keep rooms on the bottom floor that is so easily accessible. A decent place to start."

We continue with new vigor, only stopping when we spot a stream. Our chapped lips and parched throats convince us to overlook the murkiness of the water we put into our waterskins, although we do use a tiny bit of magic to purify it before taking a drink. The bitter taste coats my mouth, but I partake all the same, grateful to ease the thirst.

Without warning, Toussaint drops his waterskin and swipes a sword over my head. The clang echoes in my ears; I drop and roll out of the way, reaching for my sword.

An albino faerie towers over Toussaint, striking with speed so fast her movements are a blur. More Unseelie sprint toward us, five from what I can tell, teeth bared and weapons ready.

I lunge at the female. If we can take her out first, the others will be less of an issue when they reach us—

She bats my sword aside and pursues Toussaint, not missing a beat. The others are almost upon us; I may have to use what little magic I have remaining.

My sword sinks into the shoulder of the first Unseelie to reach me, and I kick him away to free it so I can move onto the next opponent. He tumbles backward with a shriek; two more come at me, weapons raised high. I call upon my Glamour, readying for a strike—

The female slams her hand into my chest. Air rushes from my lungs. I hit the ground instantly, head spinning. Cannot breathe. Cannot move. Darkness creeps into the edges of my vision, quickly taking over. My last thought: *My magic is gone.*

CHAPTER FORTY-SEVEN

THE UNSEELIE KING

"*H*ow did you manage to convince her to leave?" Chimere asks quietly as we watch the Troll Queen's carriage pull through the gates, followed closely behind by a caravan of goods. She brought the mirror with her into the carriage, refusing to let it leave her sight. If only she had taken Odilon with her as well. "I asssume you did not give her the princesss."

"I gave her something she could not pass up." *She would have been a fool to.* One less piece of my mother, in exchange for keeping her legacy alive.

Asra nuzzles my jaw; I scratch her head.

"I thought ssshe would never leave." Chimere pulls her cloak closer to her body, shivering. She stands closer to me since Margaux is not here, but gives enough distance to keep Asra from snapping at her. "Ssshe was too intrigued by Thaddeusss'sss ssstoriesss… essspecially the unicorn one. Ssshe asssked him where ssshe could find the royal family when he could not tell her where the unicornsss are." Chimere shakes her head. "I would be afraid to find out what ssshe would ussse them for."

"It would be better not to know," I concur, eyes fixated on the gates shutting behind the last of the caravan. Above, the sky splits, dumping more ash. The Unseelie on the wall throw their magic at it, and I lend some of mine. The gash lessens but refuses to close.

A little longer is all I need; then I will be able to restore Faerie and rid the land of the In-Between.

"Ssshe was right about one thing though." Chimere turns her slitted gaze toward me. "We would do well, ruling sssside-by-sssside."

I force myself to look her in the eyes. This close, her snake features are much more apparent, her fangs sharper and longer. I wonder if the rumors about snake faeries having venom are true. It wouldn't surprise me.

"Will you not even consssider it?" she asks fragilely. "I feel asss though we have come to know one another well, and I care for you."

At the top of the palace steps—what an odd place to make such a bold declaration. But everyone has gone back to their business, so we are alone.

"I know you do not care for me," she adds, turning to face me fully, "and it isss not asss if I love you, but perhapsss we might get there, in time. I have been a valuable ally to you, sssomeone who hasss helped you rally sssupport from the Sssolitary Fae. Think what ressspect you might gain with me as your Queen."

Asra's tail flicks, but she remains silent, just as interested in hearing my answer. Or perhaps she is as surprised as I am at Chimere's timing.

"And what would you gain?"

"Greater asssurance that my clan would be taken care of." A tentative smile graces her thin lips. "Sssomeone I can sssee myself falling for. And, of course, I would relish the title of Queen—and the privileges that would come along with it."

There is a tiny hint of relief that she wants the title more than she wants me. My mother might have liked her... or saw her as a threat to be rid of early on. She would not have left this in limbo for so long, because this is where mistakes tend to happen.

"I will not lie to you," she continues quietly, with resolve. "I have alwaysss wanted to rule, enough that I would come here to marry the legendary Unssseelie King without having met him first. I would become the queen at all costs. But then I met you..." The smile grows. "I met you, and I knew I made the right choice." Slowly, she moves closer, and for some reason, Asra does not move or make a sound. Wisely, Chimere stops there, although it would take little effort for her to kiss me if she wanted. "Think of what we could accomplisssh together," she whispers. "Consssider how ssstrong we could be."

For a moment, I picture what she must be envisioning: a powerful couple. Someone to lean on and trust implicitly, to shoulder the burdens of the crown. Equals.

That kind of vulnerability is what got my mother into this mess in the first place.

"I have considered it," I say slowly. "I have no intentions of making anyone my Queen except for Princess Briar Rose."

Her eyes widen; she takes half a step back as if I slapped her. "Ssso you do have feelingsss for her. You are falling in love with her."

"I am falling in love with no one," I correct more harshly than I intend to. "I offered her marriage in exchange for Faerie giving power to the Unseelie so I can restore the Courts."

She swallows, brow furrowing. "Ssso you take what you can get, asss long asss it isss mossst advantageousss to you."

Is that not what she is doing? "That is the Unseelie way. Blood for the throne." At her defeated look, I try to think of something to say to ease the guilt, but it is better this way, to quit tugging her along. I should have done this sooner, made it abundantly clear that there is not—and would not be—anything between us.

"What if ssshe refusssesss your offer? Would you consssider me then?"

"If she refuses me, then I will have no need of a Queen."

"What about producing an heir?" she presses. "Continue your mother'sss legacy."

Yet another thought I had shoved into the back of my mind, and here she is yanking it to the forefront. "Perhaps at some point. But we have to survive this first." I gesture to the gash in the sky.

Chimere purses her lips. Whatever she is about to say is cut off by cheers, whistles, and taunts near the gate.

Margaux has returned with Loren and Toussaint in tow.

LOREN

Dizziness. Nausea. Fire burning my wrists and ankles. I gasp, exhaling in a weak wheeze that barely makes it past my dry, cracked lips.

"Loren." *Toussaint. Why does he sound so far away?*

"He is waking. Inform the King."

"No need. I am already here."

I spend a lot of effort just to open my eyes. The room bends and sways, so I squeeze them shut tight again. Too magic deficient. Too exhausted. Yet still the land claws at me, draining whatever is still keeping me alive.

"Wake, Loren. I thought you would want to discuss your precious princess."

My eyes snap open, glaring at my half-brother standing on the other side of the cell bars. Toussaint and I are chained to the ceiling, the bottoms of our feet grazing the stone floor. By the burning sensation, the manacles have at least a little bit of iron in them.

We will not last long here.

The tall, pale faerie who attacked us—and captured us—stands behind Tristan, expression unreadable.

"Unless you are going to release her from the curse," I rasp, struggling to breathe because of the way we hang, "there is nothing for us to discuss."

The light from the torches casts harsh shadows on Tristan's face, making it seem all sharp angles. I would have to look hard to find something in him that resembles our father, resembles me. But I look anyway.

"I have already offered to release her." He looks me up and down. "I told her I would spare you and all the Seelie who agree not to harm us if she marries me instead."

I flinch like he'd punched me in the gut. "What are you playing at? Are you insane?"

"Faerie is being lost to the In-Between," he responds calmly. "Restoring the Courts under its rightful ruler will stop it."

"Then we should find another way," I argue. "If it needs balance, then perhaps we can come to an agreement."

Tristan barks out a laugh. "An agreement? You are not in a position to negotiate, not until you wear the crown, and your aunt would never make one with me."

"She is your aunt too." *She would love you just as she loves me, if you let her, if you put down your sword and showed her you only want what is best for Faerie.*

The torches burn low, the room being swallowed by darkness.

"Now that I have you," Tristan says tensely, "perhaps your princess will listen to reason."

"Tristan—"

He and his bodyguard leave without another word, slamming the door behind them. The torchlights go out completely, leaving us to suffer our pain and hopelessness in the pitch black.

"What do we do?" Toussaint asks quietly after a few moments pass.

I give him the only answer I have: "I don't know."

CHAPTER FORTY-EIGHT

BRIAR ROSE

Snow blanketing the ground is the only warning I have that Tristan is arriving. I shake it from my hair and clothes, and conjure a tea set. He was much more civil when I had that ready before, so hopefully it will work again.

Instead, Tristan rushes through the garden, heading straight toward me, trampling flowers underfoot.

"You will calm down before you speak to me," I command him, putting a little more authority in my tone than I actually feel.

To my surprise, Tristan stops short.

"Would you like a cup of tea?" I offer, unsure what else to say to fill the tense silence. When he does not answer, I settle into a chair and take a sip. "Sit."

"I do not want tea."

"That's fine. Sit."

Slowly, he obeys, back a little too straight, eyes pinning me to the chair. Whatever has him so rattled, it would be better if I don't outright ask him, I am sure. He will get to it when he is ready.

"Tart?" I conjure a few kinds, as well as some cheese and bread in case he is not in the mood for sweets either.

A tart is halfway to my mouth when he says, "I have Loren and Toussaint."

I drop everything, my teacup shattering on the ground. "What?"

"They are currently in my dungeon," he continues on, voice teetering on tense. "If you agree to the terms, then I will release them unharmed."

A hundred different questions and remarks bumble together, a few of them spilling out in fragments.

Tristan jumps to his feet and leans forward, gripping the sides of the table between us. "The In-Between is here, tearing apart the land as we speak. If you want to save them and all of Faerie, this is the choice you can make."

I stare up at him, mouth agape. "I would be betraying them. You are forcing me into this decision—it is no longer a choice."

His eyes narrow. "You are the one who said we always have a choice." He straightens, adjusting his cloak. "I will return tonight for your answer." Then he has the audacity to turn his back on me, heading out of the dreamscape as abruptly as he came.

Childish as it may be, I snap at him, "What if my answer remains no?"

"Then you doom us all."

THE UNSEELIE KING

"Stay here," I order Asra as I all but leap from the bed, unable to bring myself to look at the princess lying peacefully beside the wyvern. If she is petty enough to doom us all for the sake of what others think of her...

Faerie pulses weakly, shuddering, trying to get my attention.

Asra makes a questioning chirrup, to which I respond, "I'll be back tonight."

The war horns resound the moment I step foot outside of my bedchamber. Margaux is hurrying toward me, a scythe already in one hand. "The Seelie army has arrived."

"How did they get here without our scouts seeing them?"

We run down the hallway and stairs together, skipping a few steps at a time. She yanks a battleaxe from her belt with her free hand.

"Portals," she answers. "Flora and Fauna convinced the others to get them close enough to our castle."

That is a ridiculous amount of magic to use. Evanthe has to be one of the faeries making that happen. "If we can, send our warriors back through them. Tell them to focus on the ones keeping the portals open."

Unseelie flood the bottom floor, all sprinting toward either the weapons room or outside. A few of the trolls the Troll Queen left behind as part of our agreement make the ground shake with their excited gait.

"Blood for the throne!" is chanted repeatedly, not quite in unison, but their ferocity is aligned. Contagious, it sings through my veins. This is what we have been waiting for all these years. This is what will decide the fate of Faerie.

"Your Highnesss!" Chimere wades through the Unseelie warriors, grabbing at my sleeve. "You ssshould arm yoursssself before leaving."

Margaux looks back at me, and I wave her on. She nods once and slips outside.

"I will move better without it," I inform Chimere. "But you can get some armor and weapons from the blacksmith. If he gives you any trouble, tell him I sent you."

Her concern softens. "You... are worried about me?"

The pure adoration in her expression makes me want to recoil, but I keep still. "I am sure you can handle yourself. I only offer in case you are in need."

Most everyone is gone by now, except for a few, one of them

Odilon. Catching sight of us, he slows his pace to an amble. Outfitted in a leather chest piece and two double-bladed axes in hand, the faun looks every bit a warrior.

"Your Highness," he greets with a slight dip of his head. "Chimere, it is time."

Instead of answering him, she grabs my shoulders, pulling me into a hug. "Have you consssidered what I sssaid?" she whispers in my ear, sending uncomfortable shivers down my spine.

Odilon watches us, an unreadable expression on his face. A few others join him, curious to see the odd scene unfolding. I wonder at what I saw in the enchanted mirror, the way he was going to Chimere's room. Have I underestimated their relationship, whatever it may be?

I would become queen at all costs, she told me. Is that still the case?

"I have no time for this," I respond, trying to keep my tone even. "Chimere, Faerie is falling apart to the In-Between. The Seelie are here, at our doorstep. We have to deal with all of this before there is nothing left to save."

She grips me harder, fingers winding painfully into my hair. "Just tell me there is a chance."

Thaddeus comes into view, walking stiffly, taking in the scene. He must have waited until the other dwarves left, sneaking out to fight despite his still-injured shoulder. An axe dangles from each hand, and he stops short, gaze shifting to me.

"I can promise nothing, but we can speak about this another time." I fight the urge to shove her away; although I am unsure I could, at least not without magic.

"Chimere," Odilon says impatiently. "We are running out of time."

I can hear the pounding of my heart over the shouts and clanging of the battle raging outside. Something is wrong—if I move too quickly, I am sure whatever decision Chimere is trying to make will end poorly for me.

You should have dealt with her when you had the chance, Mother would have said. But every ally is valuable; I just need to keep her as one.

Thaddeus shoots me a questioning look, to which I infinitesimally shake my head. *I can still salvage this, just not with empty words that imply promises I have no intention of keeping.*

"Chimere, we can speak of this another time," I repeat. "Let me do what I can to make sure Unseelie is saved first."

She turns her face into my neck, the bridge of her nose brushing against my pulse. "I wisssh I could have given you more time... We could have ruled all of Faerie together, all of the world, if we ssso desssired."

"My King!" I hear Margaux roar. My Glamour flares to life, ready to envelop her and blast away the Unseelie charging at me.

But her fangs have already sunk deep into my neck. Liquid fire rushes through my veins, flooding my senses. I try to inhale but choke, my knees giving way.

A scythe sings through the air in front of me; Chimere's headless body crumples to the ground, and I follow suit. I hear the crack of my skull against the stone floor before I feel the spark of pain, made duller by the venom taking over my body.

Margaux is a white blur, painting the walls and floor with the red of Odilon and his followers, Thaddeus following suit to the best of his ability. My vision grows hazy, the edges darkening.

"Your Highness." Margaux drops to her knees and yanks Chimere's decapitated head from my neck, tossing it behind her. She covers the wound with one hand, then two, my blood trickling between her fingers. "I can't," she chokes out.

"Can't... what...?" I manage, trying to swallow. The venom has cooled significantly; the tips of my fingers and toes are turning numb.

"It's not magic," she says in a panic. "I can't stop it because it's not magic."

We stare at each other as the weighty realization settles on our chests. Healing venom would take a lot of magic, and I can't use my own to do it without risking killing myself in the process. The In-Between is coming, and I cannot stop it—

"Get Loren," I wheeze, pushing myself up onto my elbow.

"My King—"

"Loren," I say again. "My... room. Still... a... chance." If I cannot unite Faerie, it has to be Loren. With my death, the crown will rightfully fall to him. Balance must be restored one way or another.

I will not let Faerie die alongside me.

Puzzled, Margaux hesitates as I force myself onto shaky legs. Thaddeus takes my arm, holding me steady. "Go on, I'll take care of him."

She won't even look at him, too fixated on me.

"Go!" I try to yell, but it comes out as a rasped whisper. Knowing she will obey, I stumble toward the stairs, Thaddeus doing his best to keep me upright despite our height differences. I could use magic to teleport myself to my room, but I have to save as much strength as I can. One of these half-breaths will be my last.

"Don't give up," Thaddeus says through gritted teeth. "This isn't the end for you."

By the time we are at the top of the stairs, I am half-crawling, continuing on sheer will. It cannot end here, not like this. I have to make sure Faerie at least has a sliver of a chance of surviving. This will not all be in vain. I cannot let my mother down. One last sacrifice until I can finally be reunited with her in whatever comes after this life. If it is nothing, that will be a relief in and of its own.

The magic sealing my bedchamber doors responds to my touch, swinging open so fast I collapse onto the floor. Asra shrieks and glides across the room to me, chattering incessantly.

"Bed," I say, retching what little is in my stomach. She grabs the back of my shirt with her talons, flapping until she is partially lifting me off the ground. The fabric rips, but together we manage to make it to the bed. Thaddeus helps me flop onto it, and I grab Briar Rose's hand, letting myself fall into the dreamscape.

BRIAR ROSE

There is a slight breeze that brushes my neck, not enough to send a chill down my spine. Yet I adjust my shawl anyway, turn toward the playhouse—

Tristan appears, landing flat on his face. I squeak in surprise, watching him, waiting for him to get up and start another argument. But he does not move.

With quick strides, I hurry to kneel by his side, tugging on his arm. His groan is muffled, weak. "Are you hurt?" I roll him over and see my answer: golden blood trickles from two puncture wounds, his neck already coated with it. The overly sweet smell nearly has me gagging, so I hold my breath as I survey his face. Pallid, lips chapped, eyes struggling to focus.

"Tristan, what happened? What do you need? What can I do?" I pull his head into my lap. This has to be something that happened in the real world, something enough to affect the dreamscape. Already I can feel it shudder like it wants to unravel at the seams.

Hand shaking, he reaches out and touches my cheek. I gently place my hand over his, holding it there so he does not have to waste his strength. The way he stares at me, with the beginning of a smile tugging at the corners of his mouth, he seems like a different person —I can see the family resemblance between him and Loren. My heart swells.

"Tristan?" I want to stop the bleeding, to help him heal. I cover his wound with my free hand, but the magic only skates over him. Dreamscape magic is nothing to the real world; it cannot affect it, no matter how badly I want to force it to bend to my will. There is nothing to offer here but enchantments and illusions.

He wheezes, "I... release... you..."

The iciness that settled into my bones begins to lift, then snaps back into place, leaving an all-over stinging sensation. He frowns, and tries again to take the curse from me. I flinch at the second sting.

He grips my face between his hands, and his voice echoes in my mind with a spell I did not know existed. *'Evanthe changed the curse, so the magic is no longer mine to command.'*

Hopelessness seizes my heart before I can process the meaning of the words. He cannot release me from the curse... and Evanthe is too far away, probably in Seelie, trying to stop the In-Between...

He tugs the magic harder, jolting me forward with it.

"Tristan, what are you doing?" Tears prick at my eyes. There has to be something we can do, a way for us to get out of this. This cannot be the end.

The dreamscape begins to crumble, colors fading as the world breaks apart.

"Tell me what to do," I beg, squeezing his hand. "Tristan, please."

This time, he does not flinch when I say his name. The not-quite-a-smile gets closer to being one.

With one last pull, the curse's hold on me snaps; Tristan gasps, shuddering. His skin cools drastically. "Save... Faerie..."

Ignoring everything unraveling around us, I refuse to release his hand. "Tristan—"

The dreamscape is being swallowed whole by the destruction. His soul tries to cling to mine, as if he wants to save me, but we slip out of each other's grasp as the dreamscape peels pieces of me away.

Tristan disappears. I finally let out a scream—

CHAPTER FORTY-NINE

LOREN

Briar Rose, I am here… I cannot get to you, but I am here…
The darkness leaves plenty to the imagination. Every scrap of sound that makes it down here fuels my waking nightmares, taunting me.

So close, yet not enough.

Not enough.

Never enough.

I made it this far only to fail. Briar Rose is being held hostage by the curse, the In-Between is eating away at Faerie, and I am stuck in the dungeon, the iron manacles blistering my skin. Thanks to my brother's bodyguard, I don't even have magic at my disposal, not that I had much of it left. My insides ache, just as hollow as my hopeless heart.

A frenzy of shouts and chanting reach my ears as a war horn resounds. Many footsteps, hurriedly going various directions. Whatever has the Unseelie so shaken must be a serious matter. Dare I hope the Seelie decided to invade?

A cry cuts through everything. Clanging of metal follows, then heavy thumps. For a few heartbeats, there is nothing but silence.

"It sounded like they're fighting each other," Toussaint whispers.

One could only hope. I open my mouth to voice my thought, but the door clangs open, letting in dull light that makes me squint. I can barely make out the silhouette of a faerie tromping down the stairs to our cell. He raises a sword, ready to lunge at me, and I brace myself, preparing to twist out of the way if the chains will let me.

A shadow appears behind him and swipes with a scythe. With a wet gurgle, he collapses in a heap at the pale faerie's feet. She steps over him and strides toward me. "Your brother is about to die," the faerie hisses. "Will you save him if I release you?"

Die...? Her words strike clarity into the fog that hovers around my brain. "I... I have no magic."

She stalks closer to me. Her palm slams into my chest; I gasp, pins and needles pricking at my insides, making me want to double over. But the magic is still too little, barely there, and definitely not enough... "Now, will you save him?"

Did one of the Seelie manage to wound him? If so, why couldn't they use one of their healers? "How is he dying?"

"Venom from a snake faerie. He asked for you. We have no more time, Seelie princeling. Will you help him or not?" she growls. "This is the only way to save your princess."

Despite our major differences, no part of me wants Tristan dead. Maybe I can use this as leverage to get him to release Briar Rose from the curse. "I will save him. But you need to release Toussaint and return his magic as well. If the venom is close to his heart, we'll need all the magic we can get." *Not enough...*

Without a word, she frees both of us and returns Toussaint's magic as well, hitting him even harder than she did me. Toussaint grunts, falling backward. I haven't seen him lose his balance since we were children.

"Come. Hurry."

She does not wait. We sprint after her, tripping a few times as feeling returns to our legs and our eyes adjust to the dim light. She hisses at us; we follow up a long corridor of stairs, trying to catch our breath, then through an entryway littered with bodies and blood, but they are not Seelie, I realize with relief. While the clashes of battle are louder here, they are still too far away, none having made it inside yet.

I should not be surprised to see Unseelie turning on itself.

That bit of relief is stifled as I feel Faerie tremble in my soul, like it is trying to lean on my shoulder to stay upright.

My brother's bodyguard snaps at us to hurry, yanking us up yet more stairs. My thighs burn; my head swims.

What if we don't have enough magic?

The faerie takes us down a long hallway, to where I assume Tristan's room is. The stained glass windows muffle the outside battle. I am tempted to sneak a peek, but the faerie all but yanks me into the already-open bedroom.

"Save him!" she commands, slamming the door shut behind us and standing in front of it, watching our every move.

My breath catches at the sight of Briar Rose sleeping peacefully on the bed. Tristan is sprawled out beside her, his hand on hers, one leg hanging off the mattress, skin grey. The scents of blood and vomit accost my nose, so I cover my face as I move closer. A small, black wyvern near Tristan's head narrows its glowing purple eyes at me.

"Let them try to save him," Margaux orders the wyvern.

With a low growl, she scoots back a little, and the dwarf near her takes a step back. Everyone seems a little worse for wear, especially the dwarf, with bandages poking out of his ripped shirt.

Toussaint helps me roll Tristan onto his back. Four puncture wounds decorate his neck in a macabre purple, weeping blood and pus. Whatever bit him, I hope it is no longer around. And I hope he survives—not just for Briar Rose's sake.

We cover the wound with our hands and call upon what little magic we have left, dredging it from the bottom.

Let it be enough…

The pulse under my fingers is far too weak, almost nonexistent. Surely the venom has already found his heart, slowly weighing it down until it no longer has the strength to continue.

Our magic trickles in, combating it like a small band of heroes against a mighty army. I look at Toussaint, my despair mirroring on his face.

"We have to get Evanthe and the other faerie guardians if we can," I say.

"He won't last if we leave him," Toussaint replies.

"I'll stay. You two get them to come here. Hurry, before it's too late."

The faerie stares at me with those all-white eyes, unreadable. She knows I already promised to save him, so I am no threat.

"I'll watch him," the dwarf offers.

"Hurry," she says to Toussaint, and they leave. Immediately, I can feel the venom overpowering what bit of magic remains.

"Don't give up on him." The dwarf keeps a little distance, no doubt out of respect, but his rumbling voice travels. "He can be a pain, but there's good in him, no matter how much he tries to hide it. He is worth saving."

My throat closes. "I know," I manage to say.

Whether he hears me or not, the dwarf does not indicate, and I do not glance behind me. He hums, and then begins to sing somberly, voice low and rich. The words are in a foreign language, but my heart seems to get their meaning, emotions wrapping around my chest and squeezing it so tight it feels like it could burst.

"Tristan, you bastard," I whisper in his ear, resting my head next to his, "you'd better not die. Your story isn't over, and neither is Briar Rose's."

BRIAR ROSE

The dreamscape crumbles to nothing before I can reach out to my body. I claw at something, anything to hold tight to, but it all unravels between my fingers. My mind races with ideas of things to form—solid ground under my feet, a wall to brace against—but the magic is gone.

Loren, I am so sorry. I tried.

I wait for oblivion to overtake me, for the end to show itself and carry me away to the afterlife. Instead, I land on my feet, and the darkness around me moves, forming shadowy, leafless trees. My skin begins to glow dimly, illuminating a thin dirt path in front of me. The distance is hazy.

No sign of the dreamscape, or Tristan. Not even a hint of a chill. I am weightless like I have never felt before, free from the curse. He released me from it. But... why? Did someone kill him? There were terrible punctures on his throat, and blood had covered his neck and soaked into his clothes. The way the dreamscape fell apart would lead me to believe he passed away... His final act, saving me. Not entirely selfless, since he could have done it before, and it was to save Faerie, but at least he didn't leave me to rot in the curse forever.

Where am I? How do I get back to my body, to Loren?

Something invisible pulls on me, and instinctively I know: it is Faerie, beckoning me, this time in a much stronger manner, its intentions clearer than before. It is like we are connected, the shield around my heart unfurling to touch my mind once again.

There is hope for Faerie—and now the curse can no longer steal me away.

"Show me the way," I whisper.

It draws me forward, toward the haze. The In-Between. It emanates extremes, darkness and light, hot and cold, elation and despair, undying love and murderous hatred. They latch onto me as soon as I am close enough, all vying for my attention, invisible claws digging into my dress, my hair, my skin. I stumble but catch myself, and keep going. Faerie is calling me, counting on me to do this, as is Loren and so many others. I can do this. I can—

The cuts and scrapes turn into gashes and wounds. I cry out, falling to my hands and knees. There is nothing to see, no blood or missing flesh, but with each piece they snatch from me, my glow lessens.

Faerie tenderly cups my heart, trying to reassure me that this is necessary with a soothing sensation, but all I can focus on is the pain.

Keep going, it seems to encourage me.

I can't, I mentally scream. *You are taking everything from me!*

Loren's face flashes in my mind's eye, his smile bright. *"Tell me when you return."*

There is no other option. He is waiting for me—along with my friends and family—and I have to tell him what I was too terrified to tell him before.

Steeling myself, I crawl forward, my body shaking so badly I cannot bring myself to attempt standing. Tears stream freely down my cheeks and water the dirt.

The In-Between demands more, more, more. Starving, gluttonous, ravaging. It brings me to my belly, air rushing from me as I hit the earth, and still it is not satisfied, not even as my light flickers, dangerously close to being snuffed out.

What more can I possibly have to give?

Agony. I claw at the dirt, trying to pull myself toward where Faerie is leading me, but my muscles give out. Fog is all I can see, and pain is all I can feel.

Is this what you had planned for me? I want to scream at Faerie. *First you leave me to the curse, and now this? Will this make a difference?* I have no voice, no energy, nothing left to give. Even my tears have stopped, my cheeks dry and eyes burning.

Enough! My face hits the dirt, strength failing me. Three more pieces are torn from me, and my light goes out completely.

CHAPTER FIFTY

LOREN

*T*ristan's heartbeat is still there, albeit weak as ever. I keep pouring my magic into him, hoping it'll be enough to keep him alive until the others can arrive. And I try not to look over at Briar Rose, at how still she is, how pale. Is she even breathing?

Focus. Tristan first, Briar Rose after.

His eyes move behind his eyelids like he's searching for something. But the movement is erratic and sluggish, and it is hard to see much of anything in this dark room. All of the candles have gone out, naught but pools of wax.

The dwarf continues to sing, one song blending into the next, all emotional and heavy but somehow threaded through with hope.

"You have to live," I tell Tristan, sitting on the edge of the bed when my legs no longer want to hold me up. "At least long enough for me to tell you that you're terrible and insufferable and…" I swallow. "And… and that I wish I could have gotten to know the real you. That we could have grown up as real brothers instead of enemies. Our parents never gave us that chance, and we followed in their footsteps instead of trying to make our own path."

He whimpers, as if he heard. The wyvern flicks her tail, gaze trained on me. I'm sure if I make the wrong move, she will attack without hesitation.

"Prince Loren!" Evanthe calls out, and the dwarf ceases his song. Without letting go of Tristan, I turn to see her and Delphine and Irit hurrying to us. They, too, look exhausted, hair falling out of their braids and buns, clothes disheveled, skin ashen and bearing lacerations and bruises.

"He's dying," I choke out, although I'm sure Toussaint already informed them. "Please, help him, and then we can help Briar Rose."

They tear their attention away from Briar Rose and do as I ask, melding their magic with mine. The influx of magic forces the venom back; I barely keep myself from collapsing, now that I do not have to bear the brunt of it alone.

"Thank you for coming," I tell them.

"We almost didn't," Delphine states. "This is all very strange, and your aunt doesn't like the idea at all."

"What convinced her?"

"We had no choice but to believe Toussaint that this is the only way to save Briar Rose," Evanthe answers quietly. "All fighting is ceasing until we know what happens to her… and…" She tilts her head in Tristan's direction. Color and heat return to his skin, his heartbeat strengthening. My body hurts, wanting to snatch the magic for itself, to heal my wounds and ease my fatigue, but I refrain.

"We can't kill him," I say, fully aware of the dwarf and the faerie bodyguard watching us from the doorway. "There is still a chance that we can get him to undo the curse and make an agreement with us."

I know it is a lot to ask of them, after the Courts have been at odds for so long. Delphine snorts; Irit says determinedly, "We can hope."

Because that is all we have left, I will cling to it. Hope for Tristan, hope for Briar Rose, hope for Faerie.

Sweat beads at his brow, trickles down. His pulse kicks hard once, twice, banging against our fingertips, desperately trying to be noticed. The puncture wounds on his neck shift, sealing over, leaving only dried pus and blood behind.

Gasping, Tristan bolts upright. The wyvern hops excitedly, flapping her wings.

"Give him some room," I command the others, noting the defensive set of his jaw as he takes in his surroundings. "Tristan, we healed you from the venom. We're not going to harm you, but we need you to release Briar Rose."

Without turning his head, he looks at Briar Rose, his fingers running over the smooth, unblemished skin where his wounds had been just moments ago. It is strange to see him so off-put.

Gently, I say, "Please, Tristan. Faerie will fall to ruin without her. We are running out of time. Release her from the curse."

Hand still at his neck, Tristan slowly shakes his head. "I... I already did."

"...What?" But her form is too still, too pale. I scramble to the other side of the bed, cupping her face between my hands. "Briar Rose, please wake up," I implore her. "I'm here, just like I promised, and we need you to save Faerie."

Tristan said he already released her from the curse, but... there is no harm in trying to break it anyway. I gently kiss her, urging her to respond. This is how it is supposed to go, how we will get our happily-ever-after despite all the odds against us. I cannot give up on her—I cannot give up on us.

There are shouts and screams from outside. The faerie bodyguard announces, "The In-Between is here. Everyone is doing what they can to stop it."

Briar Rose's lips are cold and stiff, unmoving. I pull away, staring into her lifeless face. "You aren't dead. You can't die." *It wasn't enough. I'm not enough.*

Even if I made it in time, I still couldn't have broken the curse.

But I might have. If I hadn't messed up everything between us, I might have been her true love, might have broken the curse and saved her. Saved everyone.

"You said you released her," Delphine snaps at Tristan.

"I did," he snaps back, getting off the bed with a lot of effort. "But the dreamscape collapsed when I almost died... and it took her with it."

No. No no no no no no no.

I clutch her hand, the one with the fox charm still wrapped around it. We were so close to having it all in place—how is it that this is where everything falls apart?

"You were supposed to come back to me," I whisper, resting my forehead against hers.

The castle trembles.

"We have to help stop the In-Between," Evanthe states, panic tingeing her tone.

"I won't leave her."

I can feel their eyes on me, but I refuse to look away from her face.

"Prince Loren, we—"

All fall silent as Briar Rose's skin begins to glow, emanating a heat that burns my palms, but I keep a grip on her. The light grows brighter and brighter until it explodes into a thousand tiny lights that float downward and disappear before they hit the bed.

Briar Rose's body is gone.

"Where is she?" I cry out, hands hitting the bed as if to convince myself this is not an illusion, that she did not turn invisible again. Is all of her being taken away from me, not even leaving the opportunity to mourn her properly?

"Faerie might have accepted her."

My attention darts to Irit. "What?"

She bites the inside of her cheek. "When the previous... when it happened before..." Clearing her throat, she starts again. "That is what it looked like before, when Faerie took the human body during the last Ascension."

Dare I hope? They were all alive when the last Queen—Tristan's mother—went through the Ascension and became Fae.

Please let her be remembering correctly.

"She is still alive," Delphine breathes. "We have to find her."

"And we have to stop the In-Between," Evanthe reminds us. "If Briar Rose is still alive, she could be anywhere in Faerie."

The tremors continue, punctuating her point.

I ask Tristan, "Will you help me build a dreamscape to find her? She knows our magic well; maybe we can draw her back with it."

Tristan looks about the room, then refocuses on me, pale eyes scrutinizing.

"There is no time for games!" I point out, slamming my hand on the bed. "Faerie is falling apart because we can't find a way to get along. So help me find her, and we'll make an agreement that saves all of Faerie. But we won't have anything left to save if we don't find her."

"Very well," Tristan agrees after another pause, "but I want their word that no one will kill me."

"I will not let them," growls the pale faerie at the door.

"None of us will harm or kill you," Evanthe says, and Irit and Delphine parrot the sentiment. Toussaint does as well, as soon as Tristan raises a brow at him.

"We have to hurry," I remind them, settling down on the bed where Briar Rose just lay. "Keep the In-Between as far away as you can."

"We will," Evanthe assures us. "Bring her back to us."

"We will." *We will find you, Briar Rose.*

Tristan lies down beside me, shoulder-to-shoulder, and together we fall into the dreamscape, leaving the others behind. I conjure a field beneath our feet, just like Briar Rose likes to do, with plenty of colorful flowers under the sunny, cloudless sky. The petals brush against my fingertips as I pass by them. Even though Tristan's presence is chilling, the dreamscape remains mostly warm, not one bit of frost or ice or snow.

"Don't waste your time with those." Tristan stands still, closing his eyes, brows scrunching together.

Even if a fortune-teller had predicted I would be working alongside Tristan, I would not have believed them. Although I am not surprised he is being difficult about it.

"She likes them." I consider conjuring our playhouse, but I am reliant on Tristan's magic enough as it is, and I want Briar Rose to be able to sense me. If I completely run out...

He does not bother to look at me. "Yes, but they are not going to draw her to us."

I fight the urge to get irritated. After all, there is no time. "What do you suggest we do then?"

"Reach out your magic," he says, clapping a hand on my shoulder. A sharp, minty scent fills the air as he shares what he has with me. "As much as you can spare. If we can make the dreamscape big enough, maybe she'll find her way here."

I stare at him, again searching for the shared features our father gave us, something to connect us other than blood. Something deeper that carries meaning, something we can both silently acknowledge until we are ready to talk about it, if that day ever does come.

Tristan jerks away and breaks eye contact. "Reach out with your magic," he repeats, closing his eyes.

I follow his order, but I can't help saying, "You didn't hurt her."

A muscle in his jaw twitches. "Why would I hurt her?"

"You did curse her. Is it so big a leap to assume you might hurt her?"

His stance is all tense lines. "Everything I do has purpose behind it. What good would it do for me to hurt her when I need her to help me restore Faerie?"

He wants the same thing that we do... I send my magic out farther, skirting alongside Tristan's. Nothing, not even a hint of Briar Rose. But the brush of Tristan's magic sends goosebumps along my arms, the strength of it humbling. Even having been near death just minutes before, he carries power that I would fear to fight against. Power Faerie gives to him willingly.

"Maybe you should be King."

His eyes snap open and fixate on me. "Let's find your lover

first," he says, "then you can try to trick me with your thinly-veiled attempts at flattery."

"I'm not flattering you," I insist. "I can feel your magic—Faerie clearly chose you to rule." I watch him analyze me and my words. "Despite what our father did, Faerie still honors your birthright."

Scowling, he snarls, "Do not pity me."

"I'm not. I'm trying to tell you that we don't have to be enemies." I take a hesitant step toward him.

"Don't act like you don't see me as a monster. Can't you see I'm content in the role they've cast me as?" His tone is edged, but raw. It reminds me of the rawness I have seen in myself, the vulnerability that I was so afraid to share with anyone, especially Briar Rose.

We do not look alike, yet I feel as though I am seeing a reflection of my soul.

Using the same gentle voice Toussaint does with me, I say, "I can see you lie about yourself just as well as I do."

Puzzlement softens the harsh lines of his scowl. His gaze bores into me with renewed interest, frustration that he somehow over-looked an integral piece in his plotting. I am not the person he thought I was—who we both thought I was. No, I left that shell of a person behind when I chose to open myself up to Briar Rose.

And I hope Tristan learns to do the same for himself.

"I don't see you as a monster," I add, hoping I haven't pushed him too far. "I see you as my brother. We don't have to live in the mistakes our father made."

Tristan continues to stare at me, but I break eye contact, step forward, and pour everything I have into finding Briar Rose. Because no matter how this plays out, I want to give my all to who I am, whether that be Briar Rose's lover, King of the Seelie, nephew, friend... brother.

No more hiding.

CHAPTER FIFTY-ONE

BRIAR ROSE

*B*irds whistling. Pixies singing their high-pitched songs to welcome the morning. Soft grass beneath me, caressing my cheek. Sunlight warming my skin, coaxing me to fall back asleep for just a little longer.

Instead, I open my eyes. Brilliant colors greet me: vibrant greens of the grass and shrubs and trees; pale gold of sun rays peeking through the treetops overhead; pinks and oranges and yellows of petals of the nearby flowers. Throughout it all, there are iridescent shimmers that weave into the landscape, breathing life into it —magic.

Slowly, I stand, marveling at the breathtaking beauty around me, and the peace and harmony it exudes. Balance. Wholeness.

I hear the flutter of a pixie's wings before I see it passing by a tree in the distance, way farther than I should be able to see, and with such clarity that it is disorienting for a few moments. I lean against a nearby trunk for support, then jump away; it has a heart-beat, the same one pulsing under my bare feet.

My gaze drops to the ground in wonder, and I stop to stare at my feet. The subtle lengthening of them is enough for me to note that they are not the same as they were before, and neither are my hands. They are elegant, daintier, smoother.

Hesitantly, I reach up to trace the outer edge of my ears. The earlobes are the same, but the tops are longer and taper to delicate points long enough to peek out of my hair. *If only I had a mirror,* I lament as I run my sun-kissed honey-brown hair through my fingers. I am now Fae. *Loren will be—*

Loren. I need to find him.

Unsure which way to go, I hurry through the woods. Hopefully, I am somewhat close to the Unseelie border, so Loren and Toussaint do not have to wait long in the dungeons. Or has Queen Vivienne already sent an army to retrieve them—and me? What will they think to find me gone?

Voices catch my attention; I change direction toward them, my gait naturally graceful and sure, always knowing where to step. My heart beats in time with Faerie's, melodious and strong.

"There you are."

I halt just as Cheshire appears a couple of strides ahead of me. He floats up to get a better look at me, big eyes roaming as he grins. A multitude of colors that could create many rainbows swirl atop his fur coat.

"I had a feeling Faerie could use you once the curse was gone. If it accepted your human body, cursed as it was, that would have been the end of Faerie as we know it, consumed by darkness and the In-Between."

"I... What do you mean? Did you pull me off the path and lead me to the spindle?"

"Amusing, that you think I have power as strong as the land of Faerie itself." His smile does not falter, but the tip of his tail flicks in what I assume is annoyance.

"I can see you carry a lot of magic," I reply, staring at the colors, spells frolicking atop his body, begging to be used. "Powerful magic."

"Curiouser and curiouser…" He eyes me, head tilting askew enough to be unsettling. If I bent my head like that, I would be afraid my neck would pop out of place. "Well done, no-longer-human Briar Rose. You saved all of Faerie, and it has rewarded you handsomely. Do take care of how you use your newfound gifts."

Before I can reply, he is gone.

Toussaint might be right—he is nothing but trouble. And yet, there is something in the strange cat's words that clings to me.

The distant voices reclaim my attention. I rush forward, leaving the forest behind, and run into a clearing in front of a tall, dark castle. Not Seelie—this must be Unseelie Lands. A lot greener than I imagined. An army surrounds the castle's walls, Seelie by the look of them. Still holding their weapons and shields, they stare around them in wonder, some of them noticing me as I run their way.

"Queen Vivienne!" they call, and she appears mere seconds later, the crowd parting to let her through to me. She is clad in golden armor, and her hair looks like coils of flame braided over her shoulder.

"Briar Rose," she breathes, eyes welling as she strides toward me with open arms. I accept the hug, but cannot help asking, "Where is Loren? I have to find him."

It is disorienting, hearing so many heartbeats, so many breaths. Were the faeries this loud the entire time, and I just couldn't hear them?

"In the castle," she answers, releasing me but keeping a strong grip on my shoulders as she scans me up and down. "Toussaint said you were inside, still under the curse. They were trying to wake you." She gestures to our surroundings. "Did you do this? Did you heal Faerie?"

"I… I think so. There is a lot to explain, but I have to find him first."

Frowning, she nods. "Of course. Go. Hurry."

Seelie and Unseelie alike make way for me as I sprint past them, going straight to the castle. *I have no idea where he is,* I realize. The dungeons should be below, but what hall leads downstairs? No... Queen Vivienne said that Loren and Toussaint were trying to wake me. Where would Tristan keep me?

The main foyer has lots of blood and corpses, one of them decapitated, the head far away from its body. *Did the Unseelie turn on each other?*

"Briar Rose!" Evanthe hurries down the stairs, Delphine and Irit close behind. They quickly hug me, then tug me toward the stairs.

"We saw you arrive," Delphine says.

"Did you save Faerie?" Irit asks. "You look gorgeous, by the way. Being Fae suits you."

"It certainly does! How do you like it?"

"She can answer our questions after she reunites with Loren," Evanthe says, shutting them down. "He and Tristan should know she is here so they can leave the dreamscape."

They were trying to find me... together? In the dreamscape? Tristan is alive? My thoughts and emotions tumble over one another, and I am glad I have my faerie guardians to guide me.

They lead me to a bedchamber at the end of a long hallway, the doors wide open. The candles have completely gone out, but my new sight is undeterred by the darkness.

Loren and Tristan lie side-by-side on the bed, shoulders touching, twin looks of determination on their faces. A small black wyvern is curled up between their heads. Its glowing purple stare finds me as I approach Loren's side. A few loose curls have fallen across his forehead, and I brush them back.

"Time to wake, Loren," I whisper, then press my lips to his.

LOREN

My magic ripples across the dreamscape, seeking, yearning for any hint of Briar Rose. Tristan's follows, some melding with mine, some shooting off in other directions, just as urgent. Instead of our magics fighting against one another, they flow together, strengthen each other. Part of me wants to check on my body, to figure out what I can hear, to feel if there is any shift in Faerie's strength. But this takes all of my focus—I will not risk missing her.

I am here, Briar Rose. We can still find each other.

We expand the dreamscape farther, pressing the limits of the edges so much that our magic trembles with effort. My chest aches, and when Tristan grips my shoulder to try to replenish me, it is but a trickle.

"Time to wake, Loren." A soft, warm sensation against my lips catches my attention. I halt, barely looking at Tristan's confused expression before I let myself tumble back into the real world. Pins and needles prick me as my soul reconnects with my body, but I could not care less. Briar Rose is pulling away, so I cup her face, chasing the kiss. She smiles, shifting closer. Murmuring her name between kisses, I sit up and pull her toward me, her frame slightly different, just enough to make me stop to look at her.

Fae. Despite my relief at finding the changes subtle, Briar Rose is undoubtedly a faerie, from the pointed ears to the ethereal beauty to the power emanating from her. Her scent has shifted too, an entrancing smell of earth and flowers and *life*.

"Not quite True Love's Kiss," she says, resting her forehead against mine, "but we are both awake."

Tristan stirs, and I can feel his attention on us, but I can't bring myself to look away from her. How had Faerie managed to accentuate her natural beauty so well?

"All that matters is that we are together again," I tell her, realizing she is waiting for a response.

She grins, reaching up to tug on one of my curls. "I love you."

Tears prick my eyes; I don't bother trying to stop them. "I love you too."

Gently, we wipe at each other's cheeks. She is here, she is alive, and she is *with me*. I breathe in, and note that my magic is refilling. Not from Briar Rose—from Faerie itself. We are far from the ground, yet I can feel the thrum of the earth's heartbeat, strong and sure. Whole.

As if she cannot take it any longer, Briar Rose blurts out, "Marry me?"

I blink, processing what she said. An offer to be with Briar Rose forever, come what may? I embrace her, tilting my head for another kiss. "Absolutely, I will."

CHAPTER FIFTY-TWO

THE UNSEELIE KING

I ease myself off the bed, avoiding Loren and Briar Rose's nauseating display of affection. Asra leaps onto my shoulder, rubbing her face against mine, and I stroke her head. Despite the vitality Faerie exudes, I feel so much heavier, nearly stumbling with my first step. Margaux grabs my arm, steadying me. How did Briar Rose manage to carry this curse all of these years? Granted, I cast it on her as an infant, so she did not know any different.

She must feel weightless now. I sneak a peek at her, watching as she grins at Loren. Somehow, she looks entirely different as Fae, and yet so unmistakably herself. She radiates joy as she proposes to Loren.

I tear away from the scene, willing my stiff limbs to cooperate.

"My King," Margaux says softly, "what are your orders?"

Suddenly I am a little boy again, the crown far too big for my head, and I want to recoil. I don't know what to do, much less what orders to give. My entire life has been spent trying to make Faerie whole again, and now it is. It was not saved by blood, but by the willingness of a human girl to give everything she had.

I almost snort at the irony. One human girl turning Fae split the Courts—another restored them.

"I believe," Briar Rose interrupts, standing with the confidence of a queen, "that a peace talk is needed before any orders are given." Loren positions himself beside her, his gaze seeking mine. He had to mean what he said in the dreamscape, about us being brothers, not enemies. But how would he define that? Because I have no idea where to start.

'With a choice,' I hear Briar Rose whisper in my mind. *'We can start with a choice. We can do better than those who came before us.'*

I flinch, startled at the use of mind magic. But I cannot fault her, not when I used it on her in the dreamscape.

'I promise it will be a civil discussion,' she adds with a hint of a smile. *'I can make tea and tarts if you'd like.'*

We could leave, go to the meeting room, but that seems ridiculous to me. Why not here, why not now? We all want this sorted out as soon as possible.

Aware of the eyes on me, I ask Briar Rose, "What are your peace terms, Queen of the Fae?"

Her expression brightens further; everyone else stares at me in shock.

"I am not the only ruler here," she points out, slipping her hand into Loren's.

"I am no ruler," he argues with a shake of his head. There is no bitterness, no remorse. "Faerie clearly chose you, Tristan. It never stopped choosing you."

The others in the room stay silent with rapt attention. Even Asra keeps still. How am I supposed to respond to that, after years of fighting to be acknowledged?

"Faerie chose *both* of you," Briar Rose corrects, her words ringing true as Faerie pulses happily, filling us with magic to the point of overflowing. "It wants all three of us." She squeezes Loren's hand, and he smiles down at her.

I want to ask if she can hear it, if it speaks to her, but I save that question for another time. "How would the three of us rule?"

"The Courts are already split," says Loren. "I think we can both agree that forcing the Seelie and Unseelie back together would be messy at best—why not form an alliance instead?"

"An alliance? Against who?"

Loren shrugs. "Against whoever dares attack Faerie."

There are plenty of magic creatures other than Fae that could pose a threat—if I ever decided to break away from my agreement with the Troll Queen, this would be a viable option to help me.

But first, I will have to figure out how to get rid of this curse before it consumes me.

Thaddeus clears his throat, catching my attention.

"If I am to agree to this, then the Solitary Fae and their allies are to remain free to choose as they please," I state. "Whether that means joining a Court or remaining with their clans."

The dwarf dips his head in thanks, and steps back next to Margaux.

"Of course," Briar Rose concurs, nodding at Thaddeus. "Then does that mean you agree to the alliance? You rule Unseelie, while Loren and I rule Seelie?"

All of my schemes and plotting and tactical decisions were meant to lead me to be King of Faerie. Instead, it brought me here, and I cannot find it in myself to begrudge it. No longer having Faerie at war means I can focus on the Troll Queen and this curse. That might give me a little time to rest… maybe.

And this way, I don't have to say goodbye to Loren and Briar Rose.

Mother would disapprove, one thought says, although the next one squashes it: *But it's not about her anymore.*

"I agree."

CHAPTER FIFTY-THREE

LOREN

*T*he sun shines brightly and the earth thrums with excitement. Seelie and Unseelie alike wait outside, mostly separate on either side of the pathway leading up to where Aunt Vivienne waits with Toussaint, Evanthe, and Margaux. Margaux towers over the rest and is as still as a statue, unblinking.

It is strange to see Flora and Fauna on the Unseelie side of this ceremony, but Tristan refused to allow anything to happen to them since they were under his orders. They are his people to rule, not ours.

Solitary Fae are dispersed throughout both sides, albeit unevenly, especially the dwarves sitting with the Unseelie. And, unless my eyes are playing tricks on me, I notice a tail in the branches above, with two glowing eyes and a wide grin. I didn't think he would miss something this grand.

"Are you ready?" I ask Tristan as he steps beside me to look out the window. A small house that sits on the border of both territories, we thought this would be the best place for the coronation, neutral ground. One of many compromises made, and many more to come.

But I could get used to having my brother in my life, even if it means making some sacrifices.

Standing a little too stiff, Tristan answers, "Ready to be rid of the formalities? Absolutely."

"I can agree with that," I chuckle. He side-eyes me, his scowl softening a little.

Asra makes a chittering noise, wrapping her tail loosely around his neck.

"Is she walking with you?"

Tristan raises a brow. "Do you want to try telling her no?"

After spending time with her and Tristan these past few weeks, I know better than to try to give Asra any orders. She stares as if challenging me to try, and I say, "I would rather not be mauled on our coronation day. Or any other day, for that matter."

"Wise choice." The corner of his mouth twitches, the closest I've seen to a smile. We are not quite brothers, but at least we are no longer enemies. A step in the right direction.

"Is it time?" Briar Rose walks in, taking her place between us. Irit and Delphine have put her in an off-the-shoulder simple dress that reminds me of a sunset, bright at the top and shifting to cooler colors as it reaches the bottom, the train completely black with clusters of diamonds acting as stars. She matches both me and Tristan perfectly. Her done-up hairstyle shows off her faerie ears and the necklace she wears, with the fox and rose pendants nestled against one another. Since we were reunited, they have not left her neck, despite how much Evanthe begged her to wear something more suitable for our wedding at the very least. Briar Rose refused, much to Jovan's and my relief, declaring they are important symbols of our story.

Besides, Briar Rose could have worn anything that day, and she still would have been radiant from the pure joy on her face alone.

"You are just in time," I tell her, noting that Aunt Vivienne has begun her speech on the unity of the Courts bringing a new era of peace and prosperity, the In-Between no longer a threat. There is much to fix, and lots of territory was destroyed, but at least there is no longer the looming threat of complete destruction.

With a grin, Briar Rose sneaks a quick kiss, then turns her attention to Tristan. "I know you want this over with, so I won't bother asking how you're feeling."

Tristan smirks in response.

"Asra, I'm glad you're walking with us."

The wyvern chirrups, leaning down so Briar Rose can scratch under her chin and give her a quick peck on the forehead.

Aunt Vivienne finishes her speech, and everyone stands and turns toward us, our cue to walk. Briar Rose loops her arms through ours, and together we three stride forward. Murmurs ripple through the attendees; I catch sight of Briar Rose's family toward the front of the Seelie side, her mother gripping Jovan's arms so he doesn't try to rush forward and join us. Caspian and Sabine sit near them as humans, patches of scales on their arms and necks the only hint of their true forms.

Pixies dance overhead, tossing flower petals and leaves so that they rain down on us. Briar Rose glances up with a smile but manages to keep pace. I squeeze her hand; she squeezes mine back.

We arrive at the front and pause before Aunt Vivienne. Behind her, Toussaint, Evanthe, and Margaux all hold crowns: one of twisted brown twigs, decorated with nuts, berries, and autumn-colored leaves; one of flowers of every hue, but the most common color being pink; and one of white bark twisted with red silk and adorned with black jewels.

"For the one who found a way to restore Faerie where we thought there was no hope left," Aunt Vivienne says, and Evanthe steps forward, reverently placing the crown of flowers atop Briar Rose's head. She presses a kiss to my wife's brow, and then returns to her place.

"For the one who refused to give up even when he felt like everything was stacked against him."

With great pride, Toussaint walks to me, crowning me. He clasps my shoulder, then returns to his spot.

Instead of making another statement, Aunt Vivienne turns to Margaux. "May I?"

The pale faerie looks at Tristan for guidance. Hesitantly, he nods, and Margaux hands over the crown.

Slowly, Aunt Vivienne moves to Tristan, gazing deeply into his eyes. Tristan's throat bobs, but he keeps eye contact.

"For my eldest nephew," she finally says. Tristan's frown slips a bit. "The one who was overlooked because of choices his mother made, and in everything he does, does it for what he believes is the good of Faerie." Gently, she rests the crown atop his head and touches his cheek. "You have greatness," she whispers. "It is your choice how to use it."

Before he can respond, she steps back. "May I present King Loren and Queen Briar Rose of the South, and King Tristan of the North!"

We face the cheering and applauding crowds. Magic rushes through us, Faerie infusing us as if to give its blessing. I breathe in, and Briar Rose tightens her grip on me. I feel the cool silver of her wedding band, a human tradition we kept at her request. She could ask anything of me, and I would give it to her.

To our confusion, Tristan takes a knife from his pocket and slices his palm, raising it high as blood wells and begins to drip.

"Blood for the throne!"

Unseelie echo his chant. I look to Briar Rose, hoping she understands what is happening, but she is already taking the knife from him, copying him, so I do the same. We are, after all, trying to promote unity amongst groups of faeries that are not quite satisfied with becoming allies.

One day at a time, one step at a time.

The chants grow louder, fiercer, more joining in. Excitement increases, Asra bellowing, unwilling to be left out.

Briar Rose beams at me. She chose this—chose *me*. It is not the happily-ever-after we thought we were getting, but it is the one we have and will treasure for the rest of our lives.

ACKNOWLEDGMENTS

Originally, I was writing an entirely different book last year, but this story demanded to be told! It fits well with the *Once Upon a Reimagined Time* series—and inspired a few more fairytales I'll hopefully add soon.

As with any project, I could not do this alone! I am so grateful all of these wonderful people:

Nicole Scarano: Thank you for making the interior as gorgeous as the cover! It's like adding extra magic to the inside of the book.

Lydia Russell & Katherine Macdonald: It'd be a shorter list if I looked for things to not thank you for. All of the time spent helping with ideas, edits, feedback, encouragement—I appreciate all of it! Thank you for helping me grow as a writer.

Jessica, Mandy, Kate, Jenn, and Abigail: Thank you for beta reading. Your feedback was super helpful and made the book so much better!

Neil Infalt: As always, I am grateful for your support... and for your patience during the crazy editing schedule I gave myself. I love you forever and always!

Charlie & Maximus: My adorable fur babies, you two are the cutest writing buddies ever.

Lastly, I want to thank my readers: These stories and characters are precious to me, so thank you for taking the time to read my books and leave reviews.

Much love,
Chesney Infalt

ABOUT THE AUTHOR

Chesney Infalt has been writing stories since she got her first notebook at the age of six. While those are under lock and key, her books *The Heart of the Sea*, *The Fox and the Briar*, and *A Different Kind of Magic* are available now on Amazon.

twitter.com/ChesneyInfalt

instagram.com/chesneyinfalt

www.ingramcontent.com/pod-product-compliance
Lightning Source LLC
Chambersburg PA
CBHW051323250626
47155CB00007B/2424